Feb 24, 2003
FN

FN.

W9-ARG-980

Also by Catherine Cookson

CATHERINE COOKSON

The Silent Lady

A Novel

BOOKSPAN LARGE PRINT EDITION

Simon & Schuster
New York   London   Toronto   Sydney   Singapore

This Large Print Edition, prepared especially for Bookspan, Inc., contains the complete, unabridged text of the original Publisher's Edition.

SIMON & SCHUSTER
Rockefeller Center
1230 Avenue of the Americas
New York, NY 10020

Originally published in 2001 in Great Britain by Bantam Press

SIMON & SCHUSTER and colophon are registered trademarks of Simon & Schuster, Inc.

Manufactured in the United States of America

ISBN 0-7394-2330-4

This Large Print Book carries the Seal of Approval of N.A.V.H.

Dedication

This story was not meant to be written. I thought I had done my last one with *The Branded Man.* However, I had forgotten the machine I had set in motion fifty years ago.

This last year has proved more than trying. My blood trouble seems to have gone wild: not only have I had my nose packed frequently, but there have been more sojourns in hospital for operations to deal with the bleedings in my stomach. I will not add to these with all the other bodily afflictions . . . I was finished.

Apparently, the machine did not hear me, for one day it presented me with a very good idea for a story. It was then I said to it, 'How on earth shall I be able to get down a story now? First, I cannot see either to read or to write; only with guidance can I write my signature. Secondly, what time have I got? Doctors are forever coming and going; Tom is forever attending to my bodily needs, which do not stop at the end of the day; there is the post to be answered by my dictation, and the constant discussions on the phone about business and television; moreover, there is my editing of film scripts through dictation to Tom, who reads them aloud to me; also the editing through the same source of scripts ready for the printer; and so it is no wonder that exhaustion takes me into bouts of ME.'

A part of my mind told me that I had to face up to what 'they' were all saying: I was old and no longer fit to carry on at this rate. And so the writing of another story was definitely off.

But, try as I might, the old machine would not listen to me. 'It's a good idea,' it kept saying; 'different from the way you have tackled anything else. All right, but you are not going to be able to put it down; but thinking it through might help to take your mind off your miseries.'

I must have said to it, 'Well, what is it going to be all about?' and the answer came, 'Well, first, I think a good title for it will be *The Silent Lady.*'

'What? *The Silent Lady?*'

'Yes; and in her you have the whole story, right from beginning to end, the Silent Lady.'

Only once before has this happened to me. The result—*The Fifteen Streets.* This was after the publication of my first book, *Kate Hannigan.* The follow-up did not suit my publishers, who wished to cut it, particularly those parts dealing with religion. I wouldn't have it: I asked for it back.

So there I was on this freezing cold morning, just after the war (coal rationed to a ton a year) in a freezing cold house, and I was dead cold inside, for my mind was a void—I hadn't an idea in it.

I was in a breakdown; I was fighting against religion—I had definitely discarded God—but there I sat, huddled in a vast cold room. I've never known, even now, what made me resort to my dramatic gesture: I threw back my head and looked up to the ceiling and cried, 'If there's anybody there, give me a story!'

It might be unbelievable, but within an hour I had the complete story of *The Fifteen Streets,* right from the first line to the last, and I sat down and started on it straight away; and I did not alter one word or incident in that book over the weeks it took me to get it down in longhand.

The whole plan came over as it had first been presented to me: every character and incident in that story now has been filmed and staged all over the country, even in small village halls.

Well, the same thing was happening again. My mind gave me every character, every incident from the beginning to the end, and I found it to be a kind of salve: instead of my mind rambling on, always negative thinking—I had little to look forward to—it would pick up where I had left off in this story and continue as if I had never stopped.

This went on for some months, and one day I said to Tom, when he was trying to break the sameness of my life with reading to me, 'I have a good story in my mind, but it will always remain there.'

'Why?' he said. 'Couldn't you put it down on to tape?'

Even to myself, my voice was cold as I said, 'Don't be silly. There are times when I can hardly hear my own voice. And I am no longer able to yammer into that machine.' And truthfully, I wasn't.

But the damned rusty old wheel said, 'Here I am, grinding away listening to your complaining, your criticising, and your self-pity; and I am warning you, your self-pity will take over and bottle those all up; and one day you'll have just too much of it, when you'll find you're not able to think coherently. And then, what little time you have left will be wasted. And where has all the big noise gone—the one that keeps preaching "Never say die!" or "I *can* and I *will*"?'

Tom says he has stopped being amazed at anything I say or do, because one day, only a short time after having my nose packed, I muttered, 'Put my table so that I can handle my microphone,' and without comment or protest, he did so. And there it began.

I knew the story was going to be different: as a character was born I seemed to emerge from the womb of it and live its life. As in *The Fifteen Streets,* I knew every piece of dialogue that had to go down and every incident; and when I came to Bella Morgan, I was in her body more than I was in my own. Although, because of the comings and goings of doctors and bed attention and the like, I could put it down only in bits and

pieces, with my voice often inaudible, it became something I looked forward to; in fact,
I just seemed to live for the time I could return to this 'family' and to the Silent Lady
herself.

Then one day, after what seemed a long,
long time since I had joined them all, it was
finished, and I said to Tom, 'When did I start
this?' And he said, 'Exactly a month ago today.'

'Never!'

'Yes,' he assured me, 'a month ago today!
And now you are utterly exhausted in all
ways, aren't you?'

I lay thinking: Yes, I was. I was utterly exhausted. But how could I have got all that
down in just a month? And how could I say
to him now, 'There are two places where I
have repeated myself, and three others that
I know I must cut because the descriptions
are too long'?

He looked at me in utter amazement: 'You
can remember it all like that?' he asked.

'Yes; every word,' I said.

It went to the typist. Some weeks later I
got it back—876 pages of it.

I do not believe in the dogma of any re-
ligious denomination but, as I have said be-

fore, I believe there is a spirit coming from some power or source that runs through all of us. In some strange way that I do not question, I have been able to tap into that source. This is what has enabled me always to say 'I *can* and I *will'*; and it is working still and helping me through this traumatic time of illness; and sometimes so strongly that one could say I have been given the power to create little miracles for myself; and for it, I am thankful.

So this story I dedicate to all those faithful readers who have become my faceless friends over many years, and I thank you for your loyalty to me.

I hope you will enjoy this last effort of mine, which came as an inspiration to me when I needed it most.

Catherine

PART ONE
1955

1

The woman put out her hand towards the brass plate to the side of the half-open door. She did not look at the name on the plate, which said, 'Alexander Armstrong & Son, Solicitors', but seemed to find support from it by touching its frame while she stood drawing in deep, shuddering breaths.

When she finally straightened herself and stepped through the doorway into a carpeted hall, she made her faltering way towards the desk to the left of her, behind which stood a young woman with her mouth agape.

The receptionist did not greet the visitor with a customary 'Can I help you, madam?' or 'Have you an appointment?' because, to her, it was instantly evident that this woman was a vagrant and had no business here;

so she did not wait for her to speak but said, 'What d'you want? I . . . I think you've come to the wrong place.'

When the woman answered, 'Mis-ter Armstrong,' the girl was again surprised, this time by the sound of the voice, for it didn't match the woman's appearance. Although it was only a husky whisper it had, she recognised, a certain refinement about it.

But the appearance of the woman definitely outweighed the impression her voice made, for the girl now said abruptly, 'He only sees people by appointment.'

The woman pointed to her chest, then to her eyes and, opening her mouth wide, she brought out three words, 'He see me.'

'He's—he's very busy.'

Again the head went back and the mouth opened, and the woman said, 'Mrs Baindor.'

Again the voice made an impression on the receptionist, so much so that she turned quickly and, pushing open the glass-panelled door of her office, she picked up the phone, at the same time watching the woman now turn from the counter and grope her way to a chair that was set near a small table on which stood a vase of flowers.

'Miss Fairweather?'

'Yes. What is it?'

'There's a . . . a person here.' Her voice was very low.

'What did you say? Speak up!'

'I said there's a person here. She . . . she looks like a vagrant but she says Mr Armstrong will see her.'

'A vagrant! What makes you think she looks like a vagrant?'

'Well, Miss Fairweather, you want to look at her yourself and see if my opinion is wrong.' The receptionist was daring to talk like this to Miss Fairweather, but she felt there was something very unusual about this woman.

'Did you get her name?'

'Yes, but it sounded funny, like Barndoor.'

'Barndoor?'

'That's what it sounded like.'

At the other end of the phone Miss Fairweather sat pondering. Should she go downstairs and see who this person was who looked like a vagrant, or should she mention the name to Mr Armstrong to see if he knew any such person? She decided on the latter. She tapped on the door that separated her office from that of her employer and when that gentleman raised his head from reading a large parchment set out in front of him and said, 'What is it?' she coughed before saying, 'Miss Manning says there's an odd-looking person downstairs who says she wants to see you. Apparently she doesn't seem able to get rid of her. From Miss Manning's tone the woman appeared to think that you would know her name.'

'Well, what is it? I mean her name.'

'It sounded to Miss Manning, so she says, like Barndoor.'

'What?'

'Well, that's what she said . . . Barndoor.'

Miss Fairweather was absolutely astounded at her employer's reaction to the mention of this name, for he jumped from his seat and shouted, yes, actually shouted aloud, 'Baindor, woman! Baindor! My God!'

She saw the parchment that he had been dealing with almost slide off the back of the desk as he thrust his chair back, then he ran across the room, almost knocking her over where she stood holding the door half open.

She had been with Mr Armstrong for fifteen years and had never seen him act like this. He was a placid, middle-aged man, strict in a way but always courteous. His excitement touched her. And now she was on the landing watching him almost leaping down the stairs.

When Alexander Armstrong reached the hall he stood for a moment gripping the stanchion post as he looked across at the woman, her body almost doubled up in the chair. He couldn't believe it: he couldn't and he wouldn't until he saw her face.

The woman did not lift her eyes to his until she saw his legs standing before her; then slowly she looked up and he gasped at the sight of her. The face might have been that of her skeleton, with the skin stretched over it, so prominent was the bone formation. Only the eye sockets tended to fall inwards and from them two pale, blood-shot eyes gazed up at him.

Two words seemed to fill Alexander Armstrong's mind and body and they kept repeating themselves: My God! My God! Then, too, was added the knowledge that sitting here looking at him with those almost dead eyes was a woman for whom he had been searching—at least, for whom he and his business had been searching—for twenty-five years. No, nearly twenty-six.

The words he brought out were in a muttered stammer: 'M-M-Mrs Baindor.'

She did not answer but made a small movement with her strangely capped head.

He held his arms out to her now, saying, 'Come upstairs with me, Irene.'

When she made the attempt to rise she fell back into the chair and her body seemed to fold up again. At this he swung round to where Miss Fairweather was standing at the foot of the stairs and yelled at her, 'Call my son!' and when she answered shakily, 'He's out, Mr Armstrong; you know, on the Fullman case.'

'Then get Taggart—anybody!'

The chief clerk Taggart's office was at the other end of the building, and Miss Fairweather ran back up the stairs and along the corridor. Within two minutes Taggart was standing beside his employer, saying, 'Yes, sir?'

'Help me to get this lady to my office.'

For a moment Henry Taggart hesitated while he took in the lady's garb. She was a vagrant, if ever he had seen one in his life. But he did as he was bidden. Not only did he help the weird long-coated bundle to her feet, but, seeing that she was unable to

stand and there wasn't room for three of
them on the stairs, he picked up what the
boss had called a lady, carried her up the
stairs into the main office and laid her, as
directed by Alexander, on the leather couch
that was placed next to the long window
overlooking the square.

Then, again almost shouting at his secretary, Alexander said, 'Make a cup of
tea . . . strong, plenty of sugar.' From a cupboard he took down off a shelf a brandy
flask and poured from it a measure into the
silver-capped lid. This he took to the couch
and, kneeling down by the woman, he put
it to her lips, saying gently, 'Drink this.'

She made no effort to stop him pouring
the liquid into her mouth; but when it hit her
throat she coughed and choked and her
whole body trembled. He turned and said
to the clerk, 'Go down to the office and get
the girl to phone for an ambulance.'

It must have been the sound of the word
'ambulance' that roused the woman,
brought her head up and a protesting movement from her hand. At this Alexander,
bending down to her, said, 'It's all right, my
dear. It's all right. Not a big hospital . . . I
understand. I understand.'

She lay back now and stared at him; then he turned quickly from her and, going to the phone on his table, he rang a number. When, presently, a voice answered him, saying, 'Beechwood Nursing Home,' he said curtly, 'Get me the Matron, quick!'

'Who's speaking?'

'Never mind who's speaking, get me the Matron quick!'

'But, sir . . . !'

'I'm sorry. I'm Miss Armstrong's brother.'

'Oh. Oh yes, yes,' came the reply; and then there was silence. As he stood waiting, he turned and looked at the wreckage of a life lying on his couch, and again his mind cried, 'My God!'

'What is it, Alex?' said his sister's voice.

'Listen, Glenda. I'm sending you a patient.'

'You're not asking if we've got any room.'

'You'd have to make room somewhere. This is important.'

'I cannot make rooms—'

'Listen, Glenda. Have you a room?'

'Yes, as it happens I have, Alex; and may I ask what is up with you?'

'You'll know soon enough. Get that room

ready; there'll be an ambulance there shortly and I shall be following it.'

The voice now was soft: 'What is it, Alex? You sound troubled, very troubled.'

'You'll know why in a short time, Glenda. Only tell the staff that there must be no chit-chat about the condition of your new patient. I mean how she appears . . . is dressed. For the moment just get that room ready.' Then, his voice changing, he said, 'This is a serious business, Glenda, and I can't believe what I am seeing lying on my office couch. Bye-bye, dear.'

When he put the phone down and turned round, Miss Fairweather was standing with a cup of tea in her hand, looking as if she was afraid to touch the weird bundle lying there. He took the cup from her; then, kneeling down again, he put one hand behind the woman's head to where the cap affair she was wearing bulged out into a kind of large hairnet, which fell on to her neck. It had been half hidden by the large collar of her worn, discoloured and, in parts, threadbare coat. Lifting her head forward, he said, 'Drink this, my dear.'

Again she was staring into his face; but now she made no movement of dissent when he put the cup to her lips. After she had taken two gulps of the strong tea and it began to run from the corners of her mouth, he quickly handed the cup and saucer back to Miss Fairweather and, taking a handkerchief from his pocket, he gently dabbed the thin lips.

When he saw her make an effort to speak again, he said softly, 'It's all right, my dear. There'll be plenty of time to talk later.'

But she still continued to stare at him; and what he heard her say now brought his eyes wide, for she murmured, 'My son . . . tell my son . . . He will come.'

He knew he was shaking his head slowly. She thought her son would come to her after all these years? She could know nothing about him; yet her last words 'He will come' had been spoken in an assured tone. Poor soul.

There came a tap on the door now; and Taggart stood there, saying, 'The ambulance is here, sir.'

'Tell them to bring up a stretcher.' Alexander turned swiftly to his secretary, saying, 'Fetch that old traveling rug out of the cupboard.'

Although still amazed, Miss Fairweather

was quick, and after taking the rug from her Alexander pulled it open and tucked it about the thin body of the woman, gently lifting her from one side to the other until it over-lapped.

The ambulancemen picked up the wrapped body from the couch, making no comment, not even on the woman's head-gear, but asked politely, 'Where to, sir?'

'Beechwood Nursing Home.'

His description did not get any further be-fore one of the ambulancemen said, 'Oh, yes; we know it, sir. Beechwood Nursing Home, Salton Avenue, Longmere Road.'

It was almost two hours later and brother and sister were in the Matron's private sit-ting room; and there Glenda Armstrong stood holding the long dark coat up before her, saying, 'Can you believe it?' And not waiting for an answer, she went on, 'I can't. I remember putting this on her. It was such a beautiful coat and very heavy. I thought that even then, for it was lined to the very cuffs with lambswool. But look now, there is not a vestige of wool left in the lining, just a mere thin skin. And the coat was such a beautiful dark green; made with such thick

Melton cloth you couldn't imagine it wearing out in two lifetimes. Well, it has almost worn out in one, God help her! Where d'you think it has been?'

'I don't know. I haven't any idea, but it's been on the road somewhere. Yet, looking as she did, surely she would have been detected, especially with that hat or whatever it's supposed to be.'

Glenda now picked up the hat from a chair and said, 'It was very smart, French, a cross between a turban and a tam-o'-shanter with a brim round it. Look, the brim is still in place.' She touched the almost bare buckram-shaped rim with her fingertips, then lifted the pouch at the back as she said, 'She must have had it made for her to fit the bun she wore low down on her neck. Look at the dorothy bag! That's the same one she had with her when it happened.' Glenda pointed to the patched handbag lying on the seat of the chair. 'Everything she owned was in that bag. I remember I made her take her rings with her for she had taken them all off, even the wedding ring; and there was a necklace and a card case.'

Glenda sat down now on the edge of the

large chesterfield beside her brother. 'When we heard nothing from her I always blamed myself for not sending someone with her to Eastbourne. When I put her on the train I said, "Now, let me know, won't you, how things are, and I shall come and see you in a few days or so." And that's the last I saw of her. Do you remember when you told her husband she had gone to her aunt's, and he went for you for not seeing that I had obeyed his orders and sent her to Conway House? My God! If ever there was an asylum under the name of rest-home! Yet I would have liked to have pushed her aunt into that place when I got to Eastbourne the next day and she told me that she wouldn't give her niece house room and had turned her away. She said that Irene's place was at her husband's side, and she deserved all she had got for carrying on with other men. Dear Lord in Heaven!' Glenda now hitched herself on to the cushions as she repeated, 'Dear Lord! We know now that the poor girl dared not lift her eyes to another man, never mind carry on with him.' Then she went on, 'Oh, and the vest or the shift, whatever you like to call it. It was made by old Betsy Briggs. She used to clean for Irene's father after her mother died and Irene was still at school. It was one of Betsy's expert pieces, a long, slim, clinging woollen shift. It was more like the sort of dress girls wear today. She had knitted one for Irene's mother because she was afflicted with a weak chest, and then she made one for Irene. And what d'you think? She still had it on today, or the remnants of it, for although it was clean it was held together not with wool but mending threads of different colours. And on top of it she was wearing what was left of the rose red velvet dress she wore that night at the concert. You remember it?'

'Yes. Yes, Glenda,' Alexander said wearily. 'I remember it. How did you manage to get her undressed?'

'Without much protest, until we came to the vest. Then her strength was renewed for a time, because she grabbed at it, at least at the waist part. When I reassured her she could keep it by her, but that I must take it off for the present, she allowed us to do so. And when we put it into her hands she grabbed at the middle of it and, slowly, she turned it inside out, and pointed to a small brown-paper-covered package about two inches square. It was pinned to the garment, top and bottom, with safety pins, and she attempted to undo them. After I undid them for her she held on to the package. She held it to her bare chest, then let us take the flimsy woollen garment away from her. She made no resistance when the sister and nurse washed her. The sister said after: "It was eerie, like washing a corpse." Yet her body is covered with little blue marks, faint now but which at one time must have been prominent, you know, like the marks left on a miner's forehead from the coal.'

'Has she still got the package?'

'Yes. We left it in her hand, and she seemed to go to sleep. That was until Dr Swan came in. He stood looking down at her where she lay with her hair now in grey plaits each side of her face. I had already put him in the picture because he had attended her—you remember?—all those years ago. At the time, he was a very young man and must have had hundreds of patients through his hands since, yet he remembered her. "Dear Lord!" he said.

'It was when he took hold of her wrist that once more she seemed to be given strength, for she pulled her hand away and pressed it on top of the other, which held the little parcel. And although his voice was soft and reassuring when he said, "Don't worry, my dear, I'm not going to hurt you," there was fear in her eyes and her whole body trembled. His examination was brief, and she trembled violently throughout.

'When we were outside he said, "Her chest's in a bad way, but it's malnutrition that'll see her off. She can't have eaten properly for God knows how long. I've never seen a live body like it. Where has she been all these years?"

' "I don't know," I said to him. "That's what we hope to find out. But she has difficulty in speaking. It's as if she doesn't want to speak." Anyway, he said he'd call back later and we'd have a talk.'

Musingly, Alexander said now, 'I wonder what's in that package? Perhaps it might give us a lead.'

'Well, we'll not know until we can take it from her, or she gives it to us, which I can't see her doing as long as she's conscious.'

He turned to her and said, 'You know who her son is, don't you?'

'Yes, of course I do. And he'll have to be told: it's only right he should be. But how we're going to do it, and how soon, I don't know. The latter, I think, will depend on Dr Swan's opinion, and for the present all we can do is get some food into her. But it'll have to be slowly.'

Now Alexander rose to his feet, went to the fireplace and put his hands up on the marble mantelpiece. He looked down into the fire as he muttered, 'I'm shaking. I . . . The last two hours have brought the past rushing back at me as if it had happened yesterday.' He lifted his head and, turning towards her, he said, 'D'you think I might have a drink?'

'Of course; we both need one. Brandy or whisky?'

'Whisky, please.'

Glenda went into an adjoining room, and brought back with her a tray on which stood a decanter of whisky and two glasses. She poured out a large measure for her brother, a comparatively small one for herself.

After taking two gulps from his glass, Alexander said, 'I'd better get back to the office and put James in the picture. He, of course, knows nothing about this business; he was only a small boy when it all started.'

'Yes, I understand you must tell him, but you must also emphasise at the same time that he says not a word about it to anyone. Otherwise it'll be in the papers by the end of the week.'

His voice was serious as he answered her, 'Well, Glenda, that goes too for your staff. You must tell them that this must not be talked about, because if a hint of it got round that old scandal would erupt and no matter what the great-I-am did, he would not be able to buy off justice this time, and as much as I would like him to get his deserts there is the son to think about.'

'Don't you worry. This won't be the first secret my girls have kept.' Then she added, 'Will you come back to dinner later on?'

'No. I'm sorry, Glenda, I can't, but I'll phone before I go out because it'll be too late when I get back. All right?'

'All right; but I don't expect there'll be much change in her before then.'

2

It was about an hour later when Miss Fairweather brought in a tray of tea and set it
on the end of Mr Alexander's desk. She
looked from him to Mr James and asked,
'Shall I pour out?'

'No, thanks; we'll see to it. And,' he
added, 'don't bother waiting; we'll lock up.'

'I don't mind staying on, Mr Armstrong.'

'There is no need, Miss Fairweather. We
are likely to be here some time yet.'

It was a very stiff secretary who made her
exit, and James Armstrong looked at his father and smiled as he said, 'There goes a
disappointed lady. Is she still after your
blood?'

'Don't be silly, James; she's a very good
secretary.'

'Yes, but I suspect she thinks she'd make

a better wife. Anyway, what's all this about? I've only got to leave the office for a couple of hours and the excitement starts. It never. happens when I'm here. Taggart tells me—'

'Doesn't matter what Taggart tells you. Now, pay attention. I've got rather a long story to tell you and I'm going to start at the beginning. You were a child of six when it happened, but since you've come into the firm you've had quite a few dealings with the Zephyr Bond, haven't you?'

'Yes. Yes, I have. It's doing very nicely now and—'

'Yes, yes, I know all about that,' his father cut him off, 'but the lady who should have been receiving the interest on that bond for the last twenty-five or twenty-six years or so has never touched a penny of it for the simple reason that I couldn't find her. There was quite a bit of money spent in trying to trace her but to no avail until this afternoon when a vagrant, and yes, she must have been one for some very long time, came into this office and asked to see me.'

'Really?' The word was just a murmur.

'Yes, really. You know all about the Edward Mortimer Baindor Estate. Well, she was the wife—is still the wife—of that beast of a man. That's what I say he is, and that's what I've thought of him all these years, and although the affairs of his estate bring us in a good part of our earnings I would have told him to take it with himself to hell many a time if I hadn't been stopped by some instinct. I cannot put a name to it, except to say I felt that one day I would live to see him made to suffer for all the cruelty he had ladled out to others, and to the woman who came to us today in particular.'

His son made no remark on this, only leant slightly forward in his chair and waited for his father to go on speaking.

'My father,' Alexander now went on, 'took me with him as a young man to Wellbrook Manor, near Weybridge. He was breaking me in to the business at the time and when he received orders to go and see his client—old Edwin, Edward's father—who was crippled with gout and couldn't get around, we would make a day of it because my father had an old friend in the village of Wellbrook called Francis Forrester. He was the schoolmaster. He had taken this poor situation to get his wife away from the city because she had chest trouble. He'd had a very good job in a London school before this. Anyway, they had one daughter called Irene. She was about ten when I first saw her, a very pretty, sweet child. By the way, her mother had been something of a singer until she got this chest trouble, and her child took after her, and it was quite something to hear them singing together. The child went to the village school where she became friends with one Timothy Baxter. He was four years older than Irene, and apparently since the Forresters had come to the village six years before he had taken the little girl under his wing. His father owned a small grocer's shop in the village and when the boy was fourteen he left school and went to work for his father. His spare time was devoted to what he called his charge, who was Irene. They grew up together like brother and sister—that was, until the First World War broke out in 1914. He was eighteen then, and was only too ready to join up, but it turned out that he was colour blind. Moreover, he had had a nasty fall from his bike when he was younger and it had left him with bouts of migraine. But apparently he wasn't greatly troubled at being unable to join the Army because what he wanted to do was act. He had a good singing voice and was a natural on the stage. He had appeared in amateur concerts after he had left school and also had joined an amateur theatrical group. I don't know how it was wangled, but he got himself into a company of actors that set out round the country to entertain the troops.

'It was about this time that Irene's mother died and her father was devastated. But he looked after Irene and continued to send her for singing lessons, as his wife had wished, although he knew that his daughter would never make an opera singer. He confided to my father that, thinking the girl wasn't making any progress under the local singing teacher, he took her into town to one who had been recommended as the best. And after she had been tested the man was quite plain and honest. He said to them both it would be a waste of money to take her any further. She would do well in light musical theatricals and amateur concert singing and such, but she simply didn't have a big enough voice for anything more ambitious.

'When she told Timothy this he pooh-poohed the man's opinion and said she had a lovely voice and that he would do his best to get her work. Her father wasn't for this, and said so, so she remained at home, keeping house for him and doing light voluntary war work during the next few years. But it was on the day war ended in 1918 that she found him dead in bed. He was clasping a photograph of his wife and by his side was an empty box of pills and on the floor an empty whisky bottle.

'Since there was now less call for entertaining the troops, Timothy was home. But the war to end all wars had left many people destitute and this included his parents; the war had ruined their little business. When they left the village to join his mother's sister in the north, he stayed on because, in a way, he still felt responsible for Irene and he could still get acting jobs in London. How they both scraped through, I don't know, but I am fairly sure it was my father who helped them both financially over this rough patch. I only know for certain that she clung to Timothy, so my father said, not only as a father and brother but also as someone she loved. That he did not feel that way towards her hadn't, Father said, dawned on her. As far as she was concerned, she would always have him and he would always have her. That was her childish idea until a friend told

Timothy he could get him a job in the chorus
of a musical if he came up to town at once.
Naturally he did so.

'Anyway, Timothy Baxter did not remain
in the chorus for long but got himself a walk-
ing-on part. He was a natural actor and had
a good voice. The next thing I remember
about the whole affair at that stage was that
Timothy had got her a part in the chorus of
the same musical he was in, so their asso-
ciation continued and life must have been
bliss for her. That was until he told her that
the main members of the cast had the
chance to take their show to America and
had offered to take him with them, and of
course he couldn't refuse such a chance.
But as soon as possible he would send for
her.

'For the first six months or so they exchanged letters, hers very long, his, I understand, getting briefer and briefer. And then
his communications changed to postcards.
She was twenty when he went away. She
was nearly twenty-two when the communications stopped altogether, and I suppose
she was wise enough to know that he must
have found someone else. And also I'm sure
she must have told herself, as she told me

later, that he had never spoken one word of love to her.

'She herself by then was taking on different jobs during what the actors called resting periods. When she was twenty-three she had a part in an operetta that was getting good reviews. It was a kind of Cinderella story. She was a housemaid and she sang Offenbach's "Barcarolle," "Night of stars and night of love fall gently o'er the water." On the stage she suddenly stops and faces the mirror and sings to herself and imagines herself as a great star. Apart from that one solo it was a small part, because it led nowhere in the story, and I often wondered why it was pushed in. Although she sang beautifully her voice really hadn't the strength to reach the heights the song deserved, yet she was always enthusiastically applauded, until the real star of the show appeared. Anyway it was in that show that Edward Mortimer Baindor, old Edwin's son, saw her for the first time, and that's where I come in.'

'What d'you mean, Father, you come in?'

'Just what I say. Bear with me and you'll know why shortly.

'Well, now, first of all I'm going to go back

some years, to the manor house at Wellbrook. This is how my father told it to me,
exactly as Edwin told it to him. Edwin sent
for his son. Apparently Edward had just
come down from Oxford and had planned
to go on an extensive holiday abroad to pursue his hobby of archaeology, but the old
man had different plans for him. He wanted
him at home to carry on the name. There
were no other relatives left either on Edwin's
or his wife's side. He told his son in plain
words: "What you've got to do," he said, "is
get yourself married; and there's one ready,
if not waiting, for the chance. She is the best
bred around here, as good as her horses, I
understand, and the Spencer-Moores are at
rock bottom financially. Lillian's father'll
throw her into your lap because there's
money here. She's three years older than
you, but what's that? You look older, always
have done, like myself. And if she can breed
as well as she can ride, this house soon
should be filled with children." '

Alexander stopped here and nodded at
his son, who was laughing now, saying, 'He
actually told Grandfather that?'

'Yes, word for word. Funny, but there was
a kind of understanding between him and

my father. It was never to be the same with Edward and me.

'But anyway, I understand there was a helluva dust-up and Master Edward only succumbed after an ultimatum had been presented to him. What the ultimatum was Father didn't tell me. I don't think he knew. I should imagine it was along the lines of his allowance would be cut down to the very minimum if he didn't do as he was told. Anyway, there was an engagement announced in *The Times* and six months later there was a very grand wedding. But what neither the father nor the son bargained for was Miss Lillian's character. In a way she became a match for both of them because she showed them that horses were her priority and nobody on this earth was going to stop her riding. But young Edward did his duty as was expected of him and straight away she became pregnant, only to lose the first baby at three and a half months. Within three years she'd lost the third.

'Edward banned horses from the stables except the two that were needed for the carriage when she became pregnant again, and he practically became her gaoler. He never left the house for months on end. My father said he had the look on him of a chained and frustrated bull. He was a big man, six foot one and broad with it. Even at that age he looked like his father, though he had a violent temper, and was prone to wild bursts of anger. He had none of his father's under-standing or, at times, kindness. And it would seem he was by now more determined than his father that he should have an heir.

'Whether Lillian was very unhappy I couldn't say, because she too had a temper, which showed itself in a deep irritation to-wards another member of the household. Her husband had engaged a nurse-com-panion for her, and the woman seemed never to leave her side. Her lady's maid, a girl called Jane Dunn who had been her maid before she was married, one day un-intentionally pointed out to Lillian how she could escape for an hour or so. While stand-ing at the window, she saw Edward mount the carriage that was to take him to the sta-tion to catch a train into London for the day. After the nurse-companion had been into the bedroom to check that her charge was lying down and resting, the maid saw her, too, leave the house and make for the kitchen garden, which led to the bailiff's cottage. She had long suspected that there was something going on between those two, and that day she remarked on it to her mistress. Lillian sprang up from the bed, pulled on her underclothes, a pair of riding breeches, and a short jacket and hat. She ran out of the room, down the back stairs and into the yard, where she demanded of a fear-filled groom that he should help her to saddle an old horse, one considered past his prime who had been put out to grass.

'Lillian was out for two hours, and when she returned the nurse-companion was almost in hysterics at the disappearance of her charge. Lillian laughed at her. And she laughed at her husband when he returned and found her having dinner with his father and actually making *him* laugh. He was surprised at the bright face she turned to him, asking if he had enjoyed his temporary escape. But two days later she was no longer smiling . . . Nor was he, for he had learnt of her escapade. She was only seven months gone and the birth had begun prematurely. She was in labour for two days and the young doctor did everything in his power to ease her pain and fetch the child out alive. But he suspected it was dead before she made the last effort. Yet the midwife still did everything in her knowledge to bring life into the tiny body. But she was unsuccessful.

'Edward was in the room, and when he looked down on the well-formed male child he let out a sound like the wail of an animal, then turned his back on it. Going to the bed where the doctor was working to staunch the blood from the patient's womb, he looked down on his wife's pallid face and screamed at her, "You did it again, didn't you, and on purpose? You and your horses have killed my child. Well, I hope they gallop you into hell!" He gripped her by the shoulders and shook her like a dog shaking a rat. He let her fall back on the pillows only when the doctor's bloodstained hand came across his face and the midwife's arms were about him from behind.

'The room was a shambles and now, as he was pressed towards the door, he yelled at the nurse-companion whom he had left on guard, "I'll throttle you if you're not out of this house . . ."

'His words were muffled by the doctor yelling at him, "Shut up, man! Get out and calm yourself!"

'What Edward Mortimer Baindor did next

was to go down to the yard and beat the groom into a state of insensibility.

'Lillian died the next day and it was after the funeral that he was presented with a summons on the charge of assault and battery on one Arthur Briggs.

'It was only Father's work with Briggs's solicitor, and the offer of a substantial sum to the man made by old Edwin in order to stop any further scandal, that saved Baindor from facing the charge in court.

'Edwin, being aware of the feeling against his son in the community, willingly agreed now to his going abroad to pursue his hobby because he knew it was partly his own doing that had brought about the unhappy marriage between Edward and his dead wife.'

James rose and went to the cupboard. He handed his father a small measure of brandy. They both sat in silence sipping their drinks for a moment until James said, 'Well, I'm waiting. Go on. There's much more to come, and worse, I'm sure.'

'Yes, you're right. Well, young Edward was about twenty-seven when this happened. He would come home for short periods, then go off again, and my father said the old man never pressed him to stay. Then it was eight years later when, on one of his short stays, his father had a seizure and died, which left Master Edward in sole charge of the extensive business his father had built up. As my father said, Edward also inherited a great deal else from the old man, and that was business acumen, for now he was in control he dived into it with enthusiasm. Nothing escaped him. From the beginning Father didn't like him, nor did I, but he was a client and an important one. And what Father soon found was that the man disliked advice. He gave plenty of it himself, but by way of orders.

'Then came the night of the show I was telling you about. I was in the stalls and, happening to look up at the boxes, I saw him there. Well, that must have been when he spotted Irene and apparently fell for her, hook, line and sinker. I don't know how he arranged to meet her, I only know that from then on his whole attitude seemed to change. Not that he was any less business-like, but he was pleasanter. Yes, that is the word, he was pleasanter.

'Then one day I had an unexpected visit from her. She said the show was closing, and I said I was sorry to hear that, but she smiled and said that wasn't what she had come about. She wanted my advice. She knew that I was Edward's . . . Here she stopped herself, then went on, Mr Baindor's solicitor, and she recalled the happy times of my visits to her father. But did I know, she asked me, that she was . . . well, what was the word she should use? Being courted. And I repeated, "Being courted? Do you mean to say that you are being courted by my client?"

'She blushed slightly and nodded and said, "Yes, that is what I mean to say."

' "Well, well." I recall sitting back in my chair and smiling at her as I spoke. "So that is the reason for the change." At which she asked, "What change?"

'I said, "Well, you have altered his character already. He's lost most of his abruptness."

' "Well, I've known him less than three months, and now what d'you think? He has asked me to marry him."

' "Really?"

' "Yes," she answered, "just as you say, really. He has been very attentive and has been taking me here and there in his free time and mine. I told him about my family because he asked about them, but I didn't mention how my father died," and to this I remember replying, "No, of course not. There's no need for him to know." Then she said, "What d'you think I should do?"

'She might have been asking this question of her father, and I hesitated for a long moment before I said, "Do you like him?"

'Her answer came quite swiftly. "Oh, yes, I like him. He's so very—well, so nice and kind."

'Then I said, "Well, you like him but may I ask if you love him?" Now it was she who hesitated before she replied, "I loved Timothy first as a brother and then as a parent, both father and mother, but he didn't love me in the way I came to love him. I haven't heard from him for nearly two years now, so what feeling I had has naturally died. But do I love Edward?" The pause was longer before she said, "I don't know, but I think I could come to love him dearly."

' "Well, go ahead, my dear," I said.

'Her smile widened then vanished as she said, "But he has that great manor house and the estate, and I understand he is a very rich man."

' "In all three you are right," I said to her,

"and by the sound of it you are being offered the three, and wholeheartedly, I should say, because you have already made a change in him. I have seen him happy, and for the first time in his life, I should imagine."

' "You think so?"

' "Yes. And my father would confirm this and will, though he and my mother are away at the moment."

'She now said, "Yes, I know; but I came to you purposely because, well, you're younger and . . . and I thought you would understand my feelings. You see I am only twenty-three, but he is thirty-seven."

' "All the better," I said. "He'll know how to look after you, and probably much better than a younger man would. In a way I think you are a very lucky girl."

'At this she smiled at me and said, "I would too, if I could only realise what's happening to me. It's too much of a fairy-tale to take in, really."

' "Well," I said, "you continue to make it a fairy-tale, my dear . . ."

'Six months later they were married and our whole family was invited to the wedding. She had no relatives except an aunt who lived in Eastbourne. She looked the most beautiful of brides, but in a way very child-like. She didn't look her twenty-three years. I recall they were sent off in a glorious fash-ion at five in the afternoon to start their hon-eymoon, first stop Venice. There was a ball for the staff and their friends that night at the manor and any of the guests who had a mind to stay. This was all arranged by the butler, Mr Trip, and the housekeeper, Mrs Atkins. I remember recalling that I had been to that house a number of times with my father and never seen the staff so happy.

'But that wedding was nothing to when Irene gave him a son. Talk about a doting father! He really did lose years, and Irene adored the child from the moment she first held him. So said my mother, for she was allowed to visit her the day after the birth.'

At this point Alexander leant forward, picked up the glass from the table and drained the remainder of the brandy. Then his tone changed as he said, 'When was it I first noticed a change in her? In a way it showed first in her voice and attitude. On her wedding day, as I said, she was like a very young girl, but she was now a woman. Moreover, she was a mother who never wanted to leave her child's side, but apparently—I was given to understand much later—she had to, once her husband was in the house. It wasn't that he wanted desperately to be with her, although he did, oh, yes, he really did, but he also wanted to monopolise the boy. Wherever he was so must the boy be.

'After their honeymoon abroad, they had attended dinners and, to my knowledge, went to two balls. One was a charity affair. Your mother and I were also there, and we remarked how he danced with her, yet when she was dancing with anyone else he just sat watching her. I think the dancing must have ended when she informed him she was going to have the child, for he would have remembered what had happened to his first wife. But nevertheless they entertained and we were many times invited to dinner. It was on these occasions that I detected another change in her. She had become very quiet, her natural gaiety had disappeared. Although she laughed and chatted to her guests, there was no spontaneity in her as there had been before. There was no sign of any other babies coming, and although his manner was still cordial then, there were also glimpses of his domineering side.

When my father wasn't available and he had to deal with me, there was in his manner the unspoken words, "Why isn't he available? Doesn't he know who I am and what I mean to this firm? See that he makes himself available next time, young man." At least, that's how I interpreted his attitude, and in the end I found I wasn't far wrong.

'He rarely left home, and, I was told, when he wasn't visiting his companies and agents abroad, he spent his time with the boy. Rarely did she come to town, and when she did he accompanied her. She seemed to have very few friends of her own to visit, only us. He would leave the boy for a few hours, and a few hours only, for they never stayed in town to go to a theatre or to dine with friends. Twice they went on holiday, and the child was taken with them.

'It was about a fortnight before the boy's fourth birthday when Edward was forced to take a trip to Germany. There was to be a big takeover concerning the Flux firm, and it was imperative that he should be there. At the time I was running a charity for children's holiday camps. It had succeeded in getting a lot of poor boys off the streets or out of the gutters. It showed them a different way of life, and your mother and I were so interested in it that we had gathered together some quite big names for a charity concert. It was she who suggested we should ask Irene to come and sing. I recall her words: "Her gaoler is away, so what's to stop her? She still keeps up her singing when she can. I know because she told me. She probably sings to the boy when his papa is absent. One thing I'm certain of," she added, "she misses the stage and the company. That girl's lonely; I know she is."

'I felt I had to say to her, "I don't suppose she would dare do it without his permission."

' "Well, we can but try," was her response.

'During the past two or three weeks I had noticed that when we happened to be together Irene used to become rather agitated. It was as if she wanted to talk to me about something, to tell me something, but seemed afraid to. But this time she seemed to jump at the chance to get out on her own. The concert was to be held on a Sunday evening in one of the big theatres, and the stars would be giving their services free. It was a wonderful do—the concert, I mean.

We had gone to the manor and picked Irene up, and both your mother and I were in the nursery and were never to forget when she kissed her son and hugged him close, saying, "Mummy won't be long, she's just going out to sing for her supper." And he laughed at her and cried, "Well, Cook could give you some, Mummy." She threw her arms about him and kissed him, not once but three times. She didn't know it was the last time she would ever kiss her child.'

Alexander paused again. And then he put his hand on the table and brought his fingers into a fist and thumped the table with it three or four times before he again spoke to his son, who was now staring wide-eyed at him. He went on, 'It was a costume do and your mother had got her the most elaborate-looking Edwardian gown. It had a rather low neck, and apparently when your mother and the dresser went to help her on with it they saw there was an obstacle because Irene was wearing a kind of woollen shift affair that was, as your mother said, more like a fine woollen dress because it came to her knees. The dresser said she hadn't seen one for years and certainly not such a finely knitted one. Ladies used to sleep in them at one time, she said. Anyway, without it the costume fitted Irene perfectly, and when she put on the huge straw and feathered hat she looked the part, and for the first time in many a long day she looked happy . . . And she sang the "Barcarolle" beautifully. It was as if she had never stopped singing. In fact, it seemed that her voice had improved: it had become stronger. Anyway, she brought the house down. It was arranged that the main performers of the evening and their guests were to have a supper at the Carlton. So your mother took your grandmother out to the car that was waiting, leaving me behind to accompany Irene in a cab and join them at the supper as soon as she had finished changing. I recall the hall was soon cleared.

'As I waited, a young man who looked vaguely familiar came rushing in, wound his way between the chairs and made for a door that led to the dressing rooms. Then a few minutes later, I could not believe my eyes: Irene's husband came into the theatre. He wasn't running like the young fellow, but he was hurrying, and I recognised the look on his face. Oh, dear me, I thought.

'He did not see me. Now, what I've got

to say next is third hand. My information came later from the hysterical dresser. She said, "The lady had just got her costume off and had pulled on the cosy garment when the door was flung open and a man stood there with his arms outstretched, crying 'Irene!' and she jumped round and without hesitation rushed to him. He flung his arms about her and she hers about him, and they laughed at and with each other, and she cried, 'When did you arrive?'

' " 'About an hour ago,' he said. 'I've just heard that you were singing here, and I rushed from the hotel. I saw Mr Armstrong's mother getting into a car outside and she said you were in the dressing room. Oh Irene!' He held her at arm's length and said, 'Why, miss, did you not ask my permission to marry, eh?'

' " 'You weren't here,' she said; 'you weren't here.' Then again she threw her arms around him, and this time they kissed. Their lips were tight and their bodies close when the door opened and, at the sight of the man looking at them, she let out a sort of high-pitched scream.

' "The young fellow turned and said, 'Oh, hello. You must—' That's as far as he got because that man sprang on him. Like a tiger, he was, and the young fellow was so surprised that under the first blow he fell backwards and never seemed to regain himself, because that man battered him to the floor. All the while the lady was screaming; and then he snatched up one of the props. It was a china vase, and he brought it down on the young fellow. It hit him across the chest and the side of the face. The attacker then turned to her, and he shook her as if she was a rat. Then his fists pounded her face as he screamed at her: 'You dirty whoring slut, you!' The cleaners were rushing into the room now, but he wouldn't let go of her. By the time they dragged him from her she was quite senseless." That's all my informant remembered, because at that point she passed out.'

Alexander took a handkerchief from his pocket and wiped the sweat from his brow; but his son said nothing, just sat staring fixedly at him. Presently, his father gave a deep sigh and closed his eyes as he said, 'I can still see them lying there: her bleeding body had fallen across the young fellow's crumpled legs. His face was obliterated by blood. Somebody was yelling, "Get the police!"

Another, "Get an ambulance." Another, turning to where Baindor was leaning against
the wall, yelled at him, "You murdering bugger, you! Wait till the police get here!"

'The word "police" seemed to bring Baindor to his senses, and he was about to
stumble out when he came face-to-face
with me, and his words came out on a deep
growl as he said, "She's a whore!" and I,
forgetting for the moment who he was, cried
at him, "And you're a bloody madman!" He
just stumbled past me; and I went into the
room and said to two of the men who were
trying to straighten the young fellow's legs,
"Don't touch him! Leave him until the ambulancemen come." '

Alexander had not opened his eyes and
James, after sitting silent for some time,
said, in a very small voice, 'What happened
to them?'

'Oh,' Alexander pulled himself up in his
chair, 'it's a wonder she survived. They were
in a dreadful state, both of them. I recall
wishing the fellow would die and that mad
beast would be brought up for murder. It
happened that at that time Aunt Glenda had
her nursing home going; Father had set her
up with it. In those days she could only take

six patients and within a week we had brought Irene from the general hospital ward into Glenda's care. From the accompanying report, she learnt that Irene hadn't spoken since regaining consciousness. Nor did she utter a word for the next three weeks. It appeared that the brutal beating had not only marred her body it had also marred her mind in some way, for although she understood all that was said to her, she couldn't give a verbal answer, only make a motion with her head.'

When Alexander again paused James said, 'What happened to the young fellow?'

'Well, he was in a very bad way for some weeks. One side of his face from the front of his ear to his lower jaw had been split open, and this undoubtedly would leave a scar, but at the end of the first week he was able to speak. It appeared that the manager of the troupe he was with, which had come over for a short run in England, wanted to take the matter to court, but he would have none of it. He was thinking of Irene and did not want her name to be plastered all over the papers and Baindor's reason given as to why both she and he had been battered by the husband.'

'But didn't the police take it up?'

'No; it appeared that they went to the manor and saw him, and he said the woman in question was his wife. Had she made any complaint? And when they said no, he had asked about the other person: had he taken up the case? And again the answer was no. He said it was a family affair, quite private. It was nothing to do with them.

'I did not see him for nearly six weeks and I thought he had gone abroad; and then one day he stormed in here and demanded to see my father. At that time Father was retiring gradually and was enjoying himself, seeing to the alterations of the house he had bought next door to Glenda's in order to extend her business. The idea was to take the inner wall down and make comfortable private quarters for her and a sitting room for her nursing staff. This would still leave space for eight more bedrooms. He was like a child with a new toy. My mother had said, "Let him alone, you can manage the firm, and he's happy."

'Anyway, as I was saying, Baindor came in here like a wild bull. He stood where you're sitting now, and I sat here. I did not rise to my feet as was usual when a client entered the room, and he said to me, "Where is your father?" I, lying gently, said, "At home; he has a cold, he's in bed." I remember there was a long silence before he said, "Who gave you the authority to take my wife from the hospital and put her into your sister's nursing home?" I wonder now how I dared to answer him as I did, but what I said was, "Since you had almost beaten your wife to death and seemingly did not care any more what happened to her, I took it upon myself to move her from the hospital to quieter quarters."

' "You had no right!"

' "I had every right," I said. "It was a humanitarian act. She needed personal nursing."

'There was another long pause before he said, "I understand from the doctor that she also needs mental attention, so I am having her transferred to Conway House."

'This, James, brought me to my feet immediately and I cried, "Conway House! Attached to the convent? It's practically a lunatic asylum under the name of a nursing home."

' "It is not a lunatic asylum, it is for disturbed patients, and at the present time my wife is a disturbed woman. So will you be good enough to let me get down to the business I came to discuss with your father. As he is not available I will have to talk to you. You will have come across the Zephyr Bond?"

'I remember I couldn't speak for a moment but then I said, "Zephyr Bond? Yes, of course." The Zephyr Bond was the remnants of a company his father had bought up years ago. It never produced much interest although it remained steady but, whatever the market, it would never set the place on fire. He went on, "I wish to pass this deed wholly over to your father or to you, who unfortunately seem to be in charge now, in order that you will allot to my wife the sum of five pounds a week—no more, no less—from it. This will be paid to the matron of Conway House as long as she stays there, or to wherever they may transfer her. As a Catholic I cannot divorce her, but I wish to have no more mention of her name made to me, ever. And should she at any time in the future attempt to visit the manor there are orders—strict orders—that she is to be forcibly removed. In fact, should she resist and try in any way to get in touch with the child, I shall have the matter taken to court, and I shall be given sole custody of my son because his mother was an adulteress."

'I remember saying to him in deep anger, "You've no proof of that. She was welcoming back home after an absence of three years a man she thought of as a brother, a young man who had helped to bring her up from a child."

'The cool answer came, "So you say, but I don't believe it; and more than once she has spoken of this man with affection. In fact, I once told her, and only recently, to desist. But he is not the only man in question. There was my valet, Cox, whom I dismissed three months ago. She had him so fascinated that one day when I was out he was accompanying her on the piano as she sang."

'This,' Alexander now said, 'was news to me at the time, but I also then recalled how the poor creature had looked on various occasions when I had seen her.

'He now thrust on the table the case he had brought with him and, after opening it, he placed beside it a folded bond, and with it a long, typed letter. Pushing them both towards me, he said, "This is the old bond.

It has never been of great significance, but it has revived somewhat since the war, and will bring in enough to provide for my wife's maintenance at the rate of five pounds a week. I wish you to sign the acceptance in the name of your firm, and it can be witnessed. Send for your clerk." '

Alexander was now breathing heavily as he said, 'I recall, James, that I had the greatest desire to pick up that glass inkwell'—he pointed along the desk to where it was set in a brass tray—'and smash the thing into his face. Nevertheless, at the same time I knew that five pounds was better than nothing. She could exist on that in those days. Moreover, he hadn't mentioned anything about what was to happen to the money should she die. Were we to accept it as ours or return it to him? But I left this. That was in the future and it made no matter just then.

'The only thing I wanted at that moment, James, was to get him out of this office in case I did something that would not only ruin me but deprive the business of its most profitable client, one with whom Father had borne for years and whose business had helped greatly towards his putting me through university, buying a new home for

Mother and setting Glenda up in her nursing home. Anyway, when old Watson, the clerk, came in he showed no deference to the client, because he knew what had recently happened. Although it wasn't in the papers the news had certainly got round and, as it was no doubt also said openly, Baindor should have been exposed for what he really was. My heart went out to the old fellow for his courage because, looking down at the letter on the table, which was obviously a document, he turned to the great man and demanded, "What am I signing?"

'Baindor was taken aback; then he almost shouted, "It is no business of yours. You are paid to do what you are told to do."

'Before Watson could make any further remark on this I said to him, "It's all right. It is to do with the firm and it is in order. Just sign."

'The old fellow did as he was bidden but very slowly and reluctantly. Then, straightening his back, he gave the important client one long stare before walking out.

'I fully expected Baindor's next remark: "Dismiss him, and at once!"

' "He is my father's clerk, and that is his business," I retorted.

'His last words to me before leaving were, "Tell your sister that my wife will be collected tomorrow, and *that,* let me inform you, sir, is the last word I want to hear about her." He stood waiting for me to make a reply of some kind, but when he didn't receive one he went out without closing the door behind him.'

'I wouldn't talk any more for a moment. I'll pour you another drink,' said James, getting to his feet now, but his father stayed him with a gesture of his hand: 'No; no more.'

He smiled wanly. 'But I'll tell you something, even remembering this business has brought back to me the awful feeling I had, once that man walked out of the office. I felt so full of rage, real rage. I'd never experienced anything like it in my thirty-odd years before and I almost felt I was going to pass out. The only thing that brought me to was the fact that I had to see Glenda, as quickly as possible, and make some other arrangement for that poor girl.

'When I told Glenda she couldn't believe it. She said that Irene wasn't fit to be left on her own yet, she still hadn't spoken. Although her body had mended in a way, it was covered with odd marks and indentations. Her face, too, was still bruised, and her mind in some way was also affected. As Glenda said, we would have to get her away from the nursing home, but to where? If she took her to our place he would certainly come there. The only thing she knew about Irene's relatives was that she had an aunt in Eastbourne, the one who had come to the wedding. And it was on this basis that we got to work and talked to Irene. We had to explain what her husband was about to do, and when we asked her if he knew anything about her aunt in Eastbourne she made a small movement with her head, which meant no. Then Glenda asked her aunt's name. I can see Irene now, slowly pointing to a table on which were a pencil and pad, and as slowly she wrote down the name of her aunt, and the address. When I said to her, "Do you think you could get there—go on the train by yourself?" she made a desperate move with her head, nodding twice.

'Glenda got her into her outdoor clothes, and took her to the station. As she told me later, she kept thinking all the time that she should go with her and see her settled. But, in my presence, she had suggested to Irene that one of the nurses should go with her to Eastbourne and Irene's head had moved desperately from side to side. Then, for the first time, she spoke. Pointing to herself, she said, "All right." It was just a murmur, but it definitely was those words. Then she spoke again to me when I took her hand and helped her into the cab. Slowly and hesitantly the words came, "Thank . . . you," and that was the last time I saw her until yesterday, when she fell into this office in what looked like a vagrant's garb, but were the identical coat and hat she was wearing when she left Glenda's all those years ago. She was wearing them at the concert on that fatal Sunday night. How she has lived in them for the last twenty-seven years I don't know. But one thing is evident, she has existed on the streets.'

James's head was shaking in disbelief and his voice was low as he said, 'What about the aunt? Didn't she go there?'

'Yes, she did, but when we didn't hear anything from her for a week Glenda and I went to the house. And there I met the woman. God! My hatred for that woman almost matched my feelings about Baindor. Irene had come to her. Oh, yes, she told us she had come, but she had soon shown her the door. Irene was drunk, she said, or on drugs or something, for she wouldn't speak but wrote some disjointed words on a paper. One was "distress," the other was "husband misunderstood." So what did she say to her, this poor distressed creature? She told her that she was a married woman and must go back to her husband. Anyway, she herself was about to leave Eastbourne and live in Yorkshire.

'You know what I said to her?'

James shook his head.

'I hope you die a slow and painful death.'

'You said that?'

'I did. At that moment it was the worst thing I could wish on her.'

James now put his elbow on the arm of his chair and rested his head on his hand. They remained silent until James said, 'And you haven't the vaguest idea where she might have been all this time?'

'None whatever. And we won't have if she doesn't speak before she dies. But one thing I've promised myself, she will see her son before that happens.'

'Oh, yes.' James was sitting up straight now. 'The son. What d'you think he'll do when he knows?'

'That's to be seen. But I'm sure he's not like his father at all. He doesn't look like him or act or speak like him.'

'And he must have a will of his own to have rejected taking on the business and going in for medicine. Where is he now?'

'I don't know—in one of the London teaching hospitals, I think. I understand he's aiming to become a plastic surgeon.'

'How old is he now?'

'Oh, let me think. He was just on four when all this happened and that's twenty-six years ago, in 1928. He's thirty, I should say, just a couple of years younger than you. I should imagine he might be a consultant by now. But I don't really know when he started; I only know he was at Oxford until he was twenty-two or so. We'll soon find out, though.'

'When do you intend to see him?'

'It all depends on how the poor woman is. As she is now I don't think she'd be able to recognise anyone. Yet there must be a deep pain inside her that has lingered all these years, because that's what she said to me, the only words she spoke, "My son," which I took to mean she wanted to see him. And then she said, "He'll come." It was as if she was sure. At the moment, I only wish I knew what is in that package she keeps a tight hold of. It might give us some clue to her whereabouts all these years. Otherwise I doubt we'll ever find out.'

But he was to find out, and in a comparatively short time, and his knowledge was to come in as strange a way as the appearance of his informant herself. The story she was to tell Alexander Armstrong about where Irene had spent twenty-six of the missing years was as strange, if not more so, than the story he had just related to his son.

PART TWO
1929–1955

1

Big Bella Morgan closed the door on No. 10 The Jingles, then walked a couple of yards to her left and inserted a key into the lock of a rusty iron gate, which led into a large yard. It would have looked larger still, had it not been for the piles of broken wooden fruit boxes and the rotten fruit scattered here and there. Down the middle of the yard was a clear pathway that led to a stone building, at the end of which was a large wash-house. Thrusting open its door she cried, to the two sleeping forms lying there on thin palliasses, 'Come on! Show a leg and get on your way.'

One of the men sat up, rubbing his knuckles into his eyes and saying, 'What time is it, Bella? It's early like.'

'Aye, it's early enough,' she replied; 'early

enough for you to get to Robson's and see if you can bring some decent stuff back. I don't mind yesterday's but not the day before's lot. Give Pimple Face a kick there. He'll sleep until he dies, that one.'

Now the other man grunted, then stretched his limbs, gave a loud yawn and sat up, saying, 'God! What I'd give for a cup of char.'

'You'll have it after your first run. You know the ropes—you should by now.'

'You're a hard woman, Bella.'

'I'd be harder still if I left that bloody gate open at night, wouldn't I? Because they'd be lyin' on top of you, two double, and you know it.'

'I'll just have a swill, Bella; I've got a stinkin' head.'

This came from the big man who seemed to tower over the small fat woman, and Bella said, 'Do that, Joe, but don't make a bath of it, because you know what Robson's made of. He's as likely to hand some of the offshoots to the others who'll pay a penny a box extra. We made a deal, but I don't trust him. And, the both of you, I want this yard cleared up before you get anything to eat or a kip tonight.'

'What if, when I get to the warehouse, Baker has a job on for me? How about it then, Bella?'

'Well, it's up to you,' and she grinned, 'whether or not you eat and kip here tonight. As for you, Pimple Face, I think it's about time you gave up that whistle you play on the streets or learnt a few more tunes on it. Your takings would hardly keep a hen in corn. There are bound to be some jobs left that don't end in gaol.'

'Oh, Bella.' The smaller man shook his head. 'We've been over this, haven't we? I've been there once, I've told you, and I'm not going back again. Anyway, if I can give the cops the tip-off I'll get more than coppers.'

'Aye, you'll get more than coppers,' the woman said now, 'but as like as not you'll get a slit throat as well. The villains'll be on to you, I'm sure. Anyway, get moving.'

The two men did as she said, and pushed a long barrow through the iron gate. The woman followed them; then she turned and locked the gate again, before returning to her front door and opening it with a Yale key.

Once inside, she took off her coat and

the man's cap she was wearing, and hung them on a mahogany coat-stand by the side of the door. Then she walked across the sizeable hall, which was covered with brown linoleum, past the foot of a flight of broad stairs, one side of which was open to the hall and its banister supported by a stout mahogany pillar, then through a door into a large kitchen, which was warm and surprisingly comfortably furnished. An ornamental wood-framed sofa-couch stood against one wall, and there were two easy chairs which, like the couch, were covered with faded, worn tapestry. A wooden table stood in the middle of the room. The fireplace was a large open fire with an oven at one side and a boiler at the other. To the right of this was a Delft rack on which stood an assortment of odd pieces of china. There were four wooden rail-backed chairs tucked under the table, and to the side stood a basket chair, the seat well sunken with use. At the far end of the room was a larder with a marble-topped shelf running along one side, with, next door to it, a walled-off scullery area. Opposite was a door, which the woman opened and, switching on a light, passed through. She went down a flight of stone

steps into what appeared to be a huge cellar, and which, fifty or so years ago, had
been the kitchen of the house and the place
for the servants below stairs. Like many
such apartments for the lower classes in
those days, it was not only below stairs but
below ground and exceedingly damp.

The little fat woman now walked past the
large disused rusty stove and the various
cupboards going off the wall to her right
side, and through another door and into a
large back-yard. This had no boxes or stink-
ing fruit lying about, but in it was built a
modern flush closet. While she sat on the
wooden seat there she wondered yet again,
as she so often did, what could be done
with the yard and the cellar. Of course it
would need money, and although old Ham
had been kind in leaving her the house, he
hadn't left her any money, thinking that she
could make a living from the business he
had started long years ago of the fruit stall
outside his house. Of course he had been
right. She did make a living of sorts from it,
but the extras had to come from other
sources. Risky odds and ends, such as har-
bouring Mr Weir's vans in this very yard at
night sometimes.

Funny that. He was the only man she knew who hadn't a nickname, and he was always referred to, by his van men or those about, as Mr Weir. He was an unknown quantity, old Ham had said. They were the words he had used, Weir was an unknown quantity, and that was many years ago, because no one had ever seen him. But whoever he was he still owned remainder warehouses and sometimes dealt in questionable goods, and used more yards than her own for storing these last. However, he paid well and she couldn't but say it was a godsend at times; even though she was always glad to come down of a morning to do her business and see the yard empty. She hadn't given his main driver a key for the back door to the cellar—there was no need to. The stuff in the vans was a varied assortment of goods, cheap and otherwise, but one thing she wouldn't allow, she had stuck out against it, and that was letting them have the cellar for storage. No! She could talk herself out of a police raid by saying that she had no knowledge of what was in the vans that spent the night in her yard, but she would never get away with the same tale about her cellar, which was a part of her house . . .

By eight o'clock she had her fruit stall in place in front of the window to the right of her front door. The window had a deep sill, and boxes of fruit were piled on it. On the two front shelves of her narrow stall she had arranged various fruits. To the side stood a sack of potatoes and two orange boxes, their divisions now filled with leeks, carrots, turnips, cabbages and bunches of radishes.

There were four other decaying houses in the short street known as The Jingles, and each was used as a business of sorts. The front room of the one next to Bella's was a cobbler's shop. Next to that was a butcher's, which, it was rumoured, sold only horse meat. The fourth had been turned into an outdoor beer shop, and the ground-floor rooms of the last house held an assortment of second-hand—or you could say fourth, fifth or sixth-hand—clothing, but in them could be found something to suit all ages from the cradle upwards. It was a Paddy's market, all right, and well patronised.

The patrons of this little side-street, as one could imagine, were the lowest in the human scale, yet the businesses in it pro-

vided their owners with just enough suste-
nance to live. It was also frequented by
those who had no money with which to buy:
they came either to beg or to steal; those
deciding on the latter course were naturally
good runners.

On a Friday and Saturday Big Bella's stall
could be cleared by dinner-time, but on
Monday, Tuesday or Wednesday half her
goods would find their way at the end of the
day into the side-yard, which once had
housed a horse, carriage and tack room with
a groom's quarters situated above. These
uses had long gone and there remained now
what had been the wash-house, and was
still the wash-house.

Today was a Friday, and the boxes her
boys had brought her from the market were
naturally all seconds or, you could say,
thirds, but in their way they were good and
there was little she'd had to pick out, and
even that could be sold for a copper later
in the day. So now she sat on her stool,
which today, because the air was sharp,
was placed just within her partly open front
door.

She was not afraid, while attending her
stall, to leave her door a little way open for,

should anyone try to push it further, it was so arranged that it would knock over an old ship's bell, and this was always a deterrent more telling than a police whistle.

So her day began. She would leave the stall at ten o'clock when she would go indoors to make a drink; and again at twelve midday till half past when she would make herself a meal. At these times the stall was taken over by one-arm Pegleg, a description that spoke for itself. He was a 'remnant' left from the Boer War, who had taught himself to read and write; he could also count, so in different ways he was invaluable to the small business people of The Jingles. Moreover, he was known to be trustworthy. However, by seven o'clock that evening Bella was sitting comfortably in the old basket chair in her kitchen with a glass of porter at her side on the table. The day's takings had been gone over and found to be satisfactory. She'd had no stuff to throw into the yard, only empty boxes; and now she was giving herself a half-hour's break before she started cleaning the room, which, keeping to the pattern of years, she did every Friday night. She was looking through the pictures in an illustrated magazine. The 'boys' always brought in any picture paper they came across because they knew she liked to look at them.

She was about to take her last mouthful of porter when she heard a dull thumping on the wall to the right side of the fireplace. That meant someone wanted her attention, but why? It was only an hour ago that she had given the men their nightly bowl of soup and a shive of cheese and bread, with the warning that before they turned in they were to get that yard cleaned up as much as they could. If not, there would be no beds for them tomorrow night. With this false warning she had closed the gates on them. But now she felt something must be amiss because only once before had she heard the thumping; and that had been when Pimple Face had the jitters and Joe could do nothing with him. Joe had been concerned for his friend. The closeness of the two very different men had always puzzled her. There was Geordie Joe, all of six foot and Pimple only five foot four. She knew where Geordie Joe had come from: she herself had engaged him when she couldn't understand a word he said, for he was from the north-eastern end of the country where they spoke a different language. Where Pimple came from in London she didn't know; she didn't think he knew himself. Ham had taken him on, likely out of the gutter. At first she used to think they hadn't a penn'orth of brains between them, but she had learnt differently, for she had found they were both wily, yet also in a way wise, and they weren't greedy.

Hurriedly she picked up the keys from a little table standing by the hall-stand, and from there she took her coat, pulled it about her and went out, making sure, as always, to lock her door behind her. When she opened the rusty gates, there they both stood in the dim light waiting for her. 'What's happened?' she demanded.

It was Joe who answered her in a thick whisper: 'We've got a visitor.'

'A visitor? What're you talking about?'

Joe jerked his head towards Pimple, saying, 'He knows more about her than I do.'

'It's a woman?'

'Yes, it is.' Pimple was nodding at her, his high squeaky voice now a whisper. 'It's the one that's been knocking around the market for some time. Sleeping rough. She looks like a scarecrow. Well, you'll see for yourself. We had cleared this side,' he turned his

head towards where the stables had once
been, then thumbing over his shoulder, he
said, 'when we heard this rustle in the far
corner where the boxes are piled up.'

Joe put in, 'We thought it was rats like.
We thought we had got rid of them but you
never can, not proper like.'

That word 'like' was another thing that
identified Joe. Whether it was anything to
do with the area he came from, she didn't
know, although she could place many of the
lads who came begging by the way they
spoke.

Joe nodded towards the smaller man,
who went on, 'She's not like the ordinary
dossies. It's her get-up. It's obviously been
classy, but she's a bit wrong in the head.
The market fellows said she was dumb. And
she's not after making coppers on the game
because, they tell me, she's petrified of men.
But only yesterday I heard Mickey Robson
talking about her. He said a funny thing happened. It was early on and she must have
sneaked in in the dark and he caught her
taking an apple from a box, and he gripped
her hand, saying, 'What're you up to?' And
when she dropped the apple he said she
shivered like a jelly. He said he had heard

of her afore and thought she was one of the
meths lot, but apparently she wasn't. As
delicate as she looked she had almost torn
one of the men's eyes out when he tried to
get her to the floor. They give her a wide
berth down there now. He said he didn't
know where she kips out, but kip out she
does, because her clothes are in a mess,
but they must've been stylish at one time.
Funny but stylish. She wears a hat, velvet
one with a peak on it like a clerk's shade.'

'What d'you mean by a clerk's shade?'
Bella asked abruptly.

'Well, you know, men in newspapers and
offices, they wear a greenish eye-shade
against the light. Hers is only a narrow brim,
yet it covers her eyes. It got round too that
she's dumb, but not deaf because she
seems to understand every word that's spoken. But all the time she looks terrified,
Mickey Robson said. He had picked up another apple and handed it to her, and then
he found she wasn't dumb because she
muttered very quietly, 'Thank you', and as
Robson said himself, it was no working
lass's voice that spoke. And then Sullivan,
who was there, said he had once seen her
go into a pie and pea shop. Somebody, too,

must have told the Salvation Army lasses about her and the way she was dressed, and when they came back with one of their officers and he went to take her arm, she thrust him off and ran. And now we've got her.'

'What d'you mean, "we've got her"?' said Bella harshly. 'And how, in the name of God, did she get in here? What have you two been up to? Have you been out and left that gate open?'

It was Joe who answered: 'No, Bella. No. Except for a few minutes when I took a barrowload of muck to the tip and I left Pimple here sweeping.'

'It must've been then,' said Pimple. 'I went into the wash-house for a minute to see if the fire was all right: we had filled a pot of water, we were going to have a swill down.'

Bella was making her way through the debris to the far corner of the yard; and there she stopped and looked down into a white face from which two large eyes, expressing plain terror, stared back at her. The woman's legs were drawn up under what appeared to be a long dark coat; she looked like a bundle of rags. Bella took a deep breath, then said quietly, 'It's all right; nobody's going to hurt you.'

The two men standing to the side of her exchanged glances; and they were more surprised when their boss, as they thought of her, said, 'Come on! Stand up! Let's see you!'

When the creature made no move Bella put out her hands and, gripping the woman's shoulders, pulled her to her feet, at the same time being surprised at the lightness of her; the large coat would have suggested quite a big body underneath. When she said, 'Why don't you go in a kip somewhere?' she knew it was a stupid thing to say. If the woman had any money that's likely what she would have done. She now had to put her hand out quickly to stop the form that was standing lopsidedly before her from swaying.

Pimple cried, 'Watch it! she's gonna pass out.'

Geordie Joe's big arms prevented the woman collapsing to the ground again, and as he held her limp body he looked at Bella, saying, 'What now, eh? What now?'

'Take her to the wash-house.'

'What? You mean carry her there like . . . ?'

'Well, as far as I can see, you big stook, she's not going to fly, is she? Or trot, or run?'

'She might be lousy.'

'Well, it won't be the first time you've had them crawl over you, will it? So stop your chatter and come on.'

In the wash-house, Joe hesitated. 'Where might I put her?'

'Where d'you think? On the floor!'

So he laid the unconscious woman on the floor, and there Bella leant over her and, pushing the peak of the cap upwards, she touched the fair hair that spread from under the velvet rim. Then, her hand going to the back of the head, and feeling the large pouch there, she remarked, as if to herself, 'Must have a lot of hair to tuck in there.'

'I wonder where she's from,' said Pimple. 'I wonder what's happened to her.'

'That's what I'd like to know too, Pimple. Anyway, she'll have to stay in here tonight.'

'What? With us?'

'Yes, Joe, with you. That is, unless you'd like to sleep outside in the boxes.'

'Well, from what I hear and Pimple says, she's scared of men.'

'Then you've got to reassure her, haven't you?' Bella's voice had risen. 'Will you take it on yourself to put her back among the boxes or out into the street? Tomorrow I'll let you do it. Yes, in fact I'll tell you to do it. But for tonight I say she sleeps here.'

'There's no other mattress.'

'As I understand it, Joe,' said Bella now, 'you're sleepin' on a decent one. Well, you can let her have it for the night. Pimple there kips on two thin pallets; I'm sure he'll share one with you. That right, Pimple?'

'Aye. Aye, Bella,' the words were tentative, 'if . . . if Joe's willin'.'

'Joe has no option in the matter.' Bella's voice was loud now, and it must have disturbed the woman for she put a hand to her face; then, her eyes opening, she stared up again into the face of the short fat woman bending over her and she did not move; that was until her glance turned sideways and, through the light of the swinging oil lamp, she saw the figures of two men, one very big, the other very small. Quickly pulling her legs up under her, she shuffled her body away towards the boiler. Another foot and she would have been touching the fire door, but Bella's hand stopped her as she warned,

'Look out, if you don't want to be burned!
Now, it's all right, you've got nothing to be
afraid of from these two. D'you hear me?
D'you know what I'm saying to you?' Bella
was kneeling on the floor now by the side
of the woman and her face was on a level
with hers as she said, 'You passed out, and
you're in no fit state to go trudging the
streets tonight. You may stay in here until
the morning; and I promise you these two
men won't touch you. D'you hear me? Do
you understand what I'm saying to you?'

There was no vocal answer, but after a
long moment the head made a small downward movement, although the eyes still remained full of fear.

'What's your name?'

The woman's head drooped forward, and
Bella took her meaning: she wasn't going to
say. So, she said to her, 'Lift yourself on to
this mattress; and don't worry, I promise you
you'll be safe until the morning.'

The woman did as she was told; then
Bella said, 'I'd take off me shoes if I was
you.' But for answer the woman drew her
feet upwards and tucked them under the
long coat, at which Bella said, 'Well, have it
your way. They're your feet and as far as I

can see they're wet. Are you hungry?' But as she said this Bella thought she needn't have asked, and immediately turned to the men and said, 'I don't suppose either of you has a sandwich or anything tucked away in your pocket?'

Big Joe said nothing, but Pimple said somewhat shyly, 'Well, I've got a couple of buns in me coat.' Then he added quickly, 'I bought them, I didn't nick them. I got them along at the bakery, you can ask.'

'Shut up! Anyway, hand one over.'

Bella offered it to the woman, who was now sitting half upright propped against the warm wall side of the boiler. She looked at the hand holding the bun and her lips moved each over the other before her hand came out and picked it from the extended palm. She did not immediately put it to her mouth; but, her head turning slowly, she looked towards the small man, and there were the two words that she had been known to utter before, only this time in a croak as she said, 'Thank you.'

The effect of this on Pimple was to make him move swiftly from one foot to the other. It was as if he was about to do a jig. Then he looked at his companion, and from Joe to his boss, and what he muttered was, 'She's a different kettle of fish.'

Bella looked at him. He had a feeling in him, had Pimple: as he said, that one sitting there *was* a different kettle of fish. For a moment she wondered how long it had been since she'd had a square meal—her arms felt fleshless. On an impulse she said, 'You come with me, Joe, and I'll give you a bowl of soup for her; and if you're civil I might find a can of cocoa for you both.' And then she added as she went out of the door, 'I must be going up the pole;' and to this Joe said on a laugh, 'Just as you say, boss, just as you say: you must be going up the pole.'

Ten minutes later Joe was being pushed back through the gates by Bella. He was carrying a small straw basket in which stood a bowl of soup with a plate over it, and on the plate was a large bacon sandwich, and to the side of this was a lidded can of steaming cocoa. And as she stood locking the gates he did not walk away, but turned to look back through the rusted iron tracery and say to her quietly, 'You're a bit of all right, you know, Bella. A bit of all right. There's never been a better.'

Bella Morgan watched the big fellow disappear into the darkness; then she walked slowly to her front door, unlocked it, and entered her house.

After locking the door, she sat down in the basket chair, and she repeated, 'You're a bit of all right, you know, Bella. A bit of all right. There's never been a better.' That was a compliment and a compliment indeed. And nobody in her life, not even Ham, after she had nursed him all those years, had said, 'You're a bit of all right, Bella. A bit of all right.' It had taken that big rough galoot of a fellow to pay her the first compliment of her life. Here she was, thirty-eight years old. She was five foot two, fat, and as plain as a pikestaff, so marriage hadn't been for her. Men ignored her. No, not all men. Her father hadn't . . . She got swiftly to her feet and shook herself: she had never cried in her life and she wasn't going to start now.

2

The following morning, Bella was eager to get into the yard to see what had transpired during the night. Her first surprise was that both her helpers were up and dressed. They met her half-way up the yard, and she said to them, 'Where is she?'

'Where you left her last night, and she's sound asleep. It must be the warmth of the boiler—she's as close to that wall as to be almost inside it,' said Joe.

'Did she eat her soup?'

'Eat her soup?' Pimple put in. 'Bella, she wolfed it; and the sandwich an' all; and I gave her a can-lid full of cocoa; and she took it from me without shrinking back.'

'She shrinks from me,' said Joe. 'It must be me size. What you goin' to do with her? Give her a job of some sort?'

'Ask yourself, man, what job have I got to give her? Anyway, it takes me all me time to keep you two goin'.'

'By the looks of her,' said Pimple, 'I don't think she'd expect much, only to be warm and have a bite. I thought . . . well,' he swung his head from side to side, 'I'm sort of sorry for her. She's not like others about . . . I mean any of them sleeping rough. And she looks so scared. I've a feeling she must've had a great shock of some kind and it's turned her head, because she can speak. Well, you know, you heard her; but she won't talk; she can hear all right, though . . . everything. I'd like to know where she comes from. One thing seems certain'—his voice was firm now, unusual for him—'it wasn't the gutter, because in spite of the muck, I mean the state her clothes are in with mud and that, I swear she's known a different class.'

'My! She's got you, hasn't she?' said Bella, on a laugh.

She left them, to go into the wash-house. As they had said, the woman was still fast asleep and curled up against the wall, which held the warmth from the dead fire. She did not know whether or not to waken her, and

she asked herself, waken her to what? To
go out on the road again to scratch for food,
just as, apparently, she had been doing, and
sleeping rough? Yes; and by the sight of that
coat, very rough indeed. But, then, what
was she going to do with her? She had no
work to offer her; in fact, she thought, if, as
Pimple surmised, she was a real lady, she
might never have dirtied her hands in her
life. But if that was the case why weren't her
people looking for her? She was not one
who could be easily overlooked. Somebody
would surely have remembered seeing her:
hereabouts she must have stuck out like a
sore thumb. That coat and funny hat had
not been bought at any second-hand stall,
of that she was certain. She had felt the
cloth of the coat when she had gripped the
woman's arms. It was blanket thickness,
and under the collar it was still a bonny
green, as was the top of the cloche or turban
or whatever name you could put to the hat.

She went out, thinking, I'll leave her for a
while, but she must be out of there before
I set up me stall.

It was some time later when she had got
the can of tea and a breakfast bite ready for
her workers that the knock came on her

front door again, and there stood the two men, both grinning widely as they said, 'You want to come and see what's happening.'

'What d'you mean what's happening?'

'What she's doing, the one we left asleep.'

She handed them the straw basket holding their food and drink, then accompanied them back through the gates and into the yard.

It was broad daylight now and there was the woman. She was sweeping the remnants from the boxes into a heap in the middle of a cleared piece of the yard. A number of boxes in good condition were standing neatly piled one on top of the other against the far wall, broken ones were placed on the ground at the foot of them.

Bella turned and looked at the two men, and Joe said, 'What d'you make of that now?'

'What I make of it,' she said tartly, 'is that she's startin' to clear the yard, as you should've done a long time ago.'

'Oh, Bella.'

'Never mind oh, Bella.' She walked from them now and when she approached the woman whatever she meant to say was checked by the refined but muffled voice saying, 'Thank you—work.'

To this Bella answered, but only after a moment, 'There was no need; but thank you all the same.'

Then pointing to the rest of the disordered yard, the woman again said, 'Work.'

Bella looked from one to the other of her men; then, turning to the woman again, she said, 'You mean you're asking to work for me here?'

Now the head made a downward motion, and to this Bella said, 'But . . . but I can't afford to take anybody else on.'

Now the woman's head was shaking, and she turned and pointed towards the wash-house and then to her mouth, and it was Pimple who translated her seemingly deaf and dumb language by muttering to Bella, 'I think she's trying to say she doesn't want pay, just somewhere to kip and something to eat.'

The woman's gaze was now on Pimple, and she was nodding.

'You mean you'll sleep with the men?' said Bella.

Immediately the woman stepped back-wards quickly, her body seemed to shrink inside the big coat and her head drooped on to her chest; again Pimple translated, saying, 'She doesn't want to sleep along of us. That's awkward, isn't it, Bella, 'cos that's our kip?'

Bella made no comment, for she was experiencing a most strange feeling as she stared at this long-coated odd creature, and the feeling told her that whatever arrangement had to be made she couldn't let the woman go into the outside world, of which she sensed she was afraid and where she would certainly be taken down by some man and probably end up in the river.

She turned to the men: 'Get your bait, then before you go I'll give you a bite to put in the wash-house for her. You, Pimple, try and explain to her—I mean about me locking the gate. Make it plain to her she can't get out even if she wants to.'

'By the look of things I don't think she'll bother too hard to get out,' said Joe.

'You leave that to me; but when you're out look about and see if you can get your hands on a single mattress of some kind; but see it's clean, not walking.'

'Aye, Bella. Aye, I'll do that,' Joe assured her. Then they all turned and looked at the woman, who was sweeping again as if her work had not just been interrupted . . .

She was still sweeping, but more slowly, when at ten o'clock Bella went out to her and said, 'Drop that,' nodding towards the brush, 'and come into the wash-house and have this.'

The woman obeyed her. When they were inside Bella handed her the can of tea and a paper plate on which there was a thick slice of bread and dripping, and she said, 'Sit down and take it easy; if you mean to clean that yard it'll take days. And another thing, I don't know where you're going to sleep because you won't sleep in here with the men, will you?'

The woman turned her head away, and Bella, a little irritably, said to her, 'What's your name?' and when the head did not turn towards her, Bella said, 'You must have a name I can call you, for goodness' sake!' The woman muttered something, and Bella repeated, 'Rain?'

The woman now stared at her; then wetting a finger, she went to the dirty window and on it she traced out the letters RE, and Bella said, 'R . . . E? RE?' Then almost on a laugh, she said, 'Ren-e?' The woman's head was nodding now. 'Reenee! Reenee! Aye. Aye.' Bella was nodding too. 'I see now: not rain, but Reenee.' Then more nodding, and Bella said, 'Nice name, Reenee.' Then, being the practical woman she was, she asked, 'You found the privy in this yard, did you?' And to the unspoken confirmation, she said, 'Well, that's something. And that's a place now that wants cleaning out. Those two beggars should've seen to it. But don't you bother with it; I'll have a go at them. I'll be back around twelve.' And with this she turned and left Reenee, wondering, as she did so, why the woman should bother her. But bother her she did; as did wondering where she was going to let her kip that night. She certainly wouldn't let her stay in the house. Oh, no; she wasn't going to have any of that. But there was the cellar. It was as cold as charity, but there was the fireplace. Old Ham used to have that fire on when he brought in pieces of old furniture, what he called antiques, and at such times the fire would be lit while he worked at mending them. Well, that seemed the only solution; but God in heaven, why was she bothering? It was Saturday and she had a decent lot of stuff to sell, the best she'd had for some time . . .

At a quarter past twelve, after she had finished her own meal, she took a bowl of soup and a meat pie into the girl, as she now thought of her, with the name Reenee, and found her chopping up boxes into kindling. In the wash-house the boiler was already full of water and the fire on. She called her in, then said, 'My word, you've been busy, haven't you? And you've cleaned this place up an' all. I've not been able to look through that window for years. Now sit yourself down and have this bite.'

Reenee's eyes were on the little fat woman now and there was no longer any fear in them.

'I've thought of where you might kip. I—I mean sleep. But it couldn't be tonight because you'd freeze. It's in the cellar. There's a fireplace down there. It used to be the kitchen of the house, you know, and it's a good burner, and once that's lit . . . well . . . well, you could sleep down there. That's if the lads can get a mattress.' And then she added thoughtfully, 'And nobody would be able to get at you 'cos the door to the outside is bolted top and bottom, and the only way you can enter it is from my kitchen. So you wouldn't have to worry. You understand?'

Reenee nodded; then, her hand going slowly out, her fingers touched the little fat woman's wrist. It was only a featherlight touch but it brought a rush of feeling into Bella's body such as she had never experienced before. She did not realise it to be compassion, she knew only that she felt sorry for the creature, sorry to the bottom of her heart. But the reason for feeling like this she couldn't fathom. She was experiencing the strangest emotions. Look at last night: that big galoot had spoken to her like he did, and now the feeling for this broken reed.

Why, she asked herself sternly now, should those words come into her head—broken reed? Then she remembered seeing them in a magazine somewhere when somebody's sad life was being described. They were a broken reed, it had said. 'Get on with your bite,' she said, as she turned abruptly and went out.

Her stall was cleared by half past three in the afternoon. There wasn't even a cabbage leaf left, and the little guttersnipe gathered up the empty boxes, together with the trestles, and took them to the iron gates. When she opened them he carried the stuff inside and, as usual, went to throw the boxes into a heap, only to be stopped by Bella yelling at him, 'Stack them up! D'you hear me? Take them over to that wall where the other ones are.' She pointed to the far end of the yard and, much surprised, the youngster made three journeys with the boxes and stacked them against the wall. Then, still obeying orders, he put the trestles and the planks into what had once been a coalhouse. But he was a bit peeved when Bella added nothing to the twopence she gave him daily for running errands and clearing up.

She did not go to see what the new acquisition to her staff was about, but went into the house and made herself a cup of tea, then sat thinking about the girl and her sleeping quarters. If she let her stay in the cellar she would have to come through this house to get to it, because in no way could Bella risk giving her a key to the back door. Let's face it, she told herself, she didn't know what the creature might be up to. The word 'creature' had kept popping into her mind when she thought of the girl, probably suggested by the weird coat and hat she wore. Of one thing she was certain, the girl wasn't quite normal: something had happened to her to knock her off balance. What it was she would like to know, and she was sure she would come to know eventually; but it would take time because she would be dealing with a still very frightened creature. One thing more, there must be somebody, somewhere, looking for her: a girl like that wouldn't be without a family. Surely not. Whoever had been the cause of her distress must be known to others, and they must definitely, if they had any heart at all, want to know what had become of her. Yet she had been in the gutter, so to speak, for at least some months now. Well, she told herself, there was no use sitting here mulling over something she couldn't get to the bottom of, not as yet anyway. She'd take the girl down and see her reactions to the cellar.

When Reenee entered Bella's house for the first time she stopped abruptly within the small hall and gazed about her; and Bella, seeing this, said, 'Surprised, are you? You didn't expect to see it clean and tidy and holdin' decent pieces. Well, come and see something better still.' Pushing open the door, she said, 'This is my kitchen and sitting room. I have a parlour but I don't use it. No need to; but it would also surprise you.'

Again Reenee had stopped and looked around her. Then her eyes became fixed on the fireplace, where a large iron pan stood on the hob, something quietly bubbling within it.

'This wasn't really the kitchen,' Bella said, 'it was a sort of dining-room. The kitchen's downstairs in the cellar. Come on.'

At the top of the stone stairs, she switched on a light, then another when they reached the bottom. And this showed up the long room, bare but for a pile of broken furniture in one corner.

Bella pointed to the rusted iron range. 'That's what I was talkin' about. It's a good fire, had to be in those days for all the cookin' they did. But it eats wood, and needs coal.' The word coal immediately presented her with the idea that she could pay Reenee by giving her a bag of coal each week. Aye, that would be an idea.

She unlocked the back door and, pointing towards a door across the yard, she said,

'That's the privy, a better one than the other; but if you intend to sleep down here, don't go out to it in the middle of the night because . . . well, there might be vans in the yard. That's another thing. Don't take any notice of the commotion there might be around late evenings or in the dead of night. There's nobody trying to get in, they just . . . well, they just store their vans there until the next morning. You understand?'

Reenee indicated that she did. Then she looked up and down the large yard and the look of bewilderment on her face made Bella ask, 'What is it? I told you, nobody can get in except the vans and the men on them. Look yonder: there are two stout gates and they are locked. You'll be all right here, only always keep your door bolted because somebody might get curious if they see smoke coming from the chimney. You never know; there's always a sharp one among them. Oh, for that matter'—she was talking as if to herself now—'they're all sharp, a weird lot.' She pointed again to the lavatory. 'Do you want to go to the lav?' And when Reenee indicated that she did, Bella stepped back into the room to wait. Looking about her, she asked herself again why the hell she was doing this and going to all this trouble. Was she lonely? Did she want company? Well, if she wanted company she had picked on the wrong one, hadn't she, because the girl had hardly opened her mouth. Most of the time she talked in sign language like someone dumb.

When the girl joined her again, she walked past Bella and straight to the fireplace. There, with excitement, she pointed to the grate, then acted as if she were lighting a fire. Next, she pointed towards the ceiling and, as if somewhat exasperated, Bella said, 'Look, you can do nothing until tomorrow. That fire eats wood.'

Again Reenee pointed upwards, and Bella said, 'Aye, I know there's plenty of wood up there, but down here that wouldn't last you a week.'

Then, facing her and closing her eyes tightly, Reenee put her hand to her throat. It would seem she had to press the words upwards and into her mouth and through her lips as she said, 'Tonight.' She then put her hand on her face and bent her head, indicating sleep.

'You want to sleep here tonight?'

The indication was yes.

'But, woman, there's not a spare mattress unless Pimple gives you one of his spare pads; although they might find one when they're out and about today. And look'—she turned and swept her hand as if she were taking in the whole large room—'you'll catch your death; it would be as bad as lying in the gutter.'

The girl's head now drooped on to her chest, then moved slowly from side to side, and Bella's voice was soft as she said, 'All right. All right, lass. Come on; we'll see what we can do. They should be in about six and I'll set them to work cleaning that stove with emery paper.'

The head came up sharply and shook at the suggestion, and Reenee pointed to herself, which Bella took to mean that she would clean it. She said, 'It'll be some job. But come on. I'm freezing already down here.'

They were about to pass through the kitchen when suddenly Bella stopped and, catching hold of the girl's arm, she said, 'Look; sit yourself down on that chair and I'll make a cup of tea.'

Reenee remained perfectly still and she stared at Bella, who, looking into the pale grey eyes, saw in them an expression she could not fathom.

For a moment she thought the girl was going to cry, but the lids drooped and the eyes were closed. Then she watched her turn round slowly and sit down in the chair she had indicated.

Bella lifted the heavy pan dextrously from the hob and put it on the side plate. Then she thrust the kettle into the heart of the fire, and all the while she talked.

'If you decide to stay down there, as I said, you'll need coal. Now, you indicated earlier on when I told you I couldn't afford to pay you that you would work for your board and keep, so to speak. I can promise you a decent board but I think it's a very poor keep sleeping down there. However, it's up to you. But, as I said, that fire eats wood and won't keep on without coal. So I'll pay you with a bag of coal each week. How much you use of it each day will be up to you. Now, as regards work.' She was taking cups and saucers down from the Delft rack and placing them on a tin tray, which stood towards the end of the table and already held a teapot stand. 'When the yard is finished what d'you think you can do?

One thing, I think, is already certain: you don't want to go out and about, so you'll be no good going to the market. Anyway, they'd likely chase you in that get-up thinkin' you were on the pinch again. Oh, I heard about you and takin' the apple from Mickey Robson's box. So as far as I can see there's only housework.' She was now pouring the hot water into the teapot, in which she had previously placed three large spoonfuls of tea from a wooden caddy that resided on the mantelpiece, as she added, 'You've likely never been used to housework, but on the other hand have you ever been used to clearing up a yard like that one outside? I doubt it, but you did it. It was a case of needs must where the devil drives, I suppose.

'I don't know how long you've been on the road, lass, but you must've learnt a bit about work in that time. There, I'll let it draw a bit. I can't stand weak tea. D'you take sugar? Anyway, I'll put two in. You can help yourself to more if you want it; and there's milk there an' all. Could you clean this house, d'you think? I mean sweep and dust and polish and things like that, like a housewife does. I did it meself for years until I had to take over the stall when old Ham died. I'll tell you about him some time.'

She went to the Delft rack again and took down a plate; then from a cupboard standing to the side she took two large iced buns and put them on the plate; and this she placed before the girl. She poured out a cup of tea, and put it and the milk jug next to the plate. And her surprise was evident as she saw Reenee's hand go out to the cup but not lift it, just stroke the side of it with her fingertips, then the saucer.

For the first time, too, Bella noticed that the girl's fingernails were clean. She decided that she must have scrubbed them well under the tap in the wash-house. But why had she stroked the cup and saucer? She was an odd creature if ever there was one. And she was more surprised now to see the girl turn from the table, stand up and walk towards the wall at the left side of the fireplace, and there point to an ornamental glass rolling pin hanging by a piece of string from a hook. Tapping it, she turned to the table and made the action of rolling it, and Bella cried, in a sort of childish delight because she had translated this action, 'You mean you can cook?'

The affirmation was firm.

'Well, that's good, that *is* good. All right; sit down and have your bite and then we'll take it from there. Cooking. Well I never!'

On this Bella became silent as her thoughts raced and she began to sum up the creature, as she would still think of her. Here she was, wearing a coat and bonnet-cum-hat, which was class stuff; and her shoes, too . . . well, what was left of them . . . had been of the best. Moreover, the few words she spoke weren't common like. There was no trace of the Cockney or yet of anything like Geordie Joe's twang, or Welsh, or Scots. She would've detected Scots in the voice because hadn't Ham, or Hamish as was his name, been a Scot to the marrow? Then there was a certain twang—no, not a twang, more a haughty tone like some ladies used when jabberin' away to each other, when their words sounded as if they were comin' out of the top of their heads. No, it wasn't like that. She couldn't put a name to the way this girl spoke. One thing was sure, it wasn't common. It wasn't la-di-da either, but it certainly wasn't common. Yet she could do all these common things, and now the latest, she

could cook. Dear, dear. There was something very strange about her, very strange
indeed. And Bella would very much like to
get to the bottom of it. Aye, she would that.
But who knew? Food and warmth, and that
fear she seemed to have of men taken from
her, that might loosen her tongue.

As she said, 'Get that tea down you, and
the bun,' there was a knock on the front
door. She opened it to her two helpers
standing there, and straight away she said
to them, 'Did you get it, the tick?'

'Yes.' Pimple was nodding at her.

'Well, where is it?'

It was Joe who answered: 'We've got
one, Bella; and it's a good one, a new one.
But it won't be'—he was going to say 'delivered' when she said, 'Shut up! and come
inside,' and practically hauled the two of
them over the step, finishing, 'You want the
street to know? Wipe your feet, then come
into the kitchen and let me know the rest.'

She left them, and in a minute they followed her to the kitchen where they stood
like two awkward youngsters near the head
of the couch looking at the table, then at
Reenee sitting there. She was looking at
them, and there was now no fear in her eyes.

'Out with it!' said Bella sharply. 'What about this delivery? What're you talkin' about?'

'Well, I was in the warehouse. You know, helpin' to straighten up.'

'Aye,' Bella cut in now. 'What were you straightenin' up this time? Dinner services or chamber pots?'

The two men laughed. 'Nothing like that, Bella. Loads of Army boots, old style, and hundreds of tin plates and mugs. They must've been clearing out some barracks.'

'It must've been on the level an' all,' said Bella.

'Oh, aye, this job was on the level. Half his stuff's on the level, that's why he gets off with the other half, I suppose.'

'You're right there. Well, go on and tell me what happened about the mattress.'

'I put it to one of the fellows what I was on the look-out for like. A damaged one; I said it wouldn't matter. Well, it was just before I came away, and he called me aside and said there'd be a new one dropped off late when the vans came into the yard.'

'Oh, they're comin' tonight, are they?' said Bella. 'They haven't been for a while. What is it this time?'

'Oh, I wouldn't even guess, Bella. And I've no idea of the time; but how they get those horses and vans in there without making much of a rattle at night I'll never know.'

'Oh, aye, the horses.' Bella now turned to Reenee. 'Don't worry if you hear the jingle of harnesses and horses' hoofs. You see, they take the horses away for the night and bring them back in the morning, about seven or so. At least most times.

'But anyway, you two, for tonight you'll have to let her have one of your pallets 'cos she's goin' to sleep in the cellar.'

'In the cellar!' This came on a high note from Joe. 'It's like death down there.'

'Yes; that's why you're goin' to the depot for a hundredweight of coal; but you're not takin' one of the standard sacks; I'm not payin' for coal dust, I want roundies. Understand?'

'Aye, Bella.'

'And you, Pimple, bring your pallet round here; I'll give you the key to the gate. And bring in all the kindling she's chopped. The wash-house fire's already on; it's been goin' for half the day I should think. And you'll get your grub when you come back. All right? Stop eyeing the teapot, Joe.' Bella went to the cupboard in the dresser, bent down and took out two china mugs. After filling them with tea and four teaspoonfuls of sugar each she handed one to each of them. 'I'm doin' you an honour, for that's real good china with its name on the bottom.'

Joe made pretence of turning his mug over, then said, 'I'll empty it first, Bella.'

The men emptied the large mugs in almost two draughts. Then they were giving her their thanks as she ushered them to the front door where, in a low, changed tone, she said, 'I know it's Sunday in the morning and it's your free day when what you do and where you get to is no business of mine, but I'd like to know if you'll do something for me.'

They spoke and nodded together. 'Anything, Bella. Anything.'

'Well, will you go into that cellar down there and sweep the walls of the cobwebs and help to wash that floor, then see if there's anything worth mending among that lot of odd pieces and bits of furniture in the corner? Ham left them like that, and I must say I haven't bothered with them since—too busy. You'll lose nothing by it.'

'Oh, we'll do that, Bella. We will.'

And it was Pimple now who said, in a very quiet voice, 'She's no ordinary woman, is she? She's a sort of a lady.'

Bella looked at him closely for a moment before she said quietly, 'Aye, Pimple. I suppose in a way you could say that. She's a sort of a lady.'

3

Bella Morgan wasn't given to pondering. She had always been too busy looking for a way to fend for herself and go on living, or too tired to think at all. One thing had puzzled her when she had come to this part of London: she had been called Big Bella though she was only five foot two. Likely it was because of her voice: that was big and loud, and she wasn't afraid to raise it. But during the last month she had been made to ponder on how her existence had changed, been transformed, because this woman or girl or creature, as she had first thought of her, had turned into a sort of companion. But not only had her life, as it were, been changed, so had the lives of Geordie Joe and Pimple Face; not in their main occupations but in themselves. They were cleaner; she could even say they looked smarter, because they had been to Ginnie's clothes store down the road and rigged themselves out with some respectable fifth-hand gear. Moreover, they washed more often.

Washed. The word conjured up the first of the two incidents in the past month that had strengthened her interest in the girl, if that was needed. It had had to do with washing.

It happened on a Tuesday. There had been next to nothing to trade and it had rained all morning, and by two in the afternoon she had got her little helper to clear her stall and had presented him, to his delight, with two boxes of very questionable fruit, from which, nevertheless, she knew he'd make some coppers before the day was out; and she had walked down the now absolutely clean yard. She had never known it to be as clean in her time. As Pimple Face said, 'You could eat your bread off it.'

The rain had stopped and when she saw no sight of the girl as she usually would around this time, sitting on the log chopping the previous day's boxes into kindling, she knew she would be in the wash-house. As she neared it, she noticed the door was closed, which in itself was odd; the door of the wash-house was hardly ever closed except at night. Another thing that took her notice was that the window was covered up from the inside.

She made her approach quietly and looked at it. A sheet of newspaper was tucked into the frame. But it didn't actually fit it; there was a good half-inch gap at the side. She put her eye to this, and what came into her line of narrowed vision was a pile of clothing laid across the top of an orange box. There were two petticoats and a pair of fancy bloomers, which she immediately recognised as silk. Real silk. The bloomers had a lace frill, and round the band of the frill were garters, fancy garters, almost an inch deep slotted with ribbon. To the side was that coat. It was half open and she could glimpse the lining, of a light grey colour and the material like lamb's wool. A pair of stockings was hanging over the top of the box; the legs were a light grey but the feet were almost black, and she could distinctly see that one was badly holed.

There was the sound of faint splashing. Then the girl came into view: her whole body was bare and she was rubbing herself down with one of the two clean coarse towels Bella had given her only that morning for the boys. She was fascinated by the sight of her. She had a beautiful figure but it was so thin. She watched her now take up a garment she hadn't noticed. It seemed to be made of fine wool, and when she put it on it covered her like a skin and reached below her knees. It wasn't a chemise or anything in that line. She had never seen anything like it. It could have been a kind of fine woollen frock if it hadn't been so clinging. And now what did intrigue her was: when she saw her step into her bloomers she pulled out a little bag that was pinned to the inside of the hem, and she pulled it open by a silken cord at the top, and she put her fingers into it, then closed it again. It was like one of the small dorothy bags Bella had heard that ladies used to take to dances and such dos. They would hold only handkerchiefs and smelling salts and bits like that. When Reenee pulled her bloomers high the bag lay against her flat stomach and did not make a bulge. The first petticoat she put on was a waist one, the second had a bodice and straps, but she had no corsets. Funny that she had no corsets; and she was not even wearing a camisole that would hold her small breasts, but the long woollen garment was so shaped that it held them. At this point Bella had turned quietly away and made a hasty retreat from the yard.

In the kitchen she sat down in her basket chair. She did not bother to make herself a pot of tea but sat there; and now she did muse, not only muse but kept saying to herself that something should be done about that poor creature. She had come from good people, rich people, oh, yes. She knew finery when she saw it. And then there were the coat and hat. The coat might be mucky now but it had quality still.

And cap all this with her voice and what had you? Somebody who shouldn't be around here. Somebody who was off her head; well, not right off her head, but there was something wrong. She could speak, but she didn't; she seemed afraid to. She was petrified of men. Now that was an odd thing, for in the class she came from she would have met dozens and dozens of men. Had she been married? She didn't wear a ring but that didn't signify. Something had happened to her, an accident of some kind that had affected part of her brain, because in other ways she was sensible and she took everything in.

Ah, but then—Bella now moved uneasily in her chair—how could she account for the lady, as presented by her voice and her clothes, working as she had been like a scavenger in that yard for weeks? And now in this very house: look how she had cleaned those rooms upstairs; and, above all, look at her cooking. Somebody somewhere had taught her to cook. She could make a roast, a stew, and she knew how to bake bread.

Oh—Bella rose to her feet—she wished she could get to the bottom of it all. Nothing had ever before intrigued her like this. What she knew she should do was to go to the authorities, not the local police station, but a big central one, and tell the top brass there all about Reenee, and say somebody must be looking for her somewhere. But what would happen then? They would send men here, and she would be off! Oh, yes, in that coat and hat and her worn-out shoes, and that would be the last she would see of her. And what then? She paused for a long while before she said, 'I'd miss her. She feels like a . . .' She couldn't put the word 'daughter' to the girl nor yet 'friend', and she wasn't much of a companion for she hardly ever opened her mouth, except to bring out the odd word, and this would be accompanied by sign language. But there was something about the girl, the woman, that touched Bella in some way. She felt she wanted to put her arms around her and comfort her. Aye, she did . . . as she would a child or someone in trouble. And, oh, aye, that girl was in trouble, or at least had been, in bad trouble . . .

The second event that had aroused Bella's interest even further happened on the day the old cobbler next door died. It was about the third week of Reenee sleeping in the cellar kitchen.

The cellar had taken on a new face, thanks to the work both Geordie Joe and Pimple Face put in every Sunday: they had not only swept the walls but painted them. They had acquired, from where Bella did not ask, three large tins of paint. One was an off white and the other two a deep blue.

By erecting the trestles and planks used for the fruit stall they had painted the grubby ceiling white. This part of the business had taken them over two weekends for first they had to clear the ceiling of its layers of smoke and dust gathered over the years. Their efforts in this particular line were rather messy: they endeavoured to clean it with wet mops. However, during the second weekend they painted it. If the result was a somewhat streaky white there was no one to grumble. Following this they painted the walls blue, which was quite successful because after two coats, as Bella herself said, you couldn't recognise the place. Moreover, they scrubbed the floor, during which time Miss Reenee, as they now called her, endeavoured, as she had been doing for some time, to finish cleaning the range of rust. Also its companion fender, which had turned out to be made of brass.

What was more, among the rubbish that had been thrown into the corner of the room the men had found a seatless basket chair, and nailed some boards across it to form a seat. To this Bella had added a large pillow to soften it, but which could also be used when the girl was sleeping on the comfortable mattress that had been left, as promised, in the yard, together with a good blanket still in its shop wrappings—both, as Joe informed her the next day, gifts from Mr Weir; and he had also added that he was told the message had come from the boss personally. Undoubtedly he thought they were for Bella's use alone.

Another concession had been made to the visitor. She was eating her evening meal with Bella. Not that she ate much, and what she did she seemed to nibble at slowly as if she had to make it last. Likely, Bella thought, she had taken up this habit when she had first been thrust on to the road.

She looked at her now. She was sitting to the side of the fireplace staring into the fire, and she wondered what she was thinking about, if her muddled mind allowed her to think. She looked different, and of course she would without that coat and hat on her. Oh, what a job that had been to get them off her; she had seemed determined to go around doing the housework in them. Even to doing the cooking. She had allowed an apron to be put round her waist, but she had kept the coat on, until Bella had said, 'Now, look here, we've got to come to some new arrangement if you're going to stay with me. That coat and headgear's got to come

off, at least while you're workin'.' She recalled the pained look the girl had given her
as if she were depriving her of something
she valued. She had suddenly taken her by
the hand and almost run her up the stairs
and through one of the four doors on the
landing; and once inside the room she had
flung her arm out, saying, 'Now look at it!
There's nothing frightening up here, is there?
There's a wardrobe and a dressing-table
and a wash-stand with a little chest of drawers, together with a single bed. I can tell you,
I thought I had reached heaven when I first
slept in this room, and I can also tell you
there's not many furnished like it in this row
of houses. Now, you can come up here and
you can take your hat and coat off in the
morning and hang them in that wardrobe.
Nobody's going to go near them. But if I
were you, when you're so busy cleaning up
all my belongings, I think you should take a
brush to that coat and also sponge it down
and iron it out. What've you got underneath?
Let me see. Come on! Come on, now!' She
had unclasped the hands that were holding
the buttons of the coat; she was determined
to have her way in this instance, so she un-
buttoned the coat, opened its flaps and ex-

claimed, 'Well, now, a red velvet frock. What is there to be ashamed of in showing that? Certainly, being velvet, it's all creased and marked—velvet gets like that when it's roughly treated, which it's bound to be with you sleeping in it.'

The girl had turned from her and, pulling the coat close around her again, she sat on the edge of the bed, while Bella continued with her tirade: 'And that frock won't last for ever. Look, I know; I know it's no good suggestin' you goin' down to Ginnie's 'cos I know you won't; but I could, and it isn't all Paddy's market down there. She has a cupboard where she keeps lots of decent things. Two or three times she's tried to rig me out, but look at the shape of me. The clothes are either too narrow or too big for me; but she keeps me in skirts and things like that, and if I was any use with me needle I'd be able to alter things. I'm not, I know, never have been in that way, but there's no need why I can't bring a couple of frocks up to let you have a look at.'

When the head she was addressing drooped further down she said, 'All right. All right. But I'm goin' to insist on you leavin' that coat and hat up here. I can give you a kind of old cloak to put over your head when you go out of the front door to the gates. Now, I'm goin' to leave you here to think about it.'

As she reached the door she turned and said, 'You can take them downstairs at night when you go to your bed if you're so worried about them, but during the day when you're in the house I'm havin' to put me foot down.'

The girl had come down in the red dress, and Bella had gone on with her chattering as if she hadn't noticed any change in her new companion, and that was how she had come to think of the girl, as a sort of companion.

This particular night was a Friday night, and when her other two workers came into Bella's kitchen, as they often did now, on this occasion they were dressed in their Sunday best.

'Goin' somewhere?' said Bella, in surprise. At this they both looked awkward and grinned, and it was Joe who answered, 'We thought of goin' to the Tivoli. We hear there's some good turns on, and on a Friday night you can get up in the gods for threepence.'

'Can you now?' said Bella. 'And when did this idea attack you?'

The men exchanged glances; and then it was Joe who, inclining his head towards his friend, said, 'It was Pimple's. He'd like to hear the music, he said. He used to go at one time, didn't you, Pimple?'

Pimple nodded his lowered head. 'Well, well!' said Bella. 'It's better than the bars, I'll give you that.'

'Oh . . . I don't know if you know, Bella, but old Frankie next door died this afternoon. They said it was a heart-attack.'

Bella straightened up from where she had been going to put the kettle on the hob. 'He died this afternoon, you say? Well, well. Young Frankie will come into his own now; he's worked hard enough for the old niggard for years. Eeh, how Ham hated that man!' She laughed now. 'I wonder if they've met up wherever they've gone. Something happened between them long before I came on the scene. I only mentioned his name once in this house and never again because one night, I remember it like yesterday, he was standing where you are, Joe. I was cleaning the table there'—she thumbed towards it— 'and I said on a laugh, "Mr Francis next door offered me a job today. He said I could go and work for—" Well, that's as far as I got because . . . because he turned on me like, well, I don't know what, and he thrust out his arm and stabbed his finger towards me and growled at me, saying, "Don't speak ever again . . . about that man in my house; I can't abide . . ." '

She didn't finish, for she was looking at the two men who were staring over her shoulder towards where Reenee had been sitting in the chair, and she turned swiftly, and what she saw amazed her too: the girl was now as stiff as a ramrod. Her body was stretched out, supported by her bottom in a straight line across the front edge of the chair. From her head to her feet she was like a corpse and her arms were upraised as if she were pushing someone off her.

They all rushed towards her, the two men gripping her arms and Bella patting her face, saying, 'Come on, lass, come on.'

Then suddenly the middle of her body from her shoulders to her thighs began to heave up and down, up and down.

'She's havin' a fit,' whispered Pimple.

'Shut up!' muttered Bella.

Of a sudden they watched the whole body collapse and fold into the chair. The girl's head turned to the side and her hand came up and partly shaded the face, as if she were warding off a blow.

'It's all right. It's all right, love.' Bella's voice was reassuring. 'You're among friends; there's nothing to be afraid of. Come on; don't shrink back like that. Wake up. Come on; wake up from wherever you are.'

As if obeying an order Reenee's eyes slowly opened, and if Bella had never seen a look of terror on anyone's countenance before she saw it now. And again she was patting Reenee's face, saying, 'It's all right, lass, it's all right. You're among friends. I told you, there's nothing to be afraid of. Come on now.'

Bella straightened up and, pointing to the cupboard, she said to Joe, 'There's a bottle in there at the back. It's got some gin in it. Pour a drop out.'

As might have been expected, Reenee did not choke on the drink. She swallowed a mouthful, then lay back and closed her eyes again.

The three of them were standing apart now, and Pimple said, 'I wonder what brought that on, because just a minute before she was lookin' at you, at least at your back and the way you were pointing to Joe here and telling him about old Ham goin' for you.' Pimple nodded. 'It's funny, but it was as soon as you spoke that she suddenly stiffened out like that. It was so sudden. I couldn't say anything to you.'

'Well,' said Bella tersely, 'what could I have said that would've caused that spasm? I only said, "Don't speak that man's name in this . . ." well, in fact I didn't finish, did I?'

It was Joe who repeated softly now, ' "Don't speak." Perhaps that's why.'

'That's why what?' Bella demanded. 'Come on, tell me what you think that's why.'

'Well'—Joe moved from one foot to the other—'I can't explain, really, but you sounded like somebody givin' an order, like old Ham used to do 'cos he had been in the Army once, I understand, in his young days, and what you said was, "Don't speak!" And, you see . . . well, she doesn't speak, does she? I mean it's an effort for her to say one word. D'you see what I mean?'

Yes; Bella saw what he meant, and now she groped for the back of a chair, turned it about and sat down where she could look at the almost crumpled body of this poor girl or woman or whatever she was, and she repeated softly, 'Don't speak.' Then, looking at Joe, she said, 'D'you think somebody must've told her that once?'

'Shouldn't be surprised, Bella, 'cos look at what she did with her hand, she put it up as if to save her face like.'

There was silence for a moment until Pimple said, 'Well, whatever happened she must have ended up with her head bein' bashed. That's probably what turned her brain a bit. What d'you say, Bella?'

'I don't know what to say, Pimple. That's the God's honest truth. I don't know what to say. But I'm more puzzled now than I was before about who she is and where she's come from.'

'I think she should lie down, Bella,' said Joe. 'We've got to help her downstairs; the state she's in, you'd never be able to hold her up.'

'No; you're right there, Joe.' She got up from the chair now and, bending over Reenee, she said, 'Come on, lass. We're goin' to get you down on to your bed.'

Reenee opened her eyes. The dreadful look had gone from them, but in them was such sadness that it affected all three of them, and when she tried to speak Bella

checked her, saying, 'Don't try to get anything out, lass. Have a good night's rest and
you'll feel better in the mornin'.'

The lads helped her to the top of the
stairs, but there they knew they couldn't
help her down, one on each side of her, and
without any further words Joe picked her up
in his arms and walked tentatively down the
flight of stone steps and into the transformed cellar, where the new mattress lay
to the side of the fireplace and on it a neatly
folded blanket. To the other side of the fireplace there stood a half-full sack, and in
front of this a lidless box in which there were
some large pieces of coal. To the side of the
bag was a pail covered over with a fruit box.

After Joe had laid her on the mattress,
Bella grabbed the pillow from the old basket
chair and put it under Reenee's head, and
before she went to cover her with the blanket she pulled off the worn shoes, saying
under her breath as she did so, 'I'll get these
in to young Frankie tomorrow; he'll fix them
within an hour. The uppers are still good,
but look at the soles, they're through, and
there's hardly any heels left. Anyway'—she
straightened up—'she'll be all right now. I'll

see to her; thanks very much for your help. Get yourselves off to the show.'

It was Pimple Face who said, 'I'm not bothered any more, Bella, and you never know . . .' He turned and, looking at Joe, said, 'Do you . . . ? What I mean is, there might be need of somebody goin' for a doctor or something.'

'Aye; you're right,' said Joe. 'Yes, you're right, Pimple.'

The figure on the bed moved uneasily, and Bella pushed at them, saying, 'You see? She can hear all right again. She doesn't want to see any men at all, of any kind. Oh, I wish I knew the bottom of this. Anyway, get yourselves away.'

'We'll see,' said Joe. 'But before we go I'd better bank that fire up.' And so saying, he took a pair of old tongs from the hearth and put the roundie coals from the box one by one on to the smouldering fire until the grate was heaped up. Then he filled up the box from the sack before dusting his hands one against the other and repeating, 'We'll see, Bella.'

When the two men had gone up the steps, Bella, kneeling by the mattress, put her hand inside the blanket and took hold

of Reenee's arm, and she stroked it gently
before she asked, 'How're you feelin' now,
lass?'

The woman turned from her and when,
after a moment, Bella put out her hand and
gently turned her face towards her, it was
only to see it was running with silent tears.
She murmured, 'Oh, my lass! Don't.' She felt
in her pocket to see if she had a handkerchief, and not finding one she took the end
of her apron and wiped Reenee's face with
it; and then she said softly, 'Don't be feared
of anything, me dear. Nobody's goin' to hurt
you here. Those two lads that's just gone
away, they'll see to that. And if you don't
want to go beyond the door, except to the
yard next, well, that's good enough for me.
I won't press you in any way, lass. There
now. Don't distress yourself.'

But Reenee was gasping in her throat and
her mouth opened wide before she brought
out a single word, a broken 'Sor-ry.'

'Oh, girl, you've got nothin' to be sorry
for. You had a kind of . . .' She paused.
What was she going to call it? Not a nightmare . . . nor was it like a fit. '. . . a bit of a
turn.'

Reenee was now gripping the chubby

hand, and Bella placed her other hand on top of it, patting it all the while, saying, 'I used to have turns when I was a lass. I've never told you how I got here, have I? We all have our troubles, you know, in this life. Very few of us get off without troubles, but mine started young. By God, they did!' Again she paused, while she told herself not to go on. Then she remembered a saying of old Ham's, 'If you want people to stop talkin' about their troubles, you tell them yours. That'll soon shut them up.' Well, her troubles couldn't shut this poor creature up more than she was, but nevertheless they might distract her from any painful thoughts, so she said, 'I came from Liverpool, you know. I was thirteen and I couldn't get away quick enough, 'cos I'd had a hell of a life. I didn't have to come to this part of London to know men. Oh, no. I knew them in me own home, such as it was called. She, me mother, she never saw daylight and me dad, unfortunately, he had to work before he could start drinking in the bars. There were three rooms and you couldn't swing a cat in any of them, and from when I can remember I was crushed between lads in the bed. Top or bottom, it was the same. I slept under it for

God knows how long to get out of their way. They were all older than me, and they went off one after the other, until there was me left with a pair of them. I tried to go to school as often as I could. I got there enough to learn to read, when she didn't send me to the pawn shop or make me scour the place, which was like a pigsty. She was me mother, but she was a dirty bitch if ever there was one. A dirty, lazy bitch.

' "Love thy father and thy mother," so the big book says. If ever I hated two people in me life it was those two, especially him, for now the lads had gone he was gettin' at me. And she let him. I had the bed to meself now, and he came in one night paralytic and went straight for me. He was a big fellow, but I had means of protectin' meself. I'd used it on the lads, and by God, didn't I use it on him that night! It was a bodkin needle, you know, that you use for mats and helpin' to cut leather. It's curved at the end like. And I left a mark on him that would take some healin' for months, if ever it did, and I flew, just as I was, out of that house. Slept in me clothes. I had managed to grab me coat, me old coat, and that's all I had when I left

Liverpool around one o'clock in the morning. It was early March and cold.'

She stopped and looked down into the pale eyes that were looking into hers and she said, 'Am I talkin' too much, lass?' and when there was a slight movement from the head she went on, 'Well, that's all right, then. But I won't go on about how I got to London. I only remember that I slept in a couple of barns and scared the feathers off a number of hens. Believe me, I couldn't look a raw egg in the face now. I got two lifts on my journey; and on each one I had to show my little carved knife and—' She laughed again. 'When one of them threatened to put me off on the road in the black dark somewhere from nowhere I told him what I would do to him before he got me there and to keep on driving.' She was giggling now, like a girl, as she said, 'And you know, Reenee, he did. He just did. Although I was small made and only thirteen I knew I looked a lot older. Well, I'd had a lot of experience to make me look like that, I can tell you, girl.

'I've lost count of the days it took me to reach the big city, and also,' she added grimly, 'of the number of men who wanted to be kind to me.' Her voice was slow and low. 'I'd been brought up among drink and squalor, and all those around me lived by their wits, so now I put mine into practice. But when I think back, I must still have looked like a lost schoolgirl, except for my face. It was old. It was old then, and it has never seemed to change.'

Her smile widened here. 'But I must tell you how I came to own this house and the fruit business, and about Hamish McIntyre. I had learnt how to live rough and exist for days at a time on rotten fruit or what I could scavenge from dustbins, those near hotels. But you had to fight your way to get at them because the ones near the big hotels, as I said, they had what the posh people called their own clientele. You had to be there pretty early in the morning to pick out any-thing worthwhile, and one day a cop almost nabbed me. I'd gone into a cook shop and pinched a couple of pies and I almost ran into him head-on as I left the shop and he gave chase. The shop had been near the fruit market and I dashed through there and passed what I now know is the Opera House and up some alleys. In and out I went until I lost him. But,' she shrugged her shoulders, 'I suppose I'd lost him in the market. I was just one of hundreds of kids on the same game. Anyway, I wasn't to know that then, and I wove in and out, in and out, then up through a narrow roadway, and I recall there were shrubs on one side of it. Anyway, I was gasping when I saw a pair of iron gates and, beyond, a yard littered with boxes and rotten fruit, and I did what you did, lass: I went in and I hid in a corner behind some boxes and I waited for that bobby comin'. I could've waited till next week, had I known it, but I was so exhausted and weak with hunger that I fell asleep. I sort of dreamt that someone came and stood over me, then went away, but when I woke up there was nobody about.

'Then I did wake and looked about me. There was squashed fruit of every kind that had been swept into piles here and there, but though I was very hungry and I'd eaten worse I couldn't touch them, 'cos I wanted to be sick; and I was. I vomited but it was mostly water. After a while I sneaked out, and when I got past the gates I saw just a few yards away a man selling fruit from a stall, and again I made a run for it. But that night, not bein' able to find anywhere to kip, I thought of that yard and that pile of boxes, and when it was dark I made my way there. The gates were shut, but they weren't locked, and I carefully lifted the latch, went through them, closed them gently behind me, and took my sleepin' quarters among the boxes.'

Again she stopped. 'You all right, dear?' she said. 'Shall I go on?' When the head made a movement, she said, 'All right, then. Well, to cut this bit of the story short, I stole what I could to eat during the daytime. I'd found it was no good offerin' your services to anybody, there were so many in the same boat as meself, but each night I went back through those gates and slept behind the boxes. That was until one morning when I tried to get out and found the gates locked. Eeh, lass, was I in a pickle! The place was walled in. There was a kind of stone buildin' at the end of it, which looked as if it was droppin' to pieces, like most of the houses round about. In panic I started to shake the gates. Then there was this man. He'd come and stood in front of the gate and said, "Well, now, what can I do for you?" His voice, I recognised, was Scots. A thick Scots. "Let me out," I said, "else I'll bloody well scream!"

' "Oh, yes? Do that," he said. "By all means. That's what I want you to do so I can bring the polisman, and he can take you where you should be, behind bars."

' "I've done nowt," I said.

' "No," he answered, "only used my premises as sleepin' quarters for the last week or so."

'Eeh! I began to tremble, lass. So he had seen me that first night, but why had he left me alone till now? When he suddenly unlocked the gate and stood before me I backed from him and got me knife out. I said, "You come near me, mister, and you'll be sorry. If I do nothin' else I'll leave a mark on you."

' "Yes, I suppose you would, miss," he said. "But let me tell you, I wouldn't touch you, my dear, with a ten-foot barge-pole if I had one in my hand this minute. But seein' that you've used my premises for sleepin' quarters I don't see why you shouldn't pay for your night's rest by some work, like sweepin' up this yard."

'Well, Reenee, I stood and gaped at him. Then, me wits returnin', I said, "What'll you give me?"

' "Give you?" he said. "It's you who owes

me, miss. I've told you, you've got to pay for your sleepin' quarters."

'I glared at him. Then, as if I had any power to bargain, I said, "I'll do it if you give me a bite of food."

' "Oh! Oh, I see. You're not only askin' for a bed you're askin' for board too, is that it?"

'I nodded at him and said, "Aye."

'Now in that thick voice of his, he said, "I'll give you a meal," he said, "about ten o'clock, after I've seen what work you do. You see that buildin' down there?" He pointed down the long yard. "Well, there's a hut next to it, and it's got tools in it. You'll find something that you can use to clear up. And don't attempt to do a bunk, because if you do you won't find any sleepin' quarters here tonight. The gate will be locked. Understood?"

'I didn't answer him, but I turned away and went down the yard to find the hut with the tools in it.'

And now Reenee smiled as Bella went on, 'My cleanin' up wasn't like anything you did, me dear. But he gave me a meal, and it was a good one. Of course, he bein' Scottish, it was a bowl of porridge, and with it a slice of bread and pig's fat. Also a can of black tea—neither milk nor sugar in it, but I can tell you, it was like wine to me. And that state of affairs went on for almost a week, because after I'd done my stint and eaten the food I went out and about my scroungin'. But I always returned hungry and longed for the mornin' and that porridge. Then one day he said to me, "Where're you from?"

' "Liverpool," I said.

' "How old are you?"

'I recall lookin' from one side to the other before I said, "Sixteen."

' "You're not." His words came back like a shot. "You can't be more than fourteen. Why are you here? Haven't you got any people? Are you from a home of some sort?"

' "Aye, mister." I *was* from a home of some sort. Yes, you could say that all right. And I didn't know I was cryin', actually cryin'—me!

'He bawled, "Oh, for God's sake! Don't come that. I've never been softened by tears before, and I'm not likely to be now."

'You know what I said to him in reply? "Who's askin' you to be bloody well softened. I don't want any of your sympathy or kind words, if you have any in you, that is.

I'm me own boss and always will be. So there. Nobody's goin' to tell me what to do; if I don't want to do it, I don't do it. Get that, mister!"

'And you know what he did, Reenee? He put his head back and he laughed. He was a man, I found out later, who wasn't given to laughter. He had to have something really to laugh about. That morning I heard him laugh until he nearly choked. And then he said, "D'you want a job?"

' "What?" said I.

' "You heard. You heard, big woman. I said, d'you want a job?"

' "Depends."

' "On what?"

' "On what you're gonna pay me." I saw him swallow deeply before he said, "A shillin' a week, and your food and board. You see that buildin' down there next to where you got the brushes? Well, it's a wash-house. The first thing you do is clean it up. There's a good boiler in there. You fill it with water from the pump just beyond it. Then you chop up some of these boxes and put the fire on. You'll have to chop enough to keep it goin' because it eats wood. Then you can kip there. But first this yard's got to be cleaned as it should be, not played at like you've been doing these last few days. That wash-house is to be clean in order that you can do my washing in there, and this includes the bedding. Have you ever done any washing before?" When I didn't answer, he said, "Well, you'll learn. And if it's all to my satisfaction you'll get a shilling a week and your grub."

'Well, lass, in the next six months I learnt what work was. Aye, I did it for six months, and then one day he said to me, "Don't you think it's about time you went along to Ginnie's and got a change of rags? If you come out lookin' decent I'll take you on as me housekeeper. Can you cook?"

' "No."

' "Well, that doesn't matter very much," he said; "except you'll have to learn how to make porridge. I generally eat out anyway. But what about it?"

' "What wage?" I said.

'At this he laughed again: "Half a dollar."

' "Your housekeeper?" I repeated, lookin' up into his big hairy face.

' "Yes," he said, "my housekeeper, and"—he thumped me in the chest—"you won't need to bring out your knife. Be quite sure on that point, Bella. What did you say your second name was?"

' "Morgan."

' "Well, Miss Bella Morgan, you will be safe with me. Even when you grow up I can't see you lookin' much different from what you do now; so you have no need to worry on that score."

'I recall now, lass, how hurt I felt. I knew I was small, with a thick-set body, and me face was plain. But, anyway, that's how it started: I became his housekeeper. I must have been just turned fourteen at the time and I worked for him sixteen years—the last three he spent a lot of time ill in bed—and I knew as much about him at the end of his life as I did when I first saw him. I can only put it like this: he was a man of many parts. His routine never changed in all those years until he took to his bed.

'He didn't always attend the stall; he had a man who would come in and take over. At such times he'd be up in his bedroom. He had a little desk there and he was always writing down notes or figures. I got that much from the torn-up scraps that were in the wastepaper basket. But I also know that he didn't deal in much second fruit, it was nearly all good stuff. I understand it hadn't always been like that: he had started very much on seconds, and that's why he hated old Frankie next door. One day they had an awful row and Frankie said, "You're nowt but a bruised-fruit vendor." Anyway, as I was to find out, he had a number of different suits in his wardrobe and they were all good ones.

'He had a pattern like a timetable. The stall was cleared at five. He never did it himself, not while I was there anyway. By six o'clock he'd be washed and dressed for out. Some nights he'd be back about nine. Others he would say to me, "Don't wait up. I won't want anything." I don't think he had ever said please or thank you in his life, and he always made me feel I was of no importance, just someone to clean the house, do his washing and get his breakfast. There were nights I knew he didn't get back till twelve o'clock, and I used to wonder what he got up to. But in all those years I never saw him the worse for drink, though of course I didn't see him when he came in that late.

'At the end he had a doctor to him, who told me he had a sort of wasting disease.

I've learnt since it must've been what they call leukaemia. Something to do with the blood. Another thing that was odd, he wouldn't let me wash him except to put a flannel round his face on bad days.

'Shortly after he had taken to his bed—' She stopped here and said, 'You interested, lass?' and when Reenee made her usual nod of confirmation, she went on, 'Well, that's all right. As I said, he hadn't been long in his bed when he called up the man who saw to the stall and told him to carry on; but first, he gave him a letter to take to the warehouse for a Mr Weir. That very night he said to me, "I want you to get to your room and stay there. I'm going to have a visitor. He will be able to let himself in, he's got a key." I just stared at him and then he croaked at me, "D'you hear what I say? I'm sayin' to you, make yourself scarce. Keep to your room until my visitor goes. Your lugs will be wide open and you'll hear him leave. You understand me, now?"

'I never said a word but I went out. It was over an hour later when I heard someone coming up the stairs; it was over two hours later when the footsteps went down the stairs. Through the window I could see no sign of a cab or anything. The next day he sent for his solicitor, who brought two clerks with him. Well, as they were up there a long time I went and tapped on the door, opened it and was about to ask if they would like a cup of tea when there was a bawl came from the bed, "Get out!"

'At a glance I could see that the bed was covered with bits of paper and things like parchment rolled up, and the solicitor man was sitting on a chair to the side of the bed with the clerks standing beside him.

'I closed that door none too quietly. Sometimes I considered him a pig of a man, and that was one of the times. I forgot he had been kind in givin' me house room; yet he had never broken his neck over paying promptly for my services. Anyway, it was the very next afternoon when I went into his room that he handed me a closed envelope, and on it was simply the name "Mr Weir," and he said, "Get that to the warehouse as soon as possible."

'I went downstairs and I was about to pick up my coat and put it round me, when the bell rang and there, outside, stood the doctor. He was a nice, civil man, middle-aged and kindly, and I led him upstairs, opened the door and stood aside for him to pass. Then we both let out an exclamation. There was nobody in the bed, and to my knowledge Mr McIntyre hadn't been able to move out of it for weeks. But there he was, all crumpled on the mat at the foot of the bed and in his hand, of all things, was an open clasp knife. It was one of those, you know, like Scouts have that hold a screwdriver and a file as well as a knife. Well, on this occasion only the blade was showin', and it was still in his hand, and when the doctor turned him over he said, "Dear God, he's had a stroke! What on earth brought him from the bed?"

'I helped to carry his twisted body back to the bed, and it was no lightweight, and the doctor said, "This'll finish him surely." Then he said, "Now give me a hand. I have to get him on to his side to examine him."

'The examination proved that Mr McIntyre had certainly had a stroke all down his left side, and his face was twisted and he was unable to speak.

' "You can't manage him on your own any more," the doctor said. "He'll have to have a nurse. I'll see about it first thing in the morning. He'll take no harm lying as he does now. Don't agitate him in any way by trying to get him to talk. Will you be all right by yourself tonight? Perhaps you know some-one who will stay with you?"

' "No, I won't need any help," I said; "I'll be all right, Doctor. I've seen to him so far."

' "Yes, indeed you have," he said, "and it's been too much for anyone, let alone someone of your size."

'I tell you, Reenee, it was the most uneasy and frightening night I've spent in me life, and even before I left Liverpool, and after. I can tell you I had some frightening nights. On that road I was scared to death many times but nothing like the night I watched him die, because that's what he was doing and I didn't know. He kept opening one eye and staring at me as if willing me to do something, and I recalled the past two or three days when he had been struggling for breath. Time and again he would point through the iron bars at the foot of the bed, and twice he distinctly said the word "lino"; once I thought he said, "Lift the lino." So after he fell asleep I quietly pulled up the mat that lay across the foot of the bed. There was no break in the lino there. Then I looked around the edge of it where it was

all tucked neatly underneath the skirtin'
boards, which were agape with shrinkage
for nearly half an inch. There was no break
at all in the lino. Definitely, though, he had
been trying to get at the lino with that knife,
but why? Then I thought of the way he had
been lyin': he might have pointed to the window. Something under the window-sill?
Well, I examined that; and there was a kind
of gap between the bricks and the bottom
of the wooden sill, and I put my fingers into
this, but there was nothing there. Anyway, I
must've dozed and when I woke up I had
no need to ask any more questions: his
head had fallen to the side and I knew he
was dead. I wasn't sorry, no, I wasn't; although I still felt I owed him something for
giving me the job. Four days later he was
buried, and during that time I'd been sweating, wondering what was going to happen
now. I had a few shillings saved up, but most
likely I'd be on the streets again, because I
couldn't imagine he would have left me anything in his will.

'He was a mean man, and those, Reenee,
are the very words the solicitor said to me
the day of the funeral. He said, "Your master,

Miss Morgan, was a mean man, I'm very sorry to say."

' "Oh, I know that," I said.

' "Well, come and sit down, my dear," he said, and I can remember the kindly man leading me to the kitchen table, and we both sat down. "He hasn't left you entirely bereft," he said. "I don't know whether you'll be pleased or not, but he has left you this house."

'I gasped and said, "He's what? He's left me the house?"

' "Yes, he's left you the house, but not a penny with which to support it. He feels that there's the vegetable and fruit business outside and you should be able to make enough to keep the house going. I even dared to suggest to him that he could leave you a little something, but he bit my head off, saying you wouldn't know what to do with money."

'I think the kind man was withholding something, for I'm sure Mr McIntyre would have added, because she's a numskull. You see, I couldn't talk to him. I couldn't tell him what I thought or even anything I'd read in the papers. He didn't stop near me long enough for anything like that. Then the solicitor surprised me. He said, "You might not believe it but he has died a very rich man."

' "A rich man?" I repeated.

' "Yes," he said; "a very rich man. Your employer, I'm afraid, led two different lives."

'I remember'—she laughed here—'saying naïvely, "Well, what did he do in the other one?" and the solicitor man, he laughed too and said, "I don't suppose you know anything about what is called the Stock Exchange? Well, he worked on that, but not alone. He had a friend, a rather superior friend, and they must have worked together looking to the future, for when businesses were failing and dropping to pieces they bought shares in them and in many cases profited greatly by it. Some are still hanging fire, but will one day surely rise. But it's a pity for him he won't be here to see the result of his labours in that direction. And I must tell you too, my dear, he made no real profit out of the fruit business; he paid the man who looked after it quite a decent wage. I feel the fruit business was a cover-up for his other life, because he detested this house and also this district. I think he moved in a different circle once he was away from it. Twice I saw him with a particular man. I was very surprised, but I didn't show myself. It was his business, but he was my client, and I charged him quite high fees for my services, for I don't like mean individuals, and I found him out to be mean in more ways than one. It is more than mean of a man, I think it is cruel, to watch a business die before his eyes, knowing that with just a very small effort he could save it. No, I am not going to be a hypocrite and say I am sorry to see Mr McIntyre leave this world. I don't know about you, Miss Morgan. I think, in fact I am sure, you have more than enough to feel aggrieved about."

'You know what I said, Reenee? I even made him laugh when I said, "Me? I hope he's in heaven at this minute, Mr Travis, because he's left me this house. It mightn't mean much to you, but it's been home to me. You see, Mr Travis, I've had a bad four days thinking I'd be thrown out on the road again, because that's where he picked me up from, you know. He found me sleepin' among the filthy fruit boxes in the yard. So, yes, I do hope he's in heaven."

'The solicitor patted me on the shoulder, "You are a very kind little woman, Miss Morgan," he said; "I'm sure you'll make a success of the fruit business, because you'll look after it yourself and not have to pay anyone else. If at any time I can be of use to you, you've just to call on me and I can promise you," he wagged his finger at me, "I won't treat you as a client and put you on my charge book."

'Oh, he was a nice man, Reenee, and still is, for since then he's called in once or twice to see how I'm gettin' on. But to get back to the night Ham died. I'd been about to take that note to Mr Weir. He seemed to be the boss of the warehouse. Well, with all the fuss I never got the letter to him and I must confess I opened it. All it said was: "Come tonight." So one day when he called I asked Mr Travis, "Have you met Mr Weir?"

' "No, I've not, Miss Morgan."

' "You don't know the man who owns the big wholesale warehouses?" I asked him.

' "Yes, I know the man who owns the big warehouses, but it isn't Mr Weir," Mr Travis said.

' "Oh, I thought it was. Anything I've wanted for the house or anything like that has come through Mr Weir. Mr McIntyre used to say, "Just tell Mr Weir what you want and you'll get it if it's for the house."

' "It was Mr Weir who was the visitor who came to see him?" asked Mr Travis.

' "I don't know, sir," I said. "I only know that I wasn't allowed to see him. Mr McIntyre made me stay in my room."

' "He did? While a gentleman was here?"

' "Yes. Oh, yes. The gentleman seemed to have his own key, and I didn't come out of the room until I heard him leave."

' "Well, well. You learn something every day, Miss Morgan," he said. "Remember that." '

Bella now looked down on the white face turned towards her on the pillow, and she realised that her listener had fallen asleep. Eeh, she said to herself, I've talked her to sleep. She had heard of people being talked to death but never talked to sleep.

Gently now she lifted the blanket and placed it over Reenee's shoulders. Then she pulled her own cramped body upwards. She went to the fire and pushed the little brass tidy close to the bars to make sure that if anything fell out it wouldn't roll on to the hearth. The fire had burnt down somewhat and there was no fear of any of the coal pieces toppling forward. Well, she told herself, she'd leave it like that for a time; then

later she'd bring Reenee a night drink, although she wouldn't disturb her if she was
still asleep.

After she made her quiet way back up
the stone stairs to the kitchen, she was surprised to see Joe and Pimple sitting there.

'Why haven't you gone?' she demanded.

'Oh, well—' They rose together to their
feet, and it was Pimple who said, 'There's
always another night, Bella; we thought the
state she was in and you here on your
own . . . well, it was better if we hung
around.'

'What d'you think happened to her?'
asked Joe. 'It wasn't an ordinary fit, like, was
it?'

'No, it wasn't an ordinary fit,' agreed
Bella; 'but I don't know what happened to
cause it, unless, as you said, it was me re-
peatin' Hamish's words when he went at me
that night: "Don't speak," he almost ordered
me. Well, that's what I think it must have
been. Those words hit her then as they must
have done before when somebody yelled at
her, "Don't speak!" Dear God.' She shook
her head. 'But to knock her out of her wits
like that, it must have been something terrible that happened. Anyway'—her voice

changed—'I tell you what. If you're not goin' to spend your money on the idle life you can go and spend a bit of mine. What about goin' to the bakery for pies and peas and a roll, and bringin' them back here, and we'll have them round the fire? What about it?'

Like children who had been given a treat, their faces lit up, and straight away Pimple said, 'Oh, yes, Bella, we'd like that fine. I'll get the basins, will I?'

'Do that; and here's the money,' she said, picking up a tin box from the mantelpiece. She took two shillings out of it, saying, 'That should cover a good supper,' as she smacked it on the table.

'By aye!' said Joe, as he picked it up, then added, 'What if I scarper with it?'

'You try it, and I'll put the polis on you, that's all.'

The two men went out laughing, and Bella flopped into the easy chair by the fire and laid her head back. Then folding her hands in her lap and speaking to someone she knew not, she said, 'Thank you. I've got a lot to be thankful for this night.'

4

It was towards the end of October. Autumn was here: there had been the first heavy frost in the night and now the day was bright and crisp.

Over the past months the routine of the house had continued to run along with little change, but on that day three small incidents were to occur that would change the routine and the occupants' way of living. The first happened around dinner-time.

Reenee was cleaning the small window at the end of the hall through which the street could be seen. She was looking at four men, a street band, who were standing in the gutter. They had been playing a Strauss waltz, one man strumming a banjo, one beating a small drum, another blowing a flute, and the fourth playing the fiddle. The sound coming from the last suggested that the strings were slack. But they had stopped playing now, and one of them, the man with the drum, was talking to Joe, and they were smiling at each other. Bella had come in from the kitchen to tell Reenee to come and have her dinner break, and she had gone to her side and had looked out: 'Poor souls,' she said. 'God help them! They're walkin' on their uppers. That one's got paper stickin' out of his shoe. What's Joe on about? He seems to know the fellow.' And she went out, saying, 'I'll soon find out.'

Outside, Joe turned to her from the man. 'He's from my part of the country, Bella. Just up the coast, Whitley Bay way.' Then, addressing the four-man band, he said, 'This is my boss, Miss Morgan.'

The men all nodded, saying, 'Pleased to meet you.' Bella said nothing, she just stared at their starved faces. She had seen so many, more and more every day up this street. But this lot seemed to be welded together in their poverty.

Joe said to her, 'Would . . . would you mind, Bella, if I took them down to our place?' He pointed to the gate. 'We've still

got the soup you gave us and some pies
an' that and—'

'Stop your jabberin'. What use is your
drop of soup and a couple of pies going to
be to four of them? Take them down there,
then send Pimple back and I'll see to him.'

'Ta, Bella. Ta.' And as he turned to the
other man Joe said, 'Would you like to come
down and see where we hang out?'

'Me and me mates?'

Their faces alight, they followed Joe
through the iron gates and down to the
wash-house, which was no longer just a
wash-house: an iron flap had been welded
on to the front of the fire, and on it a tin
kettle was bubbling away. And near the wall
a bench had been constructed. On it stood
a little oil stove, a frying pan, and above that
a rack holding two tin plates, two mugs and
some cutlery. The beds had been rolled up
to form seats, a mat was on the floor and a
curtain at the window, a real curtain that
could be pulled across at night. Reenee had
made it for them.

Back in the house, Bella went hurriedly
to the kitchen and said to Reenee, 'God help
them. That's the worst lot of semi-starvation
I've seen. And one of them comes from

Joe's part, that's at the other end of the country, what Joe calls the North-East. There must be many worse than these men. There'll be trouble in the towns, you'll see; things are desperate. But what am I talkin' about? Get a tray out, Reenee, and some basins and cut up a new loaf.'

Like a well-trained servant, Reenee did as she was bidden, and eagerly. After cutting the slices of bread she pointed to a dish of margarine on the table and looked at Bella, who nodded, and she spread the bread, then stuck the slices together until there were four large sandwiches. Then she took from her own plate two shortbread biscuits and placed them on top of the bread, and Bella, seeing what she had done, said, 'Well, two won't go very far among four;' so she picked the two off her own plate and put these with the bread. 'Bring me that bowl and I'll fill it with soup. Can you manage this tray?' she said, turning to where Pimple had come in, and he answered her, 'Oh, yes, Bella. I'll manage any tray with food on it.'

'They're a poor lot, aren't they?' Bella said.

'I'd say they are, Bella. There's dozens,

even hundreds, like them on the road. But this lot, apparently, have clung together all the way from the North. Between them they haven't a sound boot to their feet or a spare shirt to their back. They've been travelling round since eight o'clock this morning and haven't taken a penny.'

'Here.' Bella went to the tin box again and, taking out a shilling, she said to Pimple, 'Give them that. It won't help much but likely it'll go towards gettin' them a kip tonight.'

After Bella had let Pimple out of the door with the laden tray, she returned to the kitchen. Reenee was shaking her head, and as if she had spoken, Bella said, 'Yes, it is a terrible state to be in. It's not right, it's the government; but what can you do with the government? I don't know, and people with more brains than me don't know either. Here! Let's make some fresh tea; that teapot is cold enough for layin' out.'

It was as they sat drinking their tea that there was a knock on the front door again, and Bella said, 'That's Joe's knock.' As she rose to go to the door she was thinking it a pity the lass couldn't push herself to open it; but when she faced Joe she said, 'What is it now? You should be back at work.'

'Aye, I know, Bella, but listen: they'll not get anywhere to kip tonight for what they've got today. They're determined to keep together through thick and thin, and they've already been through God knows what. Well, I've got two sheets of tarpaulin. They were thrown away from the warehouse, and you know there's a leak in the wash-house roof, and I thought there might come the time when I'd have to cover the roof over. So if they've got nowhere else to go would you let them lie inside the gates? Well, I mean against the wall of the wash-house. It would be warmish there. They could lie on one piece and cover themselves over with the other.'

Bella hesitated, then said, 'Well, as long as they don't make a rule of it, all right.'

'And, Bella?'

'Aye, what is it now?'

'You know you've rigged us both out with Mr Ham's things wherever they would fit us, shirts, pants and things like that. Coats an' all. I know the one you got me is a size too big, but I always wear an old sweater under it, to push it out like. One of those fellows is about my size—at least, he's big-boned, which is about all that's left of him. D'you think—'

'Yes, I think,' barked Bella; 'and I'll see what I can do. If they're not here in the morning you can tell them to call back. But don't you make a habit of this, d'you hear? You could pick up hundreds you lived next door to at your end of the country if you had a mind.'

'Aye, I could, Bella. I could at that.' He was grinning at her. 'But thanks all the same. I'll tell them. And they're grateful.'

She closed the door upon him and quickly went back to the kitchen. There she said to Reenee, 'I've got to get back to the stall, but you go upstairs now, into my room, and the big chest in the corner. You'll see it's still got piles of his vests and pants and shirts and things in it. Spread them out on the bed. Then see what coats and trousers are left. Put them over the end of the bed so I can get at them. The small chest of drawers is mine, and what I've got to hang up I put in the single wardrobe next door. That's where I used to keep me clothes before I went into the big room.' She laughed now as she repeated, 'The big room. His room. Eeh, I had a job to make meself get into that bed! I didn't for two or three weeks, you know, not after he went. Then I scrubbed the whole place down and turned the tick over. But one day I promised myself I'd have a carpet in that room, not that old lino. Now I have to go out and face the blast. It's chilly out there. I'm certainly not lookin' forward to the winter.

'Oh, don't look like that, lass. I wasn't meanin' that you should help or come out. Please don't take things to yourself. I understand your feelings. Don't worry, lass. Don't worry.' And when Reenee's hand came out and her fingers touched Bella's sleeve it was a way of saying, 'Thank you for understanding,' and Bella always took it as such, and she said, 'Of course. Of course I understand. Now let's get on with it.'

And they got on with it, and were waiting for the two lads to come in and take their meal down to their abode.

When the special knock came on the door and Bella said, 'That's Joe,' she was more than surprised, amazed, when Reenee sprang up and, almost at a run, went to the door, opened it and let the two men in.

In the hall they turned and looked at her and their surprise showed. It was Joe who expressed it by saying, 'You opened the door for us. That was good of you, Reenee. Ta . . . ta . . . thank you.'

'Yes,' put in Pimple; 'thank you very much, Reenee.'

'Will you come and get this and stop your jabberin' out there?' Bella's voice came to them, and the two men went into the kitchen smiling. Neither of them remarked on what had just occurred, but Joe said, 'I've got news for you, Bella.'

'Aye, news? What kind of news?'

'Well, you won't have any more horses' hoofs in your yard at night, that's one thing I know.'

'You do? Where did you hear that?'

'Oh, that and a lot more. There's been some fun, I can tell you, fun in the whole warehouse this afternoon. Talk about skittering! You know me and the likes of me are never allowed near the horse-driven vans when they're being loaded, but this morning I knew they had been loaded because the horses had been put into trim. Then this afternoon Mr Dixon, the real head of this end of the show, well, he comes out quick and orders the pieces in the vans to be taken out and put here and there among bits of furniture in one of the removal vans, the big long ones you know. And then two other fellows came and led the horses out of the yard to God knows where. Then the furniture van, with all household oddments as if somebody was just moving house, was driven out of the yard. Now what d'you make of that, Bella?'

'Well, I don't know,' said Bella; 'you seem to know much more about it than I do. One thing I'm glad of, though, they won't be coming here again.'

'Nor any of their removal vans,' put in Pimple, ' 'cos they could never get round that corner and into the gate. The horses were manoeuvrable.'

'Oh.' Bella laughed and, turning to Reenee, she said, 'We'll be able to go to the lav now any time we like.' And when Reenee hung her head, Bella said, 'Oh, lass, see the funny side of it.' On a sober note now, she went on, 'They've still got a key to that gate.'

'Oh, I can soon fix that,' said Joe. 'I didn't work with joiners and carpenters for nothing. I can twist a lock until it wishes it was dead.'

They were all laughing now; even the corners of Reenee's lips were moving upwards.

Although her lips remained tight it showed that she was indeed enjoying this joke.

'What about your own orphans of the storm?' Bella said to Joe. 'Have you given them a time limit to come back?'

'Aye, I have, Bella. I said if they weren't there at nine o'clock the gate would be locked.'

'Good. Anyway, if they come, I'll give them a bite before they leave in the morning, and you can tell them we've got some odds and ends of clothing that might be of use. You two have had your share and even in your case, Joe, they only fitted where they touched. But poor Pimple there . . .'

She nodded at Pimple, but he, smiling at her, said, 'Oh, I'm very glad with what I got, those lovely warm pants and vests and a decent shirt. But it's better to wear me own togs on top of them, because if people saw me decently dressed I'd get less than I'm gettin' now, and that's not sayin' much.'

'Not a good day?'

Pimple shook his head sadly, saying, 'People don't appreciate opera. I've stood outside that Opera House for hours and picked up every note, and when I play it comes out as clear as a bell although I say it meself. But do folks take any notice? No. It has to be "Tipperary" or "All Alone on the Telephone" or some drivel like that, and if they're in a picture queue they'll hum along with you. But will they put their hands in their pockets? No. Just here and there, when it'll be a penny, sometimes even a halfpenny. I feel like spittin' in their eye for the halfpenny; yet once inside they'll likely take tickets for the circle. Such is life.'

'Aye,' said Bella, 'such is life, Pimple. Could be worse.'

'Oh, aye. I'm not really grumbling, Bella.'

'Why d'you do it, then?' asked Bella. 'I mean go around playing.'

'Oh, you know why, I pick up things.'

'Oh, you've tried that game before, but what did it fetch you? Nothing. As I've said before, you could end in the gutter with your throat slit one of these nights if any of them villains you've shopped found out.'

'Aye, you're right,' said Pimple, 'you're right. But I don't know what else I can do.'

They all turned now and looked towards the young woman, who was writing or drawing on a piece of paper. Bella went and stood near her, and the other two followed. Reenee did not lift her head, but went on drawing. Eventually what she had drawn amounted to two lines down the middle of the paper with, on each side, shorter lines running to the edge, ten short lines on one side and only seven on the other. At the end of these she had made two squares. In one she was now laboriously writing the name Joe; then in the other Pimple.

'Well, what does all that mean?' said Bella tersely.

Down the middle of the paper she now wrote the word beds.

'Beds!' Bella looked from one man to the other and she repeated, 'Beds! What d'you think she means?'

It was as if Reenee answered for herself: getting to her feet, she pointed towards the steps leading downstairs, then cupped one side of her face in her hand and closed her eyes.

'I know. I know,' said Pimple quickly. 'You're making downstairs into a kip house, aren't you?'

Irene nodded, the while making a sound they took as yes.

'Oh, lass,' said Bella, impatiently now, 'and where d'you think you'd sleep?'

It was as if Reenee was trying to smile

now as she thumbed towards the ceiling, and Bella came at her, saying, 'So, you would go up there, would you? I've asked you twice if you'd take my old room but, no, you preferred to be downstairs by yourself.' Then, looking towards the men, Bella said, 'What an idea! How does she think we're goin' to get to the lav walkin' through a line of mattresses every night?' However, she turned to the girl again and acknowledged, 'It was a good idea, my dear. Aye, it was. And if it could've been worked I would have had a new business set-up, and you know where the fruit could go to, and as far beyond. But no, lass; there's no way that that can happen because the main thing for us is the lavatory. There's nobody gonna get me to go out me front door and through that back gate and down to that dirty old hole next to your abode.' As she spoke she turned to the lads and shook her head as though emphasising her decision.

'You could have a lav put up here.'

'Where, man? Where, I ask you? In this kitchen?'

Joe looked about him, then shrugged his shoulders. 'Something could be done.'

'Look!' cried Bella. 'Ten to twenty men

sleeping downstairs and that one lav across the way? What's goin' to happen d'you think in that yard? Oh, no, thanks; I'd rather have the old horses back. We could shovel up their mess.'

'Aye; you're right,' said Joe. 'You're always right. But it was a good idea;' and he turned to acknowledge Reenee.

She hung her head as if in disappointment, but brought it up sharply again when Bella almost shouted, 'And where's the money comin' from for mattresses, lavatories, new lavs up here? And that will only be the beginning. God, let's talk sense! I'm sorry, lass. I'll admit it was a marvellous idea, but what money I make now just manages to get us through, and that's with a squeeze at times, I can tell you. Go on, now, you two, take your meal and get out of it. And if those fellows turn up tonight, have you enough tea down there to give them a drink?'

'Oh, aye,' said Pimple. 'We don't have it strong, and there's quite a bit from the last quarter you gave us.'

'Well, then, go on, get yourselves away.'

'Good night, Bella.'

'Good night, Bella.'

'Good night, lads.'

'Good night, Reenee.' The two men spoke as one, and her lips opened as if she was about to speak; but no words came, yet the look on her face was telling them good night . . .

The next morning the four players stood in the hallway and looked in amazement at the pile of underwear, socks and boots that Bella had spread out on the bottom of the stairs, and at the coats and trousers that were hanging over the stair-rail.

'The vests and pants and socks,' she said, 'you can make fit you somehow, but I'm afraid the trousers and coats are way beyond your size, except for you,' and she pointed to the biggest of the men and she said, 'What's your name?'

'Andy Anderson.'

'What was your trade?'

'I was a bricklayer, ma'am.'

'Well, here! Try this coat on.'

The coat was a size too big, but it did not deter the man. He turned the cuffs up, then pulled one side of the coat over the other, saying, 'Oh, I could fix this, ma'am. Willie there is good with his needle. He'd make new buttonholes for me, wouldn't you, Willie?'

Willie did not answer, and Bella said to him, 'What's your name, son?'

'Willie Young, ma'am.'

'And what was your trade?'

'I was a baker.'

'I'm surprised you're out of work,' she said.

'Oh, ma'am, you shouldn't be surprised at anything that happens when you're among starvin' men and bairns. They broke into the shop one night and cleared the lot. It was a Sunday and the bakin' had been done for the Monday mornin'. There was nothin' left and the boss had had enough. That was the third time it happened, so there were five of us without work.'

'Dear, dear.' Bella picked up another coat, and handed it to the third man. 'That's miles too big for you, but put it on and see.'

They all laughed gently when they saw the shorter figure lost in the depths of the big jacket, but the man said, 'I'll take it, ma'am, if you wouldn't mind. I can put a belt round the middle and Willie could see to the cuffs for me.'

Bella laughed. 'Willie's goin' to have his work cut out. Now what d'they call you?'

'Tony Brown, ma'am,' and before she could ask the next question he added, 'I was a plumber.'

Turning to the last man, she said, 'That only leaves you.'

'I was a ship's carpenter, ma'am. Me name's John Carter.'

'And these trousers'—Bella had taken them from the rail—'they're very good stuff and they won't fit any of you, I'm sure, but you could pawn them. You might get a bob or so on them because they're tailored an' all.'

'We can't thank you enough, ma'am,' said Andy Anderson; 'and for lettin' us stay the night.'

'Oh, I couldn't see you had a very comfortable time of it lyin' on tarpaulin, and over you, too.'

'Oh, it's amazin', ma'am, how warm it was near that wall, and after the lads had given us a mug of tea. You've got a pair of good lads there, ma'am.'

'Yes. Yes, I suppose so.'

'They think the world of you,' said Willie Young.

'Oh, aye?' said Bella. 'Well, that's on good days. What they say about me on bad 'uns can't be repeated.'

They all laughed as they gathered up the clothes from the stairs, and it was John Carter, the carpenter, who said, 'Can we go back, ma'am, down to the boys' place and fit ourselves out?'

'Yes; yes, of course.'

'We wish we could do something for you, miss . . . ma'am,' said Tony Brown now. 'It isn't often one meets with such kindness.'

'Well, you haven't got me to thank, really, but that big thick-headed Geordie Joe who recognised a neighbour's voice. But go on now, and better luck today.'

They trooped out, still voicing their thanks; Bella returned to the kitchen, and said to Reenee, now standing at the farthest end of it, 'I doubt from the looks of two of them they'll see the winter through. It's scandalous, scandalous.' She shook her head, then said, 'Well, we can't do any more. That's the end of it, so let's get on with the day's work.'

But apparently it wasn't the end of it, only the beginning, for when Joe and Pimple came for their morning meal Joe said, very

quietly, 'Don't go for me, Bella, I'm only doing things for the best; but those lads were
tellin' me last night of some of the kips
they'd had to sleep in, and they were dis-
graceful, while the decent ones charged a
shilling a night for a bowl of soup, a can of
tea the next morning and a wash. I told them
about Reenee's idea for the kip made out
of the cellar kitchen, and how it sounded
impossible. Well, Bella, Andy the brickie said
nothing's impossible when altering a house,
and he knows that 'cos he's helped with
many, and he wondered if you'd let him . . .
well, look around and see what might be
done here and work out how much it would
cost like. What about it, Bella?'

'Oh, my God!' said Bella. 'What next?'
She looked across at Reenee. There was an
expectant look on the girl's face, so she
said, 'Oh, all right. There can be no harm in
that. Tell him to come in before they go.'

About half an hour later Bella nearly
laughed outright at the assembly of different
men standing at her front door. They must
have put the new gear on top of the old, for
even their trousers looked well padded now
and two of the men, who were wearing the
coats, appeared to be twice their size, at

least in breadth. It was the bricklayer who spoke to her. 'Ma'am, if you wouldn't mind, would you let us have a look round? We might be able to work something out, and that might help you with your plan the lads were telling us about last night.'

'My plan?' Bella cried. 'I have no plan. It was a pipe dream of somebody's.' She didn't name Reenee.

'Well, ma'am, we feel we want to do something for you, and it will be no harm leaving you with a few suggestions if ever the idea should come to anything.'

Bella was stopped from answering by seeing Reenee scampering up the stairs.

'Have we frightened her, ma'am?' said one of the men.

'No, you see, she's lost her memory, or most of it, and whatever's happened to her . . . Well, men had something to do with it, and between you and me she can't bear the sight of them. But about your suggestion. You seem set on repaying me, so if it's going to please you, do as you say and have a look round. But I'm warning you, that's as far as it'll go. I haven't any money and I have enough to worry about in keeping my little business going.'

* * *

'Now, you two, listen to me,' said Bella. 'As I've told you, I haven't the money to see this thing through. And I can understand those fellows' enthusiasm: they're in such a state they'd go to any length to have a settled place to kip and a regular bite in their bellies. It's all very fine, talk and planning, but it's happening too swiftly for my liking. No, I'm not for it. Up till now I've lived quietly without all this fuss and bother; for what is it going to come to in the end? As far as I can see, nothing. They'll be back where they started, and our lives will go on as before.'

Suddenly she turned on Reenee, almost yelling now, 'And don't you look like that, lass! It's me that has to pay the piper, as the saying goes. So let's hear no more about it. I'll tell them in the morning. They've gone mad with their measuring and planning.'

But she didn't tell them in the morning for she had something more serious to think about. Reenee had gone. My God, she would go mad!

This was the outcome of last night. Why had she allowed the men to go up in the attic to see what was there? She had given way to her own curiosity and thought she might as well make use of them while they were here. And what had they found? Everything you'd find in a children's playroom: broken dolls' houses and all kinds of toys, including two moth-eaten teddy bears, besides broken furniture.

Joe had discovered a beam running across the ceiling and through the wall into the cobbler's place, indicating that at one time perhaps the two houses had been one.

But what had caused the upset with Reenee was the larger moth-eaten teddy bear. After the four men had gone, having taken all the oddments of furniture down into the yard, Reenee had come down from her bedroom, and when she sat by the fireplace Bella had picked up the moth-eaten bear she had kept back and taken it to her, saying, 'What d'you think about this, what's left of the poor thing?' as she dropped it on to Reenee's lap, only to exclaim, 'Oh dear!' as Reenee, suddenly grabbing the bear, began to rock herself back and forth, moaning what seemed to Bella and the two men the same word over and over again. Bella was gripping Joe's arm as she said, 'God in heaven! She's had a bairn at some time.'

Neither Joe nor Pimple made any comment, they just stared at the wailing figure, for now Reenee's voice had risen as she rocked the bear.

'She'll make herself ill going on like that,' said Bella. 'We should try to get it from her.'

'I wouldn't,' put in Pimple. 'Just leave her.' And they stood watching the swaying figure hugging to her the remnants of the teddy bear until, slowly, she seemed exhausted and lay back in the chair, but still with the bear clutched to her breast, its head tucked under her chin.

Bella had approached her quietly, saying, 'There you are, lass. There you are.' She looked down into the streaming face and the tears came into her own eyes. She'd never had a child of her own, never wanted one, having been brought up among too many, so she had never known the love of a child, or for one, but she was experiencing it now. This girl was acting out of passion, of feeling. It was as if she had found her child again, long lost.

It was a good ten minutes later that the tension in Reenee's body seemed to seep away and she lay limply in the chair.

Quite suddenly, Pimple turned and walked to the far end of the kitchen, opened the door and went out, and Joe, about to follow him, said something that amazed Bella. He looked at her and murmured, 'Things happen in life that are too hard to bear. They are much worse than being hungry and frozen at nights,' and at this he, too, turned and left her.

It was at the twelve o'clock break that Bella left the stall to Peg-leg and went indoors, but Reenee wasn't in the kitchen.

Bella went to the top of the stone stairs, but told herself not to be silly, she wouldn't be down there: those fellows were probably still about. She turned round and went to the foot of the hall stairs and called, 'Reenee!'

When there was no reply she called again. Then she went quickly up the stairs and unceremoniously into the second bedroom. She pulled open the wardrobe door, then emitted the words, 'Oh, my God!' because neither the discoloured coat nor the weird cap were hanging there. But the bear was lying at the bottom of the wardrobe. What was there too was the dress Bella had got from Ginnie's a few weeks ago and had persuaded Reenee to wear round the house. The velvet dress was gone as well.

'Oh, my God!' She sat on the edge of the bed. Where would she have gone to in her state of mind? It had been bad enough until last night, but the hugging of that moth-eaten old bear must have brought back something in her past in a way that had driven her out to find it. She must send somebody looking for her. But Joe wasn't here, at least not for another half-hour, and you could never depend upon Pimple. But she must get Joe. Yes, she must get Joe.

She was running down the stairs quicker than she had done for a long time, through the kitchen and into the backyard where two of the men were standing talking; and she cried at them, 'You know the warehouse where Joe works?'

'Aye, ma'am. Aye.'

'Well, go and fetch him. Tell him that she's gone, the lass . . . the woman . . . she's gone.'

'You mean your . . . that . . . your girl?'

'Never mind who I mean, he'll know who I mean. Get yourself away!'

Within fifteen minutes Joe was standing in front of her, saying, 'You don't mean it?'

'I do. I do. Her coat, hat and the red velvet

dress. All she ever owned. In fact, just what she came in here with she's gone out with, and I don't know where to send you lookin'.'

'Somebody must've spotted her. She'll stand out, always did.'

As Joe was hurrying from her she shouted to him, 'Where d'you think Pimple will be playin'?'

'God knows, Bella; he gets around. But I'll away.'

It was half an hour before Joe returned. He stood before her silently and shook his head.

Bella plumped down on to a kitchen chair, laid her head on her folded arms on the table, and began to cry. When she felt his hand patting her shoulder she straightened herself, wiped her face quickly with the end of her apron and said, 'I—I can't tell you, Joe, how I've come to like that lass. I know half her mind's been lost in the past but I'd an idea it would come through one of these days. But till then I wanted to look after her. And it's selfish in a way because she has brought light into my life that wasn't here before I saw her lyin' that day among the boxes and the rotten fruit.'

5

During the time Bella was baring her soul to Joe, Irene was standing in a pawn shop facing an old man who wore a skull cap, and he was looking at something she had taken out of a bag inside her coat pocket. It was a ring and he looked at it for a long time before he put his hand under the counter and brought out an eye-glass. It was some minutes later when he said to her in a thick tone, 'You want to pawn this article?'

When she nodded he paused a moment or two before speaking again, then said, 'Have you any idea of its worth?' His words were slow as if he were talking to a child, and again she inclined her head towards him.

He now picked up the ring and once more put the glass to his eye. Then, after a moment, he called, 'Joseph!' and was answered by a younger edition of himself coming from a back room and taking a position by his side. When his father held out the ring silently to him the younger man looked at it for quite some moments before, taking the eye-glass from his father, he too peered through it. Then he muttered one word: 'My!'

The elderly man was speaking once more to Irene and he said, 'You will, I am sure, be asking a large loan for this article, but first I must ask you, does it really belong to you?'

The word came out quick, utterly clear and loud: 'Yes!'

Its tone was so different from the appearance of this person that the men's eyes met again for a moment, and they were still more astonished when their customer's small fist thumped her chest, exclaiming loudly, 'Mine! Mine!'

'All right, madam. We believe you, but as I was about to say, we don't often take into pawn articles of this value. Ours is a very poor district, as you can see, and really we must tell you our loans don't go much beyond ten shillings, if that. So you will understand my questioning about this most wonderful ring. Nevertheless I am used to stones, madam. Good stones.'

Again there was an exchange of glances; and then the old man gave his full attention to Irene, saying, 'What did you think about asking, I mean as a loan?'

They both waited and the same sum was in both their minds. She would ask at least for fifty pounds but they would beat her down, naturally, as it was their business to do so. But this ring here was worth a great deal of money, if he knew anything about stones. Oh, yes. Rubies and diamonds.

She surprised them both by saying, 'Thirty pounds.'

It was the son who repeated, 'Thirty pounds.' Then he looked at his father and repeated, 'Thirty pounds.'

He turned quickly to a shelf before him on which were small pockets of articles with tickets hanging from them and he pushed one here and there before he muttered, 'Don't haggle. Don't haggle, Father.'

The older man seemed to consider a moment, and then he said, 'Thirty pounds. Well, I don't see why you can't have thirty pounds. Do you mean to leave it lying for some months or a year?'

She stared back at the men who were now facing her, and they saw that she was making a great effort to speak again because her mouth opened and closed convulsively. She put a hand to her throat and such was her agitation that the elder man said, 'Don't worry yourself, my dear lady.' Yes, he had called her a lady, for he was sure, under that dreadful garb, that that's what she was, a lady, but in distress of some kind because her words came out only as syllables.

Quietly and slowly, he said, 'You mean that it may be more than a year before you come back? But I must tell you, madam, that if you do not return in a year and pay back your loan then by law we are allowed to keep what you pawned and sell it. You understand?'

They both saw that she didn't, and it was the younger man who said, 'You can insure it. I mean, you can pay so much to insure it if you don't mean to return in a year. You could cover it for a year, two years, three years or more, and it will always be here when you come back. That's if you can afford to insure it. You could perhaps use some of the thirty pounds in insurance?'

She shook her head vigorously. Then she seemed to think for a moment and, putting her hand quickly inside her coat, she fumbled about a bit before placing before them another ring.

'A wedding ring?' asked the elderly man.

She nodded.

The younger man took the ring and, turning it round in his fingers, he said to his father, 'Do you see those?'

'I would be blind, my son, if I didn't. Diamonds are diamonds, even if they're only pinhead size,' and his fingers now traced the band of small diamonds running round the centre of the circle.

'You would like to pawn this also?'

Irene's head bobbed again, and then with a great effort she brought out the word in stilted form, 'In-sur-ance.'

'Oh, yes. Yes.'

Then she added another word to it, 'Part.' This word was clear.

Both men considered; and then the younger one said, 'You want to know how much you can borrow on this ring, and you want to leave part of it by way of insurance on both the dress ring and this one?'

Irene looked at him for a long moment,

and then, taking a deep breath, she brought out again the single word, 'Yes.'

'Well, madam'—the older man was speaking again—'you know that this hasn't the value of the first ring? It is very nice, oh, very nice indeed, and of value, and it is wise that you are using it by way of insurance.' Then he turned to his son. 'For how many years would five pounds cover the insurance on the article?'

Once again the young man turned his back on his father and addressed himself to arranging the things in the small cubbyholes, and he whispered, 'Offer ten.'

'But . . . but, son . . .'

'Offer ten, Father, please.'

The older man's whispered words were audible to Irene: 'Have you gone soft in the head already? Does she hold a charm?'

'No, Father,' the younger man did not turn to his parent, 'let us say compassion of some sort. I don't know why, but compassion.'

'Dear, dear. I think, my son, you will soon have to be looking out for another post,' and the two men laughed together. Then they were both looking at Irene, whose face was now showing some anxiety, and the father

said, 'Oh, quite a small amount would cover
the insurance for a number of years, so if
we offer you ten pounds you would be able
to add most of that to your thirty. Would that
be suitable?'

They both watched the look of relief on
the face across the counter. Then it was as
if she were making another great effort to
speak. Seeing a scrap of pencil, she picked
it up, together with the newspaper that was
lying there and she wrote, very slowly, 'How
many years will five pounds cover insurance?'

'Oh,' the older man looked at his son,
then said, 'Well, that'll have to be worked
out. What d'you think, Joseph?'

Joseph had taken a pen from his pocket
and was writing hastily, and when he finished he said, 'Eighteen years.'

She seemed quite satisfied with their answer. Then the elderly man said, 'Will you
be coming back before then?'

Maybe. Her lips framed the word but no
sound came, but he seemed to pick up her
dumb language and he translated it to, 'Perhaps?' and she nodded.

It was the young man who spoke next.
'Do you live around this way?'

Her answer, he had surmised, would be a definite no; but her head drooped a little, then gave an affirmative nod. She lived around here then. Whereabouts? Why hadn't he seen her? But, then, he rarely went out during working hours; when he did it would be to visit other similar business houses that included family ties, cousins and half-cousins.

His father was now writing out four tickets, and he himself placed the two rings in a small box that he had taken from under the counter and wrote something on the lid. Then, looking at her, he said, 'Your name, please?'

She hesitated for a long moment before, on the margin of the sheet of newspaper, she wrote 'Forrester'. He said, 'Christian name?'

She wrote the letter C, and he repeated, 'C. Forrester,' as he wrote it on the box lid. Then he opened a ledger that was beside him and wrote in this too. Meanwhile his father had finished writing on the tickets, in a small neat hand, the descriptions of the pledges; and he handed two of the tickets to her saying, 'Keep them safe because, you know, they are your only proof that you have lodged your precious jewellery with us. You understand? If you were to lose them, someone else might try to claim them.'

It was the son now who put in quickly, 'We shall also give you a receipt for the insurance of five pounds on the articles.' He turned and looked at his father, who said, 'Yes, of course.' Within a few minutes she was handed another small piece of paper with 'Isaac Gomparts, Pawnbroker and Dealer' stamped on it, and above this a few words saying that she had insured the said articles for five pounds which would cover the period of eighteen years.

Irene picked up the two tickets and folded them in the piece of paper, which just covered them; then she stood waiting as she watched the younger man count out thirty-five pound notes, which he handed to her, saying, 'Count.' But she shook her head, and he said, 'I shall put them in an envelope for you, yes?'

She nodded, and after he had handed them back to her in the envelope, she put the tickets in with the money, then placed the envelope in a pocket of her coat. Then the three of them stood looking at each other, until the younger man said, 'I hope the transaction will help you.' She looked straight at him and bowed her head once to him. Then, looking at the older man, she brought out, again seemingly painfully, the words, 'Thank you.'

'Never has a customer been more welcome, madam. Good day to you.'

Inclining her head, she nodded from one to the other and went out. Then the older man, turning to his son, said, 'Well, well! And what came over you, may I ask, Joseph Gomparts?'

'I don't know,' said his son. 'I can only say we've been dealing with a beautiful maimed woman with the face of a lost angel.'

At this he turned and walked away, leaving his father patting the counter and shaking his head as he muttered to himself, 'Dear God, it is as you say, don't look for the reasons of life in your own kin. They are of you and you can't fathom it.'

Bella was sitting looking up at Joe. She was making no attempt now to dry the tears that were still running down her face, and her voice was cracked as she said, 'It was that damned teddy bear; it did something to her.

And yet, when she came down this morning, I was amazed at the sight of her. She looked so . . . well, so much more alive, much more conscious of everything. That's the only way I can put it. At one time I thought she looked excited, and I thought, Good, perhaps the bear has straightened out part of her mind in some way, and on the quiet, when she was down here, I looked in her room to see if it was on her bed—she'd likely been sleeping with it—but no, it wasn't, and when I was lookin' in the wardrobe to see if her coat was still there, I saw it pushed right into the corner. Now if it was the incident of the bear that brought her to herself, she wouldn't have pushed it into a corner, would she? She would have left it somewhere where she could still see it. Nevertheless, it must have done something to make her clear out.' She had hardly finished the last words when the door that led down from the kitchen to the stone stairs burst open and Pimple, almost breathless, hurried in and held on to the table as he said, 'She's on her way! She's on her way! She'll be here any minute.'

'How d'you know about it?' Joe demanded. 'We've been lookin' all over for her.'

'Yeah, you might have, but I didn't know anything about her walkin' out until there I was at the end of Brampton Street. It's a long street, and I saw the figure at the other end. Now, she's unmistakable in that get-up. At first I thought I was seeing things; and then she disappeared—into where d'you think? A pawn shop.'

'What?'

'That's what I said, Bella, into a pawn shop. Now, look. I'm not goin' to stop because she'll be in in a minute.'

'Oh!' Bella got to her feet. 'Wait till I see her.'

'Bella! Bella!' Pimple now spoke in a tone of command and with a voice that could have come from someone twice his size, so deep and firm was it. 'You'll do nothing of the sort. If you'll take advice, for once in your life, you'll do nothing of the sort. You'll open your arms to her because, if she went into that pawn shop, it was to pawn something, wasn't it? And who would she pawn for? Not for herself, I'm sure, but for you or whatever you're doing. At least, that's how I see her. Anyway,' he grabbed Joe's arm, 'let's get out of this. I came the back way, running like a hare, 'cos I knew she would be making for home and I didn't want her to see me. So she'll come in the front way. Now, I've told you, Bella.'

Bella gazed at him in amazement, and she watched him almost pull Joe towards the staircase door. As it banged closed the front door opened, and Bella stood trembling, holding tightly with one hand to the edge of the table to steady herself.

Then, there she was, the girl, the woman, the strange one, as she had first seen her in that long, stained coat and weird hat. Only her face looked different today. She came slowly forward and when she stood before her Bella found she was quite unable to speak. She only knew she loved this poor creature and then, just as Pimple had said, she put her arms out, and Reenee went into them. Her own arms went round Bella's stubby body, and they held each other close; and like this they stood for a full minute before Bella, pressing her slightly away, looked up into her face and said, 'Oh, lass! You . . . you did frighten me! I thought you'd gone for good, or at least gone somewhere.'

And now she made herself ask, 'Where . . . where have you been?'

Reenee's eyes were bright and her throat swelled as she endeavoured to get out the words, 'Pawn shop.'

'Pawn shop!' exclaimed Bella. And although she knew this was where Pimple told her she had been, it was with genuine surprise that she repeated, 'Pawn shop!'

Reenee now indicated that Bella should sit down, and she herself sat as well. Then, unbuttoning her coat and putting her hand inside it, she brought out a brown envelope, out of which she slowly pulled a thick wad of pound notes. She did not lift out the tickets but pressed them into a corner of the envelope, which she then doubled and returned to her pocket. Then, looking at Bella, who was staring wide-eyed at the money, she began to count it out silently on to the table. When she reached thirty she stopped; and the last notes in her hand she counted separately; then putting them to one side, she pointed to them and then to herself as she again made an effort to speak. The word she muttered now was 'Mine.'

Bella simply gazed at her. She couldn't believe her eyes. There were thirty pounds on the table; and when Reenee pushed them towards her, she exclaimed, 'Oh, lass! How on earth did you get . . . ? But why? Why had you to . . . ? I mean—' She stopped talking and gazed down on the money and said, 'Thirty pounds. Thirty pounds,' and added the word, 'How?'

Reenee pointed quickly to her left hand and the second and third fingers, then indicated what Bella clearly understood as rings.

'You've pawned your rings? You had rings? Your wedding ring?'

She watched the look on Reenee's face change: the brightness went off it, but nevertheless she acknowledged Bella's concern with a movement of her head, before she pointed again to her third finger and made two circles over the top of it.

For a moment Bella was puzzled, and then she said, 'Engagement ring.'

Again Reenee's head nodded downwards.

Bella's voice was hushed as she said, 'Must have been a very, very good ring to bring all that money. But why? Why, lass?'

On Bella's last words Reenee tried to speak. When she wasn't successful she pulled the newspaper towards her, and going to the mantelpiece where Bella kept a pencil she took it down and wrote along the border of the newsprint, 'Men's plan. Need something. Poor.'

Bella looked at her and there were tears in her eyes again as she said, 'Oh, love. Fancy you thinking of them and you frightened to death of them. There's nothing to be afraid of, they wouldn't hurt a hair . . . All right,' she held up a hand as she saw Reenee almost shrink back from her, 'I didn't mean that you should talk to them or recognise them, but I still maintain they're good blokes and they would never hurt you in any way. Oh'—she laughed to herself—'if they as much as said a wrong word to you our two would murder them, Joe and Pimple, you know.'

The words did not bring a smile to Reenee's face but she pointed to the five pounds that were to the side, and she said again, 'Mine.'

'Of course, lass. Of course you've got to keep something for yourself.' The head was shaking but in denial, and Bella said, 'It isn't for yourself, but you want to keep it? Is that it?'

The nod told Bella that she had said the right thing; and again looking at the money, she muttered, 'I'll have to put it some place safe. And, lass,' she suddenly lifted her head, 'I . . . I'll tell the lads what you've done, and for them and the others, but I won't tell them how much there's here. Oh, no, because that will put more ideas into their heads of how it could be used. Shall we say ten pounds and bring out the other bit by bit for what is needed? How d'you feel about that?'

The two nods from Reenee brought from Bella, 'Good lass. Good, we're both of the same mind. But where am I goin' to put the remainder?'

Reenee was now standing with her head slightly to one side as if thinking; then that semblance of a smile came to her face and she made a gesture that Bella should gather up the notes. She herself picked up the five pounds from the table and pushed them into her inner coat pocket. Then, taking Bella's arm, she led her down the room and through a door into the little-used parlour.

After the brightness of the kitchen this room appeared as if they had already reached late evening; Reenee led Bella to the far blank wall against which stood a roll-top desk. She pointed to the key in the lock, turned it, pushed open the lid, then pulled out one of the lower drawers that were fitted along the back of the piece and, putting her hand inside, she picked up a smaller key, pushed in the drawer and locked it. She turned and gave the key to Bella who, now smiling widely, said, 'Eeh, lass, you must have investigated all this. But that's the very place. Yes, yes, you're right.' She counted off ten of the notes and put them into her apron pocket, unlocked the drawer and laid the other twenty carefully in it, locked it, then turned . . . and handed the key to Reenee. At this Reenee shook her head vigorously and waved Bella's hand to one side. Then she pulled down the lid, locked it and handed the second key to Bella. Then once more she found herself clasped in the arms of the little woman, who was whispering, 'Oh, Reenee, if ever there was a light came into me life it's been you. But God knows, my dear, how you have suffered along the way to get here. I only wish I knew.' She put her hand up and touched Reenee's face. 'Oh, I wish you would speak and try to tell

me all that you remember. That's if you remember anything.

'Oh, dear me! What have I said? I'm sorry,
lass. I'm sorry. Don't look like that. You have
nothing to fear, ever. Whoever did what they
did to you I hope they rot in hell. But come
on, lass, come on, else we'll both be blub-
bing again. Wait till I tell the lads. And . . .
and what say I give the fellows five shillings
at the end, will that please you?'

The light slowly returned to Reenee's face
and she made one small movement with her
head, then they both left the room hand in
hand together, the slight, grotesquely
dressed girl and the little homely woman.

6

It was three weeks later and the changes
that had already taken place both in the
house and downstairs in the cellar were unbelievable. There was now going off the
kitchen a bathroom, formerly the big larder
and the long broom and oddments store.
That the colour of the bath, the basin and
the lavatory yelled their bold red at you as
soon as you opened the door was of no account. The walls had been painted what
John called a dove grey. Next to the wash-
basin was a two feet by eighteen inches
long window covered with a floral-patterned
curtain. Looking through this window across
the yard you knew something was happening to the wash-house, but that was as yet
unfinished.

Downstairs, in what had been Reenee's

sleeping quarters, a great transformation had taken place. At the far end were two doors leading into separate rooms, each holding a single iron bed on top of which was a good mattress and a quilted bed-cover. Besides this there was a chest of drawers and a curtained-off corner that acted as a wardrobe, and a repaired chair rescued from the attic. Neither Joe nor Pimple could believe that these rooms had been furnished for them alone. Such was the effect on Pimple that he had dared to put his arms around Reenee and kiss her cheek. This had been done, it must be admitted, at a rush and had taken her off her guard. But as he had stood back from her, he said, 'I had to do that, Reenee, because the miracle could never have happened without you.' He did not add 'pawning your rings'.

Along two sides of the long room were roughly constructed low wooden platforms waiting for mattresses.

Then there was the outside, the new latrines and the washplace that held two basins, each with its roller towel. The material of the towels was rough but that did not lessen the men's appreciation of them.

That the four men had worked wonders

was said over and over again by Bella. But
now there was a snag, and they were having
a meeting about this down in what was to
become the bunk-house or, to give it its
common name, Big Bella's Pad. It was Joe
who had thought up the title.

They were now sitting on forms at each
side of the long central table. This had been
constructed from two cement-covered
planks found amongst a heap of builders'
rubbish. They had picked up the trestles for
it and the forms while scrounging in the
dump yard, the same place in which they
had found the red bathroom suite. The condition of the latter had amazed them: as
John had said, probably somebody had
been unable any longer to stand the colour.
Nor could they believe their luck when the
old grubber asked only four pounds five
shillings for the lot.

Bella sat at the end of the table. To one
side of her were Joe and Pimple, and next
to Pimple sat Willie. On the other side were
Andy, Tony and John. It was Willie who now
put in plaintively, 'I wouldn't be in the way,
ma'am.'

'I know that, laddie, I know that. We all
know that. But she's a sick woman in her

head, at least half of it, and I don't know how it's gonna be overcome. Perhaps, as she got used to Joe here and Pimple, she might get used to the rest of you, if you stay that long.'

'Oh, if the plan works out, ma'am,' came from Tony, 'you've got me for life.'

'And me,' said John.

But what Andy said was, 'I wish I could say the same, but I have a wife and two bairns back there, and if things get turned round I'll have to go back. In fact, to be truthful I'd want to go back. As I've said, I miss me bairns and they're growin' up without me. But I can't see it happenin' for a year or so, not from readin' the papers.

'About the lass, though, ma'am, what are we gonna do? We can't keep out of the way all the time, can we? Now that things are about to get working? Willie there is a very good cook—I know that just from the experience of the last few weeks—but he tells me he's best at makin' bread and pastry, so if you would let him make bread,' he was nodding at Willie now, 'each man could have a shive with their broth at night and, in the morning, a slice with their mug of tea. If they wanted to buy a pie, a meat one that is, it would cost them twopence, or they might want just a bun for a penny. But he said quite a lot of money can be made out of that kind of thing, and if it got round there was a wash-up place as well as a place around a big fireguard where they could dry their boots or hang their clothes if they were wet, you would have your beds filled every night, I can tell you.'

'But would they, if they're on their uppers, be able to pay a shillin' a night?' put in Bella.

'Aye, that's a point, because there's many a night we hadn't a shilling among us, let alone one each. Yet there were other nights when we had, and what we got for a shilling . . . well, I've told you all about it. But here, what are you offering? They can have a wash straight away; they can come in and they can get warm sitting on the forms around a fire; then they can have a bowl of soup and a shive, and the soup isn't just soup, it'll be broth with plenty of vegetables in. Joe there said he could get all the vegetables he could carry from the market every morning, like he does the fruit, and all that's needed to go with them is a couple of penn'orth of bones, preferably with meat on them,' he laughed now, 'and half a pound of hough meat.'

'What's hough meat?' said Bella, looking from one to the other.

Joe said, 'Oh, it's the rough end of the cow. But one of the main things I would say, Andy, besides having a good few taties in it, is the barley. Add half a pound of barley to that and that kale pot will have more nourishment in it than any restaurant in London town. What d'you say, Willie, 'cos you'll be the one that's doin' it?'

'Oh, aye. Aye. But . . . but remember, I won't be the only one that's doing it. The missis here, she'll be running things and she'll see what is used, and know how much she can spend and what she can make in order to carry on 'cos, as she's said, there'll be no fruit stall outside once it gets going.'

'The way I see it,' put in Tony, 'the ones we'll get here are mostly those fellows with part-time jobs, and for a shillin' a night they'll be only too damn glad of the chance to come.'

'Well,' said Bella, quickly now, 'this all brings us back to the point, what about the lass? How are we goin' to get her to accept that you're goin' to be in that kitchen all day, Willie?'

'If I talk to her . . .' said Willie.

'No. No, that wouldn't be any good.' This came from John. 'I have an idea. I don't know what you'll think about this, ma'am, but I've only been in your front room, or parlour as you call it, once. To me, it was a dark, dingy place, and I'm quick at taking in things. There was a great big sideboard that could be halved in size by the middle part being taken out. They're as old as the hills, those things. One day they'll be worth money, but they're not now. And there's two big leather chairs in there, besides a roll-top desk. The window . . . well, it hardly lets any light in at all.'

'You're not touchin' the roll-top desk, John. That stays as it is, no matter what else you change.'

'Oh, aye, and it's a very good piece of furniture; but that window could be made twice its size. The sideboard could be made half its size and look better for it. Then fresh wallpaper and a bit of paint and that room could be a very comfortable place. And I saw there was quite a good grate in the fireplace, which had a tiled surround. It could be made cosy like, and I'm sorry to say it's anything but cosy to me now. Well, there you are, ma'am. What d'you think? What I'm getting at, really,' John finished, 'is that it will be some place for her to . . . well, she seems to want to hide, and it will be comfortable and nice, in fact, for you both, because there's no place in the house I can see that provides the two of you with any privacy, not even the kitchen.'

Bella looked at him, and she smiled and said, 'You must have taught yourself a lot, lad, decoratin' those boats. You've got an eye for things, haven't you?'

'Aye, ma'am, I pride meself on having an eye for how things should be in a room. It hasn't brought me very far, as you can see, but I'm never happy unless I'm fixing something or altering something to look better.'

'Well, I can say this to you, laddie, you have my go-ahead about that room. Anything you do in it, I say carry on. Only leave the roll-top desk where it is.'

'You mean that, ma'am, after . . . after we finish extending the wash-house?'

'Yes, I mean it. And was it your idea to extend the wash-house?'

John hung his head for a moment, then

quickly raised it as he said, 'Aye, it was; and it'll be fine when it's finished. We'll have two double bunks, and some bare necessities. We'll make it a comfortable pad for as long as you need us. Isn't that so?' He looked round the table.

'Yes. And we've been very grateful for it,' said Andy.

'You'll never know, ma'am, how grateful. And to think you're paying us what you can, an' all.'

'Five shillings a week isn't much, lad.'

'It's a bank roll when you haven't got owt,' said Tony. 'By, it is! But as you said last night, we know you can't go on doing that until you see how this business is going to work. So if you stop after this week we'll understand, won't we?'

John said, 'It'll be enough payment to be working on your parlour, ma'am.'

'You're good lads. They are, aren't they?'

She had turned to Joe and Pimple, and Joe said, 'Never better. But you see, Bella, they're from my part of the country, they couldn't be otherwise, could they now?'

She reached out her hand to slap his face, but he leant back from her and they all laughed.

Joe said now, 'I must tell them at the warehouse about the mattresses tomorrow, Bella, because I know they're goin' to move the lot. Supposedly for the retail business, but that lot of mattresses they've brought in was for no ordinary order. There must be a hundred of them if there's two, and they want rid of them as quick as possible. He was asking five shillings each, and I got him to phone through to the other warehouse and tell them that they were for you, and the word came back 'half price'; but that'll cost thirty bob, Bella, and there's the blankets. They're full size, there's no singles, and he wanted four bob each, but you could have them for two. That will be another twenty-four bob.'

Bella shut her eyes and put her head back for a moment, as if considering, and then she said, 'Dear Lord, I don't know where the money's comin' from. Anyway, you'd better get them, 'cos there won't be another chance like it. We can always take in sewing—there's an old Singer machine in the boxroom upstairs and nobody to use it. We'll manage. All right, then.'

But Willie stopped her rising by saying, 'I can't start in that kitchen, ma'am, knowing that I'm puttin' that lass out or hurtin' her in some way.'

'You won't have to,' said John quickly. 'You lot can carry on with finishing off the wash-house. I'll set to work in the parlour. The only thing is,' he turned to Andy, 'I'll want you for the window, but that won't be for, say, a day or so. All right?'

He had addressed this last remark to Bella and she said, 'All right, if you can do it in a couple of days; we'll manage till then.'

She rose slowly and heavily from her chair, saying, 'Good night, lads.'

'Good night, ma'am. Good night. And thanks again. And that's from all of us.'

She nodded at Andy; then, looking at Joe, she said, 'You and Pimple come upstairs for a minute or two, will you? I want a word with you.'

The kitchen was empty and Bella stood looking at the two men as she said, 'It isn't only the cookin' business that's worryin' me. It's that damn coat. She's taken to wearin' it every minute of the day. It's all since the lads have come into the yard and, of course, up in the house, and when I cornered her yesterday morning in the bedroom and said, "Look, lass, you're not naked underneath,

so why do you . . . ?" That's as far as I got.
It was the word "naked." Her eyes seemed
to pop out and then she stiffened on the
bed and, believe me, lads, she went into one
of those up and downers, you know her
stomach risin' and fallin', as if it were bein'
pumped up and down. And as she was
coming round she looked at me as if she
didn't recognise me, but when she really
came to she said, "Sorry," like she does,
you know; and then she said, "Coat," and
she hugged herself as if she was huggin'
the coat to her. And I said, "All right, then
you must wear it; but there's one thing I
can't understand, lass . . . You don't wear
it in front of Joe and Pimple." Then I saw a
look come on her face as if she was trying
to question something, you know when
you're trying to think something out and the
corners of your eyes crinkle up. She even
bit on her lip as if she was tryin' to fathom
why she didn't wear the coat in front of you
two.'

'Oh, I shouldn't worry,' said Joe, 'not so
much about the coat. The lads wouldn't
mind her wearin' the coat, but it's the business of her acceptin' Willie in the kitchen
here. And, you know, you've got to have him

because, as he says, the bit of money you'll make after you settle up everything will come from the extras on pies and things that he turns out. He says there's money in the bakery lark, but for that he needs an oven and a kitchen.'

'There might be money in it,' said Bella, 'and he's right, but what else can I do about it? There's no way of persuading her. And although John's going to alter the parlour, she can't stay in there all her days.'

'Listen,' said Pimple, 'leave it, will you? I have an idea that might bring her round. But . . .'

'Well, let's have it, then.'

'I can't, it'll just have to be worked out when the opportunity arises. Leave it for now. You might be downstairs and she'll be washing up or something, but just leave it. It might work and it might not. I only know this: half her brain's gone into the past, into a fearful past, I should say, but what's left is quite clear and she understands much more than any of you imagine. Now, just leave it.'

'Well, if you say so, mister,' said Bella, mockingly now, 'we'll do as you ask. Won't we, Joe?'

Joe did not grin, he just said, 'Well, he does get things right at times, you know, Bella.'

'Go on with you. Get along! I've got enough to think about without any more new ideas.'

After they left the room Bella turned and went into her new bathroom. She switched on the electric light, then stood looking around. Eeh! She'd never thought to have a bathroom like this. And, oh, how she would love to get into that bath. Yet, somehow, she was a bit frightened. But fancy having your own bath and being able to lie in it. She had been amazed when Tony tapped into the boiler at the side of the fireplace so they could have hot water in the bath and the basin. Of course it would mean more coal and more stoking up, all that, but she put out a hand and stroked her red acquisition and she said to herself, I'll get in one night when Reenee's in the kitchen, to be on guard, and then I'll do the same for her.

Thinking back to what she had seen through the window of the wash-house, she said to herself, She'll love a real bath; oh, I bet she will. But if only we could make her see that with Willie in the kitchen everything would run smoothly. Well, as smoothly as it can, because this is a big concern I'm taking on and, really, God only knows how it's gonna turn out.

Pimple had made sure that Bella was downstairs with the men sorting out the mattresses and the blankets, and he had taken Joe aside saying, 'Come on upstairs with me for a minute. No, not that way, she'll see us as we go in. Come on round through the gate.'

They came in quietly through the front door, and when they entered the kitchen Pimple knew that Reenee was down at the scullery end of it, washing up. He said quite clearly to Joe, 'There's nobody here. Reenee must be upstairs. So what d'you think we should do about it, Joe?'

Joe didn't for the life of him know what the little fellow was alluding to, but he said, 'I don't know, Pimple. Bella's put all she has into it, you know; she must've spent every penny; and now she's faced with buyin' new glass for that sittin'-room window because they can't get that second-hand. They couldn't get a frame small enough, and they've had to get one made. She's not goin' to like that when she hears about it. And, you know, her fruit and veg stall will stop once the pad opens downstairs. And what she'll make out of the pad business will just get her by and nothin' more; and she certainly won't be able to pay the fellows the bit she's givin' them now.'

'She won't be skinty with the broth either, that's for sure,' said Pimple, 'and although we'll get the vegetables cheap, and as much as she'll be able to take, there's the washing of them and chopping up. And then there's the shoppin' to do, which'll take her out. She's said she's got to try to make a deal with the grocer 'cos she'll want quite a lot of barley and sugar and tea; and, too, there's the butcher along there. He's not much cop, I hear, but who's to question as long as there's a bit of meat floating about in the broth. She just can't do all that herself. Willie must be allowed up here. He's used to a bakery and ordering and how they do things. It would take a load off her mind— and, as he said, there would be a further profit in the pies and oddments he would make. She'll need that if she's goin' to give them a shive of bread with the soup.'

'Well,' said Joe, 'we've been all over this

you know, and she won't disturb the lass. Anyway . . .'

There was a pause now before Pimple said, 'Such a pity, 'cos he's such a quiet, nice lad and, oh, what he'd give to get back to his own job again. I can't understand it. He wouldn't hurt a hair of her head. Look how she puts up with us, she's all right with us.'

'Yes,' said Joe, 'but it took time. Don't forget, it took time. And then there's her coat, and Bella can't get her to go about without that coat. She's tried all ways. Tried to fathom it out. It's as if she feels safe behind it.'

'I don't know about that,' said Pimple. 'She never looks safe. At times there's a look of terror in her eyes. Different words bring it out; I've noticed that, and you have yourself. Anyway, I suppose we'll get through, but not as well as we might. Isn't it funny when she was the one who thought up the idea? Remember the night she drew the lines on the paper? And the beds goin' down, and the lads turnin' up as a group like that? Who would've thought there'd be a bricky and a plumber and a carpenter and a cook? What a pity there weren't another two, such as a bank manager and a solicitor; we might have got somewhere!'

'Aye,' said Joe, on a laugh, 'if they'd had a bobby with them then we all know where we would've got. Oh, let's get down.'

'Look, I'm not goin' down the stairs just yet, I'm going to have a look at the wash-house and see how they've got on. They're geniuses, that lot, you know.'

The room was empty again except for Irene standing tight-pressed against the wall of the scullery. Her mind was in a whirl. In the kitchen all day, he wouldn't hurt a fly. He wouldn't hurt a fly. And Bella wanted him there. So much to do. All those vegetables to wash and clean. Shopping. Washing up. Piles, piles of washing up. Tin plates, tin bowls. Spoons. The words were whirling round in her mind. But my coat. I'd have to wear my coat. Oh, yes, I'd have to wear my coat. If I didn't it would come back again. All that. Oh, no! And she pressed her hand to her brow then took a long, slow, deep breath and said firmly, 'I must wear my coat.'

No one could have been more surprised than Bella, not even the men, the next morning when Reenee appeared downstairs in her coat, but over it was one of Bella's voluminous aprons, or pinnies, as she called them; and although the broad waist gave some covering to the coat, the length of it only touched her knees. And if it hadn't been that Bella knew laughter was the last thing she must give way to, she would have laughed her head off. But apparently Reenee was in a serious mood, for she had come straight to Bella and, pointing to the oven, said with some difficulty, 'Cook.'

'You want to cook, lass?'

Reenee shook her head; then to Bella's further amazement she beckoned her to come downstairs with her; and so, leading the way, she entered the room that was stacked with bedding, towels and piles of tin cutlery, besides other odds and ends.

Seated at the table were the four men, and they all rose to their feet when the young lady, as they referred to Reenee, approached them with the missis following. And, stranger still, they watched her go to Willie. She did not look directly at him, her head was bowed, but she spoke, and what she said was, 'Cook,' and she thumbed towards the ceiling. And when Willie stammered, 'Aye, miss. Aye, miss, I'd love to cook. And . . . and I won't disturb you, I promise.'

She turned swiftly from him now; and after glancing from one to the other of the three men she directed her gaze on John. Then she extended her hands to a measurement of about two feet.

Quick off the mark, John said, 'You want a board, miss, about two feet, eh? What kind of a board?' He closed his fist and started to rub on the top of the board. 'Polished?'

She shook her head vigorously; then, with her hand she made a chopping movement across the end of the table; and he exclaimed, 'For chopping?'

She now turned her lowered gaze towards Willie again, and he said quietly, 'Like a board for chopping vegetables on, ready for the broth and meat and things like that?'

She gave a quick nod, and Bella said, 'Well, I never!' and with the four men she watched the girl go up the stone stairs.

It was Willie who asked quietly, 'What's brought her round, Bella? Oh! I'm sorry . . . ma'am.'

'That's fine with me, Willie; that's me

name. Now don't ask me about the miss, I don't know. And yet I think it's got something to do with Pimple, because he said to me yesterday, "Just leave it. Just leave it." He talked as if he had something up his sleeve. And yet, although when I've been with him and Joe talking about the goings-on here, I've not heard him open his mouth about you or the cooking or anything else. But I'll find out. Oh, I am relieved, and you are too, Willie, aren't you?'

'Relief isn't the word for it, Bella. I'm dying to get my hands into some dough.' He turned to look across at John and said, 'Can you knock her up a big chopping board?'

'I've got the very thing. There's the section of wood out of the sideboard in the parlour, Bella. You'll not want to make use of that, will you? If she uses the unpolished side of that, it'll do fine. The decoration of the parlour can wait another day now that the lass hasn't got to hide herself while I do the sideboard. Dear, dear, poor lass. And, you know, she's got a bonny face, hasn't she?'

'It isn't bonny, John,' said Willie, 'it's beautiful.'

'Well, just as you say; but I can add I think

it's a Goddamn shame she's like she is 'cos somebody's to blame. It's a wonder she hasn't been searched for.'

'Oh, hush now,' Bella put in. 'She likely has, but who would think of looking in this neck of the woods? And, anyway, there would have been plenty of time to find her before she reached this part, I bet. But I say to you all, every one of you, don't probe and don't talk about her outside . . . I mean in a pub, anywhere like that. She's happy here, she feels safe. Aye, that's the thing, she feels safe, because whatever's happened to her she's afraid of the world outside, and them in it. And now let's get to work and no more chit-chat.' On this, she turned abruptly and went upstairs.

7

It was three weeks later and, as Joe said, the business was indeed going like a house on fire. They'd had to turn some customers away. The gates were opened at seven in the evening and closed on the last sleeper at half past nine in the morning. Each of the four men had his allotted task. Joe and Pimple continued to bring the vegetables from the market first thing in the morning and sometimes a box of fruit, but Joe kept on his part-time work at the warehouse for, as he said, there were pickings there from time to time that might be of help to Bella and the business.

With Pimple it was slightly different: the offerings he received from his tin-whistle playing in the local streets were meagre, but they were supplemented occasionally through his keen sense of spotting trouble here and there. His perspicacity in this line had earned him five pounds from the local police station in the last two weeks. He had heard muffled voices coming up through a pavement grid outside an empty building. What was more interesting to him was that the building was next to a bank. The street was practically deserted, so he stood for a moment, his ears strained; but he could not make out anything that was being said. And so he made it his business to take his whistle to a street not far away, from where he had been moved on more than once by its regular policeman, and sure enough, this happened again. He gave the constable some backchat and in the backchat was a message. This incident had happened a week or so ago.

When he had told Bella she had said, 'Oh, lad, that's no game to play, it's dangerous. I've told you before, they'll get you one of these days, and then God help you. You've done one stretch and you didn't like that, did you?'

'No, Bella,' he said. 'As I've told you, that's why I went over to the police's side; but as the rumour has it on the street, I'm the fellow who can't stand cops. It's a great help.' He had grinned at her, and Joe, who was there at the time, had said, 'I'll give you this, Pimple, you've got more guts than me.'

The other four men, the band, as Joe called them, saw to the admission of the men and the distribution of the food. They had formed a rota of duties that seemed to work well. There was no admission to drunks or wineys, those who stank of meths. Both Joe and Pimple helped the men out on such occasions because they knew more about the street types round the market than any of the four men.

It got that a queue would begin to form down the lane to the yard gates an hour before opening time, and on very wet or cold nights Bella would allow them to be let in earlier, even to have them put an extra mattress or two down the middle of the room rather than turn the shivering creatures away. There were written notices inside the doors in the lavatory, the urinal and the washplace to the effect that anyone known to have messed up these places unnecessarily would not be admitted again. Also, there was no fear of wet beds because the

plastic covers had been left on the mattresses.

Naturally the unfortunate men slept in
their clothes, but were they to take off their
boots and their top coat they rolled them
up and laid them alongside them in the bed,
experience at this level of life having proved
that they couldn't trust any of their fellow
men. But if a man's coat was sodden wet
he would ask if it could be laid over the large
iron fire-guard in the kitchen, and whoever
was on duty saw to it that it was still there
when its owner woke up.

The ample slice of new bread cut from a
fresh loaf and supplied with a bowl of broth
at night and the mug of tea in the morning,
was so appreciated that, as John said, it
was pitiful to see their pleasure, but nevertheless dreadful to see a man foretelling
what he expected the rest of the day to be
like when he broke the morning slice in two
and deposited half in his pocket.

Big Bella's Pad soon made a name for
itself, and when Bella was visited unexpectedly one day by an inspector all he said,
with a grin as he left, was, 'Why don't you
put sunshades up in the yard, Bella, and
make it into a holiday home?'

Bella had never been happier. There was her lass . . . her lass sitting at that kitchen table day after day chopping away at vegetables; then later, after scouring her hands, she might fill the pie tins with their rounds of pastry ready for the meat. This delighted Willie, and time and again he would whistle as they worked together . . . together but at a distance. She never stood close to him.

One day as he whistled he glanced at her face. It looked bright. She had stopped what she was doing and seemed to be looking into space, which she was, into a space where there was music and something else . . . For a moment she seemed to experience the most wonderful feeling, and then it was gone when Willie spoke, saying, 'Do you know that? It's a piece from *La Traviata?'*

As she turned to him, the sound of the music was still in her head; she was looking straight at him and her eyes were bright as she nodded twice. But when he said, 'Do you like operas?' a puzzled look came over her expression and she shook her head.

'You likely would if you heard them. I'll tell you what, some night before we open we'll get together, the four of us—no, the five of us because Pimple can make his tin whistle speak. Anyway, we'll play you some tunes. What about that, eh?'

She looked down, but the corners of her mouth were moving slightly upwards and he could see that she was pleased. A few minutes later, when Bella returned from her shopping and her ordering for the day and came into the kitchen, saying, 'It's freezing out there. You know when you're well off in here,' Willie turned a bright face to her, saying, 'Miss here recognised a piece I was whistling. It was from *La Traviata,* the opera, you know.'

'Aye?' said Bella cautiously, then added, 'Well, what about it?'

'Well, I've just said to her, one night before we open we'll get together the band and Pimple and we'll give her some tunes.' Here he paused, then looked at the straight face of the little woman and said, 'Of course, if that's all right with you, Bella.'

'Oh, it's all right with me, yes, definitely. There's nothing I like better than a bit of music.'

'Oh, we can play well together when we're given the chance. I know John's fiddle sounds a bit ropey but, as he said the other night, he'll soon be able to buy himself some new strings. The ones he has on are past tightening.'

There was a glint of laughter in Bella's eyes now but her lips looked prim as she said, 'I don't suppose you'd take on the job of playing our visitors to sleep?'

'Oh, now that's not a bad idea, missis. We could add another twopence to the bill.'

At this Bella said firmly, 'If I hear of a new idea in any shape or form coming from you lot, there'll be some sackin' to do. That I promise you.' Her attention was quickly drawn to Reenee who was bending over her table as she scraped a carrot on the grater. Bella could have sworn that she had heard a gurgle from her, so she said, 'Would you like to hear that band play their pieces, lass?'

Reenee looked up, and Bella saw the tentative smile showing around her mouth, and when her head made one small movement of agreement Bella said, 'Oh, well, then, that's that.' Turning to Willie she said, 'We'll be havin' our tea around five. Tell the men to come in and do their stuff. But inform them they're not goin' to make a practice of it. If they want to practise they can do it in the wash-house.'

Willie laughed now, saying, 'They do, Bella, on the quiet, stuffin' a mattress in the bottom of the door to dull the sound. But I tell you something, you wouldn't believe the good stuff that comes out of Tony's flute and Pimple's whistle. You wouldn't believe the tunes Pimple knows; and the two together, just them two, by, it sounds good!'

That very evening Bella had to admit to herself that, aye, it did sound good. She had brought the two armchairs to the end of the table where she and Reenee could sit comfortably and listen. The door to the stone flight was pushed well back and Joe was standing there. He could see where the men had assembled near the bottom of the stairs and when they started to play Bella's head went to the side. It wasn't like the stuff they rendered in the street, this was different. It was nice. She turned and smiled at Reenee, and Reenee nodded back at her. They played first a number of the well-known tunes of the time; one or two they had used on the road, such as 'All Alone on the Telephone', but now it was with a difference. It was all softer, clearer. Bella tried to find the word 'harmonious', but couldn't. She only knew that it was all very nice indeed and that she was enjoying it.

They had been playing for about fifteen minutes when they stopped, and then there came the combined sound of the flute and the tin whistle, and when the silvery notes of 'The Barcarolle' floated up the staircase Bella thought, Eeh, my! Fancy the two of them being able to play like that together.

Reenee had been sitting back in her chair, but now she brought herself upright and there came into her head the most odd feeling. She was floating. And as she floated to the music she heard a voice singing. She knew she was thinking like this because the voice . . . oh, she knew the voice and she knew the words it was singing: 'Night of stars and night of love falls gently o'er the waters.' Her body stretched upwards, her mind was clear. There was no obstruction there, nothing, no fear, nothing but a great emptiness and in it the voice singing:

'Falls gently o'er the waters.
Heaven around, below, above,
No more will reach the shore.'

And then it was rising. The voice was soaring: 'Night of stars and night of love,' on and on . . . and then she was standing up: her arms outstretched, her eyes wide, she was trying to walk past Bella, when Bella, pulling herself out of the chair, said, 'What is it, lass? What's the matter? Sit down.' And looking towards Joe, she said, 'It's the music, tell them to stop.'

Immediately on Bella's command Reenee's arm shot out towards Joe, and she flapped her hand at him, which meant he hadn't to tell them to stop, so he turned his puzzled gaze back to Bella, and she said, 'All right, let them go on. But sit down, lass, sit down.'

She found she had to force Reenee's stiff body back into the chair, and it wasn't until the music stopped that the stiffness went and her whole body became limp. Now Bella did say, and firmly, to Joe, 'Tell them that's enough.'

Again Bella was surprised to see Reenee's hand go out to stop Joe. Then she was sitting up and, turning towards the mantelpiece and pointing. Bella said, 'Pencil?' but without waiting for an answer she went past Joe and took the pencil and loose-leafed pad and, handing them to Reenee, she watched her slowly tear out a page and just as slowly, even laboriously, write the word 'beautiful' on it. With an effort she handed it to Joe who, looking at it, said, 'You want me to give it to the lads?'

Again there was the slight inclination of the head and he, after turning and looking at Bella and showing her the piece of paper, went down the stone steps, to be greeted with, 'Did they enjoy it?' from Tony and Pimple.

'Yes, she said to say it was beautiful; but something happened to her when you played that last piece. I swear to God she was singing. Her mouth was opening and shutting and her tongue was moving, you know, as you do when you sing. Not so much when you talk but when you sing. And I'm sure,' he looked at Pimple, 'I'm sure, Pimple, she was back wherever she came from for those few minutes and there was music there. I tell you, lads, it made me feel awful to see her.'

'What's she like now?'

'Oh, I think she's back to what she was before. Whatever it was, it was like a flash in the pan, but she must have recognised where she had once been. It was eerie. She was going to come downstairs.'

'Come down?' said Willie.

'Yes; she had her arms outstretched as if she were walking to someone and singing. It's shaken Bella. Anyway, I know nowt about music, but I can say you all played lovely. Thanks, lads.'

It was two days before Christmas Eve. The kitchen was warm, as usual, and today it had a special aroma. This was from a large basin of mixed sweet mincemeat, all ready to fill pies, for which Willie's slab of pastry had already been turned and rolled and turned and rolled.

Dressed for outdoors in a brown felt hat and a grey coat, and with a large woollen muffler round her neck, the ends of which were tucked under the lapels of her coat, Bella came in, and after taking a basket from the bottom of the cupboard she turned and looked towards the vegetable board, saying, 'Where's the miss, Willie?'

'Haven't seen her this morning, Bella.'

'You haven't seen her? When I went upstairs to get changed she was just finishing washing our breakfast things. Then she usually goes upstairs and tidies her room before coming down and starting on the veg. Well, you know she does.'

'She didn't this morning, Bella.'

Bella stared at Willie for a minute. Then dropping the basket on to a chair, she hurried out and up the stairs. She did not tap on Reenee's door but went in.

The room was empty; but she noticed the wardrobe door was half open, and when she looked inside she exclaimed, 'Oh, my God! No! No!' Her coat had gone; but she still nearly always wore that downstairs, except sometimes she would take it off in the evening when she was sitting sewing something; but the hat, that weird hat had gone, too. 'Not again, Reenee,' she said aloud; 'not again. Oh, lass, don't, please! Not at this time of the year.'

She almost ran back down the stairs and called to Willie, 'She's gone!'

Willie stopped his cutting, his hands flat on the board. 'What d'you mean she's gone? You mean the miss has gone?'

'Who the hell am I talkin' about, Willie? Yes! She's gone.'

'Well,' he swallowed deeply, 'she went off before, but she came back, didn't she?'

'Yes, she might have; but I'm gonna tell you something; she's never been the same since she heard Tony and Pimple playin' that piece. It did something to her. It must have penetrated to something from her past. At times she'd sit, her eyes crinkled at the corners as if she was thinking, thinking hard. I tell you, she's never been the same since.'

'We meant it for the best. I'm sorry.'

'Oh, lad, of course you did, and it was lovely, really lovely. And she loved it and all. Look what she wrote on that piece of paper . . . "beautiful." But it took her back somewhere, I know that. Twice she's come down without her coat on and then, as if remembering, she's gone back for it.'

Bella sat down on a chair. 'I'll go mad if anything happens to her, lad. I really will.'

'Oh, nothing'll happen to her. You know, we've talked about it when we're down there together, the lads and I, and she's got a very sensible side. We all agreed on that, and she takes everything in. It's only part of her that's got funny and, as Pimple said, that part of her is dominated by fear. Look how she won't move out among people. She's never been out of the doors, he says, for months on end. And I think we all agree,

248 THE SILENT LADY

she'll never come fully to herself until she
faces up to that fear.'

'And that's what she can't do,' said Bella,
'else she wouldn't be here if she could face
up to it, would she? And I can tell you, and
I shouldn't say this, but I dread the day she
does face up to it, 'cos then I'll lose her. She
wouldn't stay in this life two minutes if she
was all right, now, would she?'

After a moment of consideration Willie
said, 'No, you're right, missis. The likes of
us, the lads an' that, well, we're different.
Most of us have had to rough it all our lives,
but she must have been brought up different. She's known a different way of living.'

'Oh, be quiet, lad. What am I goin' to do?'

'I would just sit still or, better still, go out
and do your orderin' and your shoppin'.'

'I can't do that, I just can't. If only . . . if
only Pimple or Joe were here, they'd know
what to do.'

'No, they wouldn't, missis; no more than
you. It's my opinion that she's gone out. She
knew where she was heading for and why
she was goin'. There's part of her mind that
is as sane as your own. Perhaps it's only a
small part, but it's there. Anyway, she's likely
gone shopping.'

'Shopping! What would she go shopping for?'

'Aye, I agree. But then she wouldn't have any money, would she? Joe says she won't take money.'

'Oh, she's got money. She's got a bit of money of her own.'

'She has?'

'Yes, she has.'

'Well, then, she's likely gone shopping.'

'Look at the weather! It's sleeting, and it'll freeze her out there.'

'Well, she has that big coat on, missis, and it looks like a blanket because it's fleecy lined.' Then, more to himself, he muttered, 'It's a wonder that she hasn't been spotted before now in that rig-out.'

At that very moment Irene was being spotted in the rig-out by someone who had seen her before. She had entered the pawn shop, and there stood the younger of the two pawnbrokers. He was attending a customer, saying 'Half a dollar, I'm sorry; no more, just half a dollar,' and the customer said, 'Well, better than nothing.'

Irene stood aside and watched the man behind the counter write out a ticket, then hand over half a crown to the waiting woman, who had a woollen scarf round her head and who was definitely wearing two coats of different colours, for the upper one dropped just as far as her knees.

Mr Joseph Gomparts's smile was wide as he greeted Irene. 'How pleased I am to see you, madam. Have you come to retrieve your jewellery?'

She shook her head, and at this he said, 'No?' and again she shook her head. Then she pointed towards the shop window, and he said, 'Something in there?' She nodded; then, putting her hands together, she imitated the handling of a flute or whistle and he said, 'Oh, a musical instrument?' Again she inclined her head.

'Oh, yes,' his head was bobbing now, 'I remember there was a flute three. Yes, there was and . . .' He thought a moment, then looked along the shelves and across the shop to where there were more shelves, and he said, quite suddenly, 'He never came back for it. Can you wait? My father's in bed with a cold but he'll know whether or not he has sold that.'

It seemed no time before he was back again, almost hopping to his place behind the counter and saying, 'It wasn't sold. It's in the store-cupboard with the rest. We get a lot of musical instruments, you know. I must look it up in the book. Just a moment.' He turned to where a thick-backed ledger lay towards the end of the counter, and thumbing through it, with his finger tracing each entry, stopped suddenly and said, 'Ah, eighteen months ago, seven and sixpence. Just a moment.' Again he was gone from her; and it was slightly longer before he re-appeared. In his hand was a flute. He handed it to her.

It looked as if it were made from ivory. After stroking it she looked at the tag hanging from it which said, ten shillings; and again her eyes met his, and he, putting his head on one side, laughed and said, 'It is our little bit of profit, but in this case, madam,' his voice dropped, 'we will say seven and six. Will that suit you?'

His last words were almost whispered, but she nodded. Then, opening her mouth and making an effort, she said, 'Thank you.'

'You are very welcome, madam. Very welcome. Any time . . . any time. I will wrap it up for you. Is it going to be a present for someone?'

She nodded.

'Well,' he said, 'seeing as it's Christmas, I have a piece of Christmas paper here which,' he added, with a grin, 'we don't usually go in for. I will make it into a little parcel.'

This he did, and sealed it with a bit of wax before handing it to her, saying, 'I am sure the recipient will be delighted with it.'

She paused; then slowly lifting her hand, she extended it to him and he, as slowly taking it, pressed it gently. No word was spoken but they looked at each other; then she turned and left the shop, and as he looked after her he experienced a feeling that was new to him, but he had no words in his fertile mind to express it.

The sleet had turned to snow. It was falling in large flakes and clung to vehicles and passers-by, leaving them white-coated. Only the roads looked dark and muddy.

She had been walking for fifteen minutes before she came to the first real shopping centre. She knew she had been this way before and, instinctively, she also knew what she was looking for. Eventually she stopped outside a window, which showed winter woollies of all kinds, from pom-pom hats to large fringed scarves, woollen jumpers and even a complete knitted suit on a model. She did not linger to examine the different pieces displayed but went straight into the shop. However, once inside, she stood for a moment while her snow-covered head and shoulders dripped moisture down her coat. Then, blinking rapidly in the bright light, she approached a curved counter, at one end of which was a long rack with a notice which read, 'Half price. Making way for new stock'.

Very few customers were in the shop, and none at this counter; and the girl behind it stood looking at the figure before her. She did not see the woman's long coat and hat as odd, because they were both bespattered with snow that was still to melt, but she greeted her with a smile and said, 'Yes, madam, can I help you?'

When the customer indicated by putting her hand around her neck that she wanted a scarf, the assistant thought, Poor soul, she's deaf, but immediately she turned to a rack and brought down two scarves.

Irene could see that they were long and made of thick wool, and that they were priced at fifteen shillings each. Her mind was endeavouring to work fast: she must have four scarves; and then she must have enough money left for Bella's present, and something for Joe. She shook her head and indicated by measuring the scarf that half the length would do.

The snow from the woman's headgear had melted fast, as had that from her shoulders, and the assistant could see now that the coat she was wearing, although it appeared bulky and might be warm, also looked rather dirty.

Irene's eyes had strayed to a rack on which she saw a number of scarves hanging and the assistant, noticing this, said, 'Yes, madam. They have been reduced by more than half but some have fringes only on one end.' Then she added with a smile, 'Manufacturers' mistakes, you know.'

Irene nodded and, going to the rack, she lifted down one scarf which was about two and a half feet long and six to nine inches wide and, yes, it had fringing on one end only. There was a tag on this particular scarf, which she looked at. Noticing this, the assistant came round the counter and said, 'It is less than half price, being, as I said, a kind of mistake. They are very good value at five shillings.'

Irene laid the scarf on the counter next to the expensive one. It was only two-thirds as long and not so wide, but it was of the same quality and she nodded quickly and pointed to it, then to the other three that were on the rack.

'You'll take them all, madam, the other three too?' the assistant said. 'They're really a bargain. I'll wrap them for you.'

Irene's hand was touching what looked like a silk blouse and the girl said, 'Oh, miss, that wouldn't fit you. It's a pity, because it's a lovely material, but it comes out time and again at sale time. You see, it was made up in the sewing room here, but the customer never turned up again. There are people like that, you know, madam,' and straight away the thought flashed into her mind that she was treating this person as she would a lady. Yet there was something about her; she didn't know what. Anyway, if she could make another sale, that was all to the good, because it had been a very dull morning—people weren't out shopping on a morning like this. She unhooked the blouse from the rack and laid it on the counter. It was an odd shape for a blouse, and this she pointed out, remarking that the person who had ordered it in the first place must have been very broad and with a very short waist. But then she lifted it up and ran her fingers through one of the sleeves, saying, 'It's real silk, it's beautiful, isn't it?'

Irene stared down at the odd-shaped multi-coloured blouse, and already she could see Bella in it. Something told her it would need altering here and there, but it was indeed a beautiful material. She looked at the tag. It was marked ten shillings and sixpence and as she stared at it the assistant said, 'Believe it or not, madam, it was priced at seven pounds before it was put on the rack, and it has been reduced three or four times since. It's a gift to anybody who's good with their needle.'

At this Irene nodded affirmatively, then pressed it towards the scarves before turning again to the rack. There, fingering a woollen garment, she looked at the assistant for guidance. The girl said, 'That is really a waistcoat, madam. As you see, it's sleeveless and it's large; but it isn't wool, it's what you would call a composition. It would be very nice for a gentleman. You see it has two short leather belts on each side, which would clip in the middle.' She demonstrated how this could be done. 'These were very fashionable with men at one time, though generally in suede or leather.' And now she smiled as she said, 'It isn't everyone who can afford suede or leather, but this would make a nice Christmas present for a . . .' she hesitated '. . . for a gentleman. That is, if he had a large frame. Do you know some-one it might fit?'

At this Irene nodded vigorously: she was thinking of Joe.

The assistant said, 'Well, now, let's reckon this all up. One pound eighteen shil-lings,' she said finally. 'Is that what you make it, madam?'

Irene did not nod but, putting her hand inside her coat, she withdrew from the pocket two pound notes.

As the assistant was pushing the change and receipt across the counter towards Irene, she bent forward and exclaimed, 'You haven't a bag with you, madam? Oh, well, I can supply you with one, and I'll do so with pleasure.' She was somewhat surprised when the customer put out her hand and touched her gently on the sleeve, then pointed to some fancy wrappings on the counter, at the same time emitting one word, 'Please.'

The word had a slightly husky sound, but the assistant, after staring at this strange lady, who had an unusual, beautiful yet col-ourless face, said, 'You would like them wrapped?'

At this Irene bent her head and her lips gave a slight quirk of a smile, which brought an answering smile from the girl, as she said, 'It'll be a pleasure, madam.' And so she rolled up each in a fancy Christmas bag and closed it with a Father Christmas adhe-sive sticker. Then, from under the counter, she drew a pretty figured paper bag large enough to take all Irene's purchases, and when at last the girl handed them to her, Irene was still smiling.

When the customer's hand came out and her fingers touched her sleeve, the girl was surprised, but more so when Irene, seeming to gasp for breath, said, 'Thank—you.'

'It's been my pleasure, madam. And a happy Christmas to you.'

At this Irene's head bobbed two or three times before she turned and walked from the shop. The girl, looking at her back and seeing the long, stained coat, was wondering who on earth her customer was or had been. Yes, those were the words, had been, for although the woman could hardly get out her words, the tone of them wasn't common. And the face . . . she had never seen a face like it, and she had, over the years in the shop, looked at hundreds. But that one, that face had the most lost look she could ever imagine. What a strange incident! They won't believe it at home when I try to tell them, she said to herself.

Pimple gasped when, through the falling snow, he saw a figure he knew immediately to be Reenee's. She was more than ten minutes' walk from home. No, he wasn't seeing things, he hadn't made a mistake in identifying her; how could he with that coat? He hurried towards her, and was soon by her side, matching his steps to hers. 'You been out shopping?' he asked.

She turned her head quickly, and on a sharp gasp her lips formed his name, but they made no sound.

'You do pick your days, don't you, to take a stroll? Oh, look out!' he said, as he took her arm and, quite roughly, pushed her further on to the pavement when a lorry, its wheels in the gutter, splashed the muddied snow into the air. 'Look,' he said now, 'let me carry that bag.'

But she shook her head vigorously and held the bag quite tightly in front of her.

'All right, all right,' he laughed, 'I'm not goin' to pinch it, miss,' which, he noticed, caused her lips to move upwards into a smile, but he couldn't see her eyes for her body was leaning forward against the falling snow.

Presently, he said merrily, 'There's a saying, you know, Reenee, does your mother know you're out? I bet Bella doesn't know you're out, does she?'

Irene did not turn to look at him, but she shook her head.

'Well, look out for squalls, for there'll be hell to pay. She'll go mad, you know, wondering where you might be. She's very fond of you, but I suppose you know that. I've never known anybody so fond as she is of you. Look,' he took hold of her arm, 'let's take a short-cut else we'll be covered with mud before we get in.'

He led her up some side-streets, and then there they were in The Jingles. There was Ginnie's and the outdoor beer shop and the butcher's and the cobbler's, and then, as Pimple put it, they were at their own front door.

He rapped smartly on it, and when it was opened by Willie, he said, 'You take your time, don't you? Footmen are supposed to be already behind the door waiting for a knock. I'll talk to you later, sir.'

'You idiot,' said Willie, under his breath; 'she's nearly up the pole. Oh, miss,' and he went to help her off with her coat. She pushed him away, yet her lips were curved upwards.

In the kitchen Bella stood quite dumbfounded, so much so she couldn't speak. Not even when Irene lifted up the pretty coloured bag and brought out the word, 'Shopping,' did she utter a word; but she sat down slowly on a chair and, leaning her elbow on a table, she laid her face on the palm of her hand. She did not look at the pretty bag or at Reenee, but she turned and gazed at the two men now standing looking at her, and she said, 'It'll happen one of these days. It will. I'll have heart failure and you'll find me on the floor. Nobody seems to care what happens to me, what they do or what they don't do.'

'Oh, Bella,' said Willie now. 'And all our dear friend here has done,' he put his hand out towards Reenee, 'has been to go out shopping. Bet your life that bag's full of goodies.' And now he turned to Reenee and said, 'I hope you bought something for me.'

She actually smiled at him before turning away, walking out of the kitchen and up the stairs.

Bella asked them both, 'What d'you make of her? What can you make of her?'

And it was Pimple who answered, 'Only that she's full of love. She wants to give and there's a barrier stopping her in some way. But she overcomes it enough to go out on a morning like this to buy us Christmas boxes of some kind. That must be what was in the bag. It was just by chance I spotted her: she was walking along as if she was used to bein' out every day in Brandley Street.'

'That's away down near Holborn.'

'Yes; and that's where she's been, I imagine. And I bet you a shilling we won't know till Christmas Day what's in that bag. If I could dare to give you a little more of my wisdom, Bella, I would say to you, act as if nothing had happened. Don't go for her in any way, please.'

Bella looked at the face peering at her. Except for the cheekbones and the sockets round the eyes it had the scars of smallpox on it. But behind that marred face she now knew lay a keen brain, a wise brain, and below, the kindest heart of any man she had ever known, and she wasn't forgetting Joe as she said it to herself . . .

Christmas Eve came. The snow was lying. All but four of their patrons had told her that they had been given a ticket to this or that place for dinner, tea and entertainment on Christmas Day: some in church halls, others were going to a room taken by a number of thoughtful people to provide both the work-less and the down-and-outs with at least two hot meals that day and the next.

When Bella learnt of the plight of the four, she told Joe to tell them that they were wel-come to stay for their Christmas dinner downstairs. The four men from the wash-house had already been invited upstairs to have dinner in the parlour. The kitchen table had been carried in there and would seat eight, although four might have to sit on a bench. Moreover, the parlour had been decorated with pieces of holly, and paper chains stretching along the mantelshelf.

Pimple did not go out at all on Christmas Eve but helped Willie with the cooking and the preparations for the following day: besides a large Christmas pudding there was a still larger Christmas cake, to be decorated with pink icing and holly leaves.

It was while Bella was out doing the last remnants of her shopping that Reenee went upstairs; then returned and, placing a pound note on the baking table, she looked from Pimple to Willie, then back to Pimple again and, putting up three fingers, slowly mouthed the word 'wine'.

'Wine?' said Willie. 'You want to buy some wine?'

She nodded, but kept her gaze still on Pimple, and extending two fingers, she pointed to the parlour. Then, with only her index finger held up, she pointed towards the stairs and the room below.

It was Pimple who, after a moment, said, 'You want three bottles of wine, two for upstairs, us, and one for those fellas who are staying for their Christmas dinner?'

She nodded two or three times, and the

corners of her mouth moved upwards. He smiled widely back at her and said, 'Have you anything in mind, madam, as to what kind of wine you would like?'

She shook her head, then looked at Willie, and he said slowly, 'A dry one for . . .' he pointed towards the stairs '. . . and us, one bottle of red wine, and for the ladies one bottle of Muscat.'

'How d'you know about wines, Willie?' said Pimple.

'Because, sonny boy,' said Willie playfully, 'at one time I was a waiter too, and in a good-style restaurant. It didn't last long, just a year, but nevertheless I learnt a lot. But you won't get any of the wines along the street at the outdoor beer shop.'

'No, I know that,' said Pimple; 'but not five minutes away is a very good wine shop. I sniff it every time I pass it.'

They now looked at Reenee who was tapping the pound note as she tried to get out the word 'enough?' and they both said together, 'Oh, aye, enough. Plenty . . . plenty. And it's very kind of you,' said Willie; 'very kind of you indeed, miss.'

Pimple said nothing, but he took up the pound note, folded it and put it inside his breast pocket; then, looking at Reenee, he said softly, 'I'll see that everything goes just as you plan it. Like you planned downstairs.'

He now turned to Willie. 'You know that, don't you? It was she who planned all that outfit that you and the other three are running now. Yes, it was she who planned it on a piece of paper.'

Reenee had turned from them to go to the vegetable board. Here, she sat down and started to work at her daily chores. But there was a light on her face that neither of the men had seen there before.

Christmas Day: they had all been up since very early, and breakfast was over. Now, while Tony and Andy were seeing to the clearing up of the big room and the toilets, helped now by the four men that were staying on, Willie was at his baking table being helped by Pimple, and on one corner of it Reenee, still wearing the big coat, the sleeves turned well back, was at her board; but today she was not chopping the vegetables, she was just preparing them for boiling and braising to accompany the turkey that Bella had brought in yesterday with her shopping.

It was around lunch-time that she told the band, as she called the four men, and Pimple and Joe to get themselves cleaned up and that she would see them in the parlour in half an hour's time.

At this order, Reenee rose from her board and went upstairs. Then Bella herself went into the parlour, telling herself she was as clean and tidy as ever she would be, and there she sat looking quietly at the fire. She had never in her life known a Christmas like this, never. She was happy in a way she had never imagined possible. It was, she said smilingly to herself, like being in love for the first time. She had never been in love, never, not with a man. Yet she was now surrounded by men who all seemed to give off, and to her, a certain amount of love. You could call it respect, but then, above them all she had the gift of what she thought of now as a daughter, because that was what Reenee had become to her, a beloved daughter. She couldn't imagine life without her, and she didn't mind in the least if the girl never put her nose outside the door again in her lifetime because she felt that, one day, if she was seen out and about, someone would come and take her away.

Someone was bound to recognise her: once seen that face could not be forgotten.

The men came in one by one: first Joe and Pimple; then Andy and Tony and John and Willie. Just as they were seated the door opened and there appeared before them a lady, because not one of those men doubted but that they were looking at a lady, a real lady. Reenee was wearing her red velvet dress. To the waist it was unmarked, and not one of those men looked further to where the bottom of the skirt was badly stained. But what they noticed most was her beautiful hair. It was no longer screwed into a tight bun lying on her neck, but was laid in two loose coils on the back of her head up to the crown.

She seemed unaffected by the silence and their staring until Willie, springing forward, placed a seat for her and she sat down. That seemed to loosen their tongues and they said, one after the other, 'Happy Christmas, miss. Happy Christmas.'

She nodded to each of them; and then she looked at Bella, who now said, 'I suppose I'd better start the ball rolling. Now, I haven't bought any of you handkerchiefs or socks or suchlike, but there you are: there's five shillings each for you. You may do what you like with it except get drunk, because if you do you won't be admitted into this pad.'

At this there was general laughter, while each man, as he took the two half-crowns from her hand, offered her his thanks most sincerely.

Then it was Andy who said, 'Now it's our turn. Our presents might be very small, ma'am, but they come with our combined feelings for you,' and he handed her two boxes.

When she opened the first one she saw underneath the top glazed cover a tablet of soap, a bottle of scent, a jar of face cream, and a tin of talcum, and next to it, of all things, a little bottle of red nail varnish. At the sight of this she let out a laugh and said, 'Well, thank you, boys, very, very much and for not forgettin' me nails.'

There was general laughter now, and it was Tony who said, 'We couldn't find one without nail varnish, Bella, but there's always a first time for everything.'

'You've said it, lad; but it'll be on me toe nails I'll use it.'

Then she opened the second box and out

of it she picked up a soft woollen shoulder shawl which, they could see, pleased her greatly; but what she said was, 'Why had you to go and spend your money on a thing like this for me? You need every penny I give you.'

'Simply,' put in John now, 'we wouldn't have any money to buy anything, my dear Bella, if it wasn't for you and your kindness.'

'Nonsense! But, oh, lads, thank you very much indeed.' And she looked now from Joe to Pimple and said, 'I suppose you were in on this, an' all?'

'Oh, yes,' said Pimple; 'they made us do it. We didn't want to, but they made us do it.' There was more laughter now.

Then Willie handed two boxes to Reenee, and she put her hand on her breast as if to say, 'For me?' She put the bag she was carrying on to the floor and opened the first box. It was very similar to the one Bella had received, and she smiled at them, then tapped the nail varnish while her lips moved upwards and her mouth opened wide as she brought out one word that sent them all into peals of laughter, for the word was 'vegetables'.

And Willie said, 'Yes, I'll demand that you

paint your nails before you do any more vegetables, miss.'

Now she opened the second box. In it was a bottle of perfume and half a dozen white lawn handkerchiefs, arranged uniformly round the scent, to show the initial R. She stared down at the box, and her head drooped further. Then she gulped and brought out the words 'Thank you', before bending down quickly to the floor and picking up the bag that she had brought in with her. Now she handed the first parcel to Bella, the second small parcel to Pimple, and the third parcel to Joe. Then, one after the other, she gave each of the other four men similar size parcels. Nobody had attempted to open his own, and she looked at them, then spread out her hands.

It was Tony who said, 'Go on, Bella. You open yours first.'

Bella took out a garment and held it up, and immediately saw the odd shape of it. It was meant, she supposed, to be a blouse, and it was made of silk; it was so wide that she could see her own quite firm and large-breasted body being lost in it. She looked towards Reenee who now, with another great effort, uttered the words, 'Me. Alter.'

'Oh, yes; yes,' said Bella, 'that'll be the easiest thing in the world. But it's beautiful. Lovely material. What on earth made you buy that? It must have cost the earth, woman.'

Reenee shook her head.

'Well, thank you, love. It was so thoughtful of you. I can't get over it, I've never had a silk blouse in my life.' She turned to Joe and said, 'Well, come on, let's see what more money she spent on you.'

Joe undid the Christmas wrapping and held up what looked like a woollen waist-coat, and he exclaimed in true astonish-ment, 'My, lass! Where on earth did you get this? It's fine.' And immediately he pulled off his coat and put the garment on; and although he had to pull in his stomach quite a bit to link the two leather straps together he managed it, then said, 'It's lovely. And it's warm, and it reaches to the bottom of my back, which is where I want it. Oh, miss, thank you. Thank you.' Now they all looked at Pimple. Pimple's present looked thin and long compared with Bella's and Joe's, and after he had unwrapped it he slowly placed it across the palm of his hand and stared at it. They all stared at it;

and it was Tony who gasped as he said, 'Good Lord! It's a flute. And what a flute! Oh, look at it!'

Pimple looked at it; then he threw the Christmas paper to one side and brought the instrument to his lips. But that's all he did with it: he did not blow on it, but he stroked it. Then it was Tony speaking again: 'That's real ivory, man,' he said. 'Do you know that's real ivory? God in heaven! Where,' he turned now to Reenee, 'did you get that, miss? You . . . you could never have bought it. That must have cost a packet, and I know what flutes cost. I've never seen a better one than that.'

'Don't be so mouthy.' It was Bella speaking to Tony now. 'She wouldn't go out and steal it.'

'Oh, Bella, I wasn't meaning anything like that, but that kind of flute is rare. It's ivory!'

Reenee looked at Bella; then she moved the index finger and thumb of her right hand around two fingers of her left as if turning a ring, and Bella said, 'Oh. Oh yes, I understand lass. Gomparts.' Reenee nodded, and Bella, turning to Tony, said, 'The pawn shop. She got it in the pawn shop where she pawned her rings.'

Pimple hadn't spoken, but now he almost darted across the room, and startled Reenee as he dropped on his knees before her. Taking her hand, he kissed the back of it, saying, 'I'll keep it till the day I die, Reenee.'

And now she surprised them all: she actually lifted her other hand and stroked his disfigured face, saying with a gasp as she did so, 'Your name?'

'My name?' His voice was a whisper now. 'You want to know my name, Reenee?'

She inclined her head deeply towards him. He glanced around the company, then looking back at her, he said, 'Carl.'

At this she repeated, 'Carl', and again, 'Carl.' Then, pointing to his face, she said, quite plainly, 'No more. Never. No more.'

'You mean you will never call me by my face now, but by my name?' And at this she nodded again.

He uttered no word, but his head fell on to his chest and he remained still for quite a while. No one spoke until Andy, taking in the situation, said loudly, 'If somebody would like to know what I've got I'll open my parcel now.'

At this there was a murmur of forced

On and on the compliments went until Carl, who had turned from the window some minutes earlier, said quietly, 'Nothing could make you more beautiful than you already are, but it suits you and I hope, for all of us, we'll see you in it often.'

Reenee looked across the room at Carl and she smiled at him—actually smiled, for the length of her lips had moved up much further than ever before.

Now Bella broke the tension again with her practical common sense. 'The next item on the programme, ladies and gentlemen, is eating, and we ladies will sit here and be waited upon, so you can all get busy and scramble around.'

They all trooped out to the kitchen, laughing, to bring in the food, and there was only Bella and Reenee in the room. Reenee had sat down in the chair again, still in the housecoat, and Bella drew up a wooden chair towards her. Taking Reenee's hand, she said, 'You like it?'

There was a crackle in Reenee's throat as she turned now to Bella and whispered her name, 'Bell-a. Oh, Bell-a.' And as she leant forward and placed her head on the older woman's shoulder Bella put an arm about her and hugged her, knowing with this gesture that her day of happiness was complete. To herself, she said, Don't let anybody dare tell me that this girl has lost her mind.

8

It had been a long, hard winter, but this was a morning in March and the sun was shining and spring was in the air and the postman had left one letter. It was addressed to Mr Andrew Anderson. He was the only one who ever received a letter, and as Bella was about to take it downstairs she fingered it and looked at Reenee. 'This will be from his wife. He's been waiting for it for days, if not a couple of weeks or more. Yet I know he's quite regular in sending her every penny he can spare. And it's funny she didn't take the chance to bring the bairns and come up to see him. I told him I'd pay for their fares; and, as you said, lass, you'd put a mattress in the boxroom and they could have your room.'

Bella often referred to Reenee's kindnesses as 'she said', or 'you said', because they spoke for themselves.

As she opened the front door she remarked, as if to herself, 'I wonder what she has to say to him this time?'

She wasn't to know the answer until later that evening.

It was when Joe and Carl came upstairs to bid her the usual goodnight that Joe said, 'Andy got a letter this morning. Well, you know that, you brought it down the yard. By! There was nearly sparks flyin' when he told us about it; I've never seen him turn on anybody like he did on Tony.'

'Turn on Tony? What for?'

'Well, you see . . .' He looked at Carl, and Carl said, 'It was the contents of the letter, Bella. He must have said in one of his that he was going to make a trip home somehow and see how they were, and the answer told him that he needn't bother, that she was goin' back to Wales to live with her parents. All her people are in Cardiff, you see. Anyway, from what I gather she told him that her little job in the North-East had been cut down to three hours and that, anyway, she couldn't go on; she had no life there.

'Apparently, her sister in Cardiff has a second-hand clothes shop. She's single and she's run it for years, and now she wants some help. As Andy said, if anybody's goin' to get a job it should be somebody in the family, and she's offered it to his wife; so she's gone there and taken the bairns with her.

'When John pointed out that things were as bad in Wales as any other place in the country, Andy said nothing. But when Tony put in quietly, "I bet it's because she has a man on the side," my, you should've seen the way Andy jumped up and turned on him! I thought he was goin' to hit him, and he yelled, "She's not like that! She's not like yours!" I can tell you, Bella, the tension rose. And when Andy got up and walked out, Joe there went after him.'

'Aye,' put in Joe now, 'he was as mad as a hatter. He was grippin' the gates as if he could break them. Anyway, he says he's goin' through to Wales to see just what the set-up is. In any case, he hasn't seen his bairns for nearly four years. But he'll be back, he said. The fare will be over a pound; we're clubbing up to see to that, but he'll have to have a penny in his pocket. That's why we've come up to see you, Bella.'

'You needn't worry about that,' said Bella quickly. 'I'll see he's got enough for the journey, and a bit over.'

An incident was to arise out of Andy's decision to visit Wales. Its effect wouldn't be shown for the next three years, and then it would change Bella's little business and all those connected with it.

The coat that had belonged to Hamish McIntyre and which Bella had given to Andy had always been too big for him, but that hadn't mattered because he wore it only when he wanted to look tidy, perhaps on a Sunday when they walked into the City or the West End. But now he was facing a journey, and he said to Willie, the only man of the little group handy with his needle, 'If I were to open the side seam of the coat, Willie, and cut a piece off the front of the jacket, would it hang just the same or would it affect the shoulders?'

Willie had said, 'I don't see why it should affect the shoulder. Yes, open the seam and I'll pin it up and see how much you could take in.'

In the afternoon of that day, Andy started

on the task of unpicking the side seam of the
coat. To get a better grip on the material he
thrust his thumb and finger into the small
breast pocket as a means of pulling the material taut while he picked out the machine
stitches.

It was as his finger slipped into the fob
pocket, as these pockets were often called
in which gentlemen could keep a small
watch, that he felt a crinkle under his fingers
as if from a piece of paper beneath the lining. On closer investigation, he saw that the
lining of the small pocket had at one time
been cut and neatly stitched over.

Intrigued to know why the piece of paper
or whatever it was had been inserted in the
lining, he cut away about two inches of it.
Inside was a piece of stiff paper; he also discovered that the lining of the pocket was
quite separate from the lining of the coat. In
fact he could feel that this was a pocket inside a pocket. But now he had the piece of
stiff paper on the table in front of him, and
he saw immediately that it had been folded
up tightly. Slowly he straightened out the
folds and, to his amazement, he saw he was
looking simply at the flap of an envelope.
There was nothing on it; that was, until he

turned it over and was confronted by line after line of small writing, starting at the top of
the flap and following in shorter and shorter
lines until it reached the gummed tip.

It was a dull day and the light in the wash-
house was dim, and he realised that he
couldn't read what was written here unless
he had a light. He went to a cupboard at the
end of the room and took out a small torch.

Slowly, word by word, he picked out the
following:

My Dearest Fellow, As I'm breaking the
rule, and this is the only love letter you
are likely to receive, take care of it. I'm
in the train from Harwich. I only had a
moment's notice. There's a meeting
at four. Be at the flat at seven
o'clock tomorrow night. I can't wait
to see you, my love—five weeks is
too long, too long. Lots of pretty
bits of glass. Couldn't get word
to you sooner. Came without a
case or anything—high
command—I can't wait for
tomorrow night, my love.
Nelson will get this to you at
your business. Business? Ha!

ha! Bring quite a bit of loose
cash. Couldn't go to bank,
not supposed to be here.
Switzerland the day after
tomorrow. Can't wait to
see you. Too long away.
Must be a better cover
than fruit. Until then,
beloved.
Yours

Andrew had reached the end of the writing but could hardly make out the signature which was written across the gummed section. But holding it to the side he could discern the name 'Jason'.

Then he sat looking ahead through the window into the yard. That coat had belonged to Bella's boss—a big hairy Scot, she said he was—and all the time he was a . . . His mind stopped for a second on the word, and then he said it aloud, 'Poofter.' Good God!

There was someone crossing the yard now. It was John. He jumped up and knocked on the window first, then opened the door and beckoned him.

'What is it?' said John.

'Just this. Come in. Close the door for a minute. You'll have to take the torch, but just read that, will you?'

'Well, what is it? Where did you get it?'

'Just read it, and then I'll tell you where I got it.'

Slowly John began to read, but before he was half-way through he lifted his head and stared at Andy, then made a sound in his throat before going on.

After he had read it all he sat looking at Andy and said, 'He's one of those. Where did you get it?'

Andy showed him where he had found the hidden letter; then he said, 'Can't believe it, can you? Remember what Bella said her boss had been like, a big hairy Scot, and she did say she never liked him because he didn't give her a civil word in his life.'

'No, no; of course he wouldn't. He had no room for skirts, had he? My God!'

'What d'you think I should do?'

'I would show it to Bella, and just let her see what kind of a fellow he was.'

'You think so?'

'I do.'

They went together and asked if they

could have a word with her, and Bella, thinking it was about Andy's journey, said, 'I told
Joe to tell you everything would be all right.
If you want to come back, your place is
there, and the lads would be very pleased
to see you again, I know that, so . . .'

'It isn't that, Bella,' said John quietly.
'Andy was undoing the seam of the coat
you had given him—you remember it was
too big for him? It was all right goin' about
the place, as he said, but he was goin' to
travel and he wanted it a bit smaller across
his chest, so Willie told him how it might be
done.'

And now he turned to Andy and let him
finish the tale. Having done so he handed
her the envelope flap and said, 'Will you be
able to read that? The writing's small, but
I've brought the torch with me.'

Like John, Bella had only read a short way
when she stopped and looked from one to
the other, and before going on she said, 'You
got this out of his coat?'

'Yes, yes; I can show you the place.'

After she finished reading she sat back in
the chair and what she said now was, 'The
dirty, rotten swine of a man! He was one of
those!'

'Aye,' said John now; 'he was not only one of those but one of the worst kind. There are some just ordinary fellows in the same boat, I know. I've worked with them, and, really, left to themselves they wouldn't hurt a fly. In fact, they were terrified half the time because it would be gaol for them if they were found out, you know.'

Bella shook her head and said slowly, 'To think I worked for him for sixteen years! He used me as a cover-up an' all. He must have, mustn't he?'

The two men nodded.

'I should think so, Bella, yes. And the fruit business, as it says there. But you can't do anything about it, can you?' said John. 'And this other chap was askin' for loose cash, as if he had a pile stacked somewhere.'

'Well, I wish I knew where it was,' said Bella. 'If I could get an inkling of where he stacked his stuff I'd give him away, dead as he is, and whoever this other one is, this Jason. But I tell you what I shall do. I've told you I never liked him; I also had the feeling that his solicitor never did either. Twice, these last few years, Mr Travis has called in to see how my business is goin' because, he said, the man was a mean man not to leave me a penny to run the house on, but to say I had to keep that little business goin' in order to have a shelter over me. He . . . he left a lot of money, you know. Well, I know what I'm goin' to do, I'm goin' to show this to Mr Travis because I'm sure he'll be interested to read it. He's a solicitor and a good man. He was concerned for my welfare at the time. I'm not sure of his address, but when Carl comes in I'll get him to find out.'

Bella now tried to explain to Reenee, who had been sitting listening to what was being said, that her late boss was a bad man, and in more ways than one, and that Andy had found proof of this from the piece of a letter that had been sewn inside the lining of the coat she had given him, and which had belonged to her employer.

Reenee did not seem to understand fully what it was all about, nor did she seem interested, only in the fact that Andy was going home to see his children and that he would be coming back . . .

The following day she took eight half-crowns from the large children's money box that Bella had placed on her window-sill and into which she put two half-crowns every week, because Reenee herself had refused to handle the money, shaking her head that she did not want it. But on such an occasion as this she seemed pleased to resort to the box, and she gave the money to Willie, indicating that she wanted him to give it to Andy.

Bella had made no remark on Reenee's gesture, but Willie, in his kindly way, had thanked her for Andy, saying, 'You're one in a million, miss. We all say that.'

Before Andy returned, four days later, Mr Travis came to the house. Carl had found out where the solicitor's office lay and had taken a letter there from Bella.

Mr Travis was now sitting in Bella's parlour, on which he had remarked the moment he entered: 'What a different room this is from that dark hole you were left with.'

And she had answered, 'Yes, it is, Mr Travis, but that's thanks to the lads.'

Mr Travis knew all about the lads. He also knew about someone he had heard called the Silent Lady, someone, he imagined, who had agoraphobia and whom Bella had taken into her kindly care. And now he went on, 'You said in your note, Miss Morgan, that you have something to show me that might be of interest.'

She went to the roll-top desk and from a drawer took the flap of the envelope, but before handing it to him she explained how one of her men had come across it.

Mr Travis looked at the small writing on the flap; then he felt in his inner pocket and took out an eye-glass and, using it with his right eye, he scanned the lines. He did not lift his head until he came to the signature and, like the others, he had to turn the piece of paper on end before he could make out the name written across the gummed area. Then looking at Bella, he said, 'Well, well, well!'

'That's what I said when I first read it, but I may add, Mr Travis, I said much more than that, I swore about him. He was clearly a bad man in some other ways, from what that writing suggests, not just that he was . . . well, one of those, you know, but that reference to the pieces of glass.'

'Oh, yes,' he nodded at her, 'the reference to the pieces of glass. You know, Miss Morgan, you have done me a great service this day.' Then again picking up the flap from the table, he looked at the signature and said, 'Jason. This, Miss Morgan, this nasty piece of paper, has given me a lead that a number of people will find very helpful.'

'May I ask what you mean, Mr Travis?'

'Your late employer and his fruit business acted as a screen for part of a very big smuggling concern. You know, he was under suspicion long before he died, yet nothing could actually be tacked on him, because we did not know his associates. Only twice . . . twice did I see him with his so-called friend, and once in a restaurant. That was when I realised who Jason was, and that our Mr McIntyre was moving in very elevated social circles.

'I wondered then why a man who ran a fruit stall could be in such high company. It wasn't a restaurant in London but well outside, and it was quite by chance that I went in. Fortunately I saw them before your employer saw me, and I made my escape, so to speak. But that night I had found out something that was of great interest to those in authority.'

'The police?' asked Bella.

'Well, not exactly the ordinary police. There are all kinds of police, you know, especially among the Customs. They are

called undercover men. You know, you cannot accuse people of any crime unless you
have proof, and proof is very difficult to get.
But a Christian name can be of great help;
and the pieces of glass mentioned in this
so-called love letter, Miss Morgan, were diamonds, and this was only one kind of glass
that was being dealt with.' He shook his
head slowly now. 'No wonder his dear friend
warned him that this was the only letter of
this kind he would ever be likely to get. Your
employer imagined that he had a very safe
place for it; and he must have valued it to
hang on to it as he did.'

'Mr Travis,' Bella said quickly now, 'what
about the loose cash, a lot of it? He had no
loose cash in this house, and these last two
days I've searched the place from top to
bottom again, wonderin' if I would come
across something, you know what I mean,
like you read in stories. The only place he
would have left any money is in that'—she
pointed to the roll-top desk—'and it hasn't
any secret drawers; I've had them all out.
All the rooms, too, were linoed up to the
skirtin' boards, except this one which is a
cord carpet. But that was stripped out when
the lads painted the room: they hosed it

down in the yard and dried it and, look, it's as good as new. But there can be no loose boards underneath it, else, by gum, they would've found them! And then there was the attic. They cleared everything out of that and made use of much of it in the wash-house.'

'Yes; yes, indeed. I've seen round and they've done a splendid job. They were so fortunate to find you. Yet again, you were fortunate that they had that combination of different trades.'

She laughed and said, 'My, yes. I couldn't have picked better, could I? But to get back to this loose cash. Where could he store loose cash? Have you any idea, Mr Travis?'

'When loose cash was referred to, Miss Morgan, I think it would perhaps mean that it was in a bank, somewhere he could easily get his hands on it during the time he had before their meeting because, by the sound of it, the term loose cash might have covered several hundreds of pounds. His cover-up was the stock market. My accountant used to deal with that for him; but after the night I saw him in the restaurant I surmised he must have different channels.' He now patted the paper again. 'Oh, and the name

Jason . . . Well! That's the biggest mistake he made in sending that note to his friend.'

Bella looked at him enquiringly now and said, 'What will happen—I mean to the friend or the others he was associated with?'

'I wish I were able to tell you, Miss Morgan, but I can only say that this piece of paper has tied "Jason" in with an organisation that nobody suspected he had any dealings with. And another thing, your former employer might have kept decent clothes to change into in this house, but he had another source of income for his wardrobe. I'm sure of that now. I promise you, Miss Morgan, if anything dramatic should come out of this you will be the first to know; although I might have to ask you to keep it to yourself, which I know you will. And I would add, although I've said it before, that if at any time there's a way in which I could assist you, that is I or my company, we should be only too glad. How are you managing . . . for money, I mean, and to pay your staff?'

'Oh, that's all right, Mr Travis. I get by well and can put a little aside, not a lot but something. It means I can give these poor fellows work, as well as a dry bed to the needy, and more and more of them seem to be pouring into the city.'

'Yes, indeed, Miss Morgan, there are, the country's in a dreadful state—the world's in a dreadful state at this moment, and it seems to my mind at times that any move that is made only leads us further into disaster. But, anyway, we can't do much about it, you or I, can we? Yet we are both doing our bit in an unseen way.' He leant toward her, and his words were hardly above a whisper as he said, 'If we were to prevent hundreds of thousands, even millions being creamed off from this country to find their way to Switzerland, the place your employer's friend mentions in this epistle, we'll have done a great deal.'

Bella could only nod, saying, 'Yes; yes,' although she did not understand exactly what he meant.

They parted affably, Mr Travis emphasising again that she had only to call on him for help, and she promising faithfully that if ever the time came she would do so. As yet she wasn't to know that the time wasn't so very far away.

The following morning she was a bit late

in getting up, and when she entered the kitchen and saw Willie and Reenee busily working she apologised, saying, 'Eeh, my! I overslept. I think I've got a bit of a cold on me. You've had your breakfasts?'

'Yes, Bella, we've had our breakfasts, and all is running well, as usual, except . . .' Willie stopped what he was doing at the table and repeated '. . . except for Andy. He came back last night, Bella.'

'He did?'

'Aye, but he's in a bit of a state. He sat there with his head down and his hands hanging between his knees. Carl had just made a pot of tea, and he handed Andy a mug, which he took but didn't say anything. Yet he drank it straight down. Then John said, "Well, lad. Come on, tell us how you got on. It's better when it's out." At that Andy straightened up in his chair, and he looked from one to the other of us before he spoke. He said he had caught them on the hop. He hadn't told his wife he was comin' and he walked into a full kitchen. Of all things, they were havin' a party, a birthday party. The widower next door had a six-year-old boy, and there the two of them were, all merry and bright. So were her mum and dad, her sister—the married one—and two of her bairns, and the single one and Andy's wife and her bairns. He must have appeared like a bomb dropping on to the middle of the table. Anyway, if they were surprised by the sight of him, he said, he was surprised at the sight of that table: he had never seen such a well-laid table for years. No one would think there was a slump or anybody out of work in Wales, at least in Cardiff. It was laden with ham and tongue and tarts and cakes of all kinds.

'It was she who spoke first, he said. She jumped up from her chair and almost yelled at him, "Why didn't you tell us you were comin'?" And nobody asked him to sit down until her father stood up and told him to take a seat. Apparently Andy told them to finish their party and that he would come back later. And he went along to a pub and got himself a pint and a sandwich, and there, he said, he sat for nearly two hours. When he went back, the kitchen was clear except for her and the two bairns. They seemed to be waitin' for him, he said, for she turned straight away to the bairns and said, "This is your da."

'He must have made to go towards one

of them because he told us the younger, Betty, backed away and said, "You're not me da. I don't like you." And with this, she had run from the room.'

Willie now looked from Bella to Reenee, and said, 'What could you say to that? We just sat there like dummies. And then his wife must have said the only place he could sleep was on the couch in the front room as there was nowhere else, and she must have left him. He said to the older girl, "Don't you remember me?" and she answered that she remembered him taking them up the river on a Sunday afternoon in a sculler. His head must have drooped once more when she turned on him and in a voice, which must have been just like her mother's, she said, "I'm not goin' back there. I don't like it. I like it here and I want to stay." ' Here Willie paused, then said slowly, 'He asked Carl if there was any more tea in the pot and we all jumped up at once to pour it out. It was a dreadful experience, Bella, awful.

'And in the morning his wife said she had lived like a widow for the last four years and fended for herself for most of the time; now she was home and intended to stay there.

'He must have said something to her like,

"You won't stay a widow long, by the look of things," for she said that perhaps he was right, and her sister had pointed out earlier that long before she had met him, the fellow next door and she had been courting, and it was a pity she had ever left Wales.

'He said he doesn't remember anything more, only that he went into the front room and took his attaché case from under the couch, and then that he was at the station. And . . . and you know what he said then, Bella? I nearly burst out cryin' meself. He said he didn't feel like a man any more. He said all the rough times he'd had with us chaps long before we came here and met you, Bella, the cold, the hunger, the misery, standin' and beatin' that little drum out in the rain hour after hour, nothing like that had ever made him feel as small as he did on that station.'

When Willie did not continue, Bella asked quietly, 'How is he this morning?'

'Very down in the mouth. We told him to stay indoors and just clean up the wash-house.'

'I'll go round,' said Bella, 'and have a word with him.'

'Well, if I were you I'd wrap up well. You

shouldn't go out today at all, that cold's heavy on you.'

'Thanks, Father, I'll do that.'

After she had left the kitchen, Willie turned his attention to Reenee. She was sitting with her hands idle on her lap while there was still a pile of vegetables before her. He knew she was thinking about what she had just heard, and he said, 'I'm glad I'm not married; it must be awful to have kids and then they turn against you. Of course, you've got to see their side of it: they haven't seen him for some years. That wasn't his fault either; Bella's invited them down here more than once. It looks to me as if Tony was right about the wife.'

Willie now watched Reenee's mouth open, and then she brought out the single word 'Lost.'

'Yes, Reenee. As he himself said, he felt he was no longer a man. And as you say, he feels lost. It must be an awful feeling.'

There was a silence, then he sighed and said, 'Well, we'd better get on. Broth doesn't make itself, does it, Reenee?' She began to chop the vegetables. Yet it wasn't ten minutes before she suddenly laid down her knife and walked away from the table, bringing from him the reprimand, 'Where're you going?' and the immediate apology, 'Oh I'm sorry. It isn't my business.' Yet two minutes later, he thought it was, when she came back into the kitchen, the sleeves of that great coat pulled down and on her head that weird article which was supposed to be a hat. At the sight of her standing just inside the door he almost rushed at her, saying, 'Oh, please! Please, Reenee! Don't leave the house. Bella gets so upset when you leave.' She put up a hand and held it in front of his mouth, but she didn't touch it; she waved her hand in denial, then pointed, first to the door, then to the left as though towards the gates. With her head going back and her mouth opening, she said, 'Wash.' And again, 'Wash.'

He translated quickly, 'Wash-house? You're goin' to the wash-house?'

She nodded, and the corners of her lips moved upwards, and he suggested, 'To . . . to see Andy?' Again she nodded, brightly now, and he added, 'Nice. Nice,' and immediately went before her to open the front door, from where he watched her go along to the gates and through them.

The sight of the weirdly dressed figure

coming towards her caused Bella almost to drop the wash-basket she was carrying out of the wash-house, and she muttered under her breath, 'Oh, my God, what now? She's not goin' out again, surely.'

Andy was standing behind her and he murmured, 'That's the miss.'

'Who else?' murmured Bella. Then on Reenee's approach she said, 'And where d'you think you're off to on this soft summer's morning that would cut your throat?'

For answer Reenee pushed past her and went into what Bella would always call the wash-house, causing Andy to step back and Bella to re-enter and close the door after her.

Reenee held out her hand to Andy, and when he took it she spoke two words, almost plainly now, 'Home . . . friends.'

Bella smiled widely and with not a little pride translated, 'She means, Andy, that you're home and among friends.'

'I know. I know,' Andy said softly. He put his other hand on the one he was holding, and there was a break in his voice when he said, 'Thank you, miss. I'll never forget what you have just said: I am home and among friends and the one I hold most dear is your very kind self.' He knew he should have said the one he held dear next to Bella was herself but, glancing at Bella, he felt that she understood because she was nodding at him and her eyes were bright.

Slowly now Reenee pulled her hand away from Andy's and, looking round what was now quite a large room, she made a sound in her throat that could not be translated, for she was trying to say, 'So big and comfortable.'

She walked over to the addition the men had built on, which was larger than the wash-house itself. Against the far wall were stacked three wooden bunks; alongside the righthand wall was a wooden platform with a mattress on top, forming another bed; and in the intervening space were two renovated easy chairs and a table about three foot square.

Now taking on the role of guide, Bella said, 'They play cards in here at night and gamble for monkey-nuts; they'll have the police on them.' Then she pointed to what had been the far wall of the actual washhouse and where there now stood a large cupboard. She opened it, to disclose shelves on which were pieces of crockery.

The plates might be cracked and the cups and mugs be without handles, but nevertheless they were china; and on the bottom shelf was a box with an assortment of rough cutlery in it. The companion door of the cupboard contained an array of tins and covered dishes, and did duty as a food cupboard. The boiler top was no longer to be seen, for this was covered with what Bella recognised to be part of the spare leaf to the kitchen table. The boiler fire had an enlarged grate, on the hob of which stood a bubbling kettle, and, most surprising of all, along the left side of what had been the original wash-house was a chintz-covered sofa. That the chintz had seen better days made no difference; it looked clean and comfortable, and Bella, turning to Andy, whose whole being seemed to have lightened during the last few minutes, said, 'I've meant to ask you: how did you get that in?'

'Oh, we put it in before we finished building the end'—he thumbed over his shoulder—'and we were lucky that it never reached a tip. We saw it being taken from a house and being given to the dustmen, and we asked them if we could have it and, never letting anything go for nothing, one of them said, "It could cost you a bob," so we gave him a bob willingly.'

'Eeh!' Bella went over and examined the couch. 'It's got a carved frame. Really, it's beautifully done.' And she turned to Reenee and said, 'Haven't they made a fine place of it? And what was it, just an old wash-house? You lads are a clever lot.' She was addressing Andy again, and he answered her, without a smile now, 'Not me, Bella. I can only handle bricks; I haven't got an eye for finer things, just bricks.'

'Well, where would they've been without you and your bricks?' said Bella briskly. 'They could never have built this place with-out you. Anyway, come on now, you're not gonna sit mooning here all day. Take us back in, and tonight we'll crack a bottle. Yes, we will,' she emphasised, waving her hand; 'we'll crack a bottle to welcome you home.'

And this they did, and Andy, who yester-day had felt he was nothing, knew that among friends like these he couldn't help but grow into a man again.

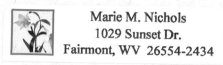
9

Bella's cold was a bad one, and she passed it on to Reenee.

Unfortunately, Reenee's cold attacked her chest, and one morning when she didn't appear at breakfast Bella went up to her room and found her in a fever, hardly able to get her breath.

'Oh, my dear,' she said, 'you've got it right and proper, haven't you? I'm sorry, lass; I'm sorry I gave it to you, but mine was never like this. Nevertheless, I know what'll cure it, a lemon in some boiling water with a drop of whisky in it.'

Reenee was past making comment of any kind: all she could do was hold her chest tight, trying to press down the pain and the tightness of it and to prevent herself from having another bout of coughing.

'Just lie quiet now; I'll be back in a minute.'

But three doses of hot lemon with dashes of whisky did nothing to alleviate Reenee's condition. As the day wore on she became worse. This frightened Bella, and when she saw Carl in the yard, talking to one of the boys, she called down to him.

When he hurried into the kitchen she said, 'Look, you know the doctors round here. I know there's only two, but who's the better?'

'Why, Bella?'

'The lass, Reenee, she's bad, real bad. I think she's in a kind of fever.'

'Oh, there's Dr Brown and Dr Harle. Dr Harle's the assistant. He's a young man, but they say he's good. Well, I know he is: I saw him pull a fellow's shoulder back into place without him havin' to go to hospital.'

'Well, go and get him. Ask him to come as soon as he can.'

It was almost two hours later when the doctor arrived, and straight away Bella liked the look of him. He wasn't all that young, perhaps in his late thirties, and he was only of medium height, but broad, and his voice was nice, as she put it to herself, kindly like.

She noticed that he seemed a little surprised at the inside of the house. Being at this end of the market area, he had likely expected it to be a muck-heap, and as they made their way upstairs, he said, 'Have you lived here long, Miss Morgan?'

'Touchin' on thirty years.'

'Really! And you've never had the doctor in?'

'No; not often, Doctor, we haven't. As I recall, you're the first since Mr McIntyre died.'

On entering the bedroom, he stopped for a moment just inside the door and looked at the waxen-faced figure on the bed. Reenee's chest was heaving; the sweat was running from her brow. Her eyes were wide open, and as she turned them towards him she pulled the rest of the bedclothes right up under her chin with a convulsive movement, making a guttural sound in her throat.

Immediately Bella went to her. 'Now it's all right, love. It's all right. This is the doctor. He's a nice man and he's come to make you better.'

The head on the pillow turned from side to side, and the doctor, having put down his bag and taken off his overcoat, gently eased

Bella to the side and, bending over Reenee, said, 'It's all right, my dear, it's all right. I'm only going to take your temperature and look at your chest.'

A sound came again from her throat, and now her two hands were flat on his shoulders and she was pushing him away. Bella, taking the doctor's arm, whispered to him, 'She's afraid of men.'

'What?' His face was puzzled.

'Just what I said, Doctor, she must've had a shock in her time, a great fright. She's afraid of men, most of them anyway. She's got to get very used to them before she'll let them come near her.'

He looked at her closely before turning back to the bed and saying to Reenee, 'My dear, I am not going to hurt you. I am a doctor and I just want to help ease that cough of yours.' He now forcibly took one of her wrists in his hand, and when he had felt her racing pulse he laid it down and said, 'I must explain to you. You're in a high state of fever and you must be examined before I can help you.' Again the hand came out to push him, and to his amazement he saw the large eyes in the pale face close tightly and the bedclothes heave up and down, not from her chest but from her stomach.

Pulling the heavy eiderdown to the foot of the bed, Bella said, 'Oh, she's gonna have one of her turns, Doctor. Her stomach always goes like that beforehand, up and down, up and down, as if it was bein' pushed up and then down.'

'Has she epileptic fits?'

'No, I've seen people in them, Doctor. What she has isn't a fit, not ordinarily, but it's something. She's . . . she's afraid of something, and she genuinely yells out in one of these turns. You see, she can hardly speak, it takes her some time to get a word out; but in the turns . . . well, she does, I mean speak, and clearly at times, but just a single word or two.'

He turned from the bed. 'She's in a very low state. She can't go on like this, I must examine her.'

'She won't let you, Doctor. She rarely takes her clothes off, I mean even in front of me. She's got a kind of what they would call phobia: she wears a big dark coat all the time, mostly in the house, as if she's hiding behind it or something. But she's a lovely girl and she's not really mental—I mean, I think she's lost just part of her memory. Something happened to her, something awful, but otherwise part of her brain's all right because she knows everything that's goin' on, and . . . and is kindly.'

He said quietly, 'I can't struggle with her and make her undress, so I shall have to give her a little jab. It will put her out for perhaps half an hour, but in that time we'll be able to see what has to be done. Otherwise, I am telling you, Miss Morgan, she could die.'

'Oh, God, Doctor! I couldn't have that . . . I love her. I love her like a daughter.'

'How long has she been with you?'

Bella had to think. 'Oh, since late 'twenty-nine,' she said. 'Two years or more. She's happy here, I know she is. She never goes out, not unless she must, and then it's only to help somebody.'

He stared at her for a moment then went to his bag, took out a phial and a needle, then gripped Reenee's arm, and jabbed the needle into it. She was now yelling, 'No! No! I won't! I won't! Please!' She turned her face into the pillow and, lifting up her arm, she covered her eyes, muttering as she did so. 'I won't, not like that. No! no, I won't.'

Slowly the arm fell from her face, her body sank and went limp in the bed. He said, 'Does she always struggle like this?'

'Oh, yes; yes.'

'Well, let's get her things off.'

'Oh, Doctor.'

'Woman!' His voice was sharp. 'I've got to examine her chest.'

'Yes, Doctor.'

Bella now pulled down the sheet and the blanket to expose Irene's body covered in the woolly shift she remembered seeing through the wash-house window. It was clinging to her skin showing her slight form, and it looked grey and dirty, but Bella knew it wasn't. This was the garment, together with her underclothes, that she washed in the basin last thing at night when they were all in bed, and which she dried before the fire and over the fireguard. It used to be that she crept downstairs in the dark at night; that was until they got the bathroom. Now, sometimes three times a week, she would bathe herself last thing at night when they were all in bed, and likely she would wash her clothes in the bath and dry them over the kitchen fire as she had before. Poor girl.

Bella couldn't tell the doctor all this, and

when he said, 'Does she always wear this thing?' she could only nod at him. 'Well, help me to get it off her shoulders; it goes right up to her neck.'

When they handled the woollen garment they found it was wringing wet. He said, 'That's got to come off; she's got to have something dry on. Come along; pull it right down.'

'It's her I'm thinking about; but I suppose it's all right, she doesn't know. Thank God she doesn't know.'

'Get a couple of towels, warm ones. She must be rubbed down.'

After Bella had hurried from the room, he examined the heaving chest and found what he already suspected. It was pneumonia. If she survived this she would be lucky. He now touched her breast where a blue mark ran for about half an inch under the nipple, and he peered at it for a moment. The breast was running with sweat, and he looked about him to see if there was a towel at hand. There wasn't, so he took a handkerchief from the side pocket of his coat and wiped it dry. Again he looked at the mark.

The other breast, he saw, showed two blue marks, but further down, and his eyes narrowed. Then he looked at the girl's stomach. It was quite flat, and he passed over it until he came to her groin. There, using his handkerchief, he again wiped away the sweat, and he could see now what looked like a dark stain on the skin. It was like the imprint left after skin had been flailed with a whip or rope. He had seen sailors' backs criss-crossed with this sort of scar from old floggings, but no, surely this couldn't have been caused by a whip or a rope?

Gently he heaved her over on to her side. There were no marks on her back but there, on her buttock, the one visible to him, were blue stains, like those on her breast. They were very like the stains left from pieces of coal that punctured miners' brows, but he knew that these marks were not from a whip or a rope, they were from teeth. He lifted the other buttock carefully, and yes, there they were again, more of them. He stood up. This woman had been abused, and savagely too.

The door opened and Bella brought in a couple of warm towels, and together they gently dried Reenee's body.

When he came to her feet he lifted up one foot and examined her ankle, and there again was scarring. Why on earth hadn't somebody found this out before? Yet who would have recognised the marks and the stained skin unless they had knowledge of how they had come about? They might have termed the bluish marks love bites, but there were love bites and love bites. These marks were in another category. Poor woman.

'Have you a dry nightgown?'

'Aye, I have a couple, but they're calico and stiff; she's not used to . . .'

'No matter what she's used to, she has to be changed into dry clothes at regular intervals during the next forty-eight hours or so.'

Again Bella darted from the room, and when she returned it was to see that the doctor had covered the sweating form with the sheet and blanket.

It was about fifteen minutes later when he sat at the little table near the window writing out a prescription. When he handed it to Bella he said, 'Get that made up as quickly as possible and give her a spoonful every three hours. The directions will be on the bottle. Also, there is a salve to rub into her chest. The main thing, though, is to keep her warm and dry. To my mind, Miss Morgan, she should really be in hospital.'

'Oh, no! No, she would hate that, she couldn't bear that, Doctor.'

He stared at her. 'What do you know about her?'

'Very little,' she admitted dolefully, 'only that she's a lady and I'm sure has been very well bred.'

He put in quietly, 'Very badly treated by someone.'

'Yes, Doctor?' It was a question.

'Oh, yes. Her body is marked where it shouldn't be. I'll tell you this much, Miss Morgan, and it might sound very crude, but if she had been a prostitute I could have understood it, but not if, as you say, she is a lady. But my examination has indicated that she has been very badly treated by someone she must have known well. Do you think she was married?'

'Oh, yes, she was married.'

'How do you know that?'

'Well,' Bella pointed to two ring fingers on the left hand, 'she went to the pawn shop once. It must have cost her something to do that: she pawned a wedding ring and an engagement ring. They must have been of some value because she got thirty-five pounds on them.'

He raised his eyebrows as he said, 'Thirty-five pounds! Yes, they must have been of value. But why did she do that?'

'She . . . Well, to tell you the truth, Doctor, it was she who suggested in her deaf and dumb way that the poor people who travel the streets or sleep rough should have a bed, and it was she who suggested starting up my business. She wrote it out on a piece of paper, a kind of design, and we had four men here, members of a little street band, and they were of all trades, building trades, I mean. So, you see, although there are times when she could be taken as being mental, she's not. She worked out that these men could do this job if there was enough money for materials. But I hadn't the money that it would cost. I said this, naturally, in front of her, and to the men, and one day she slipped away. I thought I'd lost her for ever, and I nearly went mad because . . . well, I've got very fond of her, and that's what she did.'

He stared at her before he said, 'Why on earth would she still have two valuable rings on her if she was in the condition you said you found her? Why didn't she sell these before and get a lodging or food to eat?'

'That's what I've asked myself dozens of times, Doctor, but I think they must have meant something to her.'

He turned now and looked at the bed and the face lying there, and he said quietly, 'How strange. And she's been a very beautiful woman. She still is in a way. Well, Miss Morgan, I must go now. Take that to the chemist'—he pointed to the prescription on the table—'as soon as possible, and I shall call back this evening. If she's awake I won't attempt to examine her further. At the moment, sleep is what she requires; and, as you say, she's afraid of men. And well she may be,' he said, as he took up his bag and made for the door. 'Yes; well she may be.'

For the next week Bella had her work cut out; and she didn't know how she would have managed if it hadn't been for Carl, who gave up his daily street traveling and acted as help and housemaid, running between the kitchen and the bedroom.

On the third day after the doctor had seen her, Reenee had certainly passed through a crisis, when both Bella and Carl had thought she was dying. But the next morning the fever subsided. Now, after a week, she lay limp in the bed and seemingly lifeless, and she did not protest at Bella's ministrations. Nor had she made any comment on the stiff calico nightdress that covered her. Surprisingly, too, she did not object to Carl's help, for example when he put his hand behind her head and lifted it up in order that she should drink . . .

It was three weeks before she was able to get out of bed and sit by the small fire that Carl had kept going day and night. She was wearing the housecoat Bella had given her, but her lower body was shrouded in a large blanket.

She did not make any reference to the whereabouts of her underclothes: two silk undergarments, a cotton petticoat, the woollen shift and her long stockings had all been washed and ironed. Then there was her velvet dress hanging over the back of the chair. If she noticed, she did not remark, even to herself, that an attempt had been made to clean the marks and mud-stains off the bottom of the skirt by washing it, which had improved it little.

For some days now she had been aware

that she was feeling different. More quiet inside; her mind wasn't groping so much. It seemed as if it were resting, like her body.

There was one thing that, in a small way, did disturb her. It was when she felt the approach of the strange man, the doctor. She had never raised her eyes to his face; she only knew that his chin was clean-shaven and that he always wore a soft white collar, not a stiff one, and that his voice was kind. Yet some part of her mind would remind her that this man had seen her body.

Today he stood in front of her and said, 'It's bitterly cold outside. This little fire gives off a good heat, doesn't it? But you will soon be able to get downstairs into the sitting room, where you'll feel more comfortable.'

As she listened to him, she thought she was very comfortable where she was and she would like to stay here always, just sitting, never moving, never being forced to take notice of anything or anyone, and never, never being forced to speak.

When he took her hand to feel her pulse she made no resistance. He remarked, 'That's good.' Then, as if he were talking to an ordinary patient, he added, 'But you must take care, you know, of that chest. Always see that you wrap up well when you go out.'

Outwardly she remained unresponsive. He had said 'when you go out'. She was never going out. She would never leave this house again, this security and Bella. Oh, Bella, Bella. And Carl . . . yes, Carl.

She did not tell herself that Carl was a man. No, he was just Carl . . . like Andy and the rest of the men she now thought of as family.

She knew there was a change in her, but she couldn't question it or tell herself why she should think of those four men as being part of Bella's family. But they were, and she could look at them without fear.

Something in her mind moved swiftly: the word 'fear' had stirred something. She recalled that she hadn't thought of that word for a long time—at least, it seemed a long time, although she could vaguely recall when the doctor had struggled with her.

The word 'struggled' now became prominent in her mind, and she shook herself. The quick movement of her body caused the doctor to say, 'You're not feeling cold, are you?'

She shook her head, and Bella indicated

to the doctor that he should come with her out of the room. And this he did, but not before saying, 'Well, my dear, I'm glad to see you so much better. I won't pop in again for a week, and then just to make sure you are perfectly fit again. Goodbye.'

She went to raise her head, then stopped; her mouth opened and she made a sound in her throat, but it did not form any word.

Out on the landing, Bella said, 'She often gives that shudder, and I think it is when she is recalling something, or her mind is troubling her in some way, but it didn't seem as if she was troubled today. And she hasn't been, not for days; well, I would say, since she got over the bad bout.'

'Yes, I'm sure your diagnosis is quite right, Miss Morgan.'

'If you will come into the parlour, Doctor, I will settle your bill, and gladly.'

'Oh, there's no hurry for that.'

She said, on a laugh, 'Well, if you don't take it now you might never get it. I might go out and spend it.'

'Well, I wouldn't mind if you did, Miss Morgan, because you really have had a very strenuous three weeks. And, may I say, I

don't know what you would have done without your butler.'

As they went down the stairs she said,
'I'll tell Carl your new name for him, he'd like
that.'

Then her voice sobered. 'He's a good fellow is Carl, Doctor. God, or the devil, put a
curse on him, but get behind that face and
you'll find he's got a mind and that it works.
He thinks a lot and is wise. I suppose it's
because of his reading—he reads anything
and everything he can get his hands on.'

'Well, I'm sure all you say about him is
true, but what *I* say is that in his misfortune
he has found a very good mistress in yourself, Miss Morgan.'

10

As the months wore on and another winter approached, the routine in the little business seemed to carry on much the same day after day. But outside in the streets in the daytime men begged for work or bread; at night on park benches, in shop doorways, under bridges there seemed to be more and more humanity lying huddled in disarray, for unemployment and starvation were driving men into London where, night after night, shivering creatures had to be turned away from the gates that led into the yard. This would be after they had taken in perhaps an extra half-dozen and let them sleep on the warm bare boards up the centre of the room, and perhaps another four in the men's wash-house next to the urinal. As this place was cold the men were provided with thin pallets and a blanket; but there was always a bowl of soup before they lay down and a breakfast of tea and new bread in the morning.

Things were coming to such a pitch in this way that the four men of the original band were now in Bella's kitchen, together with Joe and Carl. Reenee had gone to her room. What John was suggesting was that if Bella could afford to get the wood they would knock up a kind of shelter at the far end of the backyard. It would be a rough affair, but nevertheless it could be made to take eight mattresses. Joe had said there was to be a clearing out of the warehouse and there were still some mattresses there, which might be going cheap. He had already told her that there was something astir in the warehouse. The far sheds were being cleared of everything, but not the retail part: 'The legal and above board part,' Carl put in, thereby somewhat relieving the gravity of the looming situation.

'As I told you, Bella,' Joe said, 'they're scared about something. The mattresses, mats and things like that have all been brought over to our side for what they call a big sale. They're packed up to the roof there.'

Bella said, 'Whatever sale there is, Joe, mattresses will still cost money. As for the wood, well, I'll have to know how much it's goin' to cost because I can only do so much. You know that.' Recognition of the fact echoed through the group.

'Leave it until tomorrow,' she said. 'I'll think it over because I'm as concerned as you are about those fellows standing outside the gates at night. Talk about the Bible and the beggar at the gates. Dear, dear! Well, as I said, lads, I'll see you in the morning.'

The four men made their departure, only Joe and Carl staying behind, as they always did, to have a last word with Bella. And apparently Joe had something special he wanted to say.

'Sit down a minute, Bella. I want to tell you something, or ask you something. You've always said you hate the lino in your bedroom and that you'd like a nice carpet.'

'Yes, yes, I have. I've said many other things too that I'll never get, and often.'

'Well,' said Joe, 'there's one going. Dixon took me on the side and said, "There's a carpet left over there, lad," and he pointed to one of the stores. "It's a lovely thing—they say it's Chinese—but they daren't take it out to sell it because it's of such quality they would get nabbed for it. And then there's the size," he said. And then it came: "D'you think your missis would be interested in it?" and I said, "Well, I'll ask her; but how much?" And . . . well . . .'

'Go on,' said Bella; 'go on, spill it.'

'Ten pounds.'

'Ten pounds!'

'Aye, that's what he said. Well, what he said was it was worth hundreds. If it was sold in one of the big shops it would bring hundreds; but I know they want to get rid of it. Why they didn't take it to the other place I don't know, but I think they're cleaning that up too. There's certainly a scare on of some kind, aye. Well, Bella, the rumour is that your Mr Weir, you know the one who always lets you have things half price, he's in trouble, and I think he's on the run. He's not showin' his face anyway, we'll say that much. They're cleanin' up the place before there's an inspection by the police. You know, ours—I mean where I work—isn't the only warehouse he's got, he has two or three in the city, I understand, or he had.'

Bella was staring at Joe now, and she said again, 'Ten pounds! You couldn't beat him down?'

Joe drooped his head and said, 'I already did, Bella. He was askin' fifteen, and I said I knew you couldn't go to that, so he said he would take ten for it, ready money, if it was moved out the morrer night.'

'What if the police were to come here and find it?'

'Well, you would say you bought it second-hand from the store, and you didn't know what kind of carpet it was. It could be from Timbuktu or John O'Groats or anywhere else. But Dixon seems to know his stuff, and he said it's a spanker and that he would've had it himself, only it's too big for his front room. They're not askin' around about it, because some of his fellows might get a drink and open their mouths too wide.'

Bella looked at Carl, and he nodded at her and said, 'I think it's about time in your life, Bella, you gave yourself a treat. You've always said you hated the lino in that room. So go on. We'll all pig in and help.'

'You'll do nothin' of the sort. If I'm goin' to have a carpet for my room I'll buy it.'

Bella turned to Joe and said, 'All right, get it. I'll give you the money in the morning. But where will we put it until I get the room ready?'

'We can leave it down by the hall in your sitting room; in fact it'll go behind the couch and the roll-top desk. It would fit in lovely there, I'm sure. Anyway, wait till you see it.'

As Bella said goodnight to the two men she did not realise that the buying of that carpet was going to alter not only her life but all their lives, in much the same way as Reenee's plan had created the room down-stairs.

The carpet arrived the next night, and as it was half unrolled in the parlour Bella gazed at it in awe. It was, in a way, plainish, a sort of silver-grey with flowers woven at each corner; but the strange thing about it was the pile. It seemed to be almost two inches thick, so thick that you could not insert your finger in it and touch the canvas.

Reenee was present when Joe and Carl stretched out the carpet, and she looked from them to Bella, then down at the carpet.

Kneeling, she felt it; then again looking up, she gazed into Bella's face and nodded before her mouth opened and the word that came out sounded like something that ended in 'ease'. And it was Carl who said, 'Chinese, Reenee?' and she turned quickly to him and nodded.

Bella looked at the two men and said, 'She knows . . . She knows quality.' This to her was another proof that her dear girl came from a good home.

The carpet was rolled up quickly and placed behind the couch and the roll-top desk, and was quite unobtrusive there. When Joe said, 'We'll pull up the lino tomorrow night,' Bella interrupted him, saying, 'No; you leave that alone. Me and Reenee here will see to that.' What she didn't add was, 'I don't want two men messing around in my room when they might see more than is good for them. Her wooden box was under the bed, and she had no key to it, and what surplus money she had every week went into it. The main money for paying out the men and bills she kept in the roll-top desk.

The following day she and Reenee started to take up the lino.

They found it to be in four pieces. The three larger pieces came up easily. The last piece, to the side of the window, was, like the others, tucked under the skirting board, but no matter how they pulled at it they could not release it.

'I'll have to get a knife,' said Bella, 'and cut it right along there. Stay where you are; I'll be back up shortly and bring some tea with me. I'm as dry as a fish, and I'm sure you are too.'

Reenee was kneeling opposite the end of the window-sill, and, feeling rather tired with pulling and pushing at the sheets of lino, she rested her hand on the sill. In front of her hung an old brocade curtain that must have been put up years ago, and as she felt it she pulled it to one side, exposing the paint-work. She thought, Paint; yes, paint before carpet is laid. She rubbed her fingers up the stanchion of the window and as she did so some of the paint practically flaked away under her touch. As she brought her fingers down to the sill again she saw what looked like a round rusty patch. She had seen patches like this before, where a brass fitting had been screwed in to hold the swathes that held back the curtains during the day. She had a flash in her mind of a curtain hanging somewhere . . . somewhere. She groped in her mind but could not remember where she had seen a curtain pulled back to the brass holder and, as if in affection, she put her thumb on the patch. To her amazement she felt it move. She looked behind her to see if Bella was coming. But there was no sight nor sound of her, so she pressed her thumb again on the dark patch and when it moved downwards and she heard a rustling sound, she looked to her left . . . and saw the lino slip from underneath the skirting board. Wide-eyed and open-mouthed, she gazed on it. Then she was on her knees pulling it further from the wall and gazing down into a narrow trough in which lay neatly piled bundles and bundles of what looked like bank notes. Letting her eyes travel to the far end near the wall, she could see a number of small chamois-leather bags.

She slumped back on her knees for a moment, then sprang up and was rushing towards the door when it opened and Bella entered carrying a tray on which were two cups of tea and a plate holding two buns and a knife. She was amazed when it was seized from her hands and thrust on the bed. 'What is it, girl?' she cried. 'What's the matter with you?'

Grabbing her arm, Reenee pulled her towards the window and on to her knees, and now she was kneeling looking at a trough, all of three feet long, under the window and her mind kept repeating, Oh, my God! That's money down there, a lot of money. She picked up a bundle of the notes but dropped it as if it had burnt her.

She turned and stared at Reenee, whose face was aglow as she thrust out her arm and grabbed one of the chamois-leather bags. Pulling open the top, she dipped her hand in and brought out a number of gold sovereigns; then let them drip back into the bag.

'In the name of God!' Bella's words were awe-filled, 'Sovereigns! Gold sovereigns. What are we to do? What are we to do with all this?' She stared at Reenee and, in a trembling voice, she said, 'I must get Mr Travis. He'll know.'

Now Reenee stabbed her finger into Bella's chest and quite clearly she brought out the words, 'Yours!'

'Eeh, lass. I'd get into trouble for hoarding

all that. In any case, I wouldn't know what to do with it. God knows what it'll amount to when it's counted up.'

Again Reenee spoke, but haltingly now as she said, 'Trav-is. Trav-is.'

'Yes; yes, you're right. We must see Mr Travis. He'll know. But hide it. Look, put the lino back the way you got it. D'you know how?'

For answer Reenee pushed the lino underneath the skirting board, and there it was as it had been before; the curtain was hanging down covering the rusty patch, which seemed to have returned automatically to sill level. And Bella stood up and held Reenee's face in both her hands as she said, 'Nobody else must know about this, you understand? Until after Mr Travis has seen it. I'll get Carl to go and fetch him. I can trust Carl, but I won't tell him about this'—she pointed down to the floor—'I'll just say I want to see Mr Travis on business.'

Carl was about to go out when Bella said, 'Would you run a message for me, Carl?'

'Anything for you, Bella. You know that, don't you?'

'Go to Mr Travis's office and ask if you can have a word privately with him. Put on your decent coat. Tell him that Miss Morgan would like to see him.'

'I'll do that, Bella. I'll go and put me good togs on. Is it about the property next door?'

She screwed up her eyes as she exclaimed, 'What? You mean the cobbler's shop?'

'What else?'

She slapped his cheek playfully, saying, 'You mind your own business. Go on with you.'

After he had departed, grinning, she remained standing at the foot of the stairs: she was not looking up them, but along the passage to where the wall divided this house from the next. The cobbler's shop had been empty these past two or three months. Frankie had found that, these days, not so many people could afford to have their shoes mended, never mind buy second-hand ones, so he had put the shop on the market. Apparently there had been no buyers; well, who in their right mind would buy a place like that? But Carl had said, 'Is it about the cobbler's shop?' Oh, my God! What was she thinking? There was enough money in that cubby-hole or whatever it was to buy six cobblers' shops, she thought, then hastily reminded herself that it wasn't hers. Anyway, the idea was a good cover-up for her wanting to see Mr Travis.

She went upstairs to her room. Reenee was still on the floor, her fingers moving along the skirting board, and in this position she turned to Bella, her eyes bright, and she muttered something.

'What are you saying?' Bella said.

Reenee's fingers moved backward and forward; then again her mouth opened and, gulping in her throat, she brought out, 'Spring.'

'Oh, a spring.'

Reenee was nodding vigorously now, and she indicated the whole length of the trough and Bella said, 'Well, well,' then bitterly she repeated, 'A spring. He must have made that, the bugger; all that money there, all that time. That's what he was trying to get at just before he died. I hope where he's burning in hell now this minute he knows we've found it. Aye, *we* have. No matter who gets it we've found it. All his hidden cash that was mentioned on the back of the envelope flap,' and she repeated, 'Loose cash, indeed!'

Carl was back within half an hour. His

face was bright as he said, 'Mr Travis is a very nice gentleman. He greeted me very civilly. He said he would call upon you in the next hour and would be only too pleased to do so. Wasn't that nice of him?'

'Aye, it was. Now, don't mention to Joe or anybody else that I sent for Mr Travis, you understand?'

His face became solemn for a moment, and he said, 'Yes, Bella, I understand. And don't worry, you know me.'

Mr Travis was as good as his word, and Bella took him straight into the sitting room. Closing the door after them, she asked him to sit down, which he did, but only after she was seated. 'What can I do for you, Miss Morgan? Have you some news for me?'

'Well, in a way, I suppose you could say I have.' And she told him what they had discovered, and as she did so she watched his face lengthen and his eyebrows move upwards.

'A great deal of money?' he asked.

'I would say so, sir, a great deal. But I haven't counted it.'

He stood up. 'I am intrigued, Miss Morgan. Will you take me, please, to where you found this hoard.'

A few minutes later he was kneeling on the floor of Bella's bedroom, with Bella by his side, and Reenee standing at the far end of the room near the head of the bed. After taking up one pile of five-pound notes and straightening them out, he flipped through it quickly before turning to Bella and saying, 'You're a rich woman now, Miss Morgan. Do you know that?'

'It's not mine, sir.'

'Miss Morgan, I want to say to you'—his voice had changed—'don't be silly. This is your house, isn't it? It was left to you, and all in it.'

'But that,' she pointed down to it, 'isn't honest money.'

Here Mr Travis laughed and he said, 'It's as honest as you'll find today, Miss Morgan. Now listen to me. The only people who might lay any claim to this would be the tax man or the Customs, and they have already, through your help—oh, yes, through your help and that piece of an envelope—been able to save this country many hundreds of thousands of pounds. Oh, much more. That one signature, Jason, did so much towards clearing up what had been troubling both the Customs and the tax people for a long,

long time. There are not many people in this town with the name of Jason and who deal in pieces of glass. This Jason had been suspect for a long time but he was such a figure that no one dared put a finger on him without proof. I may tell you he was only one of a number who had to make a hasty retreat from this country, so hasty that the documents that they left condemned them. That gentleman has never yet been found, but nevertheless the powers that be remain hopeful.'

Bella looked at him in awe now, as she said, 'You found all this out by yourself?'

At this, he put his head back and laughed, 'No, Miss Morgan. But I will tell you this much. My grandfather was in the diplomatic service and an ambassador for years. I have two brothers. They are both now in the civil service. You know, there are many kinds of detectives in the civil service; my brothers are two of them. They are very ordinary-looking men, soft-voiced, but one is connected with Customs and the other with . . . oh, things along the same lines and gentlemen who, like your late master's friend, spend much time in Holland and Switzerland. We often get together, and my firm is very interested in all they have to say. Over the years we have occasionally been of help in different ways to them, through clients such as yourself, Miss Morgan, who bring into the open scoundrels such as your Mr Hamish McIntyre who, through you, led us to his friend Jason. Our firm owes you a great deal, Miss Morgan, as do my brothers. I have told them a lot about you and your business. And now we come to this.'

He pointed to the row of notes and bags on the floor, and when he saw Bella shudder he said, 'My dear Miss Morgan, you should be overjoyed.'

'I'm far from that, Mr Travis, I'm scared. I've never seen so much money in my life, and I can't believe what you say, that it belongs to me or that I can claim it, 'cos I won't know what to do with it.'

'Don't worry about that, Miss Morgan, we will deal with all that business, and to your satisfaction. The first thing we must do now is to find some place of safety for this money, at least for the moment. Have you a large holdall?'

'There is that up there.' Bella was now pointing to the top of the wardrobe. 'He used that at times.'

Mr Travis looked up at the bag. 'The very thing,' he said.

'Wait a minute, Mr Travis,' Bella put her hand on his arm. 'How am I goin' to explain to anyone, I mean the lads and . . . well, people I want to buy from, where on earth I've got . . . How much would you say there was?'

Mr Travis replied, 'I'm not sure, but at a rough guess over four thousand pounds. The sovereigns, being gold, will be of more value now than when they were purchased because the price of gold fluctuates.'

'Oh, dear God!'

'Come . . . come, sit down there, Miss Morgan,' and he pushed her gently on to the side of the bed. Then, looking straight at the figure standing stiffly against the wall, he said to Reenee, 'Don't you think, my dear, that your friend here is absolutely entitled to consider this money her own?'

To Bella's surprise, for she had swung round and looked at her, Reenee opened her mouth and said a definite, 'Yes.'

'There you are, Miss Morgan, there is confirmation, and firmly said, and from the one you say who actually found it. Now listen to me. We must think up something plausible to explain your change of fortune, but this will come later. At the present moment, we must put this money in a safe place until tomorrow morning, by which time I shall have talked the matter over with my partner. Tomorrow, Miss Morgan, I would ask you to get into your best bib and tucker and I shall take you to see him and my father. Now, let us get this money packed away.'

The following morning, Mr Travis arrived carrying a large briefcase. Bella herself had opened the door to him, and he said to her quietly, 'I thought it best, Miss Morgan, to come and help you transfer our luggage out of the house as unobtrusively as possible, because you can't carry it in that big bag. I have brought my briefcase, and between that and your shopping bag and handbag I'm sure we can get your goods from the house without any comment. What d'you say to that?'

'Yes. I was wonderin' meself how we were goin' to get it out, and I'll be glad to see the last of it.'

He laughed gently, then said, 'Well, come along and let us get on with the business.'

Half an hour later Mr Travis ushered his client into his well-appointed offices, which took up two floors of a very ordinary-looking building in a side-street off a main market piazza. He led her across the foyer, past an interested receptionist at a desk, into a lift and on to the second floor. There he was met by a tall man, who immediately relieved him of his heavy briefcase and helped him off with his coat. 'They're waiting for you in the board room, sir.'

Mr Travis had to place a firm hand between Bella's shoulders to press her forward across the carpeted hall, to a heavy oak door and into a room that smelt of leather and cigar smoke and something else to which she could not put a name.

The room seemed full of men, yet there were only four, including Mr Travis, who now took her handbag and shopping bag and laid them on the leather couch next to his briefcase, then directed her towards an armchair into which she sank. Her body seemed smaller than ever.

'This is my father, Miss Morgan.' Mr Travis directed her gaze to an old man, whose presence filled the room.

The voice that came from the chair was

more like that of somebody in his hale fifties, for it boomed at her: 'I am very pleased to make your acquaintance, Miss Morgan. Excuse me not rising. I may add that this is not the first time I have heard of you, for in the past you have been of some assistance to my family.'

What could she say to this? Nothing. She did not even smile because, as she said to herself, she was all at sea, in that lovely room, with paintings on the walls of men dressed like mayors.

'And this,' said Mr Travis, directing his hand towards the tall man sitting to Bella's left, 'is my partner and, unfortunately, my cousin,' which caused a ripple of laughter to sound round the table.

The man, standing up and bending over Bella, took her hand, saying, 'That remark is reciprocated a thousandfold, Miss Morgan. However, I must say I am more than pleased to make your acquaintance. I, too, have heard about you and the good work you do for others less fortunate.'

All Bella could find to say was, 'Thank you.'

'And this very important person, who

controls us all,' said Mr Travis now, 'is our accountant, Mr McLean.'

A small man rose from the far side of the table and came to her chair and, holding out his hand, said, 'It's an honour to meet you, Miss Morgan.' Then bending further towards her, he said, on a broad smile and in a loud whisper, 'Fortunately I am not related to the family.'

'We can thank God for that!' came the voice from the big leather chair. Again there was laughter, and Bella thought, They're just like an ordinary family.

Mr Travis now lifted his briefcase on to the table and, stooping, he picked up Bella's handbag. 'Has it only the necessary requirements in it, Miss Morgan?'

'Yes; I emptied it of all its bits and pieces.' She smiled, and he smiled back at her. Then, taking his seat close to hers, he said, 'Mr McLean will count out your little gold mine for the benefit of my father. He cannot believe that all this money was stored secretly in your house and probably would have lain there until the house was demolished if it hadn't been that you were going to give yourself a present of a carpet for the floor.'

The accountant and the other partner now began to check the money, their fingers flying over the notes so quickly that she couldn't imagine they were counting it all. When they came to the bags, the sovereigns were poured on to the table, which elicited an exclamation from the armchair: 'Well, well, well! I haven't seen so many together for years.'

At last the money was arrayed on the table piled in rows, and the accountant said, 'As the market stands now, the sovereigns would bring the amount to well over four thousand pounds; but these will rise in price, and I should imagine, once things begin to turn in the country, and they must shortly, then they could soon be worth half their value again, so it would be wise to keep them in a deposit box for the present.'

Mr Travis now took hold of Bella's hand and said, 'Please, Miss Morgan, don't look so aghast. We have had many clients in our time, but not one that shivered with the knowledge he had a little more money than he expected.'

At this her wits seemed to return and she repeated, 'A little more? That lot's too much for anybody.'

'This is what we propose to do, Miss Morgan, with your permission. We shall bank for you two thousand in safe bonds. This investment will have what you might call a proviso, meaning that should you decide to take the money out within five years you will forfeit their accumulated interest. Do you understand me?'

Bella paused for a long moment before she said, 'Just so that it's safe for five years.'

'Yes, that's a way of putting it. It's safe for five years and will eventually give you good interest. The next thousand, my accountant thinks we should use to, as he calls it, play the market when favourable. This means buying and selling shares, you understand?'

She didn't, so she just looked at him and he said, 'Well, it doesn't matter. It will mean he will try to double your money for you. Sometimes, unfortunately, he might lose some of it. How about that?'

She smiled and said, 'Well, I think,' she paused, 'we will be able to afford it.'

The laughter now was quite loud. 'Now, about the last thousand. I think this should be banked and used for your current purposes. For example, you might wish to improve your house or business.'

This she did understand, and nodded, saying, 'Yes, I was going to ask your advice on that, Mr Travis.'

'Yes?'

'Well, you see, the house next door, really it was joined on to mine, they used to be all one, and when it was divided, next door became a shoe shop. Then it went downhill and turned into an ordinary cobbler's; and now it's up for sale. I know it isn't everybody's choice, but if I could buy it I could extend my business—we have to turn a lot away most nights.'

'I think that would be a very good idea, Miss Morgan. Would you like us to see about it?'

'I would, Mr Travis.'

'Does the shoemaker still own it?'

'Yes.'

'Do you know where he lives?'

'I'm sorry, I don't.'

'Oh, well, don't worry about that, we'll find out. That'll be quite easy. Now about banking it for you,' and he turned to his father, saying, 'James has a small branch in that area, hasn't he? He could be told she has been left the money by a friend.'

'Yes, yes,' said the old man.

'Well, then, I think, Mr McLean, if you will put, say, three-quarters of this into the vault and the rest into Miss Morgan's handbag, we'll be ready to do some signing of documents and such before we go to the bank. But first, I think, we all deserve a drink, and not just coffee or tea. Would that suit you, Miss Morgan?'

She smiled. 'I never object to a gin,' she said.

Of a sudden Bella found herself relaxed and not sitting upright in the middle of her chair but leaning back. She had never experienced anything like this in her life and she knew she never would again. Well, she would be able to tell Reenee all about it, but would the lass be able to take it in? And how could she expect her to when she herself could hardly take it in?

The old man was speaking to her now, and she had to quell her thoughts to give him her full attention. He was saying, 'You have given us a very interesting morning, Miss Morgan. I know quite a bit about secret drawers and hidden hoards. You see, before he died, one of my sons was captain of a ship—and the stories he told of what sailors got up to below decks in order to smuggle in gold!

'Henry, my son, actually showed me some of the places in his ship which had been carved out, and so skilfully that at times they fooled the Customs. But Arthur there tells me that this trough under the lino was a work of art. The lino, I gather, was just a shield to cover a three-inch wide trough, fully lined with kid. He said that whoever contrived it must have been an expert in this particular field. The lengths to which some people will go to acquire riches!'

'Ah!' exclaimed Mr Travis. 'Here's Tom with our life-savers.' After handing one to Bella he then passed glasses round to the others. And when he raised his own the other men followed suit, and with him said, 'Cheers, Miss Morgan.' Then he added, 'And to a successful business life ahead of you.'

Looking at the half-filled glass of gin, Bella said, 'Thank you, Mr Travis. Thank you all,' and she nodded to each in turn; 'but I know I shall not be able to start on a business career for some time if I now drink all this.'

Oh, they were nice people. But no; she wouldn't drink it all, because she didn't want to go home under the influence, as it were. She had a lot to tell them, and plans to make, plans that would affect them all, and for the better. She would see to that.

11

Two nights later Bella got her little band together in the kitchen and told them of her
plans. She was buying the house next door
and opening it up into hers, but before anything could be done with it it must be thor-
oughly cleared out. Her solicitor had
suggested that she should get an architect
to design the best way of altering the cellar
floor and the yard. That would take in more
people than she really intended, but she had
told Mr Travis that they themselves were so
full of ideas that she would put it to them
first, to see what they thought could be
done.

With the exception of Carl, they had all
gaped at her. 'Have you come into a fortune,
Bella?'

'No,' she replied politely, 'but I have found

an oil well,' which caused them all to laugh, but self-consciously. Then she told them a tale of having been left, quite unexpectedly, a few hundred pounds by someone she had helped years ago and had never thought to hear from again. It showed you there were good people in the world. But this was the point: she hadn't money to throw away but she had enough to alter that house next door into something like this one; anyway, it would enable her to provide for more men off the street.

'I was advised to have a look at that place along the river that is run by the council,' she told them. 'The mattresses there are on raised platforms. They also have a row of single rooms which are taken by the week by men who are in some kind of work but haven't a house or flat to go to.'

'Aye,' put in John now. 'We tried to get in there one night, but it was full. The beds might be on platforms, but there's no big fire in the room, nor do they get soup and breakfast, and they still charge a shilling a head. But you can have a wash and a shower for that too.'

'And are those rooms really let as private rooms and just for men?'

'I wouldn't know anything about that,' said John.

At this they were all quite startled when Reenee made a sound in her throat and, pointing to herself, nodded.

'You know about them, Reenee,' said Carl now, 'about the rooms?'

Again she nodded.

'You stayed there?'

Her head drooped and she raised one finger. 'For one night?'

Again her head gave a slight movement.

'What were they like? I mean, how big? How many of them?'

'Give her a chance,' said Joe. Then, 'Do you want a pencil and paper, Reenee?'

She looked up at him and nodded. He went to the mantelpiece and took from it Bella's shopping list and a pencil, and when he laid them before her she turned the pad longways, then drew a long line, which she then made into ten divisions, causing Willie to ask softly, 'Those are rooms?'

She did not look at him but her head moved again, and now it was John who asked, 'How big are they, miss?'

She looked at him and thought, then pointed from the fireplace to the middle of the table; and it was Carl who got up and measured the distance, saying, 'About ten feet long?' She nodded. Then he asked, 'How wide?'

She had to think again, then pointed to the fireplace and the front of the table; and again he measured and said, 'About eight feet?'

It was John who now put in, 'Ten by eight . . . really, not bad.'

'What was in the room?' asked Bella. And at this Reenee turned over a page of the notebook and quickly drew what looked like a bed; then to the side of it a drawing of what could only be a small chest of drawers, and between that and the end of the wall, she drew a line perpendicular to the wall, with a hook on the further side; and John immediately said, 'A place for hanging up your clothes in the corner between the walls?'

Reenee nodded brightly at him. Lastly, she pointed to the wall to the side of the chest of drawers and drew a rectangle. Joe exclaimed, 'A mirror! We haven't got one in our room, have we? That's something that will have to be seen to,' which caused Tony to bark at him, 'Don't be so bloody dim, man. Everybody doesn't want to look at their face.'

Quietly, Carl put in, 'It's all right. I see my face every day in the shop windows. Don't worry, Joe.'

'I didn't mean nowt,' stammered Joe.

'I know you didn't, you great big fathead, so shut up,' said Carl, who then turned to Reenee, saying, 'What about if women came in like you? Were you in a different section?'

She now put up three fingers, which said to them that there had been three rooms for women.

'But what about if they weren't filled?' asked Willie now.

There was a quirk to Reenee's lips as she looked back at Willie, and she put her finger across her top lip, which indicated a mustache.

And he laughed and said, 'They were given to the men?'

She nodded. Then, as practical as ever, Andy said, 'Where did they wash, miss? Not in the men's place?'

She shook her head, then wrote along the edge of the paper, 'Small room off;' and

Andy said, 'There was a washbowl in the small place?'

She smiled from one to the other as she demonstrated washing her face; and now, turning over the paper, she drew a small circle with a sort of chain through it, and next to it she wrote soap.

'They chained up the soap?' Carl said in surprise.

She nodded vigorously; then swiftly her hand moved down the table and, picking up the knife and a small piece of bread, she proceeded to cut pieces off each corner until there was hardly anything left in the middle.

The room was filled with laughter, and there was a sound in her throat that might also have been laughter.

'Good for them,' said John. 'They cut pieces off it?' She nodded to him, but as she did so Bella thought, I don't think she was laughing the night she was there, poor soul. She put out a hand and placed it over Reenee's.

They looked at each other, and it was as if Reenee was reading Bella's mind because the smile went from her face and there was a silence in the room. Then, as if to break the tension, Carl said, 'How long did they leave the lights on? Right through the place, I mean.'

At this she lifted up one finger and he said, 'One hour? After closing?'

She nodded.

'They weren't givin' much away,' said Tony.

Bella broke in, saying in a firm voice, 'Well, lass, once again you've given us a pattern to work on. What d'you say, boys?'

The chorus was general and loud, 'Oh, yes, yes. We could get ten rooms across the bottom of that yard; but of course they would mean extra latrine and washin'-up places.'

'But how're we goin' to provide the soap?' Joe put in.

'They won't need to steal,' said Bella; 'there'll be ha'penny pieces of soap, and it won't be blue-mottled any more. That in future will only be used for the floors, which goes for indoors too.' She was nodding towards Willie now. 'But let's get down to facts. If the place is goin' to provide for twice as many people as we already cater for, then the six of you can't work it all alone. I've been thinking about it, and you, Joe, can give up most of your job now. And I'll put you on the same rate as the others. We mightn't be able to get much more on the cheap, but you never know, so you can still remain good friends with the warehouse people. Also, it'll be your job to see to the vegetables for both places. Get them from the market as you usually do, then it's up to you to clean them and chop them, be-cause Reenee, here, has had enough of that, I think,' to which Reenee shook her head, but Bella went on, 'I know what's best, lass, and I feel that you would very much like to help Willie with pastry and bread-making and things. Now, wouldn't you?'

Reenee was looking at Willie now, and he at her, and he said, 'I'd love to have you help me, Reenee.' And at this she lowered her head a little and nodded twice.

Bella said, 'Well, that part's settled. Now there's you, Carl. I know you like your walk-about, and you could still do it for a couple of hours a day, but the rest I'd like you to give up for me. Although you can't cook like Willie, you can make broth, which could be done in the new kitchen. Besides which you could help with the cleanin' up of the rooms and the outbuildings. But now, you other three, Andy, Tony and John. You can't see to everything and I can tell you there'll be much more work to be done than you imagine, so I'm going to employ two young fellows who wouldn't mind doin' the dirty work of the wash-houses and keepin' the yards clean. You other three'll have your work cut out with practically rebuildin' that place next door. From the little I've seen of it, it's goin' to take time and hard labour. I'll start you all off on a pound a week, and we'll wait and see how business goes. The better it goes the more your wage will go up; and when you're thinkin' of a pound a week, it might seem very small compared with what you used to make in the shipyards and places like that, but don't forget you've got board and lodgings.' And she laid stress on these last words. 'Your quarters might've been just a wash-house, but now it's as good as any house.'

'You're right there,' said Andy, a sentiment the others echoed.

'As for the two other residents,' Bella now looked from Joe to Carl, 'I really think they should pay rent for their accommodation, rooms to themselves with every convenience. Tut-tut. I'm too soft-hearted, that's me.'

They were all laughing now, and it was Joe who paid another of his rough and rare compliments, saying, 'You said that in fun, Bella, but it's right in earnest.'

12

And so on these lines began Bella's new business, which was to prosper and keep them all happy in the years that followed. That period lasted until a name became known to every individual in the western world and beyond—Adolf Hitler. War was declared on 3 September 1939, and London became a scene of activity: trains, buses, all kinds of vehicles were filled with children and families to get them away from the danger zone, because it was feared that London would be the main target for air raids. But it was not until almost a year later that London was first bombed.

When that happened, Bella found she could hardly cope with the nightly inrush of families, trying to find shelter from the heavy bombing. They would make their way down to the two large basement sleeping rooms that were considered safest because they were below ground level. Many of the families hadn't parted with their children at the beginning, while others had children who had returned, having found that they didn't like either the country or the people with whom they had been boarded. Often one of Bella's mattresses, all of which lay now on high wooden frames, would have to hold three children, with their mother lying on the floor beside them. Many openly welcomed this rescue place rather than go down into the underground stations or government-built shelters.

Bella had little fear of losing any of her men in the call-up because even the youngest among them was well over thirty-five years old. But they all signed up for civilian service in the Fire Brigade or as fire-watchers and, with the work they did for Bella, they were kept busy for never less than twelve hours a day. As for food, at first there had been no worries, because vegetables were still plentiful. By 1940, however, rationing had come in. Each person was allotted a booklet that entitled him or her to have a small amount each week of meat, tea, sugar, butter, bread, bacon, eggs and sweets, maybe small amounts but nevertheless fair to all. Vegetables became scarcer and dearer. If a night visitor to Bella's wanted fat on his bread, he had to provide it. Nevertheless, even if the broth was a little thinner and was seasoned by bones alone, it was always more than welcome to every occupant of a mattress. The tea in the morning was a different thing. Boiling water was plentiful, but there was no longer free tea and sugar.

A change had come over Reenee during this time. Although she still could not bear to be near strange men, she spent hours helping mothers with fractious children; and Bella noticed that, just as she had once hugged the old bear to her, now she hugged a child, while making a humming sound in her throat. So much had she changed in this way that Bella wouldn't have been surprised if, of a sudden, she had got her memory back, though she herself dreaded the idea of it.

Also to Bella's amazement, she seemed to enjoy the singing, especially when the four original band members got together and rattled out not only tunes from the old days, but also modern ones, especially funny ones like 'Kiss Me Goodnight Sergeant Major, Tuck Me in My Little Wooden Bed'. If Reenee could have laughed, Bella knew she would, and then wondered if she was able to laugh inside.

It took only one small incident to change all this. Reenee was near the door one night, where she had been seeing to a woman and her children who were sitting on a mattress. The small band was going out and Willie said, 'Did you enjoy it?' and Reenee was nodding to him and smiling, when one of the husbands who had come in from the outside pulled her round and grabbed at her coat, saying, 'Why the hell must you always wear that dirty black nightgown? It spoils the look of the place!'

That he was half drunk was no excuse, but before he knew where he was Andy's big fist had caught him under the chin and levelled him. Then the others dragged him from the room and to the gate and threw him outside.

By this time, away from the hubbub, Bella was assisting Reenee up the main staircase into her room, saying, 'There now . . . there, lass. He was drunk. He meant no harm, not really, he was drunk. Don't tremble so, lass. You're all right.'

In the bedroom, Reenee threw herself on the bed and, putting her hands behind her head, gripped the iron rails of the bedhead while her body stiffened and her middle began its old form of jerking up and down.

'Oh, my God!' wailed Bella. 'You've not had one of these for years! If I had him here I'd kill him meself, and not only him, but also the one who first caused you to go on like this.' And now she put a hand under Reenee's back and the other one on her stomach and tried to still the movement. But, just as she had found before, this only seemed to accentuate the motion, until Reenee suddenly let go of the railings and her body crumpled into a heap inside the old coat.

'It's all right, my love. It's all right.' Bella was holding her and stroking her face, which was wet with tears.

That's new, Bella thought. She had never seen Reenee cry like this: her eyes had always become wet, but now the tears were raining down her cheeks. Bella muttered, 'Oh, that swine! There's always somebody to spoil things. Don't worry, love. Don't worry. You'll not see him again, I can assure you of that.'

But no matter how she tried on this night she couldn't get Reenee to take off the coat; so she took off her shoes, covered her over with a blanket and said, 'I'm off downstairs, love, to make a hot drink. Now, you'll be all right.'

Bella wasn't surprised to see the six men down there in the kitchen waiting for her; and it was Carl who said, 'Has she had one of her turns?'

'Aye,' said Bella; 'the first in God knows how long. I had thought she was finished with them.'

'A bad one?'

'Yes, very bad. She's cried as I've never seen her cry before. But go on now, the lot of you, and thank you for coming up. But don't worry, I'll get her round again. I only know this, if it wasn't for the few married couples that come in together, I would see that the men kept to the room in the basement of the other house and the women to the one in this house.'

'It could be done,' said John. 'Most of the fellows are either in the Army or the Air Force or at sea. Others are on night shift and sleep in the houses during the day. We could give it a try.'

'Oh, well, I don't want to disturb them,' said Bella. 'They've got a lot to put up with, especially those with kids. Leave it; she'll likely have come round by the morning . . .'

Reenee didn't come round in the morning, or the next day, or the next: she got up and sat huddled in her coat near the window of her bedroom. It was on the third day that she went down into the kitchen, where Willie greeted her as if nothing had happened, saying as she took her place at the table, 'I don't know what we'll do, Reenee, if they ration flour. I'd hate to have to cut out the bread, wouldn't you?'

She looked at him and he looked back at her. There was an expression in her eyes that he hadn't seen there for a long, long time. He couldn't put a name to it, only that she looked lost.

No amount of talking, all the kind messages sent up with Bella from down below by the regular patrons that they hoped her cold would soon be better because they missed her, left any impression on her. She just looked at Bella, then went on with what she was doing. The patrons of what was called Bella's Pad all looked upon the poor lass as being a bit simple, not quite right in the head, but kindly nevertheless; and a number of the mothers did miss her, especially her attention to the youngest members of their families.

The air raids on London were renewed after the Luftwaffe had finished off, as they thought, the fighter airfields on the edge of the city. The four members of the band were now all fire-watchers, helping the air-raid wardens. Andy and Tony were generally on together, as were John and Willie in their turn. Each pair had their own area. It was left to Joe and Carl to see to the patrons of Bella's houses on nights when they were free of their own duties. This meant keeping watch on the gates until they were closed at eight o'clock; then, with the help of some of the regulars, distributing the bowls of soup and newly baked bread, on which each person would gladly put his own margarine or jam. Afterwards one or the other would go outside to be on fire-watch for the area.

Generally, the first siren would indicate a coming raid sufficiently early for people to take cover. But this night there was no time after the wail of the siren ended and the thunder of bombs shook the house, penetrating to the pads. Bella had been sitting in the kitchen with Reenee, who could not be persuaded to go down the stairs into the basement again.

That the bombing was quite close was evident, and Bella put her arms around Reenee and held her. She was amazed that Reenee's body was not shaking with fear as hers was. In fact, it was Reenee who put her hand on Bella's head and stroked her hair back from her brow, making sounds of sympathy in her throat.

When daylight came to London the next morning it showed the first horrors of many more to come: houses still burning, whole streets laid flat like fallen packs of cards.

The men were disturbed that Bella now had to sit out the raids with Reenee upstairs when there was more protection in the two basement rooms underground. It wasn't until Willie got the idea of getting an Anderson shelter and putting it near the gate of the yard that Bella's trouble was eased, because without any demur Reenee would go out of the front door, along the street, through the gate and into the shelter, which had been made as comfortable as such places could be.

They had arranged two separate bunks and a little calor-gas stove on which they could boil a kettle for a cup of tea. Also there were tins holding buns and biscuits, though they never seemed to eat them. There wasn't much singing done downstairs either, these days, not since Dunkirk when the remains of the British Expeditionary Force were taken off the shores of France on 3 June 1940. One young woman's husband had died of his wounds on the rescue boat coming over to England, and another's husband had been rescued from the Dunkirk beach only to be drowned when the small boat in which he was being taken to a Navy frigate was bombed.

Every now and again Mr Travis would visit Bella, but these days he was a sad man, for his two nephews, both in the Navy, had died when their ships had been torpedoed in the Atlantic while shepherding convoys of merchant ships from America.

Bella could offer little comfort; she could only take his hand and pat it. And now he said, 'I shouldn't be talking to you like this, my dear, you who've had such a rough time of your own, so much to put up with . . .'

'Oh, Mr Travis, I feel I've had nothing but luck in my life since I was fourteen. Although I hated working for Mr McIntyre, it was by luck that I came to do it, and I was very lucky then to meet you. And I look back and think what my life would have been without my dear Reenee; and there again you come into it, for not another man in your business would have guided me so honestly through that side. Had it not been for you, I know now that I couldn't have let myself claim that money. I would have been afraid. But your advice and that of your family has made me comfortable for the rest of my days, and through that I have been able to make many others comfortable too. And you know, Mr Travis, I'm going to say this, I look upon you as a friend.'

'Oh,' he said, 'then I am honoured, Miss Morgan, that you should think so of me. But what we have done for you is nothing to what you have for others and particularly for one of my brothers, and, incidentally, for the country at large.' And when, later, they shook hands at the front door, it was as close friends they parted, he promising to look in again soon, and she telling him how welcome he would be.

The war went on and so did the bombing. Many patrons of Bella's Pad had lost their homes; some had also lost relatives. But nothing so serious touched Bella and her little family till one night in 1943. The sirens had gone, the shelters were full, the bombs were dropping, the fires were blazing, and the raid seemed never-ending. At last the All Clear sounded, and some settled down to sleep while others got up to go and see if their homes were still standing.

Down in the Anderson shelter Bella was sitting on the edge of her lower bunk. She had a strange worried feeling on her. All the lads were out: Andy, Tony, John and Willie were all fire-watching; Joe was now with an ambulance team, and Carl was doing his turn in the communications office of the Fire Brigade.

Bella waited until the autumn dawn broke before she left the shelter and made her way along to the wash-house. There were no lights on in there, so she went back to the shelter and said to Reenee that she was going indoors. Reenee, too, got up. She had been sleeping in her coat, so she pulled a scarf round her head and went out and upstairs with Bella.

Bella had thought she might find either Joe or Carl indoors but there was no one.

At seven o'clock, when not one of her lads had returned, she said to Reenee, who was making tea, 'I've an awful feeling on me that something's happened. They always come straggling back, but so far there's not one of them in.'

It was as she sat drinking the tea that Joe and Carl came slowly up the stairs and into the kitchen. They were both covered with dust and looked utterly weary.

Immediately Bella was on her feet. 'Had a bad night?'

Neither man spoke, and she demanded, 'What is it? What's happened?'

'There's bad news, Bella,' Carl muttered.

'Bad news! Who?'

It was Joe now who said briefly, 'Andy.'

'Oh, no! Not Andy!'

Neither of them spoke; and Bella, her face blanched, turned to look at Reenee who had dropped into a chair and laid her head on her folded arms on the table. Bella wanted to go to her and say, Don't have another turn, for God's sake, not now, but she couldn't speak. After a moment she turned again to Carl: 'Is he dead?'

'Yes. From what Tony tells me, the house next door had had a direct hit, and this one was on fire. There was a woman screaming, and he went in. He must have got to her because after the house collapsed they were found together. Joe was helping with the injured'—he thumbed towards Joe— 'but nothing could be done. Tony was there. His hands were burnt. John and Willie had been directed there, and arrived as they were taking the bodies to'—he gulped and choked before he went on—'the mortuary. Tony went to the dressing-station, he wouldn't go to hospital. The three of them are now back in the house,' he tilted his head towards the wash-house, 'but I'd leave them, Bella, for a bit; they . . . they're so cut up. You see, they weren't just like Joe and me here, odd bods, they were more like a family, like brothers. They'd been through a lot together.'

It was a strange feeling for Bella. She felt she couldn't cry, yet she wanted to do something like scream or throw something, break something. In this moment she realised that as Reenee was like a daughter to her, those six fellows were like the sons she had never had, and that the one who had laid bricks, built walls and, although not the cleverest of the four, seemed to lead the band, would not return home again.

Andrew Anderson was buried four days later. The only mourners were his adoptive family, with the exception of Reenee who had not offered to attend and to whom no one had suggested it.

The amazing thing to all of them was that not one of his relatives had come from Wales. They had fully expected his wife to put in an appearance, but no. Carl had written to tell her that Andy had died, but did not receive a reply, although he had written on the back of it, 'If undelivered return to sender'.

After the ceremony, when they returned to the house, they found that Reenee had set out the tea table in the sitting room. She had brought out the new china tea service Bella had bought for herself before the war, and the table was set with bread and butter, corned-beef sandwiches, and a plate of Willie's buns, made with liquid paraffin, which

Willie had discovered was a good substitute for fat.

'Oh, that's nice of you, lass,' Bella said, and the men nodded their approval. What conversation there was among the six of them at the table touched only on their inability to understand how a wife and two daughters could ignore the fact that their husband and father had died saving someone from a burning house.

'Now she can get married,' Tony said bitterly. 'She'll be living with the fellow anyway.'

'He never said anything about her from the day he came back that time, did he?' Willie put in quietly. 'And I don't think he ever wrote to her again.'

'That's no excuse,' said John; 'those lasses could have sent a note, if not his wife.'

Bella put in quietly, 'He's goin' to be missed in more ways than one. D'you want to take on somebody else?'

The chorus came, 'No, Bella, we'll manage.'

'Anyway,' said John, 'we couldn't stand another fellow in his place. We'll manage, at least for a time. Don't worry, Bella; we'll rearrange things.'

'How nice it was of that Mr Travis to send that holly wreath,' Carl said, to which Bella replied, 'He's a good man, is Mr Travis, and a gentleman.'

To everyone's surprise, and Bella's most of all, Reenee went downstairs that night, for the first time in months, to help the mothers with their children. Life went on and so did the war.

The men were often asked by the 'patrons' to play again, but since Andy's death they hadn't done so.

London was bombed continually; there was hardly a district that didn't show skeleton houses or streets of rubble. Coventry had been laid flat, and many other cities, among them Liverpool and Plymouth, had been terribly damaged; more ships were sunk; food became scarcer; it looked as if the war would never end. Yet there were towns that never experienced a raid; others where a single plane had attacked, such as the one at Hereford that dropped a bomb near the munitions factory there. The spirit that prevailed over the whole nation, led by their great wartime Prime Minister Winston Churchill, was amazing.

When American troops arrived in England, Bella said many girls and women, who should have known better, seemed to go mad; and all done under the guise of making the men feel at home . . .

Then one day, 6 June 1944, an invasion fleet ferried armies of many nations across the Channel, and over the following months defeated the Germans in territories they had occupied: France, Holland, Belgium and Scandinavia. At last the Allies were winning, but at a terrible price.

It wasn't until 8 May 1945 that the slaughter in Europe came to an end. They called the day it was celebrated VE Day. The British, the Russians, the Americans and the French had won, and there began the huge task of reconstruction. In the meantime there were still the Japanese to defeat. One day a pilot dropped a bomb and devastated a Japanese city and everyone in it in one terrible flash. Now the war really was over, though the age of the atomic bomb had arrived.

13

On the day the war ended in Europe almost everyone in England danced in the streets—they'd all gone through so much together. Now it was over, though there were many who mourned that they no longer had anyone with whom to dance.

Bella's two rooms and the yard saw their share of gaiety and dancing: the boys even got their band together again and played jigs and waltzes and all the songs that were asked for . . .

But joy is an emotion that cannot be held. Normality flowed back: there were houses to rebuild and repair; there were jobs to find. Not every man returning from service life found that his old job was open to him: new hands had been taken on; women had taken men's places in many factories and were doing the work for less pay.

Bella expected that soon her beds would no longer be needed, and she talked this over with the boys. 'Wait and see,' they said. 'There are the single rooms, they are always booked up. Young fellows starting in jobs again are finding staying in those rooms is cheaper than going into digs or living with relatives. As for the beds, there'll always be tramps on the road,' to which Bella had whipped back, 'I don't want tramps, not real tramps. You lot weren't tramps: down-and-outs, yes, but there's a difference. The others do it from choice.'

'Don't worry, Bella,' they said; 'just leave it for a time. As long as you can keep us on, we're satisfied.'

'Oh, lads, I can keep you on. I can promise you that. If it comes to a push we could turn all of next door into single rooms.'

'You're right there, Bella.'

For about six months or so after the war the beds were indeed fully occupied, mostly by single men who could not find any cheaper or better place in which to kip than Bella's, so for a while they were kept busy. When things did begin to slacken off, the men cleared out the large room next door and redecorated it; then set about not only redecorating the latrines and wash-basins but tiling them. By 1947 the business was showing a big drop in those who needed a single night's kip; so it was decided, starting next door, to convert all of the downstairs into double rooms. And in each of these was to be the luxury of a wash-basin.

People had believed that rationing would end, at least by a year after the war had finished, but no, it went on, as did the black market.

And life went on in Bella's Pad according to the same pattern until 1950. Bella was now sixty years old, and feeling her age. Her boys, as she still called them, were in their fifties. Perhaps Joe and Carl were a little younger, and Reenee, she imagined, was about fifty. Bella had never been able to find out her real age when she first came to her. She guessed Reenee had been twenty-nine or thirty. Strangely, her face hadn't seemed to alter, perhaps because of its fine bone formation; but the skin was tighter and paler. But what did worry Bella at times about her dear girl, as she still thought of her, was the habit she now had of sitting for hours staring ahead. Sometimes she would blink rapidly and press her lips tightly together, as one does when trying to remember or recall something. And another thing, too, was worrying: she was eating less. Her body, Bella thought, really looked like a skeleton underneath those clothes. In the winter she'd had to call in Dr Harle again because Reenee's chest was so bad, but although Reenee tolerated him she still did not look at him unless she was forced to.

Dr Harle had not said anything to Bella about his patient seeing a doctor who could deal with her mind, but she knew that Mr Travis must have had a talk with him. It was odd, she thought, that the only man with whom her girl seemed completely relaxed was Carl. At times, she would give her hand to him, or pat his sleeve gently. These were times, Bella noticed, after she herself had scolded Carl when he had been out for longer than the two-hour walk-about, as he called it. Once she had said to him, 'One of these days you'll get done over by the vil-lains. You'll push your nose in so far that they'll see you or guess at it.' And it was at times like this that Reenee seemed to show

concern for the small man with the disfigured face . . .

World events, even events in London, did
not seem to penetrate the quiet routine and
placidity of the life that went on at numbers
10 and 12 The Jingles. That was until 1955,
when something took place that altered
their lives for good.

It was a simple incident and it happened
to Carl. He no longer played his flute in the
street, but he continued to keep his eyes
open, and once or twice had earned a few
pounds from the police. But on that day he
wasn't looking around for the smallest detail
that might have a bearing on something big-
ger, because a severe wind was blowing and
he had his head bent and his cap pulled
down over his brow.

He was walking along a residential street
in which there were a few shops, a large
public house and a hotel. A number of vehicles lined up along the kerb were deliver-
ing goods to different establishments, and
he was both surprised and shocked when
he found himself tripping face forward over
a hatchway, and then, still face forward, slid-
ing down into a cellar, there to hit his head
against a barrel, which knocked him into

blackness. He came round to a voice say-ing, 'What the hell's going on here?' and an-other voice that seemed to come from above, shouting, 'The silly bugger fell over the hatch. Is he out?'

'Aye, I'd say he's out. You don't hit your head on a barrel and say "hello".'

Another voice from somewhere said, 'Give him a drink of beer.' And the answer to this was, 'Don't be a bloody fool, I can't tap a hogshead down here. Go an' get a mug of water—that'll bring him round.'

He was round; he was lying with one side of his face flat on the stone floor, but his legs still seemed to be in the air. Someone took him by the shoulders and pulled him forward, and then, slowly, he opened his eyes and looked along what seemed to be a stone passage lined with barrels and, at the end of it, two men working. One of them yelled, 'What's all the commotion about?'

The answer came, 'This idiot's slipped down the chute. He's out for the count.'

Carl gave no sign that he wasn't out for the count; he had come round, but his eyes were fixed on the two men beyond the bar-rels, from one of which they were pulling things. He could see only half the barrel and the back of one man, and the things he was pulling from the barrel had wooden handles. But the light from a window caught the gleam from what must have been a metal tube attached to the handle. First one handle, then another came out before a voice above his head bawled, 'Get that bloody lot back! He'll be round in a minute.'

The barrel was pulled out of view and the other man disappeared with it. He now gave a gasp as some cold water drenched his face and head and a voice said, 'That's done it. He's round all right. Sit him up.'

They sat him up, but he kept his eyes closed. 'You all right, chum?'

He didn't answer, only put his hand to his head as if it were aching, and it was. The man said, 'What d'you mean by taking a slide down the barrel roll, eh?'

Still with one hand on his head, Carl said, 'I think I've hurt me ankle.'

'Well, let's get you to your feet and see.'

When Carl limped towards the bottom of the chute the man said, 'Can't see much wrong with it. Can't be sprained, else you wouldn't be able to put it down. Well, now you're goin' out the way you come in. Lie

on that board and stretch your arms upwards. Bill!' he yelled. 'Give him a hand out.'

Carl did as he was ordered. He lay face-
down on the slippery board, stretched his
hands upwards and found them gripped;
then his feet were pushed, and the next minute he was hauled into the street, with one
of the men holding him, a man with red hair,
saying, 'D'you walk about with your eyes
closed?' And then, looking at him closely,
he said, 'I know you. You're Pimple Face,
the whistle player. Haven't seen you about
for ages.'

Carl took a deep breath before he said,
'Lost me wind.'

A bellow came from the cellar: 'Get on
with it up there. What d'you think we're
waitin' for?'

The man who had been speaking to him
gave Carl a slight push and said, 'Well, get
on your way and keep your eyes open in
future.'

Carl got on his way. He had hurt his ankle
but he hurried on until he reached the house
where he told Bella of how he had tumbled
down into a beer cellar because he hadn't
looked where he was going. He made no
mention of what he had seen in that cellar.

But the next day, although he was still limping, he went out against Bella's protests for
his usual walk-about. This time he took a
different direction. It was towards a police
station; but he didn't go in, he went straight
past it, and stood on the kerb about twenty
yards away. Presently, a police car drew up
outside the station and the policeman who
got out happened to glance first one way,
then the other down the street before he
went in. A few minutes later, as Carl was
walking slowly back and about to pass the
station door, it opened and out came the
policeman as if he had timed Carl's arrival.
Carl, looking up at him, said, 'Nice day.'

'It all depends what you're doing,' the policeman answered.

Carl smiled, he even laughed, but as he
did so he said, under his breath, 'Number
six Boar's Head, very important.' Then he
added, 'Aye, it all depends what you're doing. At present I'm limping because I've got
a bad ankle.'

'Get along with you!' said the policeman,
then got into the car, and Carl got along.

But that evening, after saying he felt like
a pint, he went out again and along to the
Boar's Head. He sat on a bench near the

wall some distance from the counter and sipped at his beer. The bar was full and the men were standing about in groups. He had almost reached the bottom of his mug when a man plumped down beside him. He was holding a pint mug in his hand, and after taking a drink from it he said, 'That's better. What a day! All sixes and sevens. There are days like that, you know, when nothing seems to go right.'

'Yeah, I agree with you.' Carl had to raise his voice above the din of the room as he added, 'I've had one like that meself.' Then he muttered, 'Fell down into a cellar yesterday, wasn't lookin' where I was goin', knocked meself out for a minute or so, and then I saw something interesting.' His voice dropped to a whisper. 'I'd hit a barrel with me head and they thought I was knocked out and went to get water to bring me round.'

His partner interrupted, saying loudly, 'D'you want another?'

'No. No, thanks. I can't see you getting to the counter for the next fifteen minutes or so and I must be off.'

Then he went on, under his breath, 'The Phoenix cellar, unloadin' guns from a barrel, what looked like a beer barrel the same as the rest. The delivery lorry was from the QX Breweries.'

The man sitting next to him took a long drink from his mug, then said, 'Did they spot you?'

'No, I was supposed to be out. They brought me round by throwing water over me. Then they pushed me up and out the way I had dropped in.'

'You're sure of this?' The voice was very low and Carl answered, 'Beer hasn't wooden handles and steel pipes on the end.'

'Sure you won't have another pint?' said the man.

'No thanks; I've got to get back. I hurt me ankle yesterday and it's still givin' me gyp. Be seein' you sometime.'

'Yeah.'

Carl pushed his way through the crowd; then made his way back to The Jingles, knowing as he did so that this time he had unearthed something very worthwhile.

It was about three weeks later when there were reports in most of the papers that the police had caught a gang of arms smugglers, and that a naval patrol boat had stopped a cargo vessel. When it had been searched, the holds had contained what were supposed to be barrels of beer but were full of guns. Twelve men had been arrested. These included the manager of a private brewery and the owner of a hotel and public bar. The police were still looking for four men wanted for questioning in this affair.

Well, well. Carl had preened inwardly; he had really done something at last! What he had seen was gun-running all right.

He said nothing to anyone, but waited anxiously for the trial. They had caught three of the other suspects, who were now being held in custody, but the fourth was still to be found. Previously, two other suspects had had to be released for lack of evidence to hold them.

So important was the case that the result of the trials, three months later, again filled the front pages of the newspapers. Two of the ring-leaders were each given ten years. Of the others, sentences ranged from six to five years.

That night Carl sat on the form at the end of the bar and sipped at his pint. He wasn't a regular at this bar, but he was recognised as dropping in now and again, and the barman would have a word with him.

As usual, it was full, and after a while a man looking for a seat came and sat on the end of the form. He gave a long sigh, and said. 'Another day over; all sixes and sevens.'

To this Carl remarked lightly, 'But there's always a silver lining.'

His companion laughed and said under his breath, 'It could be gold in this case.'

It was a promise, and it warmed Carl and confirmed that he had at last done something big.

After draining his mug, the man said quietly, 'Bob's tea stall Monday, round eleven.'

Then he rose slowly and said. 'Be seeing you.'

Carl went on sipping at his mug of beer, which was only half full. It wasn't so much the money he was pleased about, although he wouldn't turn his nose up at it, it was the appreciation he had heard in the man's voice.

This was Friday night. He'd have the weekend to get over, and it would be a good weekend, a happy weekend. He'd take in a few bottles for the lads then play cards with them.

He left the bar and walked along the street. There were two blocks before he'd have to turn into The Jingles, and these he could walk blindly, even on a black night like this.

He had reached the turning when a car drew up slowly at the pavement, and its lights brought his head up. A man had got out and was now standing in front of him. He couldn't make him out, but he said, 'What is it? What d'you want?'

'Oh, we just want a chat, Mr Spotty Face. You don't remember me, do you?'

The man now pulled him to where the light was shining from inside the car, and Carl, who felt his guts turn into a knot, was looking up into the face of the red-haired man who had pulled him out of the cellar and had recognised him as once playing the whistle on the streets. 'Remember me now?'

Carl could not answer, and the man said, 'Well, it doesn't matter, chum, does it? Because you won't remember very much after this.' Carl found himself heaved up bodily and thrust into the back of the car, which immediately moved off swiftly. Another man was already seated in the car, and he said, 'Hello, chum. Did you enjoy your chat with the disguised copper? We hope you did, because it'll be the last enjoyment you'll ever know,' and immediately Carl felt a blow first to one side of his head, then to the other, and hazily heard a voice saying from somewhere in the distance, which might have been the front seat, 'Leave him be until we get him there.'

And that's all Carl ever remembered.

Bella was angry. She looked at the clock again, then said to Joe, 'It's eleven o'clock. He's never been out as late as this before. Where d'you think he's got to?'

'If I knew, Bella, I'd tell you; and I've told you afore that all he said to me was that he was goin' along for a pint. He'd be only half an hour or so, he said, and I didn't say to him, like I've wanted to many a time when he's been goin' along for that pint, that if he wanted a pint so badly we would get a few bottles in. But, Bella, you know . . . well, you know yourself, he's still doin' that other business.'

'Yes; and that's what I'm frightened of.

He'll do it once too often and it'll get him . . . Oh, dear God! Where is he?' She turned to Reenee, who was sitting by the table. There was an anxious look on her face and she pointed, first at Joe, then to her eye, and he said, 'I'm pickin' up her meanin', Bella. But where would we start to look, Reenee?'

'Anywhere,' Bella said irritably now. She did not add, 'He's likely lying in some back lane,' but she went on, 'Go and wake the lads and tell them what's happened. Then go to the bar and ask what time Carl left.'

'Aye, I could do that . . .'

Two hours later the men were in the kitchen. Nobody they had spoken to had seen Carl. The barman said he did not know at what time he had left, because the bar had been full and he hadn't noticed him going.

'Should we phone the police?' said Tony.

'I wouldn't,' said John. 'If anything's happened they'll find out soon enough; they generally do. In the meantime he might come staggering in.'

They didn't go to bed until three o'clock and Carl hadn't come staggering in; and when they all met in the kitchen again the following morning, Bella said, 'They've got him. God knows where he is, likely in the river. One thing I feel sure, we'll never hear from him again. Poor lad. What he's had to put up with. That face alone has been a drawback to him. He'd got a mind and could've used it in some business. But lookin' like that, who would take him on? And he knew it.'

'If he doesn't show up before dinner-time,' Joe said, 'I'm going to the polis station.'

Joe had no need to go to the police station for at about eleven o'clock that morning there was a knock on the front door. When Bella opened it and saw two uniformed policemen standing there, she put her hands over her eyes and muttered, 'I knew it. I knew it. Something's happened to him.'

'May we come in, Miss Morgan?' said one.

'Aye. Aye, come in and tell me the worst. Is he dead?'

They didn't answer, but she led them away from the kitchen, where she knew Reenee would be standing pressed against the wall in the scullery, and into the parlour, and there one of them said, 'I should sit down if I were you, Miss Morgan.'

She sat down, and they sat opposite, and she said, 'Well, go on, for God's sake, and tell me.'

'We've found him, in fact he was dropped outside Wall Street police station at six o'clock this morning, what was left of him, yet he is still alive.'

'Oh, my God! My God! Where is he now?'

'He's in hospital, Miss Morgan,' said the other man. 'They're doing everything possible to keep him alive. The last news we heard was that he was out of the theatre.'

'Was—was he badly battered?'

The first man said, 'I'm afraid so, Miss Morgan. They didn't mean him to survive. He must have a very strong constitution under his frail exterior.'

'May I go and see him?'

'Yes; yes, of course. But he won't be conscious for some hours.'

Her body suddenly stiffening, she said, 'This is because he was workin' for you lot, isn't it? Now, isn't it?'

They both looked away and then one of the men said, 'Yes, I suppose so.'

'You don't suppose so at all, you know so.'

Again the man said, 'Yes, Miss Morgan,

you're right. He . . . well, he was a great deal of help, more than that, in bringing those gun-runners to justice. Some of those still around were bound to take their revenge, for we cannot hope we have caught every-one concerned, but we're all very sorry that the little fellow has had to pay for it.'

'Aye,' said Bella, brokenly now, 'and he won't get any medals for it, will he?'

Neither man spoke for a moment. Then one said, 'No. I'm sorry, there's very few medals given out in this business; but I can tell you one thing, he's appreciated up top because, you know, he's one of the few straightforward . . .' he paused '. . . helpers to the force. A lot of them are on both sides: they give so much away and, under that, they can carry on with their own line. Oh, we know all that. But we've always known that the Pimple—' He stopped. 'I'm sorry, but he's been known by that name.'

'His name is Carl.'

'Carl,' repeated the policeman. 'Well, well. Anyway, I can tell you that all of us working on these very dangerous cases have appreciated his help. It's been small at times but always straight, and we were al-ways able to go on that. And now here's one who hopes he . . . well, he lives to know that we appreciate him.'

The other officer spoke now and said, 'If I were you, Miss Morgan, I wouldn't go to the hospital until tomorrow. You see, as I said, he won't be round for hours and then . . . well, I'm afraid he won't be able to speak to you much, if at all.'

'That's if he's still here,' Bella persisted bitterly.

'Well,' said one of them quietly, 'we can only hope, and we're all hoping. Believe that.'

After an awkward silence the two men rose, and she too, and as she let them out she said, 'You didn't tell me which hospital he's at.'

'He's in the Royal, in a side ward. One of our men is sitting with him all the time so that if he does recover he might give us a lead about who attacked him. Whoever they were, I'm sure they never expected him to survive.'

When she closed the door on them she had almost to grope her way to the bottom of the stairs, and there, dropping down on to the last step, she bent forward, picked up her apron, buried her face in it and began to cry as she hadn't done before, even after Andy's death.

She had known Carl before Andy and the others had come on the scene. He had been pitiable in many ways: he had had his looks to contend with, and she was convinced he had been sleeping rough for a long time. She knew that he was sharpwitted; later, she recognised he was wise in many ways and also that he had a brain, that he was intelligent. When she felt the arm go round her she turned and put her head on Reenee's shoulder; and Reenee held her and rocked her gently, and her face, too, was wet. Presently, she pushed Bella away gently; then she brought out the word, 'Dead?'

Bella's throat was so tight she couldn't speak, but she stood up and tugged Reenee to her feet. Then she said haltingly, 'Not . . . yet,' and repeated, 'not . . . yet.'

Reenee now put her joined hands against her breast as if she were praying, and the guttural sound that came from her throat repeated the words, 'Not yet.'

Bella was in her best coat and hat. Joe had on a good suit; he'd even had his hair cut, and his brown shoes were well polished.

The police had arranged that they would be met outside the Royal Hospital's main entrance at eleven o'clock this morning and they were now waiting for the taxi to take them there. Willie was in the hall, Reenee was there, too, but standing further back near the kitchen door, and Bella, turning towards her, said in quite a loud voice, as if she were some far distance away, 'Don't worry, love, we won't be long; and if he's awake we'll tell him you're thinking about him.'

'Here's the taxi,' said Willie, as he opened the door. Then, looking at Bella, he said, quietly, 'She'll be all right.' Then even lower, he added, 'Don't expect miracles; he likely won't know you.'

For a moment she stared at him as if in disbelief, then went out into the street, with Joe following her, and they got into the taxi. The driver had not bothered to leave his seat and open the door for them, an action that seemed significant—fares from this end of town wouldn't expect courtesy.

However, his manner changed, just the slightest, when he drew his cab to a stop and was turning to ask for his fare before they let themselves out. To his surprise, a

policeman hurried along the pavement towards the taxi, opened the door and gave
his hand to the woman. Then, looking at the
taxi driver who had now opened his door
and was about to get out, the policeman
asked, 'What is it?' The man, inspecting the
meter, gave him the price, and at this the
policeman turned to Joe, saying, 'It's all
right, I'll see to it.' Bringing some silver out
of his pocket, he picked from it the exact
amount and said to the driver, 'You were a
bit late in opening the door, weren't you?'

The man glared at him, reached back and
banged the door shut, then drove off.

Bella had recognised the policeman as
one of the two men who had called at the
house yesterday to give her the dreadful
news, and she said, 'Thank you. Thank you,
Officer.'

Placing a hand gently on her elbow, and
with Joe walking at her other side, he guided
them to the main door of the hospital.

Although she had lived in London all these
years she had never seen the Royal London
Hospital and she was awed by its size, but
more so by the bustle that was going on all
around her as they were led through corri-
dors and past wards until the policeman

brought them to a halt. He stopped a nurse, and said, 'We have permission to visit Mr Carl Poze. He is, I understand, in a side ward.'

The nurse looked from him to the little woman and the tall man and she said, 'Oh, yes. Wait a moment, I'll get Sister.'

The sister came and the policeman addressed her, 'Good morning, Sister;' then, motioning to Bella and Joe, he explained, 'These are relatives of Mr Carl Poze and have permission, I understand, to visit him.'

The sister looked at the two visitors before she said, 'Yes; just come this way.'

She led them into a short corridor, but paused before opening the door and, looking at Bella, she said, 'Please don't be distressed by the condition in which you'll find . . . your son?' she enquired.

'Yes, you could say so,' said Bella softly.

'I must ask you, if possible, not to disturb him in any way by . . . well, your reactions. Also I think that ten minutes will be sufficient.' She now opened the door to allow them to pass into the room.

A man was seated at the far side of a bed. Bella had taken only three steps towards it when she found she couldn't move further. Joe's arm came about her, and with the sister's help, he placed her in a chair.

She sat staring at the thing in the bed. At first, all her blurred gaze could make of it was that it was attached to wires and tubes, all joined to the head and face and neck. The little of the face she could see was just a slit that might have been the mouth, and if there was a body it was lying under a cage, with the exception of the arms. Yet here again there was no flesh visible, because right down to the wrists they were bandaged, and from there the hands lay in what looked like bags.

There was a whirling in her mind. The sister had said only ten minutes: that was a long, long time ago; something was happening to her . . .

For the first time in her life, Bella had fainted.

She knew she was dragging herself up out of some terrible blackness. She had never felt like this in her life before. What was the matter with her? Where was she?

She opened her eyes and gasped for breath, and a voice said, 'That's it. Take deep breaths. That's it, deep breaths. You'll feel all right in a moment. I'm sure you'd like a cup of tea.' It was a nice voice, soothing. She felt relaxed. She didn't know why she was here. What had happened to her? Then slowly, slowly, there came into her mind the picture of the thing she had seen lying in the bed, and she wanted to cry out against it. But the soothing voice was going on: 'Ah, here comes a cup of tea. Now will you sit up? That's it. Open your eyes. There, that's better, isn't it? I'll put this cushion behind your head. Now sip this tea; you'll feel better. That's it, open your eyes.'

She opened her eyes and looked up into a bright round face, a young face, and what she said to it was, 'Joe?' and Joe's voice came to her from the foot of the couch or whatever she was lying on, and he said, 'It's all right, Bella. It's all right. I could've passed out meself. I could that.'

She looked up again at the bright face. She had to put her head well back, for the nurse was standing, and she said, 'Is . . . is he gone?'

'No, no. Don't worry. The doctor's just finishing on the ward; he's going to come in and have a word with you. Now, just finish this tea,' she said, placing the cup on a small table to Bella's side.

'Thank you.'

'Rest there now; I'll be back in a moment.'

'Joe.'

Joe went to her and knelt down by her side. He took her hand, and said, 'They say he's holding his own. Try not to worry.'

'But, Joe . . . did you see him? There . . . there must be nothing left of him.'

Joe did not answer for almost a minute. Then he said, 'He's tough inside, is Carl, and he's got pluck. I always knew he had much more pluck than me. Me, I was all brawn and mouth, but Carl, well, he had brains— and pluck.'

For a moment she forgot the picture in her mind as she patted his hand and said, 'You've always been a good man, Joe, always. You were like two brothers together, and he was very fond of you. Very. He—he once told me that you were the best mate anybody could have.'

'He did, Bella?'

'Yes. Yes, he did, Joe, and that's the truth.'

When the door opened, Joe pulled himself to his feet and looked to where a young man in a white coat, accompanied by the sister, was coming towards them.

'This is Dr—' Bella did not catch the name, it sounded foreign, but the sister went on, 'He is seeing to your son, Mrs Morgan.' She now pulled a chair forward and the young man sat down on it. Leaning towards Bella, he said, 'How are you feeling now?'

'I—I couldn't really tell you, Doctor. It was the shock.'

'Of course. Of course.'

'Will . . . will he live, Doctor?'

The young man did not answer for a moment; and then he said, 'If we can possibly make him, he will live. If he gets over the next three or four days then we'll be able to say he's going to be all right.'

'He must've been in a dreadful state.'

Again there was a pause before the young man said, 'He was, Mrs Morgan, in a dreadful state. Whoever did this to him didn't intend him to live. Even if for nothing else, I would hope that he does survive to give us some idea of the culprit or culprits whose intention was to murder him. Perhaps you noticed that there was a policeman sitting by his bedside. They, too, are hoping, even willing him to live so that justice can be done. Anyway,' he patted Bella's hand, 'rest assured everything that possibly can be done medically will be done.'

As he went to rise from the chair Bella caught at his hand and said, 'How—how long will it be before . . . well, before he will know anybody?'

'That's hard for me to tell you at the moment, Mrs Morgan, but give us a week and then I'm sure we shall know much more. And may I suggest, for your own good as well as the patient's, that you don't come to see him for, say, another three or four days? Will you agree to that?'

She stared up at him. 'Yes,' she said flatly.

As if to lighten her anxiety, he said, 'But you can phone every day and Sister will tell you how he is. All right?'

She nodded and he said, 'Goodbye, then, Mrs Morgan.' He inclined his head towards Joe, then went out with the sister.

Bella sat up on the side of the sofa and realised she was in a rest room. 'Let's go home, Joe,' she said.

Quickly, he replied, 'Stay there a minute while I go and see if the polis is still there, 'cos we'll never find our way out of this place on our own.'

The policeman was still there, and he got

them home; and now, her hand in Reenee's, Bella was sitting facing her four boys and listening while Joe related to them what they had found in the ward and how Bella couldn't stand it and had passed out; and he gave them word for word what the doctor had said about Carl, finishing with, 'There's nothing for us now but waitin'.'

At this point Willie put in, 'Aye, and prayin'. I've never prayed in me life that I can remember, not even from a bairn, but I'll do it now.'

John added his voice. 'I won't do any prayin'; I can only hope that the police catch those buggers before one of us get wind of who did it, because what they've done to him would be nothin' to what we'd do to them. I can promise you that,' then turned and went down the stone steps to the room below.

Without further words, the other two followed him, and Bella was left with Joe and Reenee. She whimpered, 'It was awful. Awful, the sight of him. He wasn't there; it was a mummy of some kind, all wired up.'

'Don't distress her, Bella. Don't distress her.'

'I'm not! I'm just tellin' her. The only good

thing about it, he's under a very good doctor. He's a nice fellow, young, and he said I
can phone every day, but . . . but we haven't got to go yet.'

Bella phoned every day for a fortnight. The
first week the sister's replies were mostly
the same, kindly but firm: there was little
change; she would be advised not to visit
for a while. At the end of the week a different
voice came on the phone and a nurse said,
'Oh, I think he's turned the corner. Anyway,
they're taking him down again to theatre this
afternoon, so he must have.'

Bella had repeated, 'Theatre! Another op-
eration?'

'Oh, yes. But they wouldn't be giving it
to him if he wasn't fit to have it, you see, so
it's good news in a way. Don't worry.' She
rang off.

Such were the answers, too, during the
following days. The sister must have been
absent, for different nurses answered Bella's
calls and they all said yes, definitely he was
holding his own; and they had great hopes
for him, and perhaps, yes, they would tell
her tomorrow when she could come and see
him again.

* * *

Carl came to himself gradually. He knew he had no body, but he could move a few fingers on his right hand; but then they stiffened. All he had left was a head, and it ached. Sometimes it ached so badly that they would stick another needle into him. He welcomed the jabs, because they took him away from everything and into a warm blackness where there was nothing. But one morning he woke up to see a face looking at him. It wasn't a nurse's face, this face he didn't know, but he knew the voice and what it was saying, because it was saying, 'You're feeling better this morning, not all sixes and sevens.'

Sixes and sevens. He was sitting once again on the bar bench and a man was saying, 'Oh, it's been a day. All sixes and sevens.' And whenever the man said that Carl would give him a message. What kind of a message? The man's voice came to him again, saying, 'You won't remember me, because I don't look as I did when we talked in the bar.'

He could see only out of one eye, for the other was bandaged, and he fixed it on the face. This was a thin face, sharp. The chin was pointed. He always noticed people's features. He could see that the man was smiling at him, and the voice said, 'If I told you I had thick tidy brown hair, a mustache and plump jaws, and I talked with a Cockney accent, saying, "It's been a day, all sixes and sevens," would you recognise me? A wig and some gum shields and an imitation 'tache can change a man.'

The man in the bar, the police bloke.

His voice was soft. 'I'm sorry about what happened to you. Sorry to the heart, chum. You did a good job but, my God, you've had to pay for it! And I'm still looking for them; but, believe me, I'm grateful for what you did. That's a poor way of saying thank you, but if, in the future, there's ever anything I can do, you've just got to say, "What a day it's been! All sixes and sevens," ' and he laughed, still softly, then said, 'We were wonderin' if you could remember anything that happened before the attack.'

Carl thought . . . Before the attack. Before they murdered him. He knew they had been going to murder him. Oh, yes; yes. It was the ginger-haired fellow, the one who had pulled him out of the brewery. He didn't know the other two with him, but his face he'd never forget. It was the last thing he remembered. Carl's eye turned towards the man and he muttered, 'Ginger-haired.'

'He was ginger-haired?'

'Yes.'

'Sure?'

'Yes . . . and . . .'

'Yes? Can you remember anything more about him?'

Could he remember anything more about him? The teeth? Oh, yes, the teeth, because that day he himself had had the toothache, which was why he was walking with his head down and his hand across his mouth. And that's also why he saw the tooth like a tusk. When the man said he had remembered him playing the whistle, he had grinned, and there, at the side, yes . . . yes, he had seen what he had thought looked like a little tusk. It must have been two teeth growing together. Two growing out of the one place. He remembered thinking it was a good job the point went straight down else it would have ripped his lip. Yes. 'The tooth.'

'The tooth? Something about his teeth?'

'Yes. This side.' He was trying to lift his hand up to his face, but found it too difficult. Then he said, 'Right side . . . No, left side.

Two teeth, one—' He paused for breath and the man said, 'Take your time, don't hurry. Just try to remember,' and his voice sounded excited.

'Well . . . two from, like, one root. One half over the top of other, like—like a fang.'

'Oh, Carl. You're a marvel! You really are a marvel. I must tell you, straight away, I've got them. I know where he is, and where I get him I'll get his mates. I've got him. Red hair and a crooked tooth. God!' He put his hand on the bandaged arm and said, 'You're a wonderful fellow, so observant. You should've never been in the position you are. I must go now, but you'll see me again, and many others of my lot, I promise you. And I promise you this also, if I can do anything about it, he'll get life.'

The detective hurried from the room and almost bumped into the doctor, who said, 'My, you're in a hurry! What is it?'

'You wouldn't believe, Doctor! He's just given me a piece of most vital information. He's actually given me the features of the man who intended to murder him, and I know exactly who this fellow is. We've grilled him for four days, but he got out of it—supposed to be in the house with a cold or something, never near the brewery. And he was backed up by his mates.'

'And you know where he is?'

'Oh, yes! We can put a finger straight on him.' He leant towards the doctor. 'He thinks he's safe, lying low, he's assisting in a brothel.'

The doctor laughed gently now and said, 'How exciting for him.'

'Yeah. And there's more excitement to come. I'll keep you in touch, Doctor. Well, anyway, it'll make headlines shortly, if I've got anything to do with it.' He jerked his head back towards the door. 'That poor fellow in there. He should've been in the police force, in the special end. He's got an eye for small details, and it's small details that can move mountains. Well, be seein' you, Doctor.'

'Be seeing you,' and smiling now, the doctor went into the room, saying to the nurse, 'There goes a happy man.'

He turned to the figure on the bed.

'Good morning, Mr Poze. Oh, you're looking a bit brighter. How are you feeling?'

'I still don't know, Doctor.'

'Of course not. But you are improving, and as you know, you're for another ride down the long corridor this afternoon. We're going to see to that nose of yours; you won't recognise yourself when they're finished with it. And also, as I said yesterday, we'll be dealing with some of those marks on your face. It could've been done years ago if you'd only come to the hospital.'

'Too old, Doctor.'

'Nonsense! How old are you?' He turned to the nurse. 'How old is he, Nurse?'

Before the nurse could say anything, Carl said, 'Kickin' sixty.'

'Oh, what's sixty? By the way, what is your Christian name, Mr Poze?'

'Carl, sir.'

'Oh, that's a nice name. Well, our acquaintance has been very close of late so I don't see why you shouldn't be Carl.' The doctor straightened up. 'Is there anything you need, Carl, I mean anything you fancy? You've got to eat, y'know.'

Carl attempted to shake his head. Then his eye turned towards the table, banked with flowers, near the wall at the foot of the bed and he said, 'Who sent those?'

'Oh, well, I've seen your mother bring some in.' He knew now that Mrs Morgan was really Miss Morgan and that this poor fellow here was not her son. Yet presumably she had cared for him for years and thought of him as her son. But his name was Poze, foreign in a way. He turned to the nurse, saying, 'Who else were the flowers from?'

The nurse went to the table and said, 'Someone called Reenee, and this other one, the last visitor brought yesterday, and there are just two initials on them. Well, they're not initials, they're numbers, a six and a seven.'

The doctor said, 'Do you know what those numbers stand for, Carl?'

And Carl said simply, 'Yes, I know who they're from. It's very kind of him.'

The nurse said, 'There's another bunch with a card on. "From the lads. Come home soon." '

Carl closed his one eye. Come home soon, they said. Would he ever be able to walk? As it was, he still felt that he hadn't any body left on him; he was numb from the neck downwards. Perhaps he was paralysed. He didn't know and was afraid to ask.

The voice above him was saying quietly, 'That's it, rest. I'll see you this afternoon. Don't worry, you're going to be fine.'

The young doctor left the room and

walked briskly along the corridor; but at the end he was stopped by the little woman, Miss Morgan . . . She was looking quite happy at the moment, so different from when he had first made her acquaintance. She must indeed love that fellow very much, son or no son. It was a strange world. 'Good morning, Miss Morgan,' he said. 'On your way once again? You'll find him much better this morning.'

'Oh, thank you, Doctor. Thank you.' Her hand went out now and caught at his wrist. Looking up into his face, she said, 'I'll never forget you as long as I live and what you've done for him, and what you're doing for his poor face.'

'Oh, the credit is not due to me, Miss Morgan, I can assure you. Professor Baker is the plastic surgeon, I just assist him.' He leant towards her now, saying, 'I've not yet reached the eminence of being a consultant. I have nearly two more years to go as a registrar.'

Quite slowly she brought out his name, but in two syllables, 'Bain-dor. It's a difficult name to remember and, I must tell you, I've made a mess of it a number of times.'

He was laughing now. 'You're not the only

one, Miss Morgan, and it's clever of you to pronounce it so accurately, because it is sometimes Baindoing, or I have even known it to be Barndoor.' She laughed and Joe did too. 'But, then, what's in a name? Nothing, really.'

'There's something in yours, Doctor. As I said, I'll never forget it, or what you have done for my lad.'

'Well, go along now and see your lad. You will find him much brighter. He's even asked about the flowers on the table.'

'He has?' Bella was surprised.

'Yes.'

'Eeh! Well, that shows he can think.'

'Oh, yes, of course he can think. Whatever those brutes did to him they didn't manage to knock his brains out. He has still got those.'

'Thank God for that, and you.'

He waved at her and walked quickly away, and she, turning to Joe, moved on along the corridor, saying to him, 'Isn't he a lovely man?'

'None better,' Joe said; 'and I understand from one of the porters he's from the top drawer. His father's a millionaire and they live in a mansion.'

'No!'

'Aye; one of them told me yesterday when I spoke about him. He said he was well liked, not like some out of the top drawer, who think they're God Almighty because they have the tag of doctor on them and hold their noses in the air. Not him. It was rumoured, the porter said, he had to fight his father to take up this career. But he still lives in the mansion.'

'Well I never!' said Bella. 'And he talks so ordinary. Well, I mean not ordinary but kindly.'

'Aye; well, he's a gentleman.'

14

It was the same evening, and John, Tony and Willie had come upstairs to find out the latest news from the hospital. Bella regaled them with the incidents of her visit. First, of Carl's apparent improvement and of how plain now were the few words he could utter; and of how interested he was in the flowers. And, lastly, of their meeting with the doctor in the corridor. She laughed as she said, 'He was . . . he was so nice, so lovely, and I think he was pleased that I got his name right. It's a very funny name and everybody seems to get it wrong. He said some people called him Barndoor. Did you ever hear anything like it?'

'What is his real name?' put in John.

'Well, it sounds foreign, but it is pronounced Bain-dor. I suppose when you say it quickly it could sound like Barndoor,' and as she repeated the name she turned to include Reenee in the laughter, only for her face to change quickly as she got to her feet, saying, 'No, no, lass! No!' because Reenee's body had stiffened. It wasn't jerking, as it usually did, it was just stiff. She seemed to have no middle; her head rested against the back of the chair and her heels were stuck in the rug on the floor, and from her heels to her head she was stiff.

With Willie now to one side of her and Bella to the other, they endeavoured to break the rigidity by forcing her to sit up again; but she remained as she was. Then slowly her right hand moved up to her head and her mouth opened to emit a guttural sound; then she brought out a word. They couldn't understand what it was, but John immediately suggested, 'She's been struck again by something that was said. Perhaps it was the name of the doctor or something.'

'How could it be?' snapped Bella. 'It was only his name.'

'Well, that could've done it,' said Tony.

'Done what?' demanded Bella.

'Stirred her memory. It's things like that that do.'

'Oh, my God!'

'She's comin' round,' said Willie. 'Lift her back in the chair.'

They eased her back; but she didn't open her eyes, she just sat there, her body limp now but her hand still to her head.

'I'll have to get her upstairs to bed,' said Bella; 'that's where she should've been long before now 'cos she coughed her heart out all last night. I'll have to get the doctor to see to that chest of hers again. And, what's more, she's not eating. Oh, there's always something! I thought things were goin' too smoothly. Help me to the bottom of the stairs with her, Willie. I'll manage after that.'

Reenee did not need much helping upstairs. She walked, each step slow and deliberate, and in the bedroom she went straight to the bed and lay down on top of the eiderdown. Bella said, 'Aren't you goin' to take your things off, lass?' And when there was no reply, she said soothingly, 'All right, then. All right. I'll just take your shoes off and cover you up, then perhaps you'll get to sleep and feel better in the mornin'.'

She lit a night-light, then turned off the electric table lamp and went quietly downstairs.

The men were still there, and it was John who said, 'That doctor's name is an odd one. I've never heard a name like that before, and nobody's ever spoken such a name in this house, have they?'

He was looking at Bella, who flopped down into a chair as she said, 'But he's a doctor, and he must be thirty if a day. And she's been with me . . . well, how long? It must be all of twenty-six years. I don't know how long she was roaming before that.'

It was Willie who asked now, 'And she had no sign of identification on her clothes, Bella? Not on her underwear or anything?'

'No. It's worn to ribbons now with her wearin' it, like that coat, but it was of very high quality at one time. All her underwear was silk. She used to have a little bag; it was pinned to her knickers.'

She thought of that little bag. She had seen inside it the time the doctor had come and given her that dose that had knocked her out, and all there was in it was a cheap-looking necklace affair, like a chain dog collar, and on the end of it there hung three red balls. It was like something you would buy in the market. There was a flat case, too. She didn't know whether it was brass or gold, and no matter how she had tried to open it she couldn't. She had gone round the sides of it and pressed it as if it might have a spring. She had even inserted one of her nails between the two pieces of metal, but could make no impression. She stopped at using a knife because perhaps it wouldn't close again, and then the lass would be upset and know that she had been messing about with her things. So she had put them back in the bag.

'It's a long time since she had a turn, isn't it, Bella?' said Willie.

'Oh, yes; and ages ago since she walked out.'

That had been another scary time, Bella thought. It was the day after she had said to her, 'D'you know how long we've been together, lass? Nearly seventeen years.' The next morning she was gone, dark coat, funny hat and all. Bella had nearly gone round the bend again, and once more it had been Carl who had warned her that Reenee was on her way back; and she hadn't been gone an hour. She had asked him if he knew whether she had been to the pawn shop. He had said he didn't know; he had just seen her turning the corner on her way back

up the street. And yet, that was an odd
thing, she recalled now. She'd had to call
the doctor in to her because her chest had
gone very bad again, and she had looked
in the bag, and that cheap-looking chain
had gone; as also had the case that she had
been unable to open. But in its place there
was a piece of brown paper folded neatly;
and when she opened it there were four
pawn tickets and a faded piece of cardboard. She remembered she couldn't quite
make out the figure on the cardboard. She
thought it might have been that of a little
boy; then again, no. It was as if it had been
torn off a postcard with a picture on it, but
the years had dimmed the colours and it
had seemingly been wet, so it had a smudgy
look. But that was all that was in the bag,
and it had been wrapped in this square of
brown paper. She had wondered about it for
a long time. She must have gone to the
pawn shop again and pawned those things.
They must've been of some value else they
wouldn't have taken them. But she didn't
come back with any money this time. Nothing at all. So why had she pawned them?
Bella remembered Reenee had taken off her
hat and changed her shoes, then rolled up

her coat sleeves and gone downstairs to the
kitchen and got on with her work as if nothing had happened. She had been a puzzle,
that girl. She had been the light of Bella's
life, but at the same time she had been a
worry, and now here she was going off her
head again because of the mention of a
name, Baindor. Why should a name like that
affect her? Oh, dear me, she'd have to keep
a close watch on Reenee else she'd go off
on her wanderings again. In her mind she
must be looking for somebody.

She wished Joe was back. He had gone
out to get himself a pair of shoes.

In her mind Irene was looking for somebody
connected with that name of Baindor. Baindor. Was it her own name? Yes; yes, it must
be her name. It *was* her name. She was Mrs
Baindor. And there was a child. Oh, yes;
there was a child.

She turned over in bed, grabbed a pillow,
hugged it to her and rocked herself as she
said, a child, a child, a birthday . . . Richard.

The name filled the room, it filled the
world. Richard. Richard. The echo was like
bells ringing. Dozens and dozens of church
bells. They became a din. She dropped the

pillow and put her hands to her head, covering her ears. Richard, he was a child. He was four. Yes. She knew he was four. Where was he?

There came a great rush of feeling in her, and she could hear a voice saying, 'It's all right, dear. It's all right. We are going away, far, far away, on a boat. No one must know.' He would kill her. He would kill her. Who? Who would kill her? She was staring into the blackness . . . the blackness of her mind where a face was forming, a large face, a terrible face; and then it was staring down into hers, and she was crying out against it. Then her body stiffened and she could hear herself shouting, 'No! No! No more! Not that! I won't! I won't!' Her body was paining all over; and she became stiff. That was until the great hands were on her stomach and were on her back, pushing her up and down, up and down, the voice crying at her, screaming at her just one word: 'Respond! Respond!' Then her body was lifted and thrown about, and she screamed again, 'Not that! Please!'

There were arms about her and a different voice was saying, 'There, lass. There, lass. You're dreaming. Come on. It's a nightmare.'

She fell against the body, then she clung to it, and her shaking was making the body shake; but she gripped it tight because she knew it would save her.

'There now. Just look at the sight of the bed. And that chest of yours. You'll have to see the doctor again. Come on! Let me take your coat off.'

'No, no!' The words came hoarsely from Irene's throat. She must never take her coat off. He must never get at her body. No man must get at her body, ever, ever, ever. Timothy.

Timothy. Who was Timothy? She opened her eyes, then murmured, 'Oh, Bella!'

'Yes, love; it's me. You're quite safe. Now, be a good lass and let me take your coat off; just your coat, that's all; and I'll get you a hot drink, and give you one of your tablets to ease that chest . . . That's a good girl. I'll hang it up.'

Bella took the worn threadbare coat to the wardrobe and hung it up, shaking her head as she did so. All this because she had used the name of that doctor. It had done something. It had hit Reenee's mind—her other mind—and she had recalled something. Oh, she hoped it would stop there.

She settled Reenee down and covered her up, saying, 'Lie quiet now; I'll be back in a minute.'

Reenee lay quiet, and her mind was repeating, Bella. Bella. She loved Bella. But there was a name that had come back. Timothy. Who was Timothy? Slowly the sound of the name seemed to soften her. For an instant, she felt warm inside; the name was acting like a balm on her troubled thinking.

It would come back, she told herself. Oh, yes, it would come back, because he wasn't in the nightmare. No, that man, that dreadful, dreadful man; she didn't want *him* to come back, not into her mind. Oh, she didn't want to see that man again. He was cruel, dreadful. Oh, she hated him. Why? Who was he, the one who brought the blow on to her head and knocked her into darkness, into another world, into another life? And her child had gone. Yes, her child had gone. But now he was back. Bella. Bella had brought him back. Baindor. Baindor. That was her name. That was her child's name. But he was not a child, not any more. Bella said he was a doctor. How long ago was it since she had held him and rocked him, the child? Weeks, months, years, aeons of time. Words were coming into her head that hadn't been there before.

'Is your head still aching, dear? Take your hands down. Now drink this cocoa and take this pill. It'll ease your chest, and you'll have to see the doctor again. Now lie down and go to sleep; everything will be different in the morning. Don't worry; your coat's in the wardrobe.'

She lay quietly. The door had closed; the night-light was glowing softly in the room and her coat was in the wardrobe. Her shield was in the wardrobe. She couldn't live without her coat; they would get at her if she wasn't covered up. Men with hands that clawed at you. His hands had clawed at her all over. Oh, what his hands had done. Whose hands? The hands of the face. The hands of that awful face. She was tired. Bella said it would be all right in the morning. She would think a lot better in the morning. She knew she would.

She woke at dawn. It was as if she had spent the hours of sleep in a life that must have been hers at one time. She got up and went to the wash-stand and, pouring some ice cold water into a basin, she washed her face and hands. She got into her velvet dress, then put on her coat and what was left of her hat, pushing the bundle of her greying hair into the net at the back of her head. Amazingly, the net was about the only part of the hat still intact. Then she took the money-box from the mantelpiece and, turning it upside down, she twisted the lever at the bottom until there was a gap, and a shower of half-crowns fell into her lap. These she dropped into the inside pocket of her coat, then replaced the box on the little mantelpiece.

She went down the stairs as softly as a cat and let herself out of the front door, but once the cold morning air hit her she began to cough, and so, her hand tightly over her mouth, she hurried away down the street into the lightening day . . .

How long it took her to reach the hospital she didn't know, she had twice lost her way; once she actually stopped and, opening her mouth, she forced herself to speak to a woman, saying, 'Royal Lon-don hos-pital.' And the woman, obviously puzzled by the weird-looking creature, pointed, saying, 'Along the main road there. Then two streets . . . no, three. Somebody will show you the way after that, but keep to the main road here.'

Irene nodded her thanks, then walked on.

However, when she reached the hospital she was neither amazed nor distressed by the bustle of people around her—she seemed to have been here before—but a number of times she was pushed aside or jumped at the sound of an ambulance or a car horn, before a porter who was helping someone into a car banged the door closed and, in standing back, nearly fell over her.

He was about to say, 'I'm sorry, miss,' when he stopped and surveyed her. She was coughing desperately and he said now, kindly, 'You want the Outpatients?'

She did not answer him, but he said, 'Well, come along this way.'

He led her to a door and into a kind of hallway, and at the reception desk he said, 'She's wandering about; I think she's looking for Outpatients. She's got a bark on her like a dog.'

Exhausted, Irene leant on her forearms on

the desk and brought out the word, 'Doc-tor Bain-dor.'

At the desk two girls were attending to phones that seemed never to stop ringing, and the receptionist said to her, 'Dr Bain-dor?' Then she said, 'You want Outpatients.'

At this Irene shook her head and repeated, 'Bain-dor.'

The girl stared at the weirdly dressed individual: she was definitely a vagrant of some sort, but she wanted Dr Baindor.

She pressed a button at the side of her desk, and to the woman who came to the counter she said, 'This one wants Dr Bain-dor; she doesn't want Outpatients.'

The newcomer leant forward on the desk and surveyed the dirty-coated, weird-hatted individual. She looked at the deathly white face, and then Irene again put her head back and brought out the word, 'Baindor.'

'Get ward six,' the woman said; 'and find if he's on duty.'

Irene stood waiting. She heard the receptionist speaking on the phone and she heard part of what she said; one of the words was 'weird' another was 'insists'. Then the woman was nodding into the phone; and after she had put it down she came to the desk and said, 'Dr Baindor has gone off duty for the weekend; he won't be back until Monday.'

Irene looked at her for a long time, then slowly she turned, tottered out of the hall and made for the entrance. Outside, she was confused. There were so many cars, so many ambulances, so many people. She walked down a side-road, but before she reached the end of it she knew that she was going to fall. She looked about her: by the kerb was a large wooden box, as if someone had just delivered it or put it there to be picked up. She dropped on to it and sat with her head bowed and her hands in her lap. What was she to do? She couldn't wait here until Monday and she couldn't walk back to Bella's; she didn't know the way. But she had money, she could get a taxi.

At the sound of laughter, her head lifted. Three men had turned the corner into this side-road and were coming towards her; and at the sight of them her whole body seemed to leap into the air: the man in the middle, yes, the man in the middle, that was Richard! He looked like her father; he had her father's features and his mouth. This she had always said and been so proud that it was so.

She wasn't aware of jumping up and of approaching the men, or that they had stopped and one was saying, 'What now? Look at this!'

What she did, and to all their surprise, was grip the wrist of the man in the middle, who, now more surprised than the rest, said, 'What is it? You want Outpatients?'

She stared into his face. It was Richard. He was just like her father.

A man to the side of her said under his breath, 'She's a nut. She's begging.'

She turned towards the man, and such was the look she gave him that he stepped back; and now opening her mouth wide, she brought out, 'Rich.'

'What did I tell you?' said the man. 'She's begging. She says you're rich; she's heard about you.'

'Shut up!' said the man in the middle.

But the man on the other side had put his hand in his pocket and was handing her a shilling. She looked at it, then slapped the back of his hand so hard that the coin went spurting into the air, bounced on the ground and rolled into the gutter.

The man in the middle said, 'She's . . . she's not after money. She's in trouble of some sort. Sit down,' he said, and, his wrist still held tight, he led her back to the box. As she started to cough again he said, 'Oh, my goodness! You must get to Outpatients. They'll see to you there.'

She shook her head, and the talkative man now put in, 'It's you she's after. You do this to the women.'

'Shut up, Alex! For God's sake, shut up!'

This was Richard; he looked like her father. Her father was never handsome like him but the features were the same.

The young man now loosened her fingers from his wrist, saying, 'I've got to go. I've got a car waiting, but my friend here'—he now pointed to the other man—'my friend here will take you to Outpatients.'

He backed away from her; then, turning to the man called Alex, he said, 'See to her, will you, Alex? That chest is bad, very bad.'

Alex. Help. Alex helped. He helped her father. Alexander? Yes, Alexander. For the moment she saw the dreadful face hovering over her; then in its place came another, a nice face. Alexander. Armstrong. Her head went back and she said the word aloud, 'Armstrong.'

The kindly man said, 'You want to see Mr Armstrong?'

She shook her head. Then in a flash it came to her, Alexander Armstrong. He was a solicitor. He came to the house, the great house. Alexander Armstrong the solicitor. Beverley Square. She had been to Beverley Square. The young man bent over now and said, 'Come along, my dear. Come along; you can't sit here all day. And that box will soon have to be moved.'

She looked up at him and said one word, 'Taxi.'

'Taxi?'

She nodded, then put her hand inside her coat and brought out some silver and showed it on the palm of her hand.

'Oh, I see what you mean, my dear, you can pay for a taxi. Do you know where you want to go?'

She put her head back, then tried to bring out Beverley but couldn't. Suddenly he said, 'Could you write it?'

She nodded, and he brought from his inner pocket a small book with a pencil. It was an address book, and turning to a plain page, he said, 'There. Write it there.' And so, in large letters that almost covered the small sheet, she wrote 'Beverley Square. Armstrong, Solicitor.'

After reading it he did not say anything for a moment; then he repeated to her, 'You want to go to Beverley Square and a solicitor there called Armstrong?' She bowed her head deeply, and he said, 'Come along. I'll get you a taxi.'

When he stopped a taxi, he opened the back door, then said to the cabby, 'This lady wants to be dropped at Beverley Square near the office of a solicitor called Armstrong. Will you do that?'

The cabby looked from him back to his passenger, and he muttered, 'That's what I'm here for, sir.'

'She has enough money to pay you, so don't worry.'

About ten minutes later the taxi entered the square and cruised slowly, until it stopped opposite a flight of steps at the top of which was a large brass plate with, imprinted on it, Alexander Armstrong and Son, Solicitors.

He got out and opened the door for her, and again from her pocket she brought a palm full of half-crowns. Being a moderate man, he took only what was his due, one half-crown, and when she nodded to him, he said, 'Thank you, ma'am,' and watched her stagger up the steps and into the remainder of her life.

PART THREE
1955

1

She lay, as it were, between two worlds. One in which soft voices spoke to her as they dripped food into her mouth and washed her body. That was a nice feeling. Why had she ever been afraid of her body? But had she been afraid of it? Oh, yes; she had in that other world that kept coming and going. She was still afraid of her body, and of hands going over it. Nails digging into her. Leather straps striking her. But these hands were as soft as the words that were spoken. The voices talked above her head as if she couldn't comprehend. She could, though; she had always been able to comprehend, hadn't she, even in the other world? She mustn't try to bring back that world because in this present one were Mr Armstrong and Glenda. Oh, yes, Glenda. Glenda had put her on the train, but she hadn't told her about the other world. And her son. Her son was coming. Glenda had promised her that. And he was grown-up. He was more than four. She closed her eyes tightly. Of course he is, she said to herself, in a very strange voice that seemed to come from the past. Don't be silly. He is a doctor. You've held his hand. But Alex has promised to bring him back and we will have dinner together.

Will Mrs Atkins be there to serve it? Mr and Mrs Atkins knew a lot of what was going on, and she was so kind, she wasn't like an ordinary housekeeper. And Trip knew too. Oh, he knew what was going on. He hadn't been a butler to father and son for nothing. He and Mrs Atkins talked. They talked about her, but kindly. They knew what she was going through, especially Trip. He was the only one who slept in the main house, and he must have heard her at night.

There it was again, the face! Oh, no! She didn't want to see it. She was in this soft, soft bed. They were washing her body, or they had washed her body. Yes, they had and she was resting. But why? Why had he to come again? He was haunting her. She heard her voice yelling, yelling, 'Don't! Don't!

You filthy swine! I am not an animal. I hate you! I hate you!' Then the lifting up and the throwing of her body here and there. And now she was in that last night when she knew it was the end. She had planned to escape and she was going to escape or she would die under his hands. And he was shaking her as she yelled at him, 'You are worse than any animal. You are a filthy pervert!' Yes, she had yelled at him; and that was when he shook her until her brains seemed to rattle in her head. She could feel them, and his voice must have vibrated through the house when he said, 'Don't you ever dare speak again.' Then there was more shaking, and, his voice deeper, louder, more terrible, now screaming, 'Don't you ever dare open your mouth again!'

She couldn't remember how those words finished, only that they put a stamp on her mind. She must never speak again. Never, never, never. He had screamed that at her, and he had beaten her body back and forward on to the bed, his great hands lifting her shoulders, then throwing her back; and then he had done what he usually did, and she could fight no more.

But there was one hope. The escape was

planned. Mr Cox, dear Mr Cox, whom that devil had sacked just because he played the piano for her. Cox had taken the money, more than a thousand pounds. She had saved this over the years, not spending her lavish allowance, and now he had booked a passage on a liner and she and Richard were going to America where Timothy was. Timothy was her very dear childhood friend. He was married, oh, yes, but that wouldn't matter. He would hide her somewhere, because her husband would have her followed. But it was all arranged. She only wished she could tell dear Alex. But Trip knew, at least she thought Trip knew. But Freda McArthur could be trusted because she, too, knew what went on at night and how she suffered, because she had helped to bathe her on many a morning, when the tears had run down her face. And she would have helped her anyway, because Freda was in love with Mr Cox and, she knew, she was going to leave soon and they were to be married. It was all planned. They were just waiting for his next trip abroad, and it had come. She had been so full of joy that she wanted to please Alex and sing at his concert. And how she had enjoyed that. Oh, it was in defiance, because he would never let her sing; never mind stand on a platform. The beast, the horrible filthy beast of a man. And then she hadn't time to think about the plan of going to America to see Timothy, because there he was and she was in his arms, and then the world broke up: there was nothing but screams and blows and terror and the voice yelling again, 'Don't you dare speak!' She had tried to explain the surprise visit but the voice had bawled her down. Then a great weight had come on her head and she had fallen into another world; and there she had remained until now.

And the old world was on her again and she screamed out, 'I hate you! I loathe you! You dirty, dirty . . .'

She knew her voice had trailed away.

The prick in her arm brought her back into the softness of the bed, and there were voices all around her, some saying, 'Dreadful. Poor creature.' Who were they talking about? It didn't matter, she was going to sleep.

2

'I can't do this on my own, Father. I just can't. You'll have to talk to him.'

Alexander sighed and lay back in his chair. Then he said, 'Shall we have him here?'

'No,' James said. 'I don't think this is the place to break such a story. I think it should be at Glenda's, where he'll be able to see her clothes and the rags and tatters she must have worn under that dreadful coat. Dear Lord! Well, you'd better get on the phone and invite him to hear the change that's going to take place in his life. Where d'you think he'll be?'

'Back in the hospital,' said Alexander. 'But it's Monday and they'll all be on different times. I'm certainly not going to ring his home; for if he shouldn't be in I'd be put through to his father, and the thought of that man makes my gall rise.'

He picked up the phone but didn't, as would have been usual, ask his secretary to get him the number, but dialled the hospital himself.

He was told he would be put through to Dr Baindor's ward, where a curt voice said, 'Yes, Dr Baindor is on duty, but he's busy.' Alexander almost shouted, 'Well, please will you tell him wherever he is that Mr Alexander Armstrong wishes to speak to him on a very important matter, and now!'

There was silence, and when he glanced across the table at his son, he saw that he had covered his ear with one hand. James said softly, 'They're probably too frightened to bother the great man if he's on a ward round.'

Alexander turned quickly to the phone, saying, 'Hello there! Is that you, Richard?'

'Yes. Yes, it's me. And what a way to send a message. You are a bully of a man, you know. What is it now?'

'Richard, when will you be off duty?'

'In half an hour's time.'

'Well, I would ask you, in fact I would tell you, that you must come straight to the nursing home where James and I will be waiting for you. There is a patient here you must see.'

'A patient in the nursing home? But, Alex, what have I to do—'

'Be quiet! Just listen to what I say. This is most important.'

'Something to do with me?'

'Everything to do with you.'

'Concerning my father?'

It was almost a yell into the phone, 'Yes, concerning your father! Now don't ask any more; and, please, don't phone home and tell them where you're going. We'll expect you . . . well, within the next hour. Now get here, Richard, as quickly as you can.'

There was silence at the other end of the line for a moment; then came the words, 'As you say, Alex. As you say.'

They were in Glenda's sitting room, Alexander in an easy chair and James at the end of the couch. Glenda was standing by the sofa table, and her fingers were beating on it as if keeping time to something. She was saying, 'I hope she comes back a little to herself before he arrives, because she's had an awful turn. I wouldn't like him to hear her repeat what she was saying. His father must have been quite inhuman. At one point she must have imagined she was in bed with him. Dear God! It was awful. You know what she said?' Glenda now looked from her brother to her nephew. Then, her head drooping, she said, ' "I am not an animal! I won't be treated like an animal!" And then her body heaved in that strange way again, up and down, up and down, and then she was begging him, actually begging him, not to do something. Then quite suddenly she croaked—in her mind she must have been screaming, you know, like in a dream—but she croaked, "I hate you. You're worse than any animal. You're a filthy pervert!" Then her body began to lift from the bed as if she were being pushed back and forward. We had to try to hold her down in case she injured herself. I don't know where she got the strength, because she's so frail. And then she was gasping, "Don't dare speak! But I will! I will!" And then it was as if her body seemed to be lifted in the air and thrown on to her face, because she heaved herself round in Sister's arms and fell on her face. I had to give her an injection. It'll be a wonder if she survives this one. This is the first time I've seen her in this state.

'Before that, she imagined she was back in the house talking to Mrs Atkins and Trip, and she mentioned Mr Cox, the valet, and was on about something like an escape he had planned for her. Do you remember Cox, the valet?' She looked at her brother.

'Oh, yes. Yes.'

'And she mentioned her lady's maid and the nurse. She was talking to the nurse as if she were standing beside the boy's bed. It was pitiable. Her chest has eased a little but she can't last much longer. This has taken away the very little energy she's got left.'

Her fingers were again beating on the table and she said, 'What I'd like to know is how Richard's been kept in ignorance all these years, I mean of what actually took place.'

'Simply because, my dear, his father is a clever man. If you remember, he took him straight away to Italy, and they stayed there for more than two years. The boy was seven or so when he brought him back and put him in that Catholic boarding-school. It was only he who visited him, and immediately the holidays came he was whisked off abroad or away somewhere. He was about twenty when the war ended; but before that he had made up his mind as to what he wanted to be, once he got out of the Army, and he stood his ground against his father for the first time. He was going to be a doctor and, of all things, he chose plastic surgery. This caused such a row that things have never been the same between them since.'

Alexander now pulled himself to his feet and stood with one hand gripping the mantelshelf as he looked across to his son. 'Whether you are with me or not in this, James, our firm is no longer going to see to the Wellbrook Estate. I know what it'll do to the firm's income, but as it is, we both know we're doing quite well now and can live comfortably without his business.'

James's reply was quiet: 'I'm with you there.'

'There's the bell,' Glenda put in. 'That'll be him. I'm away. You can call me later, if you like, but I can't be in on this. I just couldn't sit through it; and anyway there was my share, and I'm not proud of it. I'll never forgive myself for letting her go alone on that train to Eastbourne.'

When Richard Baindor entered the room

his handsome face looked strained and his voice held an anxious note as he said, 'Well, here I am, at your command, Alex. And I'm still wondering what it's all about.'

'Sit down.' Alexander pointed to an armchair; then he resumed his seat, as did James. There followed a long, awkward silence as they surveyed each other; then, haltingly, Alexander said, 'What do you know about your mother, Richard?'

'About my mother? Only that I was about four years old when she left me and . . . well, she went away. My father told me later that she had died and that he didn't want to hear me speak of her again. It seemed to annoy him. Even as a child, I had noticed it when I asked him something like "When is Mama coming back?" And this happened a number of times while we were in Italy; and because at that time I was a little afraid of him, even more than a little, I kept my thoughts about my mother to myself. Then one day, some years later, without any lead-up, he said, "Your mother is dead, Richard, and I don't want you to mention her name to me ever again." I don't know how old I would have been then, ten or eleven. It was during a school holiday, and I remember, when back at school and hearing other fellows talking about their mothers, feeling a bit lost somehow, as if I had missed out on something.'

'You had indeed missed out on something, Richard. You had indeed.' Alexander was nodding at him. 'Now, I'm going to start at the beginning, and it'll be the second time I've had to go through it, and this is a painful process. I told James here the story and he found it almost unbelievable, as no doubt you will yourself.'

Richard said quietly now, 'You're going to tell me about my mother?'

'Yes, I'm going to tell you about your mother, and also about your father. And I warn you that you will be disturbed. But you must know the truth before it is too late.'

And so Alexander began. For a full half-hour he talked, and for a full half-hour Richard Baindor sat staring at him, not uttering a word or asking a question, not even when Alexander finished, 'Nearly twenty-seven years have gone by. We don't know what has happened to her in all that time, only that she must have worn the same clothes practically every day, I think, and that, for a time, she must have been sleeping rough. Very rough.'

Again there was a painful silence. Then

both Alexander and James watched the young man fall back in his chair and cover his face with his hands. They made no move, but waited until the spasm had eased. Then they watched him pull a handkerchief from his pocket and wipe his face. He did not say he was sorry or make any apology for his tears, he just sat staring at them. It was some minutes before he spoke: 'It's . . . unbelievable,' he said.

'Yes,' said James, 'it does seem unbelievable, but when you see her, Richard, you will believe all right.'

'He turned her mind?'

'Yes,' said Alexander. 'He definitely turned her mind. It is slipping back now, into Wellbrook Manor when you were a boy of four. I recall the night she last held you: she put her arms around you and hugged you while she promised you you were both going on an adventure. I didn't know anything about it then. She had told me nothing, but her manner had been rather odd—odd for her, that is, because usually she was not placid exactly, but just quiet. That evening she seemed excited, even highly excited, especially when she went on the stage, and she had never sung better. In her heart she must have known it would be her last appearance there because she was going to escape. It was only some time after the terrible scene in the dressing room that Cox called on me and gave me what money was left over from the purchase of two second-class tickets to America. At that time, your father was away, but she was determined, even if he hadn't been, that she would still make a run for it, and take you with her. Trip has told me that he was in on this.'

'Trip? Old Trip?'

'Yes, old Trip.'

'Why has he never said anything to me?'

'Because, I should imagine, he knew what it would do to you: you thought she was dead and it was better to leave it like that. He didn't know what had happened to your mother and, what is more, he was middle-aged even then, and the manor had been his home since he was a boy working in the yard. He had no other home, but he knew that if he dared to say anything to you he would be out on his neck; and so would Mrs Atkins.'

'And . . .' Richard hesitated '. . . have you thought she was dead all these years?'

'Not really. No. For years we had detectives looking here and there, but we decided, at least I did in my own mind, that when one reported that a strange lady had been sighted on the London docks, she must have gone abroad after all. But no; she must have just been wandering there, knowing with half her mind that that was the place of escape.'

Richard rose to his feet and began to pace the room almost from the window to the door. Neither Alexander nor James did anything to stop him or uttered a word until he looked at them and said, 'I can't take it in. You say she looked like a vagrant and probably had been exactly that for years, judging from the condition of her clothes?'

It was Alexander who answered, saying, 'Yes, Richard, and we shall show you the clothes so that you will see what I mean by a vagrant.'

Now Alexander rang a bell, and when a maid arrived he said, 'Would you please ask Matron if she will step in here a moment?'

Glenda came in. She looked at Richard, who was now standing by the far window, gripping the framework.

At her entry he turned slowly.

She did not speak to him and it was a moment or so before he murmured, 'Oh, Glenda. Glenda.'

'I know, Richard. I know just a little of how you must feel, because I, too, am staggered.'

It was here that James broke in, 'Do you think you could get the coat and hat and other garments?'

She paused, then said, 'Yes, I can do that,' and went off.

It was more than five minutes later before she returned, and during that time not half a dozen words had been exchanged between the three men.

Glenda drew away the white sheet covering the garments that were laid across her arm. She put them on the couch and, turning to James, she said, 'Hold that up, will you?'

He took the dirty-looking, worn coat and held it so that Richard could see it. Then, when Glenda took the weird contraption of a hat and placed it on the neck of the coat there came a loud exclamation from Richard. 'I've seen her! I've met her! Oh, dear God! Yes.' He put his hand to his head and turned to face them again. 'She was sitting on a box on the drive of the hospital. She—' He couldn't go on: his eyes were tightly closed and his lower lip was caught between his teeth, before he recovered sufficiently to say, 'She gripped my wrist. She must have recognised me somehow. Why she was there, I don't know; but the chaps—there were two with me—they thought she was begging. And'—he closed his eyes again—'one of them offered her a shilling, and she knocked his hand flying and the shilling went into the gutter. She still had hold of my wrist and was trying to say something.' He looked at Alex now and asked, 'Is . . . is she partly dumb?'

'In a way, yes, Richard, or, at least, she's fearful of speaking.'

'She kept opening her mouth and putting her head back, and one of my friends suggested that what she said was "Rich," and went on to explain: "She thinks you're rich, she's begging." And I remember now how that dreadful pale face changed. I—I had to ease her fingers from my wrist and I kept telling her she must get to Outpatients. She—she needed attention for her chest. Intermittently she was absolutely croaking, and I recall I backed away from her saying I had a car waiting. And, you know, I almost went at a run. And she had come in those clothes when she first saw you?'

'Oh, yes. Just like that. She must have worn them for years.'

Richard now took the coat from James's hands and, holding it in front of him, he stared at it before pulling it to his chest and saying, 'Poor woman! I'll—I'll kill him! I know now that I've always had two overriding emotions with regard to my father. Fear and dislike. But not any more. It isn't just dislike. I'll kill him!'

He laid the coat gently over the arm of the couch and said to them, 'But where has she been all this time? She couldn't have been going round in such a state. She would have been picked up by the Salvation Army or some organisation like that.'

'We don't know where she's been, Richard,' said Alexander, 'and I doubt if we'll ever find out, because she still has great difficulty in speaking, though I think part of it is her weakened state. She's in a bad way.'

Glenda was now holding up the tattered remains of two other garments. She hadn't brought the drawers with her; that would've been too embarrassing; but she had brought what was left of the woollen shift, and he took it in his hands, and saw that it had been stitched here and there, with stitches over stitches. The woollen garment was still long but very fragile and worn.

Glenda said to him: 'It's as I told Alex, she

has terrible memories, and she thinks she's back in the manor, and what she reveals happened at night in it becomes more horrifying. But how, I ask myself now, did she ever expect to escape from that man? I'm sure he would have hunted her to the ends of the earth and taken you back, Richard. Then God knows what he would have done to her, because he must have certainly intended to kill both her and Timothy on that night of the concert. When I saw her body I couldn't believe it. I know she has a delicate skin, it still shows in her face, but I don't think she bruises easily. But her body is almost covered with marks left by deep cuts and tears of some kind. Even after all these years they are still evident, faint but evident, like stains on the skin. They're especially noticeable around the ankles. I'm telling you this, Richard, to give you some indication of the reason for her mental condition. The last battering must have turned her mind and impeded her speech. But why she has worn these clothes all these years, I don't know. At some time she might have had a change in circumstances, but we'll probably never know. She has clung to these clothes as if . . . well, I have my own theories, but we won't know until we find out where she's been.'

Richard sat down, his elbows on his knees, and rested his face between his hands. No one spoke until he lifted his head and, looking at Glenda, asked, 'May I see her?'

Glenda hesitated before saying, 'Well, she's asleep now; she became so agitated that I had to give her a jab. It might be an hour or so before she's round. But of course you may see her; and,' she smiled now, 'it will be wonderful, I'm sure, when she wakes to see your face.'

'She must have recognised you that day, as you say, when she gripped your hand,' Alexander said.

'But how? If I was four when she last left me.'

After a moment's thought Alexander said, 'Probably because you bear a strong resemblance to her father. Yes,' he nodded, 'the more I look at you the more I see Francis, your grandfather. And you have her mouth. But there's no sign of your . . . . begetter in you, and none as yet shows in your nature, and I've known you since you were a baby.'

'Well, I suppose I can thank God for that,'

said Richard bitterly. 'But when I think how my poor mother was allowed to suffer so much all those years . . .' In quite a different tone he appealed to Alexander, 'What am I going to do?'

'You'll have to see him and tell him.'

'Tell him? If I were to see him at this moment I'd strangle him. I'll have to think, because this puts an end not only to my way of life but also to his.' He stood up again and once more began to pace. Then he stopped and, looking at them, he said, 'I'll never live in that house again. I'll set foot in it once and that will be to tell him what I know of him and think of him. I've felt guilty all my life about my feelings regarding him because everything he did seemed to be for my welfare. Until I decided for myself what I was going to be he was for pushing me on into business so that in time I could take over his empire. And it is an empire he's got, as you know only too well.'

He turned to Alexander now. 'And what has he made most of his money out of? Property. A lot of it in the slums, dropping to pieces. That has always upset me; but I was so afraid of him for years that I daren't say anything to him. Twice only I have witnessed how he reacts when he is thwarted in any way. On each occasion he became violent. Once only, though, did he attempt to lift his hand against me, when he kept his doubled fist in mid-air before dropping back to his seat. It looked as if he was going to have a seizure. I recall now, it was in my teens on the day I dared to say to him, "I would like to know more about my mother, Father." That day I was once more forbidden ever to mention her name again: she had been a wicked woman, he said, she had left me without a thought. On and on he went, before finishing in a dreadful, terrifying voice, "Don't ever speak her name to me again as long as we live."

'From that day I began to question, but daren't voice my thoughts. It was Trip who, one day, took me aside and said, "Your mother was not a bad lady. Just remember that." I could never get him to go on and tell me more, although I begged him, and he said . . .' Richard paused. 'He said, "I've lived in this house all my life, as has Mrs Atkins. We both came when we were very young; we look upon it as home. We want to finish our days here in peace, Master Richard. Do you understand me?" I didn't, but I said yes. It would be easy to condemn his attitude, but when I think that only a few days ago I pushed her off me, I want to bury my head in shame.'

'Don't be silly!' Alexander said sharply. 'You weren't to know.'

'Come along, Richard,' said Glenda, 'but she won't be round yet.'

A few minutes later he was entering his mother's bedroom. He walked slowly to the bedside and looked down on the emaciated face with the two long grey plaits lying, one each side of it. He was so pale himself that the sister pushed a chair towards him.

As he sat there, staring into the face of his mother, there was no way to describe the emotions that flooded him. He could say the main one was love, but there was sorrow, anxiety, remorse and, through it all, a strong vein of anger. For a moment he felt it would overpower all his other emotions, because it was linked with hate, and deep within him he knew that, if nothing else, he had inherited those two emotions from the man who had begotten him, and he knew he would use them to the full.

How he would do this, he did not yet know. He knew only that he wanted to lift the figure from the bed and hold her in his arms and tell her he remembered her. Oh, yes, he remembered her. He could even now recall the last time she had held him in her arms. She had looked so lovely, and she had worn that coat and that hat, which had made her extraordinarily beautiful then. He could even recall his nurse of that time . . . Flora. Flora Carr. But where had his mother been all these years? Why hadn't she come back and sought him out?

Well, she had, hadn't she? She had sat on the box on the hospital drive and held his wrist. In some way her mind had cleared and she remembered the past. But who or what had brought her into the present?

Someone was speaking to him. He turned to see a nurse at his side who said softly, 'Matron says will you stay to dinner?'

He couldn't give her an answer, his mind was in a whirl. He muttered, 'I don't know. I'll see.'

He recalled that he had promised to meet Jackie later on for dinner; he wasn't due back in the hospital until nine tomorrow morning. But he wasn't going back to the hospital and he'd have to tell them. But Jackie? He'd have to get word to her as well. Just now, though, the only thing that mattered was that he meant to stay with his poor mother for as long as she needed him.

During the next hour he drank two cups of coffee, sitting where he was, holding the long-fingered, blue-veined hand. It was the hand of an old woman, yet the face did not show many wrinkles. The skin was too tightly drawn for that. He was staring down into it as the lips moved and the eyelids lifted; and then she was looking at him. Now her mouth opened and she brought out one word in a husky whisper, 'Richard.'

As his arms went about her, hers went around his neck and he murmured, 'Oh, Mother, Mother.'

The sister and a nurse were standing at the foot of the bed. Both turned away and busied themselves at a table by the door. It was too much to witness.

'My love, I should have known you the other day.'

The arms tightened about his neck.

How long they clung together he didn't know; only when she released her hold on him did he let her slip back on to the pillows and, stroking her damp hair from her forehead, said, 'I'll never leave you again. Never.'

'Richard.' The name was clear although throaty.

'Yes, talk to me. Tell me where you've been all this time. Just a little bit at a time.'

She put up her hand and stroked his cheek, and now she said another name, 'Bella.'

'Bella? Who is Bella?'

He watched her eyes close and her lips move up into what could have been a smile, and the next word she used was, 'Good.'

Again he repeated, 'Good?' Then said, 'Bella was good?'

She made a small motion with her hand.

Glenda was by his side now and she said softly, 'Don't tire her, Richard. It's wonderful. She spoke clearly; I could hear it. A little at a time. Let her rest.'

He leant forward now and placed his lips on his mother's forehead, and again her arms were up and around his neck.

'Richard.'

'Yes, dear Mother? I'll be here, all the time. I'll not leave you unless you're asleep. Try now . . . try now to rest.'

Slowly her arms slid from his neck and on to the counterpane, and again the smile was taking up the corners of her mouth.

Passing the sister, he went to the window and stood looking out. He knew what was about to happen to him: he was going to cry again, and he mustn't. His heart was so full of love for her that it had become an unbearable pain. He knew what it was to love. He loved Jackie; but it had never caused this pain. Pain that was built on sorrow and regret for the years that had gone and would never return. Years during which he had missed the love of a beautiful girl, a beautiful woman, who was now lying behind him, a mere skeleton of herself. But at least now she was here although it could never fill the great gap that had built up in him since he was a boy . . . It had closed a little when he met Jackie, who had filled his heart with warmth.

Glenda was by his side once more, and she said softly, 'She's asleep. Now, come and have something to eat.'

'I'm going to stay tonight.'

'Yes; I'll have a chair-bed made up for you alongside her. But you can't go on if you don't have rest and food; you know that. Come on now.'

She took his arm and, after one more glance towards the sleeping figure in the bed, she led him from the room.

She was saying, 'Alex is still here; I'll bring a drink into the sitting room before we eat. Go on in.'

'Presently, Glenda. I must get in touch with Jackie; I promised to meet her. I must also get through to the hospital. But tell me, how long do you think she's got?'

'Oh, I couldn't say, my dear. Dr Swan says that if we can get a little nourishment into her and if her chest eases, she could hang on for a few weeks.'

'A few weeks! Really? Oh, well, then, I shall ask for leave.'

'What are you going to tell Jackie?'

'You mean about this business? Nothing at the moment. I'll . . . I couldn't talk about it to anybody else, not just yet. I'll try to explain to her. Will you excuse me? And may I use the phone in your office?'

'Certainly. Go along.' She pushed him down the short corridor, and at the corner, she said, 'It's the end door.'

He went into the small, neatly arranged office, sat down on a typist's revolving chair at the end of a desk and pulled the phone towards him. His first call was to the hospital and his head of department. He knew that David Baker would still be at work and he asked to be put through to him. When the voice came on the phone, he said, 'David . . . it's Richard.'

'Yes, Richard? You want to have a word with me? Anything wrong?'

'I can't put you in the picture yet. Something very important has happened, and I want to ask if you think I could take my leave as from now for the next month or six weeks.'

'For four to six weeks?'

'Yes. I know I'm asking a lot, but I was due for a month anyway.'

'It's all right. Tell me honestly, are you in trouble?'

'No, I'm not in trouble, not that kind of trouble, but someone I love, should have loved for years, I have found and she is dying . . . and . . . and I want to be with her.'

There was silence at the other end of the line; then David's voice was saying, 'Someone you have found? You intrigue me.'

'I'm sorry, David. I would like to give you the whole story now, but I shall later on, I promise you. I must ask, though, if it would be putting you out too much.'

'No, no. I'll fix something up. Your main work was on the little fellow, but he's getting on amazingly and a few weeks more in bed won't do him any harm. Anyway, he's got to learn to walk. But may I keep in touch?'

'Yes, of course.'

'Where are you now? At home?'

'No.' Richard's voice was harsh. 'No, David, I'm not at home; and I'll never be at home again. I can tell you that much.'

'Oh, my goodness. Anyway, where'll I find you?'

'At Beechwood Nursing Home.'

'Oh, yes, I know it. And I can get you there?'

'Most of the time.'

'Well, go ahead. I'll phone you again in a day or two.'

'Yes. Thanks, David, thanks very much indeed. Goodbye.'

For a moment longer he sat thinking, then rang a number and a stiff voice said, 'Beaumont Lodge.'

'This is Richard Baindor. Is Miss Jackie at home?'

The voice at the other end changed: 'No, sir. She left for her office not half an hour ago. Would you like to speak to his lordship?'

'No, thank you. I'll contact her. Thank you. Goodbye.'

In answer to his next call the voice that answered was abrupt, but said, 'Yes?'

'Is Miss Franks in her office?'

'Yes. Who's speaking?'

'Richard Baindor.'

A moment later and Jackie was on the line. 'Hello, Richard. What's up? We haven't to meet for another hour, have we? I've been home to get all togged up, but there are some papers I need for tomorrow's journey and I thought I'd pick them up before I went on to your little grey home in the west and . . .'

'Jackie, stop it and listen to me. I can't see you tonight.'

There was a pause, and then she said, 'I knew it. One of those blasted nurses has got you at last! I said they would.'

'Jackie, please! Stop kidding. Listen to me. Something serious has happened. I can't tell you what it is on the phone and I can't see you tonight.'

'What d'you mean, something serious has happened? To your father?'

He barked, 'No, not my father.'

'All right! All right, don't shout!'

'I can't explain now, but just believe me, I'm desperately sorry about tonight but—'

'Where are you? Where are you speaking from?'

'Glenda's nursing home.'

'Who in there can be keeping you, then?'

'Someone very important; but I've told you I can't talk about it over the phone, and I'm in no state to see you tonight. What's more, whatever you do, don't phone the house.'

'Well, you'll see me tomorrow, will you? Look'—her voice was soft now—'if you're in trouble of some kind . . .'

'No, I'm not in trouble, Jackie, of any kind. I'm only in—Oh, I can't explain! But look, do me a favour, go off on your assignment to Wales tomorrow. It's a very good one. You know it is; you've been looking forward to it.'

'To hell with Wales and assignments! I'm not going to leave you—'

'Jackie. Something good and something awful has happened to me . . . well, not to me, but has come into my life. It's something you'll have to share, but it's something I'm so upset about at the moment I wouldn't be able to talk to you coherently. Now, do as I ask, you'll be there only for a day. He's a big catch. Get his story, then come back;

and as soon as you're home ring me up. Then we'll make arrangements to meet and I'll tell you all about it. It's a long story and it's going to change our lives.'

'Our lives? You mean we're . . .?'

'Oh, no. No, I don't mean we'll have to part or anything like that. I could never part from you, Jackie, you know that. Believe me, I'm going to need your help and your advice. So will you do as I ask?'

There was a pause before she said, 'Yes. And I'll say it again, I love you very, very much whatever happens.'

'And I love you, Jackie, more than words will ever express. Goodbye, darling, for the present.'

'Bye-bye, my love.'

Richard put down the receiver, took a long, deep breath, then again rested his elbows on the table and put his head on his hands.

3

Bella was at her wits' end. She'd had them out searching all day and nobody seemed to have seen the odd figure in that awful dirty coat and weird headgear. They must have made Reenee stand out, yet no one seemed to have noticed her. Bella was tired. They were all tired. She couldn't go to the hospital today to see Carl; she had sent Joe to tell him that she had a filthy cold and was lying up for a day or so, because she knew that once he heard that Reenee had gone again he'd be upset because he was unable to do anything about it . . .

The following morning she asked them all again to go out looking and asking if anyone had caught sight of her, and they all returned with the same message. John refrained from mentioning again that he had been to the river police to ask if they had come across a body in the water.

They were about to break up that evening when Willie remarked, 'She's never gone off like this for years, has she, Bella? Then you mentioned the doctor's name and she went into one of her turns.'

They all looked from one to the other, and Tony said, 'None of us knows her real name. I wonder, do you think that might be her name? You never know.'

'No,' said Bella quickly; 'it was the name of the doctor.'

'Well, the doctor, that special doctor, works in the hospital an' he's been lookin' after Carl, hasn't he?'

'Yes.' She nodded.

'Well, d'you think she might have gone to the hospital to try to see Carl?' asked Tony.

'If she had,' put in Joe, 'I'd have been the first one to know. But it wasn't Carl's name that upset her, it was the doctor's. And I think our next step, Bella, is to go to the hospital tomorrow morning and find out if she's been there.'

The following morning Bella and Joe took a taxi to the hospital. They did not go straight to Carl's ward but to the reception area and enquired if a woman had been asking to speak to Dr Baindor.

One of the girls behind the desk looked at her and said, 'Lots of people come here enquiring for this doctor and that.'

'Yes, I know what you mean,' said Bella, 'but this woman would look different. She would look very odd to you with a weird hat and an old dirty coat.'

'Was she ill?'

'Yes; she had a very bad chest.'

'Well, she would likely go to Outpatients. Look, go outside and you'll see the directions to Outpatients.'

'Thank you.'

In the outpatients' department Bella put the same question to a girl standing behind the counter, but the girl took no heed of her because she was busy dictating something to a doctor who was at the end of the counter writing on a pad; and when again Bella put the question, the girl said, 'What? An odd woman? This is a place for odd people.' She laughed and turned to another receptionist, further along the counter, who was using a phone.

'But this person would stand out,' persisted Bella stiffly. 'She was wearing a long, dirty-looking coat and a weird headpiece.'

'Well, I'm sure I haven't seen anyone like that.'

The girl who had been using the phone put it down and said, 'Oh, yes. I was on the main desk the day she came. She was asking for a doctor, a special doctor. She wouldn't go until we made enquiries about where he was. When she was told he had gone on leave she went away.'

Bella turned and looked at Joe, who said, 'Thank you,' but then added, 'Do you know whether or not she left the hospital?'

The woman thought for a moment, then said, 'I suppose she did. She went,' and she pointed to a window, 'down the drive there.'

Outside, Bella said, 'I can't go and see Carl, I'm too upset. But she must be about somewhere.'

They were walking down a side drive when they heard running footsteps behind them. They turned and saw a young man in a white coat. He called, 'Pardon me, but . . . but I think I have seen the woman you are looking for. She was dressed very oddly, had a weird contraption on her head.'

'Yes, yes,' Bella was nodding at him, 'that's her.'

'Well, you see, she was enquiring for Dr Baindor.'

'Yes, I'm sure she would be, a doctor of that name, yes. You see, I know that doctor, he's looking after one of my boys.'

'Oh,' the young man said, and Bella went on, 'Do you know where she went?'

'Yes, I do, as it happens. I was with Dr Baindor at the time. She seemed to recognise him and hung on to him. But he had a car waiting and he asked me to see to her. She should have been in hospital, she had an awful chest.'

'Oh, my!' Bella said. 'And you don't know where she went?'

'Yes, I do, because she had difficulty in speaking, as if she were partly dumb.'

'That's her,' said Joe now.

'Do you know where she's gone?' asked Bella quickly.

'Yes, because she asked me to get her a taxi. She wrote the address in my diary here . . .' He put a hand into his breast pocket and brought out a little book. He opened it, and said, 'There,' pointed to a page and read, ' "Beverley Square. Armstrong, Solicitor." I got her a taxi and I told the driver where to take her. That's the last I saw of her.'

'Oh, thank you, young man!' Bella grabbed his hand and shook it up and down. 'You have been a help! Thank you. And you helped *her* too.'

'I hope you find her,' he said; 'I'm sure you will.'

Fifteen minutes later they were walking up the steps and into the hall of the solicitor's office.

The receptionist asked Bella, 'Have you an appointment?'

'No, I haven't, but I must see him,' said Bella curtly.

The girl looked at the pair, the tubby little old woman and the big, gangling middle-aged man, and she said, 'He never sees anyone unless they have an appointment.' She didn't like the look of either of these two. Common. 'What is your name?'

'Miss Bella Morgan.'

Once more the young girl picked up the phone and contacted Miss Fairweather. 'There are two people down here,' she said softly, 'who want to see Mr Armstrong. The woman's called Miss Bella Morgan.'

'Have they an appointment?'

'No.'

'Well, what are they like?'

The receptionist's voice was very low now as she answered, 'Common.'

'Miss Manning, please don't judge people by their dress. Remember the other day?'

Yes, Miss Manning remembered the other day all right, and that weird woman, and all the fuss and the ambulance and everything, as if she were somebody important; and apparently, from the little she had heard, she was. Then why was she looking like a vagrant? Nobody could explain that to her. She again spoke into the phone: 'Well, what am I going to do?'

'Get them to wait.'

Miss Fairweather now tapped on her boss's door and straightway went in, saying, 'There are two people in the foyer, Mr Armstrong, and their appearance doesn't seem to impress Miss Manning. She described them as common.'

'Did she now? And those two common people want to see me? What is their name?'

'If I remember rightly, it is Miss or Mrs Bella Morgan.'

'Bella?' He repeated the name again, before saying, 'Send them up straight away.'

Bella and her companion were shown into
Alexander's office. He was standing ready
to greet them and immediately he offered
Bella a chair. Then, after looking from one
to the other, he sat down and asked quietly,
'How can I help you?'

'A woman came to see you the other day,'
said Bella. 'She was very oddly dressed in
a long dark coat and a weird hat or whatever. Am I right?'

'Yes, Miss Morgan; you are right; she did
come to see me and—'

'And you know where she is now?'

'Yes, I do indeed. She's well tucked up in
bed in my sister's nursing home, and I must
tell you, my firm and I have been looking for
her for the past twenty-seven years.'

Bella took a deep gulp of air and said,
'Twenty-seven years? And that's nearly as
long as I've had her.'

'No!'

'Yes. Yes, sir, it is. She's like . . . well,
she's more than a daughter to me, more
than a companion. She brought something
into my life that I'd never had, and I've
looked after her. She wasn't right in the head

then, and I'm afraid it hasn't improved much, but I've looked after her to the best of my ability. The only thing I couldn't get her to do was change her clothes, I mean that coat and the hat. But she has never been out of my house for . . . well, nigh on ten years until two days ago, and only two times before that.'

Alexander was gazing at her in amazement and his voice was just a whisper as he said, 'She wore the coat all the time?'

'Most of the time, yes. It was a sort of protection somehow. You see, she was afraid of men. I've got five lads—well, I call them mine—and I've looked after them for years. One got killed in the war, but Joe here, and Carl, they were lads when I took them on years ago because I had a fruit stall attached to the house. It took her some time to get used to them, but she had only to see another man or anybody come to the door and she flew out of the way. It was as if she was expecting somebody to come and do for her, or something like that.

'Oh, it's a long story, sir. Joe here, and Carl—he's in hospital under Dr Baindor— they found her lying in a dirty old yard of mine that was filled with broken fruit boxes and quite a bit of rotten fruit. She was sleeping among the boxes. I don't know how long she had been on the road or sleeping rough, I never could get that out of her, but it must have been for some months because she was in a dreadful state. But, anyway, I've had her, sir, for all these years. And I thought I'd lost her for good.'

She stopped for want of breath, and Alexander said, 'Miss Morgan, at this moment I don't know anybody I'm more pleased to see than you and your friend there'—he nodded towards Joe—'because you've filled in the great gap of her life. And, do you know, twice she has said the name Bella.'

'Has she?' Bella's face was a-beam now.

'Yes, it was as if she missed you.'

'Would . . . will I be able to see her?'

'Of course. You'll be very welcome. I'm sure you've got a long tale to tell us, and I've got, I can assure you, Miss Morgan, a longer and more terrible tale to tell you.'

Her face drained of colour. She looked at him and said, 'Aye, I bet you have, sir. I knew something terrible must have happened in her early life because she used to go into spasms at the mention of a name or a word that seemed to recall some terrible past. Her body would go into contortions as if she was fighting somebody.'

'And indeed she was, Miss Morgan. But you'll know all about it later. Now, I'm not going to ask you if you would like a cup of tea here, I'm going to take you to my sister's nursing home where you'll be made more than welcome, I can assure you. And there you will see your—'

'I call her my lass.'

'Well, you'll see your lass.'

He rang a bell, and when Miss Fairweather entered he said, 'I am going with these good friends to my sister's, Miss Fairweather. And when Mr James comes back, tell him to come straight along, will you, please?'

'Yes, Mr Armstrong.'

He took his hat and coat from a hallstand near the door, and led them out, down the stairs and into the hall. There he paused. 'Will you just wait one tick, I forgot to tell my secretary something.'

At this he went back up the stairs and surprised Miss Fairweather by going to her desk and saying in a low voice, 'I've left quite a number of letters I've already drafted on the desk. Some others I haven't got down to yet, but they're not very important and you'll know how to deal with them. Will you see to them for me?'

'Of course, Mr Armstrong. Don't you worry, just leave them to me.'

'Thank you, Miss Fairweather.' He patted her arm then left her with a strange look on her face. He would have been surprised if he had seen her eyes turn to her arm where he had laid his hand, for it was the first time he had made such a gesture to her in all the long years she had worked for him.

Bella could not believe all this was happening to her and Joe. Wait till she told the others! The car was a large one, though she did not appreciate the luxury of it for she was so taken up with the fact that in a short while she would see her lass. The words kept repeating themselves in her mind: she would see her lass . . .

The lady who was introduced to her as the solicitor's sister was kindness itself. She took them both into a fine sitting room, where she informed them that before they did any visiting they must have a cup of tea and a little talk with her and her brother.

The little talk filled Glenda and Alexander with astonishment. For twenty-six years this little woman had looked after Irene. They could hardly believe it, nor that the poor dear thing had lived in a house for years and years without going out of its doors. But was it any more astounding than the life the patient was revealing to them all bit by bit, demonstrating the time she had suffered under that brute, that filthy brute of a man, who was now a multi-millionaire and sitting comfortably in his mansion?

When Glenda opened the bedroom door, Richard rose to his feet from the side of the bed and stared at the little woman and the tall fellow by her side, and exclaimed softly, 'Bella?'

She stared at him: this was Carl's doctor, Dr Baindor, whose name had knocked her lass into one of her turns. Baindor. This, then, was the boy, the son. She thrust out a hand towards him and he grasped it; then he put his finger to his lips and pointed to the chair. She sat down, still looking at him, before she turned slowly to the bed and looked at the face that was lying there. That dear, dear face, but how different: the long plaits hanging down each side of her shoulders, the pretty nightdress, the long sleeves ending in frills at the wrists. Gently, she lifted up the thin hand from the counterpane and held it almost reverently against her breast.

Slowly the eyes opened and to her utmost delight there was recognition in them, and her name came out quite clearly, though slightly huskily. 'Bella. Oh, Bella.'

The arms lifted and were about her neck, and she was enfolding her lass, crying as she did so, 'Oh, my lass! Oh, my love! To see you here lookin' so lovely! I've been so terribly worried. I thought I'd lost you.'

'Bella. Bella.'

'Yes, I'm your Bella. I'll always be your Bella.'

Then the face below hers turned and looked at the man standing to the side of the bed, and Irene said, 'My son.'

'Yes, lass, your son.' Bella was looking up into Richard's face and she said, 'I can't believe it, but I always knew she had a child somewhere;' and turning back to Irene, she said, 'Remember the teddy bear?'

'Teddy bear.' Those words were clear too.

'You hugged it and rocked it, and I knew then you had a child.'

Bending down to his mother, Richard said

softly, 'Bella and I have met before. I look after one of her boys. You know . . . Carl.'

'Carl. Oh, dear Carl.' The name, too, was clear.

'Bella came to visit him.'

'Carl here?'

'Not here, Mother, in the hospital.'

Irene looked at Bella and, lifting one hand, she stroked her cheek, saying as she did so, 'Kind. Kind.'

'And who wouldn't be kind to you, lass? Who wouldn't? The lads'll be overjoyed. Joe's here.' Bella looked over her shoulder. 'Joe! Come and say hello.'

Irene now looked up into the big rough face, and the smile came to her lips again and she said, 'Joe.'

'Yes,' put in Bella, 'Joe and Carl. They were pals. Always pals.'

'Lovely to see you, Reenee . . . 'tis,' said Joe. 'By! We've missed you.' Then, bending closer to her, he said, 'Worn my shoes down lookin' for you.'

The lips went higher up into a smile. Then Glenda's quiet voice broke in on them: 'I would let her rest now.'

After they had left the room, Richard sat by the bed, and Irene, looking at him, said,

'Bella . . . so kind, so kind,' and he answered softly, 'Yes, I'm sure she is, my dear; and she loves you.'

Irene's eyelids drooped and there was a smile on her lips as once again she drifted into sleep.

It had been agreed between Alexander, James and Glenda that before he approached his father Richard should talk to Jackie and give her the full picture, because although the result of the interview might not alter his choice of profession, it would certainly affect his way of living. The old swine would definitely cut him off without a penny.

They imagined they all knew exactly how Jackie would react, but it was better, they thought, that it should be put to her, so here he was at the station, greeting her from the train.

After their warm embrace Richard said, 'May we go to your flat?'

'Yes, of course; but what about yours?'

'I . . . I don't want to go back there.'

When she glanced sideways at him, he said, 'It will all be made plain to you shortly.'

'Well, I hope so; you've had me worried for the last forty-eight hours.'

'How did you get on?'

'Well, I suppose you could say the interview was successful but to sit for two solid
hours in the company of a man who has the
intelligence of a rabbit and an ego the size
of an elephant, there you have my answer.
I suppose he was born with a photographic
mind and at school he could read through
a book and remember every page of it, so
was dubbed one of the clever clogs, and he
has built on that. He could tell me every law
that has been passed since 1066, oh, and
long before that, and that has got him where
he is today. But ask him to solve any of the
problems that are being created by his lot,
and he'll give you an answer by reference
to page so-and-so in a book by so-and-so.
There were times when I had to tell myself
to sit still, to stay put, that this was a job: I
wasn't there to dissect his character, only
to know how he felt about his new title.'

Her tirade stopped as he brought the car
to a halt outside her flat, but as soon as she
was indoors and they were settled in a comfortable but small and rather cluttered sitting
room, she went on, 'I was saying about how
that had got him where he is today. Now,
Richard, give my father his due, and I know,

as do a few other people, that in a way he bought his title. You don't shovel heaps of money into your party without expecting something in return. He has always aimed at being somebody, after having pulled himself up by his boot-laces, and not having had much of a so-called education. Yet he's got more intelligence in his head than many of his so-called friends in the House of Lords, especially that big lump of egotism I've been dealing with all day. Well, now, that's the answer to your question at the station; and now it is your turn to tell me whatever is making your face the colour it is. Before that, however, d'you want a drink? Something hard? Or tea or coffee?'

'Coffee, please. It'll keep hot longer.' He gave her a wry smile.

'Oh, that means it's going to be a long session.'

'Yes, it means just that.'

It was an hour and a half later. They were both still sitting on the couch and they were silent. He had told her everything, right from the beginning, as Alexander had told him, up to the present day when his mother had given him four pawn tickets and a faded picture of himself when he was a boy. As yet he didn't know what the pawn tickets represented; but he or Alexander would find out. And lastly he had told her what he meant to say to his father, and that he knew he would be disinherited.

Slowly she put out a hand, caught his and held it against her cheek. She said softly, 'The usual thing to say would be that I can't believe it, but I can, every word of it; and I'll tell you now, darling, I might not have said so but I have always disliked your father. As for my old man, he can't stand him either, for he knows only too well your engagement to me would never have been countenanced if it hadn't been for his title.'

'I'll not have any income other than what I earn, you understand that?' Richard said.

'Of course I understand. But very shortly you'll be a consultant, and I haven't seen your present superior or any of the others like him living from hand to mouth. And then there's me. I have my job, which I might tell you I'm going to change.'

He took her other hand. 'What d'you mean you're going to change?'

'I'm . . . Oh, I'm going to stay in the same business, but I'm not going to go on tour any more. That one assignment abroad finished me. I realised then that I wasn't made to witness children dying of hunger or people fleeing for their lives, and one tribe slaughtering another. I thought I was until I got there; but no. It takes years to find out what you do best, and I've just found out what I can do best'—and now her voice changed—'and one of the things is staying near to you, because I love you, Richard.'

He was now holding her tight, and they were lying on the couch and his eyes filled as he said, 'I'm ashamed of myself. I'm doing this so often.'

'You can't find a better way of release. Go on, darling, let go. As long as you want to cry on my breast I'll be happy all my life.'

After a moment he muttered, 'It's . . . it's her . . . Mother. I . . . I can't get her out of my mind. The sight of her and what she must have gone through at his hands. To have turned her mind, because it is still not right. She slips back and forward between the past and the present, and nearly always a terrible past. It's pitiable to see her fighting and struggling when she's remembering him again. I don't know how I'm going to face him, Jackie, I really don't. I know I must; but how am I going to keep my hands off him?'

'You will. After what you've told me you'll be able to cut him to shreds with your tongue. The final fact that you're walking out on him for ever will finish him.'

They lay quiet for a moment before she asked softly, 'Will you take me to see your mother?'

'Yes, darling. I'll take you to meet her, and you will be able to see for yourself the devastation that one human being can wreak on another.'

It was nine o'clock the next morning when Richard rang the number of what was called the house phone. This was placed in Mrs Atkins's office so that she could deal with the ordering and the household necessities quite apart from what was called the main phone.

When she picked it up and heard Richard's voice saying, 'Is that you, Mrs Atkins?' she exclaimed, 'Oh, Mr Richard, the master has been so worried—' only to be cut off by his voice saying sharply, 'Listen, Mrs Atkins. I need your help and Trip's. Now, listen carefully: get Trip to the phone, but don't let the master know I'm calling. You understand?'

'Yes, Mr Richard. I'll get him.'

When Trip came to the phone, he said, 'Oh, sir, I'm glad to hear you. We wondered what had happened to you.'

'Listen, Trip, there isn't much time. Has he got anyone looking after him now?'

'Not at the moment, sir. You know he's had nurses, but the last one left a week ago. He's been seeing to himself since.'

'Well, now, I want you to do something for me; and should it go wrong and he finds out that you have helped me, let me assure you and Mrs Atkins that you will not lose by it. What is more, there is a position awaiting you both at Beaumont Lodge, Miss Jackie's home, you know. Now, listen, I want you to get my cases, or better, tell Mrs Atkins to take a maid up with her and fill the cases with as much of my clothing as they can get in. Don't bother with any folding or messing about; just throw everything in from my drawers and cupboards. Then I want you to have them carried down the back stairs where my car will be waiting near the old barns. Who can you trust? Benson?'

'Oh, yes, sir. Benson, of course.'

'And old Tollett?'

'Both of them. They would do anything for you . . . like myself.'

'Thank you, Trip. Thank you. As I say, don't worry. Whatever happens, you'll all be taken care of. That's a promise. I shall be there within the next hour. That should give Mrs Atkins time to get those cases downstairs, shouldn't it?'

'Oh, yes, sir. You are leaving, then, sir?'

'Definitely, Trip. To put you in the picture, I shall tell you one thing: I have found my mother. Yes . . . yes, I heard you gasp. I gasped too. She was turned into a vagrant on the roads. It's a long, long story, but if you stand in the hall this morning, you and Mrs Atkins, you will hear all about it. But do this for me first and as quickly as possible. You will, won't you?'

'Oh, yes, sir, we'll see to it. Don't worry.'

Richard put down the receiver, and stood breathing deeply. Then he looked at Glenda, who was standing nearby, and said, 'Glenda, I'm full of fear, like a soldier who has been sent into battle and ordered to kill somebody.'

'Oh, Richard, don't talk like that; and you're not full of fear, at least of him, are you?'

'Oh, no! Not of him. Never again of him, ever. But I've a fear of myself and what I might do.'

'Well, you know what Jackie said to you: slay him with words, that will be enough. And another thing, you're not sleeping on that chair-bed any more. There is a room vacant, it's just two doors away, and you're going to take that as yours for the present.'

He put out his hands to her and drew her gently to him and said, 'You're a lovely person, Glenda Armstrong, a lovely person. And, like your brother, you are the best friend a man could ever have, and I'll never stop being grateful to you.'

'Get yourself away! We don't want any more tears, do we? That'd be the end of me if my staff see me with a wet face; they'll know they have made a mistake and that I'm human after all.'

She pushed him away from her on a laugh, and he too, entering her mood, laughed and said, 'Poor staff; I understand how they feel.'

The road along which he drove was so familiar. He knew every hedgerow, every copse, every field. He felt he even knew the cows in the fields; the same ones seemed to have been there for years. And then there was the river gleaming in the distance. How many times had he fished in there? But never again. When he came to the gates of the manor he drove past them and for some distance until he came to two more iron gates. These were plain ones and were open; he drove through them and along an avenue of beech trees. They ended at a high wall, beyond which were the kitchen gardens. He drew the car to a stop, picked up a case from the passenger seat, then got out and walked round the side of the house on to the terrace.

Within a few seconds he was standing at the front door. He had no need to ring, it was open, and Trip stood there as if he had been waiting for him.

'Where is he?' asked Richard quietly.

'In the drawing room, sir. He's been using it a lot of late.'

'Are my things in order?'

'Just as you arranged, sir; and your sports gear, too.'

'Thank you very much, Trip. We'll be talking later. Don't worry,' and he put out his hand and patted the old man's shoulder as he emphasised, 'And tell Mrs Atkins the same.'

It seemed a long distance before his steps had covered the hall and he was at the drawing-room door. He did not knock but went straight in and closed the door behind him. Then he stood looking at the man who had brought himself forward in the big armchair, muttering, 'Richard.' His name, though, wasn't spoken in welcome but in a growl of disapproval. As the great bony figure pulled itself up from the chair, the voice went on, 'And where do you think you have been, sir, on your month's leave? Answer me.'

'I'll answer you, sir,' Richard replied, in a similar tone. 'I've been seeing my mother. I've been by her bedside for days now.'

He watched the face before him change colour as if it had been lit by a red-hot fire beneath the skin. The voice that came now was not from the throat but as if from some distant high place: 'You're mad! What is this? A game? Your mother died years ago.'

'My mother did not die years ago. Under your treatment my mother lost most of her mind and became a vagrant. And for more than twenty-six years she would have remained as a vagrant had it not been for the kindness of a poor woman who took her in and has looked after her all these years. And such was the condition of my mother's mind that she never left the little house where that woman lived but four times in all those years. And during all that time she wore the same clothes she had worn the night you attempted to murder her and her friend.'

'Her lover! He was her lover. I saw them.'

'You saw them meeting after years of separation. He had come to the theatre on a surprise visit, just as you had. But long before then you had not only bruised her body, but tortured it! And also tortured her mind, and to such an extent that she became afraid of men. Her only shield against them was the coat and hat she had bought herself, and which you didn't approve of. Remember? It was too striking; it brought men's attention to her more than usual. You couldn't stand it. But she defied you and wore it. Here it is, sir!' and, bending down, he opened the case and brought out the dirty coat and the hat, and swung them before his father's eyes, saying, 'Look at it! It's in a terrible state; but how else would you expect it to look after all this time? You will recognise the shape, at least that of the hat, the French hat you forbade her to wear. But she defied you, as she did in many other ways.'

'That could have been anyone's coat and hat. Somebody found it. The woman is an impostor.'

'Such an impostor sir, that she still has nightmares, which have been witnessed by two doctors, who have sometimes to hold her down because she continues to fight you off. You! With your filthy, rotten, perverted hands. That is just what you are, a filthy pervert. All your life you have been one.'

'How dare you?' It was a scream that filled the room and echoed from the walls.

'I dare! And I'll go on: it is known that you as good as murdered your first wife. I have talked with her maid, who saw you ignore the dead son she had just pressed from her dying body, then take the poor woman by the shoulders and shake her, almost throttle her, until you were dragged from her. But she, too, had defied you, hadn't she? She died within hours, and what did you do? You left the country. People talk and you couldn't bear it. You should have been locked up then.

'But my mother's case was worse; oh, much worse. You must have instilled in her the fear that burnt into her brain: you commanded her not to talk. "Do not speak!" You ordered her. And those words, after all these years, she still repeats. And added to them is a description of the things you did to her body. You are *vile!'*

'Shut up!' It was another scream. 'It's you who are mad! How dare you say such things? You know nothing about it; you were only a child.'

'But she wasn't, was she, Father? She wasn't a child. You married her when she was twenty-three. Following that she had five years of torture with you, at least after the first year, when you started to show your true self. Your toothmarks are still on her body, faint maybe, but still evident to two doctors.'

'I will not have this! I shall go and see her and prove she is—'

Now it was Richard's turn to raise his voice, 'You move one step towards her, you make one enquiry as to her whereabouts and I'm telling you, believe me, I shall see that the whole story is in every paper in this country, as well as in France and Germany and Italy where so many of your assets lie, and where you are known as a great businessman. I shall tell the world exactly what you are: a filthy pervert who used a young woman so vilely, and the mother of your child at that, that you turned her brain. Now I promise you: make one move out of this house and I shall do as I've said. I shall see your story reaches America—there first. So, I'm warning you, for the rest of your life you will live in this same cage in which you have tortured two women.'

'Do you know what you are doing? I'll—I'll disinherit you.'

The laugh that came from Richard was scornful and he cried, 'Disinherit me! Do that by all means—you'll be doing me a service, for I am no longer under your control, your ownership. That's what you think, don't you? That you own me, as you owned your poor wife. Well, you made a mistake with me because—let me tell you now: yes, you are my father, and I've feared you, but I have never, never liked you. Now, sit and think about that. I no longer fear you, nor do I even pity you; and this is going to be your gaol, this house, which, if you are wise, you won't leave, because once I know you have I'll do as I promised and carry out my threat, and there won't be a country in which you'll be able to hide your head under your money-bags any more.'

He gazed around the room now as if looking for something, and then his eyes fell on the Ming vase standing on a tall carved-wood Indian pedestal. This vase, he knew, was one of his father's greatest treasures, because he had won it from other collectors who had gathered in London many years ago at an auction to bid for it. It had cost a fortune then, and today it would be priceless. So much did his father value the vase that he would not allow even Trip to dust it. Only he himself handled it.

With a dive, Richard grabbed the precious object, and lifted his arms high, before bringing it down on the marble-tiled hearth.

It was with a cry of rage that his father now sprang at him, but Richard's arms were up and his fists ready.

Of a sudden the great man, who was now almost towering over Richard, stopped. His face had lost its fiery colour and had drained to a sickly grey, and when slowly his arms dropped to his sides, Richard turned from him, grabbed Irene's coat and hat, thrust them into the case, then made for the door.

In the hall, huddled together, were three maids, Trip and Mrs Atkins.

Edward Baindor tottered backwards and fell into a chair. There, gasping for breath, he brought out a sound that was recognisable only to Trip. But it was only with measured tread that he entered the drawing room. When he saw the condition of his master he hurried forward, saying, 'I'll ring for the doctor, sir.'

At this the great head was shaking and the word that came out was 'Solicitor.'

Trip gazed in amazement at the pieces of china splayed all over the hearth rug and the hearth, and he thought, Oh, my God! *That* vase. It will kill him. But he turned and hurried to the phone and rang Alexander's office. 'Let me speak to Mr Armstrong straight away, please,' he said.

When Alexander came on the line he said, 'This is Trip, Mr Armstrong. The master wants you. I will take the telephone to him.'

When he handed the phone to the gasping man, Edward Mortimer Baindor said, 'Get here! Now!'

'I'm sorry, Mr Baindor, but I can't, not just now.'

'Now, I said, Armstrong,' and then there were only gasps to be heard before the voice came again, 'Listen! I want you *now.*'

'I have to be at a meeting in fifteen minutes' time. It's very important. I am sorry, I can't be with you today at all. Perhaps tomorrow.'

'Don't dare!' There was another silence before the voice came again: 'Leave meeting, everything. Get here now!'

The phone at the other end was put down, and only then did Edward Baindor turn his head towards Trip and gasp, 'Doctor!'

It was two o'clock in the afternoon and Miss Fairweather was sitting at the end of Alexander's desk taking down in shorthand a letter he was dictating when the door swung open and a very presentable young woman bounced in, saying, 'Sweetheart, I just had to—' At the sight of Miss Fairweather rising quickly to her feet she said, 'I'm very sorry, my dear. You're busy.'

'I'm always busy, but not too busy to see you. Come and sit down, you . . .'

What the end of his sentence would have been Miss Fairweather did not wait to hear. She gathered up her notebook and swiftly left the room, closing the door noisily behind her.

'I've annoyed her—you were busy?'

'No, no. But what on earth are you doing here?'

'I've come to look for my intended.'

'Well, I too would like to know where he is.'

Jackie's tone changed now as she said, 'I'm getting a bit worried. I knew he had gone to see the old man and that he had made arrangements with Trip to have all his things brought down to his car. Well, I've been to his flat and can't get in. And then I went along to Glenda's and she, like you, hasn't seen hide or hair of him since he left the house just after nine this morning. And you know, as she says, he has hardly left his mother's side for . . . well, not for this long anyway. Glenda was a bit worried that she hadn't heard from him. She phoned Trip and he said Richard had left the house by car with his luggage as arranged just after eleven this morning.'

After a moment, Alexander said, 'He

phoned me . . . the old man. It must have been just after Richard left, and he told me he wanted me there immediately. Well, I knew what that meant, the changing of the will, and he meant it all right. In fact, Trip phoned not fifteen minutes later to say that I had to bring documents and my clerk. I had already told him that I had a meeting and that I wasn't coming today, but you know him: he speaks and you obey or else. Well, this time it's or else: I told him I wasn't able to get there until tomorrow.'

Jackie sat back in her chair, closed her eyes and said, 'One tries to put a cheerful face on things but, oh, I really am worried about Richard; he was in such a rage inside. I've been saying to him, do your blows with your words, they'll be more effective, but I'm afraid that something may have happened and they came to blows and . . . well . . .'

'You needn't worry about that,' put in Alexander, 'because as I said, Trip told me he had left the house.'

Jackie said slowly, 'I saw her yesterday.'

Alexander had no need to ask whom she had seen but said, 'Yes, and what did you think?'

'I . . . I seemed to stop thinking. It was a

shock to see the face so emaciated. Twenty-six years of living in the dark, you could say, being afraid to speak. Probably the fear kept her from recalling the past, which Glenda tells me she's doing frequently now and also talking a little more clearly, linking her words together as she hadn't done earlier. But, oh dear, dear! What a tragedy; what a wasted life! I wanted to cry just looking at her.'

'Did she speak to you?'

'Yes, she did; and it was odd how Richard transmitted her meaning, because when she put out her hand towards me and said, "Nice," I didn't know how to answer, but Richard, looking at her, said, "Yes, isn't she? She's very nice," to which she again nodded and repeated his words, "Very nice." When Richard said softly, "She's going to be your daughter-in-law and you're going to be at our wedding," she turned to him and her face was very sad when she said, "Soon." He looked at me then, and said, "Yes, soon." It was too much; I just had to get out of that room. I knew I was going to cry, as he had.'

Alexander's voice was low and soft as he leant across the table, saying, 'You're a very nice person, Jackie, and Richard is a lucky man to have found you.'

'I'm lucky, too, Alex. My work takes me among a lot of men, especially in offices, and some of them are . . . well, pigs; they are the kind that look down on women as an inferior species and, being so, won't object to a little mauling.'

'No-o.'

'Oh, yes. You in your small world don't know what goes on in the big one. I learnt how to give an upper-cut by the time I was twenty.'

'You didn't!'

'Oh, yes, I did. But, going back to your remark, I know, Alex, I'm a lucky girl in finding Richard.'

At this there was a buzz from the button at the end of his table and a voice said stiffly, 'Miss Armstrong on the phone for you, Mr Armstrong.'

He picked up the phone and said, 'Hello there.'

'He's back.'

'Oh, good! Where on earth has he been?'

There came a short laugh; then, 'Two places. To a locksmith to have the lock changed on his flat, because he wouldn't put it past the old fellow to send somebody down to clear it, for he, too, has a key and, of course, it's his property. The other is'— here she began to laugh as she continued —'he went and had a drink. It must have been more than one. Oh, he's not drunk, although he's not far from it; he would need something after that ordeal, I should think. I wish you had been here. He went in to his mother and, Alex, I'm sure she nearly laughed.'

'Why was that?'

'Because after apologising to her for being away so long, he said, "Mother, I'm drunk. I'm drunk because I've achieved something today that I've wanted to do for years."'

'I'm sure she didn't know what he was talking about, really, but she made a sound like laughter in her throat and put her hands up to his face and held it, before drawing him gently into her arms. It was good to see, Alex. I'll tell you all about it later.'

After he put the phone down Alexander looked at Jackie and said, 'Did you get the gist of all that?'

'He's had a lock changed or something and he's drunk.'

'Yes; and that's about the whole of it,' said Alexander, laughing.

'Poor Richard. He must have gone through it. I'll go now, because I'm dying to see what he looks like tight.'

As he led her towards the door, she said softly, 'I love him so, Alex.'

He had opened the door and now, when she lifted her head up towards him and kissed him, she added, 'And I love you too.'

'Go on!' he said, pushing her, and she went past Miss Fairweather's desk, meaning to give the woman a smile, but Miss Fairweather had her back towards her and was doing something at the filing cabinet.

For the next half-hour or so Alexander got on with the special business of the next day, when he must go to see that damned man. As the will stood, there were no other beneficiaries; everything was simply left to his son, Richard Mortimer Baindor. Alexander rang for Miss Fairweather to come and take the dictation on the rest of his letters.

After about three minutes, when there had been no reply to his signal that he was waiting for her, he rang again; and when, once more, there was no reply he got up and looked into the next room and towards her desk. She wasn't there. At the end of the corridor there was a rest room where the staff had their breaks, but he didn't like to go in. However, he had no sooner seated himself at his desk again than his door opened and James came in.

James did not sit down but addressed his father straight away: 'What have you done or said to Miss Fairweather?'

'Me! What have I said to whom?'

James's voice rose, 'To your secretary.'

'What did I say to her? I only dictated the letters. What are you getting at?'

'She's going to give her notice in. That news to you?'

'She's what?'

'You heard what I said, she's going to give her notice in. She says she's had enough, over fifteen years of it.'

'Had enough of what?'

'Enough of you, Father.'

James pulled a chair close up to the desk and sat down. 'You are sometimes very blind and stupid about other people's needs behind that keen law-filled mind of yours.'

'Would you mind telling me what you are talking about?'

'I'm talking about your secretary and your conduct towards her.'

'My conduct? It has been impeccable.'

'Yes, damn you, and I mean that . . . too impeccable. You've never unbent with her all these years: Miss Fairweather this and Miss Fairweather that. Miss Fairweather will see to this and Miss Fairweather will see to that. Yes, and Miss Fairweather, let me tell you, will be a very great loss to the firm. Go down into the storeroom and look at the files. She can lay her hands on anything, right back practically to the day she came. She was twenty-five years old then, and a highly trained secretary, and since that time she has looked after our interests in a way nobody else would or could. Do you know that?'

Alexander sat back in his chair. Then he said, 'What in the name of God are you getting at?'

'I'm getting at you, Father.' James's voice sounded weary. 'Even when Mother was alive that girl had a crush on you.'

'*What?*'

'Well, call it what you like. As I said, it started before Mother died, and that's ten years ago.'

'But what have I done today to make her change her mind?'

'Only that you are, she understands, about to marry a girl who is young enough to be your granddaughter.'

'I'm *what?* I've never said anything to her about marrying again or—'

'No; but you've had a young lady in here today, haven't you?'

'Yes, I have, and that young lady was Richard's fiancée. She came looking for Richard, just as we've all been doing.'

It was James's turn now to sit back and he spluttered as he said, 'Oh, that's it, is it? How did you part with her?'

'Part with whom?'

'With Jackie, of course.'

Alexander sat thoughtfully for a moment, then he suddenly began to chuckle and he said, 'Oh, my God! Just before I opened the door she'd told me how much she loved Richard and we'd had a long talk about this and that and then . . . well, as I opened the door for her, she leant up and kissed me and said she loved me too.'

'Well, that must have done it. Miss Fairweather's been in the rest room crying her eyes out. But she means it about leaving.

Even when she knows that it was Richard's girl, it won't make any difference. I think, as she said, she's had enough.'

'And what d'you expect me to do?'

'Melt.'

'Melt?'

'Yes. You treat her like a machine. She is Miss Fairweather. She is the one who can lay her hands on anything you want at any moment. Because of her you can walk out of this office at any hour of the day and the work will get done. She is just Miss Fair-weather.'

Alexander sat back in his chair, an expression of wry dismay on his face. Then he voiced his thoughts: 'Look at me,' he said, 'I'm almost sixty. She's a woman in her prime—she's only forty.'

'She's older than Jackie.'

'Oh, Lord!' Slowly Alexander shook his head. 'If there wasn't enough trouble here and there as it is. Now this. How on earth am I going to face her?'

'That's up to you, but she'll give you her notice in the morning, I know that, if not to-day. Apart from Jackie, and I'll explain that to her, I don't think it'll make the slightest difference. She knows and I know and you know that any firm in this city will just jump at her once they know she's free. And I'll tell you something else you didn't know. Rankin—yes, Rankin, your kindly associate at the Bar—offered her a job about three years ago and at much more than she's getting here.'

'Rankin did that? The swine!'

'No; he's a businessman. He'd lost his secretary and he'd heard about her. None of your papers ever went astray nor was a word misspelt, nor the grammar anything but perfect. Oh, no, he knew what he was after. He put it to her quietly one day. "If ever you want a change, Miss Fairweather, just come and see me," he said. I was there; well, I was within earshot when he said it; and I remember when I passed him I said, half in fun and wholly in earnest, "Do you want your throat cut?" He burst out laughing, and he said, "All's fair in love and war" '

'Well I never!'

'Yes; that's something else for you to think about. So, if I were you, I wouldn't ring for Miss Fairweather tonight. I would put your things on and get yourself away home, or along to Glenda's.'

'What I want to say to you now,' said Alexander tartly, 'is, go to hell!'

'Yes, I know you do; but I'm going along now to tell your secretary, who is going to be your secretary no longer, that she made a mistake. Not that it'll do any good. I'll be seeing you, Father.'

James went out, laughing now, and Alexander put his head in his hands and said, 'Oh, my God! What have I done?'

Glenda was laughing heartily as she said, 'And what advice do you expect to receive from me, dear brother?'

'Oh, Glenda! Don't take it as a joke. I'm in a fix here . . . Miss Fairweather and me!' His voice had sunk to a scornful note.

'It's as James said, you're a blind idiot.'

'Oh, he's been on the phone already and told you?'

'Yes; and you deserve all you're getting. It's as he said, even when Miss Fairweather knew who the girl was, she was still adamant that she was going to leave. And, you know, I don't blame her. When I've been in your office I've noticed your manner towards her. You *do* treat her like a machine.'

'I do nothing of the sort. I've been a very good boss to her.'

'Moneywise, oh, yes, perhaps, but there are other bosses who'll be glad to give her the same, or more, to get somebody who's so efficient. James may have laughed about it, but I can tell you he's right.'

'But what can I do about it, Glenda? Look at me. I'm nearly sixty. I've never thought of anybody since Mary went, and she's . . . well, she's not forty yet, I don't think.'

'She's forty and she's a very good-looking woman. I've seen her out of her office gear and she's attractive.'

'Then why the devil hasn't she been married before now?'

'Because, you idiot, she fell for you and, what was more, years ago she was tied to her home and her mother. Her mother was riddled with arthritis, and she stayed at home after office hours and saw to her. Did you know she was brilliant at school and heading for university when her father died? He wasn't as well insured as he should have been, leaving barely enough to keep them both, so she had to change her thinking. She went to a managerial college for a year and sailed through. Then she became a secretary and she landed with you when she was twenty-five.'

'How do you know all this?'

'Because we've chatted. The first time was when I met her in the restaurant round the corner from Beverley Square and she recognised me from my visits to you at the office. That was when James was just starting and I came and set up his office for him, if you remember, for he had as much idea then of order as he has now. He's very like you.'

'Look here,' put in Alexander now, 'you're going too far. You'd think we were a pair of idiots.'

'Well, that's what you are when it comes to running an office. You're all right on the law and on the courtroom floor, and with the clients, because it's already been set up for you.'

'Good God!' Alexander got up from his seat, went to the sideboard and poured himself out a whisky from the decanter standing there, threw it back and said, 'How strange it is that our firm has managed to get where it is.' Then, as if asking a question of the air, he continued, 'How on earth did we manage until fifteen years ago?'

'All right, but you were very much smaller then, and even so you were often in a muddle; changing secretaries and other office staff as often as your coat. You look back.'

He sat down again and his voice now had an almost pathetic note about it when he asked, 'How am I going to get through the next month with her?'

And the answer that came was, 'That's up to you, Alex. Have you ever thought of looking at her? Have you ever asked yourself if you like her?'

'Oh, I like her. Yes, I like her. I admire her. But honest to God! I've never thought past that.'

'Well, once again,' said Glenda, 'have you ever *looked* at her?'

He thought. Yes, he had looked at her. She had an oval face with a very small nose. It was a snub nose. He couldn't remember what her mouth looked like. Her eyes . . . he couldn't remember the colour of her eyes either.

Glenda's voice came at him now, saying, 'Try looking at her during the next few days.'

As he was answering, the phone rang. 'Yes? This is . . .' She got no further for a voice said, 'Is Mr Richard Baindor with you?'

'Who's speaking?'

'Dr Bell.'

'Yes, Richard is here.'

'Well, will you tell him his father is dying and that I think he should be here.'

'I will do no such thing.'

'What did you say?'

'I said, I will do no such thing. He saw his father this morning.'

'Yes; and the heart-attack and stroke have followed that meeting.'

'Dear, dear!' she said; then, 'My brother, Mr Baindor's solicitor, is here. Would you like a word with him?'

She handed the receiver to Alexander. 'Yes, this is Armstrong here.'

'Hello there! We know each other.'

'Yes; yes, we do, and I understand from the little I have heard that your patient is dying.'

'Yes, he is.'

'Do you like him? Have you ever liked him?'

'That is a very odd question to ask of me.'

'But I am asking it of you. Do you like him?'

'No, I don't. Never have.'

'Good. Well, I can say the same.'

'Nevertheless, no matter how we like or dislike anyone, it isn't good for a man in his state to die alone.'

'He deserves nothing else. You say he's dying; well, so is his wife.'

'What d'you mean? His wife died years ago.'

'His wife didn't die years ago. It might be news to you, Doctor, that she's lying here, but she is also dying, and her son is with her. When your patient tried to murder her he didn't finish off her body but he almost finished off her mind. She lost her memory and for a time was a vagrant on the roads and would have been still but for a kindly woman who looked after her for these twenty-six years or so. That'll be news to you, and I would ask if you will keep it to yourself until I see you, which will be after you have rung to tell me that your patient has died.'

The voice that came over the phone was very low now as Dr Bell said, 'Will you tell his son?'

'No; not until you phone me finally.'

'Very well. Goodbye.'

Alexander turned to Glenda and said, 'So he's going. Thank God I didn't answer his demand this morning, for Richard would now be without a penny.'

'That wouldn't have troubled him.'

'It mightn't have, but it's his due and he can now use his father's ill-gotten gains to put things to rights. I'll see to that.'

It was three o'clock in the morning and the voice on the phone was Trip's. The night nurse took the call and Trip said, 'Could I speak to Miss Armstrong, please?'

'She's asleep. But I could give her your message as soon as she wakes. Is it important?'

'No. Not all that important. Just say Mr Baindor died at half past two this morning . . .'

By nine o'clock Richard had telephoned both Alexander and James and asked them the same question, should he tell her? And the answer was similar from both. It was up to him. If he thought it would ease her mind, yes. But what did Glenda think? Glenda thought she should be told and added that she had had a quiet night and seemed rested this morning.

Now, as he sat in Glenda's office, Richard

said to her, 'I don't know how I'm going to put it to Mother because, although I have no regrets whatever, I know our meeting yesterday morning caused the attack.'

'He would have had it in any case, and shortly. I spoke to Dr Bell first thing and he told me that of late he'd had minor heart-attacks and that he wouldn't have been surprised if he had dropped dead straight away. But he rallied, then had the stroke.

'Knowing him, he'd make himself rally until Alex appeared and he'd had time to change his will. But all I can say is, thank God for the stroke. So don't let his going worry you in any way.'

'It's not. It's not; believe me, Glenda. And you know something? It wasn't what I said that upset him most, I'm sure it was the breaking of that vase. I only wish there had been more of the wretched things I could have smashed.'

There was a tap on the door now and a voice said, 'May I come in?'

When it opened Jackie entered, and Richard, getting to his feet, said, 'You're early. I thought you'd be at work.'

'I've taken the day off . . . no, the week off.' And then she added, 'How d'you feel?'

'All right. All right in one way but worried in another. We've just been discussing if it would be wise to tell Mother of his going.'

Taking a seat near Glenda, Jackie looked at her and said, 'What d'you think?'

'I think he should tell her.'

'So do I.'

'Will you come in with me?' Richard asked her.

Jackie paused, then looked at Glenda and said, 'Yes, if it's all right with you, Glenda.'

'Of course. But I would suggest that you get it over as quickly as possible.'

Irene was lying with her eyes closed, but she wasn't asleep; she was thinking, thinking it had been a strange night because of the dream she had had, and she could remember it. That was very odd because she often dreamed but when she woke she could never recall details. Her mind was mostly in a jumble, and she made it worse when she tried to think.

She had seen herself as a young woman walking through some kind of hall; she went upstairs and into a room where a man was lying on a bed; and she walked up to the side of the bed and looked at him. She saw that he looked frightened; then she realised why—he was wearing handcuffs, and they were clamped to each side of the bed. Yet, strangely, his plight did not move her to pity for him, or sympathy. His brow was running with sweat, but she made no effort to wipe it.

She had no feeling whatever for the figure on the bed; so she turned away from him, and was now in a garden, a beautiful garden, and there was pulsing through her such a feeling of relief that she wanted to skip and dance. But she shouldn't, you only did that when you were a child. But there she was, she was jumping over narrow streams; she was running through woods; and then, of a sudden, she stopped and found herself back in the bedroom. But there was no one in the bed, the man had gone. She turned about and ran down the stairs and out into the garden again. She looked up at the sky and began to sing—she could hear herself singing—and then a voice spoke to her, saying, 'Would you like a drink, dear?' She had looked at the kind nurse and shaken her head slightly. Then she had gone to sleep again, and went once more into the garden. But now she was walking slowly and her body had a strange feeling. There was a lightness about it as if it were about to fly away from her. It was as if she had been released from somewhere. She sat on a seat. Everything about her was peaceful.

Then she was on her feet again, walking once more into a kind of light. Beautiful light. Rosy light. She was watching the dawn breaking, feeling so happy to be in the light, for the night had been so long, so very long. She was still walking in the light when a nurse's voice said, 'There you are, dear. Let me put a pillow behind your head. That's it. Now drink this. That's right. You've had a good night. The night nurse told me you only woke up once, and that was early on. Do you feel better?'

For a moment she did not answer, because she was asking herself if she did feel better. She felt something, she felt different, she didn't know how, or why she should feel different, but she did; and she enjoyed the tea. Her answer was plain and clear, 'Yes.' And then after a moment she added, 'Thank . . . you. Thank . . . you.'

'Oh, that's splendid! Your throat's a lot better. Now rest easy; we won't disturb you for a while, you look so comfortable there.'

It was odd, but she did feel comfortable. Her body did not seem to trouble her any more. She made a great effort to swallow some porridge when breakfast came, which brought murmurs of approval from the nurse; and further murmurs when she ate three teaspoonfuls of the beaten-up softly boiled egg mixed with thin pieces of bread and butter.

When later she was washed and her hair combed and she was lying waiting for the time when her son would come back into the room she slid into a light doze, to waken and see not only Richard but that nice girl he was going to marry looking down at her. It was the girl who said, 'Good morning.'

And she answered her with a smile and said, 'Good . . . morning.'

'Oh,' said Richard, 'you sound much better this morning. That proves your chest is easier.'

He turned from the bed, pulled a chair forward and motioned Jackie on to it so that she could be closer to his mother's head; and he took his mother's frail hand and, bending over her, said in a low voice, 'You do sound stronger this morning, Mother; do you feel better?'

She looked at him, then nodded. He turned now and looked helplessly at Jackie. Jackie knew he was afraid to start, so taking hold of Irene's other hand, she stroked it for a moment before saying, 'Richard's got something to tell you, my dear, and he's afraid it might worry you.'

Irene was staring at her son and to his amazement she said, quite clearly, 'I know . . . He's gone . . . dead.'

They stared at each other for a long time; then slowly she withdrew her hand from his and stroked his face, and there was even a smile on hers as she said, 'Free.'

He turned from the bed and walked blindly towards the window. All the tears of his childhood that he'd had to clamp down on for fear of his father seemed to have formed a well inside him that was now over-flowing, and he seemed unable to stop it.

He heard Jackie saying to his mother, 'You're wonderful . . . wonderful.'

And she was wonderful; but, he realised suddenly, she would soon be leaving him.

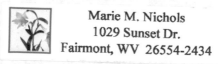
4

The funeral of Edward Mortimer Baindor took place four days later. It did not make headlines in any paper, but in one of the leading journals it was stated in so many words that it was a great surprise that the financier had been cremated with less attention than would have been given to most men of his position. It was a private occasion and was attended only by his solicitors, Alexander and James Armstrong, and representatives from his businesses in America, Germany, France, Italy and Holland. It was regrettable that his only son had been unable to attend the service; he was indisposed. A near neighbour, Lord Blakey, father of Miss Jacqueline Franks who was engaged to Mr Richard Baindor, was also present.

Mr Richard Mortimer Baindor would inherit what amounted to a financial empire.

After the funeral, Alexander, James and Richard had been tied up for hours each day talking to the managements of the overseas companies of the firm. They had come to the conclusion that a chief executive should be appointed to oversee all the separate businesses and report back on whether some of the companies should be dissolved or sold off.

When at last the three men had the office to themselves, Richard burst out, 'I can't handle this, Alex. You can see they all expected me to take his place and run them all more or less as he did.'

'As I've told you and we've told them, a new chief executive will take his place,' said Alexander.

'Well, it'll be a very tough man who could deal with that lot. What I suggest you do, Alex, is sell as many of the companies as you can.'

'I'll do nothing of the sort. As for a candidate, I know the very man.'

'You do?'

'Yes.'

'Well, why haven't you mentioned him before?'

'Because I couldn't. I haven't spoken to
him yet. But I know he's a man who will be
delighted to analyse these various companies and get the general feel of the best way
forward.'

'And who is he?'

'George Peacock. He's the senior partner
of a firm of accountants across the square.
He's only in his late forties. Like me, he was
pushed into a family firm to follow his father's footsteps. What is more, he's had
wider experience than I ever had; he's a very
good accountant with receivership experience and investment banking contacts.
Now he would just jump at the chance to
immerse himself in the reorganisation and
scaling down of the Baindor empire. Anyway, we can talk to him, but I know before
I start what his answer will be. And he can
quite easily leave what he's doing to his
younger brother, who, like his father, has a
feeling for the more general side of account-
ancy.'

'Whatever happens,' said Richard, 'I'm
going on with my career. I've only another

two years or so and I'll be fully fledged, and I love the work.'

'Well,' put in James now, 'I see no reason why you shouldn't go on and leave it to Father and me to fleece you, because we will, you know.'

'Yes; yes, I know that.' Richard smiled now and looked from one to the other; then, turning to Alexander again, he said, 'When can we see this fellow?'

'I'm going over to see him today.'

'The sooner the better. Now I must get back to Mother. I've hardly seen anything of her these last few days.'

'Get along there then,' said Alexander. 'James and I will join you tonight. By the way, one of us must go and see that pawnbroker. I meant to do so before the funeral, but one thing and another held us up.'

'Why not forget about the things there? She'll never need them again.'

'She didn't carry those tickets about with her for years for nothing. Glenda said that she mentioned the tickets yesterday, at least she said, "Gomparts," and then followed this with "Tickets, pawn tickets." So she knows that those things are still in pawn, and I'm sure she would like them. So I'll go tomorrow.'

'All right.'

'Lastly,' put in James, 'you really can't carry out your intention about the manor, Richard.'

'I can, James.' Richard's voice rose as he opened the door. 'The minute she's gone I'm going to burn the whole damned place down.'

In the silence after his departure neither of the other men spoke. Then, looking at his father, James said, 'He means it.'

'He can't do it.'

'Who's going to stop him? It's his place; he can do what he likes with it.'

'It would be a sin, and what good would it do?'

'Apparently it'll do him some good. What's more, doing it is a kind of last tribute to her.'

'By the way,' Alexander said, 'she's failing. I would say he won't have very long to wait.'

James sighed as he rose, but at the door he paused and, looking back at his father, he smiled and said by way of a little light relief, 'May I ask how things are going with . . .' his voice dropped '. . . Miss Fair-weather?'

'Oh, now, don't start on that again.'

'I won't; but how *are* things?'

'I can do nothing. She told me that she's going at the end of the month and I told her how sorry I was, and asked if I had upset her in any way, and so on, and so on.'

'And what did it come to?'

'Nothing, except I told her that I would miss her a lot.'

'Did you say just that, or did you add, "in all sorts of ways"?'

'Get yourself out before I start swearing. Go on!'

'In today's paper it says that your star's in the ascendant.' Then James made a hasty escape before his father could make any comment.

It was on the Saturday evening, and through the misty autumn twilight Alexander and Richard hurried in to Beechwood.

They were taking off their overcoats when Glenda appeared from her private quarters, saying, 'You're back, then. How did it go? Did you get them?'

'Yes; Alex did,' said Richard, smiling at

her. 'Come along and see how she takes them.'

'No, no; I can't. Anyway, Bella is with her. The boys dropped her off. She has bought them an old banger, which they have done up. Really, it's a marvellous little car. Talk about four kids with a Christmas box. Anyway, they're going to pick her up later. And I have visitors, too.'

'Anyone we know?' asked Alexander.

'Of course. Anyway, go and get this business over. She's had a quiet day, but take it easy with her, not too much emotion, mind.' She had spoken the last words to Richard. He did not answer, but both men turned and walked towards the stairs.

As soon as they opened the door Bella rose from the bedside, saying, 'Oh, I'm about to be on me way. I've stayed too long as it is; I always do. But she's lovely today, aren't you, love?' She bent over Irene and kissed her, and Irene put up her hand and stroked the grey-white hair.

'You stay where you are,' said Alexander, 'because you know more about this little business than we did a couple of hours ago.'

Richard was bending over his mother now and asking, 'All right?'

'Fine. Fine, dear.' She smiled up at him, and the hand was once more raised, but touching his cheek now. Alexander had pulled up two chairs to the bedside, one on each side of Bella, and it was Richard who said, 'Do you know where Alex has been?'

Irene gave a slight movement of her head, then contradicted this by saying slowly, 'Yes . . . and . . . no.'

Richard now put his hand into the inner pocket of his coat and brought out the small brown envelope. After opening the flap he took one of her hands and tipped the contents on to it; and she was looking down on her wedding ring, her engagement ring, the beautiful necklace that Bella had taken for a fairground trinket, and the little card case. She stared at them for a long moment before lifting her eyes and looking from Richard to Alex and saying, 'Mr Gom-parts?'

'Yes.' Alexander was nodding at her. 'I saw the two Mr Gomparts, two gentlemen indeed. You know, they have kept these for you all these years because, as the son said, he fully expected you to come back one day for them. The necklace had insured the other pieces for two lifetimes. They had kept them in their private safe all these years.'

Richard, now touching the articles she was holding in her palm, said, 'Alex says the younger one spoke so wonderfully of you. You know what he said? He has never been able to get you out of his mind, and he's always thought of you as . . .' He paused here and his voice dropped. There was a crack in it as he said, 'The Lost Angel.'

Irene's eyes closed. The lids were pressed tight and when a tear fell from beneath her lashes Alexander said quickly, 'Now, now; we were warned. Glenda told us she would throw us out if we upset you.'

Irene opened her eyes, and said, 'Dear . . . Mr Gomparts . . . so good.'

Then, looking down at the jewellery in her hand, she lifted up the wedding ring, handed it to Richard and said, 'Hated that.' There was a long pause while they waited, because they knew she had something more to say. When she spoke again her words were blurred but audible: 'I . . . kept it . . . because it had . . . giv-en me you.'

'Oh, Mother.'

Alexander's voice said, 'Steady. Steady. She has more to say.'

Richard straightened up. He watched his mother pick up the beautiful engagement ring and, lifting it towards Bella, whose head was on her chest and whose face was already wet with tears, she said, 'Bella . . . my friend . . . for . . . you.'

Bella lifted her head and looked at the ring, and, being nobody but herself, she could only exclaim, 'Oh, my God!' Then, looking from one man to the other, she said, 'Eeh, no! I couldn't. Not that. It's worth a lot of money.'

'Take it.' Richard's voice was low. 'She loves you, and it is the only way she has of showing her thanks.'

Irene had to push the ring into Bella's hand, and all Bella could do now was pull her bulky self to her feet, lean over her dear lass and kiss her, saying as she did so, 'I really want no presents. You were my present.'

The tap on her shoulder from Alexander brought Bella slowly back into the chair.

Now picking up the little card case, Irene offered it to Alexander, saying, 'Small . . . but . . . full of . . . grat-it-tude.'

He looked down at it in his hand. Then,

doubling his fingers over it, he said, 'It will always be my most precious possession.'

Irene smiled at him, then said haltingly, 'You will . . . never . . . open it.' And he, looking back at her, said, 'I won't?' Then, opening his hand again, he pressed round the edges as Bella had once done, and tried every way to open it.

Irene put out her hand and took it from him; then she squeezed the middle of the little case twice, and it opened slowly. She smiled at him and said, 'Clever.'

Taking it from her, Alexander looked at the inside for a spring but couldn't see one; then, looking at her with a broad smile, he said, 'Yes, indeed, Irene . . . clever. Wherever the spring is it must be so minute that no one could ever find it. It's wonderful.'

Irene now gave a long sigh. She lifted up the necklace, put it back into the brown paper envelope and laid it by her side on the counterpane; then, looking at Richard, she said, 'For . . . someone else . . . Jackie.'

'Yes, Mother. I'll bring her after dinner.'

Alexander now put out his hand to a small bell-pull, and when a nurse appeared the men left the room. Bella remained, wordless now but holding Irene close . . .

A minute later the three stood outside the door; and now Alexander said to Bella, 'Don't cry. Don't cry, my dear. She's happy. Dry your face and come along. Glenda's waiting. She says she's got company.'

'Eeh, no! I couldn't meet any company, Mr Armstrong, and the lads'll be waiting.'

'The lads can wait,' Richard put in. 'Come along.' And he took her elbow and led her down the stairs to Glenda's sitting room. But once inside they all stopped as, surprised, they looked at the company. It consisted of Jackie, Miss Fairweather and James.

Jackie was no surprise to Richard, but Miss Fairweather was to Alexander. However, before he could make any comment Richard, looking at his fiancée, said, 'Where on earth have you been all day? I've been trying to contact you.'

'I've been at work.'

'I thought you'd left.'

'There're more jobs than one. I've been offered two since I left the magazine, but I've turned them both down.'

'Why?'

'Because I've got another job in view.'

'For goodness' sake!' put in Glenda now. 'Sit yourselves down and let's get this over with because, if I know anything, tempers are going to rise.'

'Why should they?'

This came from Alexander, and his sister said, 'Wait and see.' Then turning to Jackie, she said, 'Well, fire away. Get it over with.'

Jackie was sitting next to Miss Fairweather and they exchanged glances. Then Jackie said, 'I've been very busy these last two weeks.' She was now looking at Richard who had seated himself opposite her on the couch.

'But so have we all,' said Richard.

'Yes, Richard, so have we all, but your projects have been different from mine. Do you want to hear about them?' and she paused for a moment, then said, 'Why am I asking that? Because whether or not you want to hear you've got to be told. First, though, I must ask you a question, and I'll have to stand on my feet to do it.' She rose from the chair and, looking straight across at him, she said, 'Are you still determined to burn down the manor when your mother goes?'

He did not respond immediately, but rose slowly to his feet also before saying, 'You know I am. Absolutely determined.'

There was a long pause, and an uneasy feeling began to fill the room, when Jackie's next words brought a gasp from all those present. 'Well,' she said, 'Richard Mortimer Baindor, if you persist in carrying out your scheme of hate, then I shall never marry you, and I won't repeat that, but I'll just emphasise it by saying that I meant every word of it.'

He glared at her. Then harshly, he said, 'What's come over you? You've known all along what I meant to do. You've never said anything against it yet.'

'No. But I've thought all the more, and I knew from the beginning that should you do such a thing it would break us up.'

'But why? In the name of God, why?'

'Simply because you imagine it will recompense your mother for all she has gone through, but you have forgotten the nature of the man who caused it, for I know he would be glad to see it burn to the ground rather than be used for the purpose I have in mind.

'He looked down on his servants as menials. Besides being a bad and evil man, he was an out-and-out snob, a social climber, and it irked him that he had never been given a title. Well, now, if you will listen to me for a few minutes more I shall tell you what I have been doing during the last two weeks—at least Margaret and I . . .

'With the help of Miss Fairweather and her cousin, who is an architect, I have, or rather we have, planned the rebuilding of the manor and would hope to make it into something that would burn your father up still more, wherever he is, because we propose it should be turned into a convalescent home for the poor.

'And when I say the poor, I mean the poor: not anyone who can afford to pay something towards having attention after an illness or any such thing. It's the poor I have seen this last week or so under the guidance of Bella there. She has shown us parts of the city which make her little house appear like a middle-class mansion, and she has introduced me to people who have never known anything but the life lived in a slum. And they are your slums now, some of them. Oh, I know you mean to do something about it, but you won't be able to change the whole world or even London, and there will always be those people who, after being in hospital or lying at home with no one but their family to see to them, who are so poor that they can't afford a week, a fortnight, a month of attention and comfort and the feeling that they are being cared for, that they are no longer the dregs. And Bella knows a lot about the dregs, because all her boys were taken from there. What did surprise me, among all the debris I saw, was how they managed to approach life with a smile and a joke.

'Well, there you have the rough outline. For more details I must tell you that Maggie,' she nodded towards Miss Fairweather, 'and George, the architect, have worked out a plan. By the way, do you know how many rooms there are in your mansion, Richard?'

When he did not answer but still continued to glare at her, she said, 'Sixty-five! That isn't counting the kitchen and the servants' quarters. And did you know that that house was built in three parts? The kitchen quarters were the original part, built at the end of the seventeenth century. It was a little homestead. Then at the beginning of the eighteenth century along came somebody and bought all the land around it, and added on an east wing. Not satisfied with that, somebody else in the nineteenth century stuck another wing on the other side of the kitchen. From the outside you would think it had all been built at the same time, because at the end of the last century a new façade was put over the lot.'

Here she paused for breath and bowed her head for a moment; then she went on, 'The proposition is this, that two-thirds of the house could be turned into a convalescent home with rooms for twenty patients, with others for nursing staff, et cetera. The other third could be a strictly private house. The original kitchen quarters could be attached to the convalescent home and that would be a big asset. The other part, the east wing, which consists of the drawing room, dining room, billiard room and so on, besides the bedrooms upstairs, could be private quarters, a home, not a showplace. Then there are the gardens. There's the river where male patients could fish, and the gardens could remain for patients to wander and sit in. The private house would have its own garden at the back. As for the cottages outside, we'll come to them later; but these, when altered, would be homes for Bella and her boys.'

Jackie looked down at her tightly joined

hands which were lying in her lap; then jerking her head upwards, she returned Richard's stare and said, 'Well, Richard?'

For answer he swung round from her and made for the door. At this she jumped up and cried after him in the loudest voice she had ever raised to him before, 'That's always the coward's retreat. Why don't you stand and face an opponent?'

He turned on her, saying, 'I am not retreating, miss. I am going next door to pour myself a very stiff whisky and to ask myself how, in the name of God, I ever got mixed up with you.'

At this both of them were startled by Glenda's voice, almost as loud as Jackie's: 'Whose house is this anyway? Jackie and I will go next door and see to drinks, not only for you but for all of us, for we certainly need them. Come along, Jackie.'

When the two women were outside the door they leant against each other and Glenda said, 'Dear Lord, girl, you did give it to him!'

'It was the only way, Glenda. I know him. He would have burnt that place down, I know he would, and everything in it.'

'And you wouldn't have married him?'

'No, because what I've seen this last fort-night has wrung my heart. You know, I didn't realise that I had been brought up with a silver spoon in my mouth. Because I pushed myself into journalism I thought I was a working girl. I found I know damn all about work. I know damn all about living. It's Bella who knows about living, and the lads; and so does Margaret, in her way. I have an idea in my head and I mean to carry it out, not just the conserving of the house, but some-thing else. I'll tell you about it later, but let's get that drink, because here's one who needs it.'

In their absence Richard had slumped on to the couch in the sitting room. His head was down, his joined hands hanging be-tween his knees, and there was silence in the room for a moment, until Miss Fair-weather spoke.

Looking across at Richard, she said, 'Dr Baindor . . . I am perhaps speaking out of turn, but I must say that she is right. That house could be used for so much good. It could vindicate all your dear mother has had to suffer. Miss Morgan here knows what it is to live in poverty, what it is to live in the gutter, as she has said. And there are still many people in such a situation. I, as you know, work during the week, but both Miss Franks and I and my cousin have spent the last two weekends under her guidance traveling through parts of London one could not believe existed. I'd like to stick my neck out further, by saying you have a great lady in your fiancée.'

Richard now raised his head, loosened his hands, lay back in his chair and looked at Miss Fairweather.

'Thank you,' he said. 'I—I suppose you are right; in fact, I know you are. But that . . . my way . . . was the only way I could see to getting him and the house entirely out of my life.'

Alexander meanwhile was looking at his secretary and what he now said to her in a soft voice was, 'You are a very secretive creature, Miss Margaret Fairweather.'

Miss Fairweather's colour changed slightly, but she kept her eyes on Alexander's face as she said, 'One learns that, Mr Armstrong, when working in the law.'

This caused an immediate guffaw from James, who put out his hand and patted Miss Fairweather's shoulder as he said, 'Maggie, all I can say is, you're marvellous.

I've always known it; I haven't been blind like some people.' He grinned now as he went on, 'What we're going to do at the end of the month, I just don't know.'

'I shouldn't worry, Mr James. I've decided to stay on for a little longer until Mr Armstrong finds a suitable substitute.'

Alexander's voice cut in, addressing his son: 'You're enjoying yourself, aren't you? Well, I would thank you to mind your own business for a time, and I mean that. You understand?'

'Oh, yes, sir, I understand.'

James was still grinning when he stood up and said, 'Here come the drinks. Thank God for wine, whisky and women.'

Immediately after dinner, which had been simple and short, Richard, speaking to Jackie for the first time since their heated encounter, said, 'Mother would like to see you. Will you come along?'

Her face straight, her voice matter-of-fact, she said, 'Yes; of course,' and together they left the others. But before they reached Irene's bedroom he pulled her to a stop and, taking her by the shoulders, he said, 'I want to shake the life out of you, even slap your face and tell you that you are an interfering busybody; and for two pins I would take you at your word and go ahead with what I meant to do. Yet at the same time I know damn well I couldn't, because I can't live without you.'

She did not say anything to this, but she put her arms around his neck and his went around her waist and, their lips and bodies held close, they stood swaying for a moment; then she said softly, 'I took a risk. I knew I might be blighting my life but I had to do it, not only for my sake but for yours, because I knew that that was the last thing your mother would want you to do, and that what she would love you to do is help the poor, the lost and the lonely, as she herself was helped for so many years.'

Again he kissed her, but softly now; then they went into the bedroom where the sister was putting the last touches to her patient's comfort for the night. Turning to them, she said quietly, 'I'll leave you for a little while, but she's very tired.'

Richard nodded to her; and then she left them. Now, bending over Irene, Richard said, 'You wanted to see Jackie.'

After making a slight movement with her

head, Irene took from beneath the counterpane the paper envelope that held the necklace and handed it to Jackie, saying slowly, 'For you.'

Jackie gasped as she stared down at the beautiful gold and ruby necklace, saying, 'Oh! How . . . how beautiful. For me?'

'Wedding . . . present . . . soon . . . very soon.' And when, after a deep breath, she ended, 'A week,' Richard said, in surprise but softly, 'But, Mother, we have nothing prepared. I mean, there have been no arrangements made or anything.'

Irene turned from him and looked towards Jackie. 'Licence.'

At this Jackie nodded quickly, saying, 'By special licence?'

Again Irene nodded, but now she was smiling as she brought out, 'Good girl.'

Jackie laughed softly; and, bending towards Irene, she held up the necklace, saying, 'I'll always treasure it. Always. And I won't be happy until I can call you Mother-in-law.'

Irene closed her eyes, and when they watched her lower lip tremble Richard said, 'Now, Mother, please, don't upset yourself, or else we'll have Glenda in here knocking our heads together.'

Irene opened her eyes, swallowed deeply and said, on a slight laughing sound, 'Dread-ful . . . woman.'

There was a tap on the door and Sister entered. Her voice was low but brisk as she said, 'Time, please.'

Richard bent over his mother and kissed her gently. She held his face in her hands for a moment but said nothing. Then Jackie was looking down into her eyes, and in a soft whisper she said, 'You are a beautiful lady, and I thank you for giving him to me.' Swiftly she kissed her, then turned, and Richard followed her.

They were on the landing now and Jackie stood with her face against the wall. Richard put his arms about her and pulled her round to him, and, with tears rolling from her eyes, she muttered, 'Don't say one word. Not one word.' Then, tugging herself from his arms, she said, 'I'm going to Glenda's bedroom to tidy up. You tell them.'

'Yes, darling. I'll tell them.' He let her go, then made for the sitting room where the rest of the small company were having coffee. When he entered the room he closed

the door behind him, but did not immediately step further in. He said, 'She—she
wants us to be married right away. Special
licence.' Then slowly he walked towards the
couch and said to Alexander, 'I know nothing about this, how to go about it.'

Alexander put up his hand and caught
Richard's and pulled him gently down to his
side, saying, 'Don't you worry. We'll see to
everything.'

5

It was amazing to them all how Irene seemed to come alive during the next few days, after Richard and Jackie had told her what they proposed doing with the manor house. Her interest was aroused and she nodded to every plan they explained to her. And when, after one or two short sessions with her, they hadn't mentioned Bella or her boys it was she who said, 'Bella . . . What . . . about Bella?'

At this Jackie had laughed and said, 'Oh, Bella was our first thought; Bella and her boys could never be left out of this scheme. You know the six cottages at the end of the estate?'

Irene had made a small nod.

'Well,' went on Jackie, 'the first two are to be made into one, in fact gutted and re-

built. They are to house Bella, Joe and Carl.
And provision has been made for Carl's
wheelchair.'

Irene had nodded in agreement. 'Nice . . .
Yes; nice.'

'And the other cottages,' Jackie had gone
on, 'are to be gutted in the same way, and
Tony, John and Willie will have one each,
which they mean to rebuild themselves, like
they did the wash-house, you know.'

There was a smile on Irene's face now
and she repeated, 'The wash-house;' then
again, her head moving, 'The wash-
house . . . warm.'

'And what is more,' Jackie went on, 'Trip
and Mrs Atkins and the two old gardeners
who have worked outside for years are to
carry on as long as they want to. In fact,
they'll all keep on the same services in our
part of the house and look after us because
there'll be a special staff for the convales-
cents. It is all being arranged. You know
Miss Fairweather, Alex's secretary?' and she
smiled widely at Irene now. 'She and her
cousin, the architect, have done marvellous
work.'

'Nice . . . woman.'

At this remark, Richard said, 'Yes, she is,

Mother, a very nice woman; and between you and me'—he leant over her and smiled into her face—'we all hope that soon she will not remain Miss Fairweather.'

'No? . . . Marry?'

Richard smiled at his mother, and she, looking up into his face, asked softly, 'Who?'

And the reply came just as softly, 'Alex.'

'No!'

'Yes . . . we hope.'

Now Jackie put in, 'If he's got any sense.'

Irene lay back in her pillows and drew in a long breath before she said, 'Exciting.'

'And that's what we're doing to you, exciting you too much, and we must go, because if that sister comes in, or a nurse, we shall be in trouble.'

Irene closed her eyes and put out her hand to them, which they both patted before going quietly out.

Eight days later they were married in the local register office, attended only by Alexander, James, Glenda, Bella and Miss Fairweather.

When they kissed they did so gently, looking into each other's eyes; then they thanked the registrar and went out. There had been no talking; they went through a hall and down a flight of stone steps to the waiting limousine, followed by Bella, James and Glenda.

Miss Fairweather was about to follow them when Alexander drew her back into the hallway. Looking straight at her, and without any lead-up whatsoever, he said, 'Maggie,' and to this she merely answered, 'Yes?'

It was a question, and the next thing he said was, 'Would you marry me?'

There was a long pause before her laughter came: it was soft, but nevertheless it was laughter; then she said, 'The answer, Alex, has been a foregone conclusion for years.'

'Oh, Maggie!' He now had hold of her arms. 'I've been a selfish damn fool, and I never guessed, because you didn't give me an inkling. But really I had never thought I could feel this way ever again for anyone. But is it too late for me to say, and for you to believe, that I love you and have gone through the devil's own torture these last few weeks?'

She was smiling broadly as she put her hand up and touched his cheek, saying, 'I have no sympathy for you whatsoever, and

I hope you go on suffering, because I've done my share of it over you for a long time now.'

'Oh, Maggie.' He glanced round the hallway. There was no one in sight, so quickly he thrust his arms around her and kissed her. Then as he turned towards the door, who should be standing there but James, and at the sight of him Alexander gave a short laugh and said, 'Dear God! You would have to stick your nose in, wouldn't you?' And at this, the three, laughing together, walked down the steps and towards the second car. Before they reached the pavement Alexander, his voice a hoarse whisper, now said, 'James, please . . . please don't say a word yet. Please. It's their day.'

And his son, looking at them both, said, 'All right,' and they continued the few steps to the car, which would take them back to Glenda's for a wedding breakfast.

6

Irene's joy lasted only ten days more; yet during that time it was noted that she seemed to be more at peace and happier than she had ever been.

She died in her sleep, but right to the last she was aware that her son was holding her hand and had been holding it for a long time and that his dear face was near hers.

When she closed her eyes, it was a gentle fading away, for she did not stop breathing until four hours later.

Irene was buried next to her mother, whose grave and small headstone had been obliterated for years now with moss and overgrown weeds at the far end of the cemetery, which overlooked the river.

Of her father's grave there was no trace.

He hadn't had a Christian burial because he had committed suicide; yet there must have been some part of the cemetery where he lay, although there was no record of it.

The church was crowded, and so was the cemetery, with many photographers and journalists, the latter having found it difficult to get anything out of the close-mouthed family and friends who had surrounded Irene during her last days.

It had come as a great surprise to everyone that Mrs Irene Baindor had been still alive. There was a mystery here, but not one that even the cleverest journalist was able to probe, although it was felt that there must be a great sentimental story here. The nearest they could get to it was that her son had been with her when she died . . .

A fortnight later there was another gathering of all those concerned. It was in Glenda's sitting room. They were there to discuss their futures as far as it was in their power to do so.

It had already been arranged with Alexander and George Peacock that the businesses abroad that remained would eventually be managed by the accountant. The London office would be run by Alexander and his wife Margaret, leaving his own business in the hands of James.

A new post had been created for George Green, Maggie's cousin. His position now was managing director of the company that had been set up to oversee the demolition of old slum properties and the erection of new ones. His first job, however, was to get the convalescent home into working order.

Lastly there were Richard and Jackie. It was decided that Richard would finish his training during the next two years with the next step his appointment as consultant plastic surgeon. Jackie had not yet voiced her plans, but now she did, saying, 'What am I going to do? Well, I'll tell you. I've taken up a new career.'

'A new career?' This came from a surprised Richard.

'Yes, dear husband, a new career.

'First of all, I propose to be a wife and mother, but my new career is to be that of a writer.'

'Writer? What d'you mean?' said Richard. 'As a journalist, you write now.'

'No, I don't; I merely report. But now, I propose to write a book.' She had everybody's attention, and Alexander said, 'A book? A novel?'

'No; not a novel, Alex, a biography, of a man who was once known as a great financier and of how he turned his wife's brain and for twenty-seven years put her into limbo. But most of all, the main character will be Miss Bella Morgan, who was dragged up in the slums of Liverpool, and knew what it was to sleep rough. One day, when she was nearly forty years old, she came across a strangely dressed woman lying in a filthy yard, trying to find shelter under dirty fruit boxes. She took her into her life. She not only cared for her but she loved her and protected her and lived daily with her; and her charge only set foot out of the house four times in twenty-six years. The only thing, it seemed, that Miss Bella Morgan could not do for her was to get her to discard the old, tattered dress and coat and weird hat in which she had left home: her idea was that the coat protected her from men. And such was her love for it that she asked to be buried in this outfit. Her wish was granted.

'And of how, in the end, one word, one name that Miss Bella Morgan happened to mention brought back, at least partly, some of her charge's past and revealed to her that she had a son whom she hadn't seen since she had last held him in her arms as a boy of four years old. And so she went searching for him and she found him, and the great silence that had held her almost dumb was broken. And,' she finished, 'I'm calling the book *The Silent Lady.'*

No one spoke, and Richard, who had been standing by her side, dropped on to a chair and bowed his head; then, looking up at her and taking both of her hands, he brought them to his face and kissed them. Then he said, 'You are the most wonderful woman in the world.'

She stared back at him, then to break the silence that had fallen on them all she reverted to her usual joking manner and said, 'Oh, I've just been waiting for you to recognise it.'

They all laughed until Alexander said, 'And how long do you think it is going to take you to write this epic?'

'I've worked it out. Four years. In between times I hope I will have other family business to attend to: the nursery is all ready.'

Epilogue
1959

Covering the whole of Wellbrook Manor was an air of excitement: from the nursery at the top of the house, where lay two-and-a-half-year-old Alexander Franklin Baindor and his sister, one-year-old Belinda Baindor, through the convalescent area where the patients were about to celebrate with a party; to the main room in the house which was a sixty-foot drawing room and was now crowded with people. Standing in groups there were Mr Trip and Mrs Atkins, members of Glenda's nursing staff, Alexander Armstrong and his wife Margaret, James Armstrong, and in their company was Bella's kind friend and solicitor, Mr Travis, together with George Green, the architect. Lord Blakey was there, and next to him Timothy Baxter, who had flown in from America, a man now in his sixties but as handsome as ever; close by Dr Bell was talking to Dr Harle; and near the end of the long table was Mr Joseph Gomparts, his face alight with pleasure. Bella's five lads, Joe, Carl, supporting himself on two sticks, John, Tony and Willie were there; and close behind Carl stood his friend, now a high police official, Raymond Smyth, jokingly known among the family as Mr Sixes and Sevens. A group of Richard's friends had come from the hospital, and included three doctors and two nurses; and there was Bella, resplendent in blue velvet. Finally, there were Richard and Jackie, and Richard, having received a signal from Trip that the cars were on the drive, announced to the company that they must now all be on the move.

It took them exactly an hour to reach the centre of the City and their mystery destination, which had been a closely guarded secret. It was the Merchant Tailors' Hall where a reception was to be held to mark the publication of Jackie's book.

It began at half past seven with drinks and introductions to Jackie's publisher, his associates and literary friends, and Jackie's journalist friends and acquaintances she had made in the magazine and newspaper world.

The mingling with drinks went on from seven thirty to eight fifteen when dinner was announced; it was a sumptuous meal accompanied by the soft music of a string quintet that played in the background.

This was followed by the speeches, which took no more than half an hour. The last to speak was Lord Blakey, who talked of the qualities of his daughter, her husband, and of Miss Bella Morgan and proposed a toast to their health. Such were the brevity and wit of his words that they brought a hail of laughter from the assembled company and gave a final touch to a magnificent evening.

Now cameramen and television journalists were mingling among the tables. But many of them had naturally gathered in front of the top table. Cameras were clicking, lights were flashing, and, amid the hubbub of voices, one was raised above the rest.

With a camera pointed at Jackie, the man cried, 'Lift it up!'

He was pointing to the book on the table, but had the good sense to add, 'Please, Mrs Baindor, lift it up!'

At this request Jackie took the book from the table, looked at it for a second, then suddenly thrust it at Bella, who was standing by her side.

Shaking her head, Bella cried, 'Oh, no! No!'

With a broad smile and a quick lifting of a hand Richard told her to do what the photographer was asking.

Bella stared down for a moment at the cover: There was her lass, draped in the long dirty coat; but the beauty of her face shone out from the dark background and drew the eye upwards to the cloth crown, all that was left of the weird hat. In the seconds that she stared at it her heart cried, 'Oh, my lass, my lass. This, as your son says, will vindicate your life.'

And on this thought her arms swung up and outwards as if she were about to launch the book into the air.

* * *

Such had been Bella's gesture that the following morning one newspaper showed the exact picture, and the editor, being in poetic mood, added, 'It was as if the little woman was opening a cage and letting free an imprisoned bird.'